Arthur Ness

and the

Secret of Waterwhistle

The Complete Edition

wilf morgan

BRING A WORLD OF ADVENTURE TO YOUR SCHOOL!

Want to do something cool for your school? Show this book to your teacher, reading co-ordinator, librarian… heck, just barge right into the Headteacher's office! Then say these words;

"Hi! (Sorry for knocking over your goldfish). If you send an email to **free-books@88tales.com**, you'll get a free 88Tales Press book for the school! One per school, Terms and Conditions on the **88tales.com** website. Okay, I'll go and get a mop."

Then sit back and await hero status. Easy!

88TALES PRESS
Southwell, Nottinghamshire,
NG25 0DF
www.88tales.com

First published in Great Britain
in 2017 by 88Tales Alpha
an imprint of 88Tales Press

First Edition

A catalogue record for this book is
available from the British Library

ISBN 978 1 9997590 5 6

www.88tales.com

www.arilon-chronicles.com

Thanks to Tia, Jake and Joe for pestering
me until I wrote this book!

(Now, go and tidy your rooms.)

Acknowledgements

Thanks to all the kids (even the adult-sized ones..!) who read early versions of this book and gave me invaluable feedback. I literally couldn't have done it without you.

Akeira, Andrea, Anna, Chloe, Debbie, Fola, Gareth, Jacob D, Jakey, Jane, Jocelyn, Joe H, Joseph M, Josh, Kaleb, Lewis, Lionel, Mark, Murray, Sam, Samuel D, Tia, Usman

Special thanks as well to the Bookcase in Lowdham, Nottinghamshire for all the support and advice and also to the staff and pupils at Sneinton C of E Primary School for all the priceless input!

THE ARILON CHRONICLES : BOOK 1

WILF MORGAN

ARTHUR NESS and the Secret of Waterwhistle Part 1

88TALES

Over 2000 years ago, in Rome, a man called Virgil said

'Fortune favours the bold.'

or to put it another way;

'Be brave! You never know - you might just get lucky and win.'

PROLOGUE

Arthur Ness ran.

He ran so fast that his chest was bursting, his head was pounding and his legs were burning up from the inside. *You'd best stop running right now,* his legs threatened him. *Or we'll never work for you again!*

But Arthur Ness did not stop running. One of the witch's spells blasted right past his head. Its bright, white light slammed into a nearby wall and the explosion blasted stone and mortar in all directions.

Arthur Ness ran faster.

Somewhat unnecessarily, the talking cat next to him shouted, "Keep running, Arthur!"

There were times that Arthur Ness needed advice – like what to do about the boys at school that bullied him. Or whether it was okay to feel bad that his father was off fighting Hitler in the war (when he knew he was supposed to feel proud). Or how to handle being scared of everything all the time. Yes, all those things Arthur gladly admitted that he could do with some advice on.

Being chased by an evil witch and several huge, snarling bull-creatures that ran on their hind legs and brandished giant swords and axes..? No, he didn't need advice on that. He knew *just* what to do.

"Arthur Ness!" screeched the witch. "You cannot escape! There is nowhere to run to!"

"Don't listen to her, Arthur," the cat called. "One thing I've learned in all my lives is that there's *always* somewhere to run to! Just keep going!"

Easy for you to say, thought Arthur, *you've got four legs!*

Nevertheless, having the cat with him, even though they were running for their lives, somehow made Arthur feel better.

A little.

"This way!" the cat shouted impossibly loudly while darting left through a stone doorway. "We're seconds away from a grand escape!" Arthur huffed and puffed and put his head down and sprinted after him. The doorway was ancient and medieval-looking just like the rest of the castle and it was identical to a hundred other doorways they'd passed. Arthur didn't have the spare energy to wonder just how the cat knew his way around this place or where they were going. But even though he'd only known the creature for a short time and even though this was, admittedly, the first talking cat he'd ever met and even though he'd never really liked cats in the first place... Arthur trusted him. So he followed the cat through the doorway.

It led outside.

To a cliff.

Which meant that they were-

"-trapped..!" Arthur gasped in-between deep gulps of breath. "I thought you said this way was a grand escape?"

"Jumping off a cliff isn't a grand escape where you're from?" The cat shook his head. "You're a picky one, Arthur Ness."

Instead of safety, the cat had led them to a dead end. Arthur looked around quickly as his rasping, heaving lungs fought to suck air back into his body. But while his breathing slowed, Arthur's brain began race as he noticed the strangeness of his new surroundings.

They were outside the castle now and Arthur saw how big the place really was. Dozens of grey, forbidding battlements and towers clawed their way up to the sky. A perfectly black sky with no stars. Just a big, round, white moon.

And yet...

The moon's harsh, white light burned at Arthur's eyes and he had to quickly look away. There was only one thing that burned so brightly you couldn't look directly at it, Arthur knew. That was no moon. That was a sun.

A sun at night.

Arthur looked down and tried to blink away the green and yellow spots the ball of white flame had sent dancing across his vision. As his sight cleared, he saw that the cliff they were standing on stretched away down to... well, nothing. No ground, no sea. Just more blackness, the same as the sky. Perhaps it was so dark, the bottom was just hidden, Arthur thought. But no, the cliff face didn't fade away into darkness. It just... stopped. Right where the darkness began. It was as if the black, empty sky was wrapped all the way around them – above and below.

The final thing Arthur noticed was a cable attached to the ground, right next to where he and the cat were standing. It was a massive thing – wider and thicker than Arthur's body – and it stretched up and away into the black sky. Unlike the cliff, the cable did fade away into the darkness and Arthur could tell it went out a long way, further than he could see. But what on Earth was it attached to? What was sitting out there, out of sight, holding on to this thing?

Given all this strangeness, Arthur was more than a little unsettled that the cat was so unshakably calm. Especially as the witch was now emerging from the doorway behind them, her massive, armed Yarnbulls flanking her, left and right.

"Ah, Eris," said the cat, "so glad you could keep up. I thought we might have lost you what with all the twisting and turning and... you know... trying to lose you."

Lady Eris raised a hand toward them, energy sparking dangerously between her fingers.

"So, Arthur Ness..." she sneered, her eyes dark, her breath not at all heavy or rasping like his, "...and you, my feline tormentor... your running is finally at an end."

That's when the huge, stretched-out cable began to shake.

And shake.

And shake.

And the cat smiled.

ARTHUR NESS
AND THE
SECRET OF
WATERWHISTLE

PART I

THREAD ONE

THE CAT IN THE CARPET

THE BIG HOUSE
AT THE END OF THE VILLAGE

Arthur Ness was scared. Of everything.

It was almost Christmas of 1940 and Arthur was a long way from home. Enemy planes were flying over London every night and bombing everything, including his own neighbourhood. His mother was still there, alone. His father, a pilot in the RAF, was somewhere in the skies above, facing constant death, battling the enemy. So, perhaps it could be argued that Arthur had many good reasons to be scared of everything.

Unfortunately, Arthur's fear had been around a lot longer than the war. It had been with him for his entire life. He'd been scared of his first teddy bear (and his second... and his third). He'd been scared of his neighbour because she was too old. He'd been scared of going under his bed. He'd been scared of climbing trees. Of going swimming. Of animals. Of the strange way his cousin's dolls looked at him.

Now, right now, Arthur was standing on the doorstep of a big house. It was nighttime and it was raining. He was in a village he'd never heard of, in a part of the country that was miles away from his home. He was standing on that doorstep getting wetter and wetter and colder and colder.

And he was too scared to knock.

"You have to be brave," his mum said as they stood on the platform in the train station. There were other children, other parents all around. The platform was packed with them. Some he recognised from school, most not. Arthur didn't look at his mother. If he didn't look at her, the conversation couldn't finish. If the conversation didn't finish, she couldn't put him on the train. If he didn't get put on the train, he wouldn't get sent away like all these other children.

But his mum gently took hold of Arthur's chin and turned his face toward hers. And she smiled at him.

"Be brave, okay?" she said. "For me."

And Arthur nodded.

And then the conversation did finish. And he did get put on the train. And he did get sent away with all the other children. And even though he knew it was making him safe from the bombs, Arthur had never felt so alone. Or afraid.

Arthur sneezed.

The rain was beginning to soak through his clothes. His cap, his coat, his shorts – even his socks inside his shoes. All beginning to get squelchy and horrible and cold. His little, battered suitcase was looking exceedingly soggy. And the label that was hanging from the top button of his coat that made him look like a bedraggled, misplaced parcel that nobody wanted. The label that read:

Arthur Ness to :
Lord and Lady Roberts
No.1 Church Lane
Waterwhistle
Nottinghamshire

Even that was getting hard to read – all the inky words now running into each other in a black, blobby mess.

Blinking against the rain, Arthur forced himself to look up at the house. It was huge and dark with horrid sharp edges and massive windows that looked like evil eyes staring out over the countryside. It even had a small turret at the top, near the roof. Arthur shivered – and not just from the cold.

What kind of a person could possibly live here?

The kind of person who will be very angry with you for waking them up at this hour of the night.

That was the voice. Arthur's voice. Not the one he talked with. It was the one he *thought* with. The one that sat inside his brain and constantly reminded him how scared he was. Arthur never argued with it. It was always right.

But scared or not, Arthur knew this couldn't go on. If he didn't go inside, he would freeze to death. And he didn't *like* freezing to death, not especially.

He took a deep breath and raised his hand toward the wooden door – but before he could knock...

CLANK! CLUNK!

Arthur nearly jumped out of his skin as the deafening noise burst from behind the door. The noise of someone pulling open large, old, heavy locks. Then the door scraped slowly open. And there, emerging from the darkness inside the house into the half-light of the rainy night was the tallest woman Arthur had ever seen.

"Arthur Ness," she said. "You're late."

LADY ERIS

As soon as she said his name, something dark and heavy seemed to land on Arthur's shoulders. His knees went weak and his head felt fuzzy.

"I'm sorry," Arthur muttered, dredging his voice up from the murky depths of his fear. "There was no-one to meet me at the train station in Nottingham. This man with a lorry-full of sheep gave me a lift to Lowdham, but then I had to walk the rest of the -"

"In," she said.

So, in Arthur went. The door slammed shut behind him.

Even though it was nighttime, it was somehow darker inside the house than it was outside. A couple of murky-looking lamps struggled to illuminate a long, high hallway. It was nothing like the houses in London. Not like the ones he'd ever been in, anyway. It was big and quiet and reminded Arthur of being in a church. But not the friendly kind where he went with his parents every Sunday. Here, there were no welcoming smiles or biscuits. Just a wide, sweeping darkness.

Arthur's teeth chattered uncontrollably as he stared up at the dark, towering figure that was glaring down at him.

"Get used to the cold. You are forbidden to put on any heating in this house," the tall woman said to Arthur in a hard, impassable voice. "You will sleep tonight. Tomorrow you will begin work. Every day, you will clean, tidy, cook and wash. You will not speak to me unless it is absolutely necessary. You will stay out of my room. You will stay out of the drawing room. All other rooms are your responsibility to clean. Am I making myself perfectly clear, Arthur Ness?"

"Yes, Lady Roberts," said Arthur. "But, I…"

"I am not Lady Roberts," she said, annoyance crawling all over her voice. "You will call me Lady Eris."

"I'm sorry, Lady Eris," said Arthur, lowering his eyes to the floor, confused and embarrassed.

"Do you have any questions?" she asked. Arthur forced himself to look up at her. She was really very pretty, he thought, but in a dangerous, cruel kind of way. She reminded him of the creatures he'd read about in ancient Greek mythology – Sirens. Beautiful creatures on the outside but nasty and evil within. Her strong jawline and long, black hair framed dark eyes which pinned Arthur, petrified, to the spot. She had on a long, midnight-black dress that seemed to suck in the light around it. It was so long, in fact, that her feet were completely hidden from view. Arthur wondered if she even *had* feet.

"Let us be perfectly clear, Arthur Ness," she said, looking down her nose at the boy. "I do not want you here. It was the previous owners of this house, Lord and Lady Roberts, who volunteered to take in evacuee children from your war. Despite my objections, I was unable to have you sent elsewhere when I… took over."

Arthur nodded, his gaze returning to his feet. *Your* war? What an odd thing to say. Surely, it was everybody's war. Arthur found himself wishing that those Roberts people were here now. They, at least, sounded kind.

Arthur shuffled from foot to foot, unable to settle or calm himself down. Then, quite suddenly, a chill like a hundred daggers swept right through his body. Incredibly, he felt as though Lady Eris was looking *into* him. Into his brain, into his mind. It felt for all the world as though she were spreading his thoughts out like a newspaper on a table and flicking through the pages at her leisure. And then, just like that, the feeling passed and Arthur felt alone in his head once more.

He looked up at her to see a horrid, satisfied grin across Lady Eris' face and he knew just what she was thinking. He knew because he was thinking it too:

You're scared of her, scaredy-cat. Really, really scared. So scared, you'll do exactly as she says. You won't cause her any trouble.
And she knows it.

Lady Eris unfolded a long arm and pointed a slender finger up the stairs.

"Your room is the first on the left," she said. "Mine is across the way, up in the tower. Never go there."

Arthur looked up towards where she was pointing. When he turned to look back at her, he was startled to find her face just inches away from his.

"*Never*," she repeated, "go there."

Arthur nodded, mute.

Suddenly, he noticed her hair. Up close like this, it almost looked like lots and lots of pieces of straight, black…

…string?

Lady Eris returned to her full height.

"Go. Unpack. Sleep," she said. "Tomorrow, you begin."

Without waiting for another word from her young houseguest, the scariest woman Arthur had ever met turned and went into the drawing room – one of the two rooms he was already banned from.

As the door to the room swung slowly open, Arthur caught a glimpse of something inside – the biggest, most elaborate tapestry he had ever seen. Okay, he had to admit he hadn't seen many tapestries. But this one was absolutely huge. A great piece of material, like a wall-mounted rug. It stretched from floor to ceiling and was made entirely from multi-coloured cotton threads, woven in and out to make a huge picture.

Actually, Arthur noticed, it was lots of little pictures, all connected to each other from one end of the weaving to the other. But the pictures were too small for Arthur to make out at this range. All except one.

The picture of a small, black cat.

Arthur wasn't sure why that one caught his eye. Maybe because it looked kind of different from the other images. A different style. The cat was looking off to one side. Very enigmatic, Arthur thought. Impressive. Mysterious.

A drop of rainwater plopped off the end of his cap and landed on his nose, making Arthur sneeze.

When he looked back up at the cat again, Arthur was somewhat startled to see that the cat was looking back at him.

And - **click** - the door closed, leaving Arthur standing in almost total darkness.

With a sigh and a shake of his head, the young Londoner picked up his heavy bag and suitcase. He was exhausted. Scared. Not thinking straight. Clearly, he'd looked at a different picture the second time. Clearly, it hadn't *actually* moved. Clearly, he needed sleep.

And so Arthur trudged up the stairs, his case banging on each step as he went.

OUT OF THE TAPESTRY
(from the chaotic thoughts of the Cat)

The ship was on fire.

If I had to make a list of sentences I want to say while aboard a ship, they would include 'I'm going to take a long nap', 'Yes, madam, you're right, I *am* handsome' and my all-time favourite, 'I see that everything on the menu is made of fish.'

'The ship's on fire' wouldn't even make the top one hundred. When I got aboard this morning, the Captain had assured me his vessel was sturdy and strong and reliable and absolutely *not* going to be on fire by late afternoon. Still, I suppose it wasn't entirely his fault. I'd say the fault lay more in the hands of the Royal Battle Ships that were attacking us.

Now, as bad as things were – and, make no mistake, being under attack from the Queen's Royal Vanguard is very bad indeed – things could actually have been worse.

'You were on board a ship that was on fire!' I hear you cry. 'How could things have been worse?!'

Well, mainly because nobody knew I was here. I mean, yes the Captain and his crew. But they just thought I was a normal talking cat. They thought the same thing everyone thinks when they see me. What a nice cat. What a small cat. What a harmless cat.

In reality, I'm none of those things.

So, since the Captain and the crew thought I was just a regular (if dashingly handsome) cat and since the Queen's soldiers – like the Queen herself – thought I was already dead (more on that later) then that meant they hadn't attacked the ship because they were looking for me.

Like I said, that was a good thing. It meant my mission could go ahead. Well, once I'd dealt with the whole 'trying not to be on fire' thing.

'And how did you do that?' I hear you cry.

Well, have no fear. I may be a small, black cat (or I may not) but I'm perfectly capable of taking care of myself. Little cat. Flaming ship careening toward the docks at full speed. No problem.

I've been in plenty of scrapes in my time – most of them courtesy of the Queen. I've spent more years than I care to remember fighting her. Yes, many years and four lives. Fighting either her or one of her Noir Ladies.

In fact, when it comes to the Noir Ladies, I've got a one hundred percent record. I've seen off each and every one of them. Lady Aerie. Lady Kray. Lady Taranteen. Several others. All defeated. And each time, the Queen doesn't get the hint. She just goes ahead and brings out a new model. The latest one, though… ooh, she's a toughie.

Lady Eris.

By far, the meanest, coldest and most dangerous of all the Queen's Noir Ladies. We've been battling for some months now. Even in that short space of time, though, we've gotten to know each other quite well, I'd say. Best of friends. Do anything for each other.

By 'best of friends', of course, I mean, 'worst of enemies'. And by 'do anything for each other' I mean 'kill each other on sight'.

In fact, the last time we met (a couple of weeks ago on board a runaway train heading into the heart of an active volcano, very exciting) she dealt me what baddies like to call a 'killer blow'. She thought she'd finally defeated me once and for all. Thought I was on my last life.

She'd miscounted.

However, even though I escaped (fantastic stunt, it was, remind me to tell you how I did it), I have to admit that none of the Queen's other Noir Ladies have ever come as close to defeating me as Lady Eris. And under her stewardship, the Queen's schemes have actually started to get quite... well... *lethal*.

Up until now, my battles with the Queen were lots of fun. She'd come up with some villainous scheme and I'd stop her. She'd rant and rave for a bit. Then she'd come up with another villainous scheme and the whole shindig would start all over again.

Except now, with Lady Eris at the helm, the Queen's villainous doings are actually starting to work. I can't defeat her quite so easily.

Occasionally, I can't defeat her at all.

More and more of my allies are getting captured, killed or Bound. More and more of hers are running wild. She's always had her agents – you know, the soldiers, the Yarnbulls, the Sharp-Eyes (oh, and the Rainhand – if you can count that terrible, terrible creature as truly *hers*...). But now, everything feels like it's almost in the palm of her hand. The sun, the islands and all the NothingSpace in between. (By the way, I'm glad you're from Arilon – if you were some random human, you wouldn't have a clue what I'm going on about).

Anyway, I keep getting sidetracked.

Me. Flaming ship. Speeding towards the docks on Noir Island. Location of Noir Castle. Home of Lady Eris of the Noir Ladies (okay, I'm sure you'd figured all that out).

Now, let me assure you, once again, that I'm really very amazing and extremely talented when it comes to getting out of tight scrapes.

'But how?!' I hear you cry. (You really ought to stop with all the crying. It's bound to get us discovered).

You see, I had a plan. Well, it wasn't really a plan – I just ran as fast as I could and hoped no-one saw me. I hate plans. Plans are boring. Knowing what's going to happen in advance? Where's the fun in that?

So, anyway, I had the utmost confidence in my abilities and I *did* manage to get off the blazing ship before it crashed into the island. And I *did* manage to do it without being seen. And I *did* manage to evade all the soldiers and Yarnbulls roaming the castle as I made my way to the Main Hall.

And I did manage to get into the tapestry and make my way over to the Human World. All the way to Waterwhistle.

And guess what I saw as I arrived in the drawing room in the house in the village in the Human World? Guess what I saw standing there, shivering and dripping wet?

I saw a young, frightened human boy.

And I thought '*brilliant*'.

Because I knew I'd just found the best weapon against the Queen I could ever have hoped to find.

THE SILENCE OF
WATERWHISTLE

One day into his stay, Arthur had decided he hated the countryside. After another four days, he'd revised his opinion. He *really* hated the countryside.

Arthur had muddled his way through most of his first week in Waterwhistle and he was really beginning to miss the city. Right now, as he trudged through the village, pushing a wheelbarrow over the rough gravel of the village square, Arthur felt the nasty, oppressive nature of the countryside.

First of all – and most scary – were the hills. They were just...*there*. Right there, all around. Looking at him.

There was nothing like them in London. And if there were any hills, they were sensibly covered up with lots and lots of buildings. Here, the hills were left standing bare and proud. And the open spaces – wow, the open spaces just went on and on and on for miles. It was most unnatural.

And as if that wasn't enough, there was also the village itself. The streets were tiny, the buildings were small and most unnerving of all, there were animals wandering around. And not just dogs and cats (they had those in London, he could handle those). It was the *big* animals. The geese. The sheep.

The cows.

Arthur didn't trust the cows. They constantly looked as though they were whispering about him. He kept his distance from the cows.

As strange and disorienting as all this was, though, none of it compared to the worst thing about Waterwhistle. Because the worst thing…

…was the silence.

Arthur had always thought that people in villages were meant to be friendly. Full of community spirit and 'how do you do's and forever lending each other cups of sugar.

Well, not *these* people.

On the very first day, Lady Eris had sent him into town with a wheelbarrow to fetch some compost from the village grocer. And right from that very first day, the silence had been deafening. At first, Arthur had wondered if he'd been imagining it. Was he just used to London noise? People shouting at each other all day (and most of the night)? But no, surely something was definitely wrong.

"How much for six apples?" someone would ask.

"Six pence," the shopkeeper would reply.

This constituted the longest conversation Arthur had yet overheard. But when money and apples changed hands and then shopkeeper and customer went their separate ways without even a 'Thank you, bye!', Arthur knew something strange was going on.

Even the children didn't make any noise. He'd seen some on his first day. They were in the park. Some were sat on swings, some on the roundabout. A couple on a see-saw. And they were swinging and see-sawing and roundabouting. But not talking. It was like their bodies were there, but their minds were mostly somewhere else.

Arthur had hurried on by.

So, all in all, Arthur wasn't a great fan of the countryside. When faced with all that, being told to scrub floors and polish staircases all day didn't seem so bad. At least he was inside.

Unfortunately, though, Lady Eris had given him another job to do. One that needed compost. And lots of it. So here he was, collecting what felt like his hundredth bag.

"Good morning, Mr. Smith!" Arthur chirped his greeting as he pushed his empty wheelbarrow in through the doorway of the grocer's. As always, the place was full of people buying fresh fruit and veg in almost total silence.

Arthur said, "I'm here for Lady Eris' compost, as usual." He always tried to be polite, even though the response was always exactly the same.

Mr. Smith was a tall, broad man with a receding hairline, a firm jaw and no hint of anything remotely resembling a smile. He pressed something on the till and it **ping**ed open. He held out his hand. Arthur dropped the coins into it. Mr. Smith put the coins in the till. He closed it. Then, he turned and disappeared out to the back of the shop.

All without a word.

Arthur shrugged as his eyes caught the front page of the newspaper someone had left on the counter-top. *More Bombings in London* read the headline. Arthur began to crane his head around to see if he could see any-

SNORT!

Arthur's head shot up - what on earth was *that?* A horse, it sounded like. Really close… like, right behind his head! But – he span round – there was nothing there… No horse. And, strangely, even though it had been so loud, no reaction from any of the other shoppers.

"Did…" he stammered to a woman next to him examining some potatoes, "…did you hear that?"

The woman turned and looked at him, quizzically. Her eyes looked Arthur up and down, probably trying to figure out if he was a little bit crazy. Eventually, she shook her head.

"Didn't hear nuthin'."

And she turned back to her potatoes.

A sudden **THUMP** jerked Arthur's head round once again – but it was just Mr Smith. He'd returned with the compost and had dumped the sack into Arthur's wheelbarrow.

"Oh, er…" Arthur gathered his composure again, "…thanks, Mr. Smith."

But Mr. Smith wasn't taking any notice. He'd gone back to staring out of the window.

Grunting, Arthur lifted the handles of his wheelbarrow and left the shop with its strange customers and even stranger sounds.

That's when he heard *another* sound.

Thunk.

Thunk.

Thunk.

This one made Arthur smile, though, because he knew exactly what it was.

Someone was bouncing a football!

THINGS YOU CAN'T SEE

At last! Someone normal!

"Hey!" Arthur called out, plonking his heavy wheelbarrow down on the cobbled street. "Over here! Give us a kick!"

The boy looked up from his one-child game of football. Immediately, a look of fear crossed the boy's face. Arthur had to admit, that hadn't been the expression he was particularly expecting.

The boy looked Arthur up and down, trying to figure the stranger out. Then…

…he rolled the ball over.

Grinning, Arthur flicked the ball up and did a series of keepy-uppies with his knees, feet and (to the boy's amazement) his head. Arthur finished off the show by chesting the ball down, letting it drop to the ground and trapping it under his foot.

"Wow!" the boy uttered his first words, an awestruck grin plastered across his face. "That were brilliant!"

Arthur shrugged, modestly, "Something I saw Ted Drake do when my dad took me to see the Arsenal last year."

For the first time since he'd arrived in Waterwhistle, Arthur felt something other than abject fear. He'd finally met someone who seemed kind of normal. He rolled the ball back to the boy who picked it up, staring at it like it had just been dropped from outer space.

"What's your name?" Arthur asked.

"Sam," said the boy as the smile finally melted off his face. "You're Arthur Ness, aren't you? You live up in the big house. With *her*."

Obviously, the locals felt the same way about Lady Eris as Arthur did. He nodded.

"Yes. She's keeping me busy, that's for sure. Every day, I have to get compost and spread it all over the garden. And she gives me these weird seeds. They're all nobbly and spiky. Horrible things. Never seen anything like them. I don't know what they're meant to grow into...except..."

Sam had a somewhat wary look on his face as Arthur talked but he didn't interrupt. So Arthur – not knowing what else to talk about – decided he might as well press on.

"...well, sometimes, when I go into the garden, there are big holes there. I mean, massive. Almost big enough for me to fit into. Like something's been pulled out in the night. But...well, it can't be, can it? Because there's nothing growing there during the day."

Sam stood there, turning the football over and over in his hands as he watched Arthur, his earlier grin of admiration long gone. The awkward silence made Arthur look down at his feet and start tapping a stone with the toe of his shoe.

"Everyone's afraid, y'know," Sam suddenly said. Arthur looked up, intrigued.

"Afraid? Afraid of what?"

"Not of 'what'..." said Sam, "...of *'who'*."

"Alright, then, of *who*?"

The ball suddenly stopped dead still in Sam's hands.

"Lady Eris."

SNORT!

Arthur snapped his head up – that noise, again! It had to be a horse, it was so clear this time, so loud!

"Did you hear that?" Arthur said. When he looked back at Sam, he expected to see the same look of bewilderment that the grown-ups in the grocer's had had. But, Sam didn't look bewildered. He looked scared.

"I didn't hear nothin'," he said, evenly. And Arthur could tell right away. Sam was lying.

A horrible feeling was beginning to build in Arthur's stomach but he didn't know exactly why. Something told him not to ask Sam why he was pretending he couldn't hear the noises.

"So…you were saying," Arthur said, "about Lady Eris..? That everyone's scared of her?"

"Well, not *exactly* everyone," said the boy, a new note of pride in his voice. "My sister weren't."

Arthur was immediately interested. Brave people always intrigued him.

"And where is she?" he asked. "Your sister?"

The boy held his ball in one hand and pointed gingerly over toward the village square. "She were standing there. Shoutin'. Tellin' people how Lady Eris were doin' somethin' to 'em. How she were makin' the town all…silent."

Aha, thought Arthur, so the silence *wasn't* normal.

"And were people listening?" Arthur asked.

"Oh, yeah." The boy nodded. "People were startin' to gather. There were a bit of a crowd. As Teresa – that's me sister's name – as Teresa talked, you could see some people noddin' and agreein' with her."

"So, what happened?"

"She vanished."

Arthur was taken aback. "What do you mean, vanished?"

"One second she were there," said Sam, quietly, "the next second, she weren't. It were like she were taken. Taken by things you couldn't see."

Arthur shivered. He didn't like the sound of this.

SCRAPE

Arthur jerked his head again. What was that sound? Like hooves on cobblestones. Perhaps it-

GRUNT

It was just village noises, he thought. It had to be. In fact, at the far end of the street, there was a farmer with a horse and trap cart. He was lifting heavy sacks onto the back of it. It must have been him grunting and his horse's hooves scraping.

Except, it had sounded so *close*...

"What did the people say?" Arthur asked, ignoring the noise once again. "When your sister vanished? What did they do?"

"Nothin'." Sam shrugged. "They just walked away. No-one even talks about it. Like they can't remember it ever happenin'."

Sam was talking nonsense, Arthur decided. He had to be. People forgetting something the instant after they watched it happen? This all sounded so unlikely, so pretend, so crazy.

And yet, there were the noises...

"But *you* remember," said Arthur. "Didn't you see what took her?"

Sam was silent for a long time. Then he finally looked Arthur in the eye and whispered. "Sometimes, it's best not to notice dangerous things. If you can't see them, they can't hurt you."

Arthur felt cold all over. Then…

SNORT!

… a blast of warm air rushed down his back. He span round. That one was right behind him!

"Arthur," Sam's tone was suddenly desperate and urgent, his voice still a whisper and it made Arthur turn to face him again. "I think it were Lady Eris what took Teresa. You're livin' up there. Can you look? Can you look for her? She must be up there somewhere!"

"But…" Arthur didn't possess the words to describe to Sam how scared he was of Lady Eris, "…she's very strict. She tells me what to do and where to go and…"

"*Please*," Sam was standing right in front of Arthur, now, his voice even more desperate. "She's me *sister*…"

Arthur's mind was swimming. He didn't see how he could possibly help Sam. But given that this was the first person to speak to him in a friendly way, he didn't see how he could possibly *not*.

He opened his mouth to answer when Sam's eyes suddenly widened in horror. He was looking directly above and behind Arthur. Shot through with fear, Arthur span round. What was it? What was there?!

Nothing.

Nothing was there.

His heart thumping, he turned back to Sam but the boy had already begun walking off. He wasn't bouncing the ball now. He was acting like everyone else. Silent. Scared.

Suddenly, Arthur decided his nerves had taken enough. He jogged back over to his wheelbarrow, hefted the handles up and made his way as quickly as he could back through the village. He had to get this wet, stinky stuff back to the big house. Then he had to spread it all over the garden before he got in trouble. Time to put this nonsense out of his mind. Because, it *was* nonsense, wasn't it?

He took one last glance over his shoulder. He looked at the spot where he thought he'd heard strange noises and felt strange things.

But it was just empty space.

What was it Sam had said?

Sometimes, it's best not to notice dangerous things.

LADY ERIS' ROOM

"Put your back into it, Arthur Ness!" Lady Eris scolded the young boy, her voice devoid of any mercy. "I want that floor scrubbed and scrubbed and scrubbed again."

Not even daring to pause to catch his breath, Arthur, down on his knees, dunked the scrubbing brush into the bucket of dirty water. He sloshed it around for a second before putting it back on the hard, wooden floor and carried on scrubbing.

He'd been at this for almost an hour. Not the rest of the floors in the house, just this one area. The upstairs landing that linked Lady Eris' room and his. He had started outside his own room, worked his way along the corridor, up the four or five steps to the higher part of the landing and was now finally outside the turret on the corner of the house. Lady Eris' room.

Arthur's knees scraped against the rough, wooden floorboards. His back was aching, his shoulders and arms were burning and his hands and fingers were red raw from pushing this blummin' brush back and forth, trying to clean wooden panels that – to Arthur, anyway – really didn't seem that dirty.

Arthur had been in this house for a couple of weeks now and in all that time, he barely saw Lady Eris anywhere other than her room and the drawing room where the giant tapestry was. She barely spent any time in any other part of the house. And yet, Arthur had to spend all his time keeping it all clean. And what for? She didn't care about how clean the place was, that much was obvious.

In fact, Arthur had the distinct impression that she was simply keeping him busy and out of the way while she did…

…what?

Could Sam have been telling the truth? Could Lady Eris be up to something in this place? And if she was, Arthur thought, shouldn't he do something about it…?

Like what? What could you do about it, scaredy-cat? Absolutely nothing. Because you're unimportant.

Arthur knew the voice was right, so he kept on scrubbing.

"And don't even think about eating dinner until this entire floor is spotless, Arthur Ness," she said.

"No, ma'am."

"And after you've eaten, don't you dare go to bed until you've cleaned the downstairs hallway again."

"No, ma'am."

And with that, Lady Eris turned and went into her room, her unseen feet banging out a firm **click clunk click clunk** with every step. Not daring to look up or stop scrubbing for even a second, Arthur waited for the sound of Lady Eris' bedroom door closing. At least then he could rest for a second. He waited and waited. But the sound never came. He glanced up.

Lady Eris had left her door ever so slightly ajar.

From his position, Arthur could see right into her room for the first time. Nervously, he craned his neck forward a little and stole a peek further into the room. It didn't look anything special. But he saw something much more interesting than what kind of wardrobe she had.

Lady Eris was dancing.

Arthur couldn't believe his eyes. This horrid, stern woman was actually, actually dancing! A weird dance it was, too. All in the arms. It was like she was playing some kind of huge, invisible harp. He could almost see her plucking the strings this way and that, first on one side of the room and then the other, back and forth.

Suddenly, a brief glimmer of light caught Arthur's eye and he noticed something else in the room – a safe. It was in the far wall, beyond Lady Eris. And it was slightly open. Even from where he was, Arthur could see that there was only one thing inside the safe. A small, shiny hand mirror.

Arthur started to wonder what was so special about a mirror that it would be the only thing to be put into the safe when he suddenly noticed two things –

One) at some point over the last few seconds, he'd stopped scrubbing…

…and Two) Lady Eris was standing still as a statue.

Staring right at him.

Arthur's heart leapt in his chest in embarrassment and he quickly shifted his eyes back down to the floor and went back to scrubbing twice as hard as before. He didn't dare look up and all he heard was the **click clunk** of Lady Eris walking towards him and a **BANG** as the door was slammed shut, leaving him alone on the landing.

THE CAT

The rest of Arthur's day was like all the other days in the big house and it went like this;

CLEAN
SCRUB
WASH
SPREAD COMPOST
CLEAN
SCRUB
SCRUB
SCRUB
SPREAD COMPOST
WASH
CLEAN
WASH
SCRUB
SPREAD COMPOST

And it ended with

CLIMB THE STAIRS
CHANGE INTO PYJAMAS
COLLAPSE INTO BED

Arthur had done CLIMB THE STAIRS by forcing his tired, aching arms and legs up the staircase one agonising step at a time. Exhausted, he then slowly did CHANGE INTO PYJAMAS (it made him sad that his pyjamas now no longer smelled of home – they just smelled of here). Finally, he started COLLAPSE INTO BED by turning toward his bed and –

"Woah!" Arthur jumped in fright and almost fell backwards when he saw what was on his bed.

A cat.

"Where did *you* come from?!" Arthur tried to calm his suddenly thumping heart. "I've never seen you before. How did you get in here?"

The cat was small and black and radiated an air of regal calm. It sat on Arthur's pillow like it was a throne. No longer would the pillow be used for anything as mundane as resting Arthur's head on – it had been upgraded to something far more important, now.

It blinked at him.

Surprising himself, Arthur laughed.

"Listen to me, I'm going crazy." He allowed himself a tiny smile, his eyes still looking at the feline. "I'm talking to a cat!"

"Yes," said the cat. "Imagine if I talked back."

"Aaaahh!"

This time Arthur *did* fall over. Right over. Onto his backside, knocking his empty suitcase and sending it skidding across the floor. His eyes and mouth were wide open and he pointed a shaking finger at the small, black creature.

"You…you…" Arthur stammered, "you…you…"

"Me, me, me?" said the cat. "Ah, fantastic! You're a clever one. You just worked out my favourite topic of conversation. Let's talk about *me!*"

"You can… you can…" Arthur continued to struggle to build a sentence.

"I can…what..?" The cat cocked its head. "I can dance? Well, I suppose I do enjoy a good tango. Or a waltz. I'm not great at it, though – I've got four left feet."

Even to Arthur's shocked brain, he could tell that the cat was making fun of him.

"No!" said Arthur. "I mean, you can… you can…"

"Sing?" said the cat. "Well, no, not really. Tried it once. Made a child cry. She thought I was in pain. Very embarrassing."

"No, I mean you can-"

"Read? Oh, I love a good book. Especially if it's about a handsome cat who defeats criminals and eats lots of fish."

"No, you can-"

"Arrange flowers?"

"No, it's that you can-"

"Sew on loose coat buttons?"

"No, you-"

"Sell lemonade out of the back of a manure cart?"

"*Will you stop interrupting me?!*" Arthur suddenly shouted. The cat rested one paw ontop of the other and looked decidedly unimpressed.

"Well, spit it out, then," it said. "I don't have all night."

"You…can…" Arthur breathed slowly, "…*talk!*"

BANGBANGBANG

Straight away, Arthur stiffened with fear. Lady Eris was hammering on her bedroom door from the other end of the hall.

"Arthur Ness! Stop that racket!" she shouted from her doorway. Arthur's door was closed but her voice was so strong and loud, it sounded like she was right there in the room with him. For a moment, not even a talking cat could distract Arthur from how terrified he was of Lady Eris. Just like every time she said his name, he felt cold and hot all at once. Weak kneed and sick in his stomach.

"If I hear another peep out of you," Lady Eris' voice boomed, "I shall hang you from the roof by your shoelaces!"

"Yes, Lady Eris!" Arthur called. "Sorry, Lady Eris!"

Arthur held his breath in silence for a moment and eventually, he could hear Lady Eris' door click shut again.

"Oh, bravo well done," said the cat. "You know, it's a good thing you kept your nerve and didn't tell her I was here."

"Why?" said Arthur returning his gaze to the feline. "Because she'd think I was crazy?"

"No…" The cat yawned then licked its lips. "Because she'd cast a spell and kill us both on the spot. Ooh, nice bed, this."

"Cast a…" Arthur shook his head. "You mean, she's a witch?"

The cat looked up at Arthur, somewhat puzzled. "Couldn't you tell?"

"Stop talking nonsense," Arthur laughed again but was careful to keep his voice low. "Witches aren't *real!*"

The cat looked at Arthur. "You do realise you're conversing with a talking cat?"

"Witches are from fairy tales!"

"Again… talking cat."

Arthur looked around, shaking his head as though he were trying to shake this crazy conversation out of it. He didn't know what to think.

"Do you have a name?" Arthur finally found himself asking.

"Yes, thanks," said the cat, staring around the room.

"…and it is…?"

"None of your business."

"So, what should I call you?"

"Call me what everyone calls me. Call me the Cat."

"Everyone calls you 'the Cat'?" Arthur stood, hands on hips. "Why does everyone call you 'the Cat'? People don't call me 'the Boy'."

"What *do* they call you?"

"Arthur…Arthur Ness."

"Well, Arthur Arthur Ness, unlike you, my name is hidden. Locked away nice and safe where no-one can use it against me. So, in the absence of a name, people call me the Cat. Because I'm a cat. It's really quite simple, even a human should get it…"

Arthur shook his head. "What do you mean, 'use your name against you'? People don't use my name against me!"

"Oh, really?" said the Cat, raising an eyebrow. "Whenever Lady Eris says your name, how do you feel?"

Arthur was about to argue that he didn't feel anything – but then he remembered that he *did* feel something. The weakness, the jelly knees, the hot and cold feeling. The fear.

"But that's…" Arthur stammered, "…that's nothing… I mean, it's not… it's not magic or anything…"

"Do you want proof she's a witch, Arthur Arthur Ness?" The Cat suddenly got up from the bed and strolled over to the open window. "Right-o. Come on, then."

And without another word, it leaped out into the darkness and disappeared. Arthur stood there, his mouth hanging open in shock.

You can't climb out there! You'd fall and break your legs!

You don't even like climbing that small tree in your back garden at home!

"Come on out!" the Cat's voice drifted in from the darkness. "It's very easy!"

Arthur looked at the empty window. For a moment, he wondered if anything from the last few minutes had actually happened.

It might all be a dream, Arthur thought. Yes, a strange dream brought about by inhaling too much furniture polish and compost fumes. If he went over to his bed right now and jumped in and closed his eyes tight, it would probably all go away. Yes, Arthur thought, just go to bed. Let it all go away.

But before he knew it, he'd walked not to his bed...

...but to the window.

Okay, he'd take a *little* trip out. He could always wake up later.

He swung his legs out and started the climb down and straight away he found the cat had lied. It wasn't easy. In fact, it was very, very hard. But it immediately became clear that once he'd started, it was easier to go forward than to go back. And before he knew it, his bare feet touched the cold, damp grass.

The cat was sitting there, waiting patiently for him. His green eyes flashed in the dark as he watched Arthur dust himself down.

"Right, Arthur Arthur Ness," he said. "Follow me."

YARNBULLS

The moon was high in the sky as Arthur Ness and the Cat sneaked through the empty lanes and streets of Waterwhistle.

"Keep to the shadows," whispered the Cat as it walked silently ahead of Arthur, "or they'll see you."

There were still some people out and about at this time of night, Arthur saw, though not as many as there would be back in London. Sticking to the shadows as the Cat suggested was the best plan since he didn't want to get told off for being out of bed and sneaking around in his pyjamas.

Although, to tell him off, the villagers would have to actually speak to him. That being the case, he probably didn't have anything to worry about.

"So…" the Cat said as they went along, "Arthur Arthur Ness. It's a bit of a mouthful isn't it?"

"My name isn't Arthur Arthur Ness – it's just Arthur."

"Can I call you Artie?" asked the Cat.

"No."

"Art?"

"No."

"Bob?"

"That's not even my name!"

"Art?"

"You already said that one," Arthur sighed. "And I said no."

"Good grief," said the Cat. "I can tell *you're* going to be hard work."

They carried on in silence for a little while – past Mr Smith's grocer's where Arthur got his compost. Past Mr and Mrs McGugan's sweet shop (which never had anyone in it as far as Arthur could tell). Past Mrs Pettifer's Post Office and Mrs Shepard's garage (Arthur suspected one or both of these ladies had husbands who had gone off to fight in the war – but as no-one spoke to him, he couldn't be sure).

Soon, they both arrived at the village square – the place, Arthur remembered, where Sam's sister, Teresa, had apparently been kidnapped by things no-one could see.

"In here, quickly," said the Cat as it disappeared into a bush. Arthur crawled in behind, flinching every time he thought he saw some kind of creepy-crawly. And there they hid, looking out over the square.

They could see the stone cross in the centre – a memorial, listing the names of all the soldiers that had died in the first World War. Arthur looked quickly away from it and tried not to imagine his father's name being written onto one of those things in the future.

"So…" the Cat said, eventually. "Can you see them?"

Arthur nodded. "Yes. I can see a few people walking about. There's the man who's always walking his dog. So what?"

"Oh, dear."

Arthur frowned. "What?"

"Well, I'm really sorry to have to break it to you," said the Cat very seriously, "but you appear to be a complete and utter dimwit."

"Hey!"

"I'm not talking about the villagers!" scolded the Cat. "Look again!"

"But...what am I looking for?" Arthur asked. But the creature didn't answer. So, Arthur kept looking. And kept seeing nothing.

Eventually, the Cat said, "Are you scared?"

Arthur realised he was shivering – and not entirely from the cold.

"Yes," he admitted, "a bit."

"Well, being scared is okay," said the Cat. "But try to fight your fear. Pretend your fear is like...like a balloon. Give it a punch. It won't pop. But it will wobble."

Arthur shook his head in frustration. It always annoyed him when people said it was okay to be scared. What nonsense! Being scared stopped him from doing things. Things he sometimes really wanted to do. He didn't want to be scared of *anything*. He wanted to be like... like that girl. Sam's sister. What was her name? Teresa.

He wanted to be like Teresa. Yes, Arthur thought, *she* wouldn't be scared. She'd give his stupid fear balloon a punch. He imagined being her and wondered what she'd see if she were here. Would she be able to pick up whatever it was that this silly cat was going on ab-

And that's when Arthur saw it.

It looked like a bull. It had a deep, thick forehead sitting over two, tiny, beady, black eyes. Its neck was super-wide and pulsing with muscles – as was its entire body. It was standing on its hind legs, like a person and it was easily seven feet tall, taller than a doorway. And in its hands, it was holding an axe the size of Arthur himself.

It looked around, silently, menacingly, left and right. Up the village and then back down the other way.

Arthur opened his mouth to shout out *Run! Run for your lives! There's a dangerous creature!* But that's when he noticed something that was even stranger than the beast itself.

Nobody else could see it.

A man walked right by it and didn't so much as glance up at it. An old woman was carrying a basket of something or other. She took a break and put the basket down right in front of the creature's hooved feet. She stood up straight, stretching her back. The bull-thing looked down at her, threateningly. Then she picked up the basket and went along her way, completely oblivious to the creature's presence.

It shifted on its hooves, **clatter**ing them on the cobblestones. And it **snort**ed. Those noises! That was what Arthur had heard before, when he'd been in the shop and when he'd been talking to Sam..! It had been this thing! Standing right next to him, looking down on him and he'd never noticed!

"What... what is it?" Arthur whispered, his mouth completely dry.

"It's called a Yarnbull," said the Cat, quietly. "And I'm afraid the bad news is... it isn't alone."

Arthur looked again and his eyes opened wide in shock. He could see them. He could actually see them.

Loads of Yarnbulls.

Dotted all over the village. Some were holding axes, some had swords. They were stood still or they were striding up and down the streets and lanes. Some alone, some in pairs. But they were all completely fearsome and terrifying. And they were watching the villagers.

Very closely.

"How come..." Arthur struggled for breath, "...how come nobody can see them?"

"They're too scared," replied the Cat. "It's the perfect way to control people. Make them so scared, they forget there's anything out there controlling them in the first place."

"But what are they doing here?"

"They're guards."

"What are they guarding?"

"They're here to make sure nobody cuts the Threads."

"Threads..?" Arthur was confused. "What threads?"

The Cat looked up at Arthur, quizzically, "Can't you see them?"

"Are... are they big?" Arthur asked.

Now it was the Cat's turn to be confused, "How can you see the Yarnbulls but not the Threads?"

"I don't know," said Arthur, getting a little annoyed. "You're the talking cat showing me the armed bulls, you tell *me!*"

The Cat didn't say anything. He looked at Arthur as though he was trying to figure something out.

"Are they here all the time?" Arthur asked, eventually. "The Yarnbulls?"

"Oh, yes," said the Cat. "*All* the time."

"Where do they come from?"

The Cat fixed its green eyes on Arthur. "What do you think you've been growing in the garden for Lady Eris?"

"Th..*those things?*" Arthur couldn't believe it. "I've been growing *those things?* But... there's nothing in the garden. It's empty!"

"No, it just *looks* empty," said the Cat. "Because, as you can see, they're good at staying hidden. But trust me. That garden's *full* of them."

Arthur looked back at the village, back at the Yarnbulls all over the square and the surrounding roads. No wonder this place was so silent. Everyone was petrified. And they didn't even know it.

"When she first got here, months ago," the Cat said, "Lady Eris put the village under her control. The Yarnbulls are here to make sure it stays that way."

"But, how did she control everyone in the first place?"

"She Bound them."

"Bound?" Arthur said, a little puzzled. "You mean, like, tied-up?"

"Yep," the Cat nodded. "With the Threads."

Arthur sighed, frustrated. The Threads, again.

"But…" Arthur looked back out toward the village, puzzled, "…no-one's tied up."

"You can see the Yarnbulls because you forced yourself to be a little bit brave," the Cat encouraged. "The Threads follow the same rules. Go on, try again."

Arthur shook his head, a growing sense of defeat beginning to build ominously in his belly. "Sorry… I still can't see them…"

"Well, they *are* harder to see," the Cat admitted. "The Yarnbulls are a real danger so, if you try, you can see them quite easily. But the Threads are a very clever kind of danger. And all clever kinds of danger are hard to spot."

Arthur suddenly started feeling more and more angry. Why could he not make himself more brave? He could see the Yarnbulls – why not the Threads? Why did he always fail when it came to being brave? He just wanted to scream at the top of his lungs… but, of course, he was too scared. The Cat didn't miss Arthur's growing frustration.

"Listen, Arthur, I need your help," it said. "It's okay to be scared, but-"

"*Stop saying that!*" Arthur had to force himself not to shout. "It's *not* okay! *You* try it, sometime!"

"Arthur, listen-"

But Arthur didn't want to listen. He scrambled out of the bush and without even dusting himself down, he ran all the way back to the house. Keeping to the shadows, Arthur kept out of the way of the Yarnbulls… but as he ran, he noticed that, actually, he couldn't see them anymore.

Of course not. You heard the Cat. Only brave people can see them.
Just because you pretended to be Teresa, that doesn't make you brave.
You don't have any bravery of your own –
you had to borrow someone else's.

Arthur got all the way across the village, up the lane and back to the garden of the big house and, of course, could see no Yarnbulls growing there at all. He looked up and saw his bedroom light was still on. His bed. An escape from this madness. He took a step toward it – and almost went sprawling to the ground as he tripped over the Cat, which had appeared out of nowhere.

"You think you're the only person who gets scared?" the small, black creature said, its eyes flashing an angry green. "Look at all those people out there! They're so scared, they can't see the Yarnbulls at all!"

"Yes!" Arthur scrunched his hands into fists. "Because Lady Eris has Bound them! That's what you said! Cast some spell on them! But what's *my* excuse, eh? She hasn't cast any spells on me! And do you know why not? Because she doesn't have to! I'm *already scared!*"

"Arthur, I need you," said the Cat. "I need your help. There are things I have to do and I can't do them without you."

"Well, I'm sorry to have to break it to you," Arthur said, a stinging feeling building behind his eyes, "but you're a dimwit. Because out of all the people you could have picked, you've gone and chosen the most useless person in the world!"

The Cat stared at Arthur for a long while, never blinking. Then it shook its head.

"Maybe I am a dimwit," it said. "Maybe I'm getting old. Used up too many lives. I'm starting to make stupid decisions. Fine. Go to bed. Go to sleep. And when you wake up, convinced this was all a dream, then you'll go back to how you were before. Too scared to see the Yarnbulls. But at least you'll be safe from them. Yes, Lady Eris will control you like she's controlling the entire village. But it'll be okay. Because, like them, you won't even know she's doing it."

And with that, the Cat turned and disappeared into the night.

Arthur stared into the darkness for a moment, feeling colder and smaller and more alone than he'd felt in a long time.

Eventually, tired and drained, he turned towards Lady Eris' house and headed for the drainpipe that would take him back to his room and his bed.

SCARED AGAIN

The next day went in a bit of a blur.

Arthur scrubbed the kitchen floor, polished the silver in the front room, fetched some more compost from the village, dusted some cobwebs from the ceiling in the hallway, brought the coal in from the shed and a dozen other back-breaking, mind-numbing tasks. And all the time, the idea of talking cats, Yarnbulls and Lady Eris being a witch seemed like the most absurd nonsense ever.

Polishing the door knobs to all the downstairs rooms, Arthur thought about Sam and his foolish stories. Silly tales made up by a bored child. And everything that had seemed strange actually had a simple explanation when he thought about it logically:

1) The snorting and scraping noises Arthur had heard were just from all those animals that these crazy people had walking around their village. (Almost certainly, it was the cows. Arthur did not like the cows).

2) It wasn't a witch's spell that made the villagers not speak to each other. The reason was simple; they were just rude.

3) Then of course, all this led to him having such a lucid dream last night. It had been vivid, he'd admit that. It felt very real. He could still feel the icy fear of seeing those Yarnbulls. But a vivid dream is still just a dream.

4) And then there was the cat. A talking cat, no less. Arthur wasn't overly fond of cats so it made sense that his fear of living in Waterwhistle should manifest itself in his dreams as a black cat. To lead him out of normality and into craziness. To keep calling him 'Arthur Arthur Ness'.

Arthur suddenly found himself grinning.

It was such a silly joke – Arthur Arthur Ness – and yet, strangely... it *did* made him feel a little better to think of it. Yes, it had certainly all been a strange, fantastical dream. And yet, Arthur found himself wishing that the talking cat, at least, was real.

The door handle Arthur was now polishing had a stubborn stain on it. He gave it an extra hard rub and

click

the handle pushed down and the door drifted open an inch. Only then did Arthur realise that the doorknob he was cleaning was actually on the door that led to the drawing room. So now, in front of him stood a thin, vertical-strip view of the place he had first been forbidden to go.

His initial thought was to quickly pull the door closed again before Lady Eris came down and caught him. His second thought was to push it open and take a look inside.

Unbelievably, he went with his second thought.

The door glided open silently and Arthur peeked his head round. The room was large with a high ceiling, just like the other downstairs rooms he'd been cleaning. But he didn't much care about the wallpaper or the carpets or the chairs.

Arthur wanted to get a look at the tapestry.

The wall-mounted woven rug was *huge*. It went from the floor right to the ceiling and seemed to stretch almost as wide as the room itself. It was kind of old and dirty, Arthur thought. It reminded him of the worn-out rug in the hallway back home. Obviously that was a lot smaller than this – and it was meant to be walked on rather than looked at – but they both had pictures woven into the fabric.

Arthur was a lot closer to the tapestry now than he was on the night he arrived and he could see the pictures on it very clearly. There were lots of little islands – floating islands, hanging in space. The threadwork was so intricate, you could even see little people on the floating chunks of land.

The islands were all connected to each other by hundreds and hundreds of little, black lines that cris-crossed all over the picture like some kind of gigantic spider's web.

Arthur's eyes opened wide with wonder. This thing was *amazing*. Who had made it, he wondered? How long ago? What for? Arthur knew, somehow, that this thing hadn't belonged to Lord and Lady Roberts. It had definitely been Lady Eris who had brought it into the house.

Arthur thought that maybe somewhere deep down, he'd wanted to look at this tapestry because he thought there might be something special about it. Magical, even. But now he could see it properly, he could see that, impressive as it was, it was nevertheless just a big piece of fancy material. Seeing the cat on it before, thinking it had moved… it had all just been a trick of the light. A result of his exhausted, homesick mind.

Strangely enough, though, as Arthur cast his eyes up and down the tapestry, he couldn't see the picture of the cat anywhere. It had to be here somewhere…

Creeeeek

Arthur's breath caught in his throat – the top step!

Lady Eris!

Barely daring to even breath, Arthur darted out of the room, pulled the door shut and went back to polishing the handle. After a few seconds, he realised Lady Eris wasn't coming down the stairs after all. It must have just been the old, wooden house making noises on its own, the way old, wooden houses do.

Breathing a sigh of relief, Arthur scolded himself.

Keep your nose out of things, scaredy-cat!
There's nothing going on! Do as you're told!

He hadn't seen the picture of the cat on the tapestry, but Arthur knew it must be on there somewhere. And it explained why he'd dreamed of a cat – because he remembered seeing it on the tapestry on his first night.

All in all, the young Londoner knew that nothing strange was going on in the house or in the village. Last night was just a fantasy, created by his own mind. There was no magic, no witch, no bull creatures, no talking cat and definitely, definitely no spark of bravery from Arthur.

He finished with the polishing and headed outside.

He still had compost to spread.

STILL SCARED BUT...

It was while spreading his fourth shovel-load of compost when the thought suddenly struck Arthur.

Threads!

The word suddenly felt like it was emblazoned across his brain, like he could see it written in huge, firey letters in the dull, late afternoon sky.

1. On the tapestry – little islands, connected by threads.
2. The villagers bound by invisible threads.
3. Yarnbulls – yarn, being a type of thread.
4. Arthur remembered being close to Lady Eris' face on that first night and thinking that her hair did look like lots of threads.
5. Even the tapestry itself – a huge picture made of threads.

Lots of things to do with threads. Co-incidence?

Or something more?

What are you still thinking about this for?
I thought you'd realised it was all in your head!

Something made Arthur suddenly look up at the house. At Lady Eris' bedroom window.

There she was, staring down at him. Just for a moment.

Then her face disappeared behind the curtains again.

Arthur looked around him, around the garden. Could there be dozens of Yarnbulls here, right now? Growing out of the ground?

Of course not, don't be stupid.

What if…what if he tried to be brave right now? Would he see them?

Go on, then. Try it. I dare you.

No, he couldn't see anything. Maybe he wasn't brave enough. Or maybe, he was stopping himself being brave on purpose. After all, last night, he'd forced himself to be a tiny bit brave and had seen the Yarnbulls for a moment. But it had scared him so much, his bravery had vanished again and the creatures were hidden from sight once more. He'd even managed to convince himself that they weren't real.

Last night was a dream, *stupid! Stop thinking about this stuff!*

And that was the problem, Arthur realised. The villagers were all scared so none of them saw the Yarnbulls. And that kept them safe. If you happened to be brave enough to see them – like Teresa was – then the Yarnbulls would come after you.

Being brave enough to *see* the danger meant you were *in* danger.

…stop it…stop thinking about this nonsense…get back to your work…
…please…?

But, Arthur wasn't just like the villagers, was he? They were scared mostly because of the Binding spell that Lady Eris was casting on them (Arthur suddenly wondered if that's what his host's strange 'dancing' had been all about). The magic was helping keep the villagers scared but what about Arthur? She hadn't bothered with him, had she? The only thing keeping Arthur scared...

...was himself.

"Arthur Ness."

The thin, sharp voice made Arthur jump. He hadn't even heard Lady Eris come outside and here she suddenly was beside him. He looked up at her, fearfully.

"I am going into the village," she said. "I will not be long. I want this entire garden done by the time I get back."

"Yes, Lady Eris."

The tall, thin woman cast her raven-dark eyes down over Arthur Ness and just for a second, a cruel, self-satisfied smirk crossed her lips. Then she turned on her heel and left, heading out towards the village lane.

Arthur replayed that smile in his mind. He knew what it meant. It meant that Lady Eris was pleased with herself for guessing that Arthur would do as he was told. That he would be too scared to cause her any trouble.

She was pleased for being right.

The smile replayed itself over and over in Arthur's mind and he felt something that surprised him. A sudden urge. An urge to show her she was *wrong*.

Show her?

No, not her.

Show *himself*.

... but you can't...

Yes. He could.

He threw the spade down into the soil and ran as fast as he could into the house and straight towards Lady Eris' room.

A FLASH OF BRAVERY

Arthur sprinted all the way through the hallway, up the stairs, along the landing and burst into Lady Eris room in just a few seconds.

His heart was beating hard in his chest and his head felt a little woozy – but not from the run. It was from the fear. Fear of what he was daring to do. But, for the first time in his life, the fear felt a little different. It was more like… *excitement.*

The first time in his life? Actually, no. He had felt it once before, just a teeny, tiny bit. Last night, when he'd climbed out of his window after the Cat.

Still, he had no time to waste marvelling at his newfound bravery, however brief it might turn out to be. He had come in here for a specific reason. After all, if Lady Eris really was a witch and really was binding the villagers with invisible threads, then what would be her biggest fear?

Well, thought Arthur, it was quite simple. Her biggest fear would be the villagers *seeing* the threads. Teresa had seen what was going on. That's why the Yarnbulls had kidnapped her. If the villagers were somehow shown what was happening, the fear might disappear. And Lady Eris would be powerless.

Arthur might have thought that there was no way to make the threads visible if not for one thing he had happened to see by chance yesterday. A mirror in a safe. Because why else would Lady Eris be keeping it locked away unless it could cause her trouble?

Immediately, Arthur ran across the room and put his hand on the safe door handle. What if it was locked? This would all just be a waste of time. He might even get caught and it would all be for nothing.

Yes… just let go of the handle and get back to the garden.
If you leave now, Lady Eris need never know
you came up here.

The thought of Lady Eris coming back and finding Arthur exactly where she left him and smirking again at how easily she had controlled him… Arthur shook his head and the urge of defiance flooded into his body again. He twisted the handle and pulled…

The safe door opened.

This showed how confident Lady Eris was that Arthur's fear would keep him in line. She knew he'd seen the safe and yet she hadn't even bothered to lock it!

Arthur reached inside. The mirror handle felt cold against his fingers. He took it out and looked at it properly for the first time.

It was beautiful! The handle was silver and ivory and lead up to a gold-framed mirror. The glass had a strange, unearthly sheen to it. Different colours danced across its surface as Arthur tilted it back and forth. And all around the edge of the mirror were carvings and incriptions in a language Arthur couldn't even recognise, let alone read.

SLAM!

That was the back door. Lady Eris was back, already!

Quick as he could, Arthur stuffed the mirror into the front waistband of his shorts and pulled his jumper over the protruding handle. He ran out into the hall and no sooner had he silently closed the bedroom door than Lady Eris appeared at the top of the stairs.

She looked at Arthur with dark, distrustful eyes.

"What are you doing up here, Arthur Ness?"

Again, Arthur felt the cold weakness come over him. He had to fight every urge to simply drop to his knees and confess everything.

"I was just...I was just..."

Just what? Think fast, scaredy-cat.

"I was just going to clean the hallway again," Arthur said, suddenly. "I trampled compost in here from the garden."

Lady Eris climbed up the final step and moved slowly towards Arthur, her eyes never leaving his. It felt like she was doing that thing again, thought Arthur, flicking through the pages of his brain, looking for something.

The mirror slipped a little bit in his shorts. Arthur tried hard not to sweat.

Please don't fall out...*please*...

Then, Lady Eris simply walked past Arthur and off towards her room.

"Finish in the garden, Arthur Ness," she said without looking back. And she closed the door behind her.

Breathing a sigh of relief, Arthur reached into his shorts and pulled out the mirror. Then, without waiting even one more second, he ran downstairs as fast as his legs could carry him.

THE MIRROR

Arthur didn't stop running when he got to the bottom of the stairs. He didn't stop running when he got out of the house. He didn't even stop running when he got to the garden and was shocked to see several Yarnbull horns peeking up through the soil.

He kept running all the way down the lane towards the village, his hand on the front of his jumper, the mirror hidden underneath.

Arthur did finally stop running, however, when he got to the village and saw something that, even though he'd prepared himself for it, still sent shivers of fear throughout his body.

Yarnbulls. Everywhere.

There were even more than last night – or maybe he could just see more than he could last night. Back then, he'd pretended to be Teresa and tried to use some of her bravery. Today, he was just being himself. And all the bravery he'd managed to gather together was now in danger of seeping away as he watched the huge beasts strolling about the village.

But none of them made a move toward him. *They don't realise*, Arthur had to remind himself. *They don't know I can see them.*

And so, with a deep breath and a marshalling of his nerves, Arthur walked as slowly and calmly through the middle of the village – and the middle of the Yarnbulls – as he could.

He tried to keep himself as casual as possible. He walked past Yarnbull after Yarnbull, each time keeping his gaze facing forwards, doing his best to ignore the huge creatures as they watched him go past. He could feel the hotness of their gaze on him as he walked. Watching him, watching all the villagers for any sign that they weren't as scared as they should be. But Arthur kept his cool. He made himself seem just like the rest of them – completely unaware of the monsters standing about on the perfectly green village lawns.

Eventually, Arthur made it to the village square and, checking no-one was watching him, ducked down behind the bush next to the bin. It was the same bush that he and the Cat had shared the night before.

Taking a deep breath, Arthur took the mirror out. Time to find out if this really was something special.

He looked into it. All Arthur saw at first was his own face. He turned it slightly so he could see over his shoulder and get more of the village behind him. And his heart almost stopped.

Everything was absolutely *covered* in threads. It was like a cotton factory had exploded and thrown reels of the stuff everywhere. Fine, black strands cris-crossed all over the place, connecting everything to everything else. They covered roofs and streetlamps and shop fronts. They wrapped up gardens and gates and entire cars. They even went into the ground and came back up wrapped around the carrots and turnips growing in Mr. Babbage's yard. And then Arthur saw Mr. Babbage himself. He had to put his hand over his mouth to stop himself crying out in shock.

Mr. Babbage was almost completely enveloped in threads. His entire head was wrapped up like an Egyptian mummy in tight, black wrappings. Eyes, nose, mouth, all covered. It was the same with parts of his body and hands.

And yet, he was moving around, working in his garden, completely unaware there was anything wrong.

But if his eyes were covered, Arthur thought, surely he couldn't see anything at all. Yet, there he was, sprinkling water on his vegetables and picking out weeds that were poking up from between the plants.

Arthur looked away from the mirror glanced over at the old man with his own eyes. Nothing. No threads at all. Completely normal. He looked back into Mr Babbage's reflection in the mirror and there they were. Threads, all over the man's face and arms and hands and covering his eyes.

Maybe what the old man was seeing, Arthur thought, was just *like* real life… without actually *being* real life.

Arthur looked from person to person in the reflection of the mirror and it was the same with them all. All tied up. And not a single one of them knew it.

So this was what the Cat had meant, Arthur realised. This was being Bound.

The entire village was caught up in a giant spider's web of threads and all the strands rose up into the sky and headed off eventually into one direction. They coalesced and joined together at a single point of origin. And that single point was the big house. The turret on the corner.

Lady Eris' room.

"Scary, isn't it?"

Arthur nearly jumped out of his skin at the sound of the Cat's voice.

"Don't do that!" he breathed as he glanced down at the small, black creature, appearing from nowhere.

"So," said the Cat, "you fought your fear, realised the mirror was important, sneaked into Lady Eris' room, grabbed it and came out here to see what it could show you. Not bad for the most useless person in the world. And you did it all without any action music!"

"Action music?"

"You know," said the Cat, "like in the movies. The music you imagine in your head when you have to do heroic and awesome action stuff! Doesn't everyone do that?"

Arthur stared at him, blankly.

"Okay..." said the Cat, returning his gaze to the villagers, "...just me, then..."

"Every single person's been Bound," Arthur said, looking into the mirror, again. "Everyone but me."

"And that," said the Cat, "is exactly why it's down to you to do something about it."

Arthur felt his head swimming as the situation began to sink in. The bit of bravery he'd managed to grab onto was, even now, melting in his hands like a sliver of ice, "But...but, what good can I do? Lady Eris hasn't Bound me because she knows I don't pose any threat. She knows I'm worthless."

"Ah, well, she's already wrong, isn't she?"

"What do you mean?"

The Cat locked eyes with Arthur. "*Nobody's* worthless."

Arthur felt a little numb. Could the Cat be right? Arthur had managed to get this far by stealing the mirror. Now he'd started, could it be like clinging onto the side of the house after following the Cat out the window – easier to go on than go back?

Uncertain, Arthur looked into the mirror again.

And saw a Yarnbull raising its axe towards him.

"Move!" yelled the Cat.

Arthur dived to the ground and the massive axe whistled past his ear, missing him by millimetres and

CRASHed into the bin next to them, smashing it into smithereens with a single blow.

Arthur lay on the ground, looking up at the biggest, most fierce creature he had ever seen. The creature, all snarls and anger and bared teeth, raised its axe over its head once more. And the Cat said, "I'm not sure, but I think we might have been discovered."

YARNBULL CHASE

Arthur rolled to one side as the Yarnbull's axe flew down again. With an almighty **THUD**, it embedded itself into the ground, Arthur on one side of it, the Cat on the other.

The creature grunted and hefted the huge, metal weapon back into the air a third time. Without thinking, Arthur grabbed a handful of soil and threw it into the Yarnbull's beady eyes. It howled in rage and staggered back for a moment, taken by surprise.

"Run!" yelled the Cat.

And run, they did.

In seconds, the pair were out from behind the bush and off across the village square, the Cat in front, Arthur sprinting as fast as he could behind. All Arthur could hear was the **boom Boom BOOM** of the Yarnbull's hooves as it pounded the ground in pursuit. Then came its snorting. And its deafening **ROAR**.

Arthur thought it sounded very angry. But then he suddenly realised it wasn't just bellowing in anger.

It was calling for help.

"Look out!" cried the Cat as three more Yarnbulls crashed out of a side-lane and onto the main road, ahead of the fleeing pair, forcing them to skid to a halt.

"Help!" Arthur cried out to the passing villagers. "Somebody, please, help us!"

A couple of passers-by glanced up at them but they soon turned away, completely disinterested.

"It's no use!" the Cat shouted. "They can't see them!"

Four Yarnbulls now surrounded the pair and began closing in, snarling and brandishing their weapons.

"This way!" the Cat suddenly cried out. He ran straight towards one of them and disappeared in between its legs. Arthur felt a sudden, freezing flush at the thought of doing what the Cat had just done. And yet, off he ran, straight towards the same Yarnbull.

With a deafening bellow, the creature raised its sword towards Arthur and brought it down with pulverising force – but Arthur was no longer there. He'd already skidded through, in between the creature's legs after the Cat.

There was no time to congratulate himself, though, as Arthur followed the tiny, black shape.

"Don't dawdle, Arthur!" the Cat yelled back as he ran. "It's not just a haircut they're trying to give you!"

Howling with bloodcurdling fury, the Yarnbulls pounded after the pair.

"Where are we going?" Arthur cried out as he ran.

"Back to the house!"

"WHAT?! Back to the place where the Yarnbulls actually *come* from?!"

"It's the only way out!"

"Out? Out where?"

But the Cat didn't answer, he just kept running. Hearing the Yarnbulls getting closer, Arthur thought running was probably the best idea right now. Talking could wait.

And so they ran, all the way back up the lane and towards the big house. Somehow, short, fast legs managed to keep ahead of long, slow ones. Within moments, they were dashing through the garden. As fast as they could, they weaved in and out of the Yarnbull heads and horns that were poking through the ground.

With a cry of fright, Arthur dodged past one Yarnbull head that roared and snapped massive teeth at him. Luckily, with the rest of its body still buried in the earth, roaring was all it could do.

Finally, they reached the house. Quick as a flash, the Cat was through the kitchen window. Arthur crashed into the back door. He flung it open, ran through, slammed it behind him and ducked as a massive axe smashed it to pieces. Arthur ran past the window as another Yarnbull shattered it, reaching massive arms in for him.

Arthur ducked the creature's monstrously large hands (with fingers each as thick as Arthur's wrist) and ran after the Cat out of the kitchen, into the hallway and along the corridor – only then realising where the Cat was taking them.

The drawing room.

Bursting in, the first thing Arthur noticed was the tapestry.

The second thing he noticed was Lady Eris.

The third thing he noticed was the fact that Lady Eris was floating in mid-air.

In shock, Arthur dropped the mirror (he was mildly surprised to realise he was still holding it) and it skidded across the floor, stopping face up in the middle of the room.

"So, it appears I was mistaken about you, Arthur Ness," Lady Eris said, looking down at him. The Cat was nowhere to be seen. "You have proven to be a problem after all."

Arthur looked down at the mirror and saw Lady Eris' reflection. He was surprised to see she wasn't actually floating at all. She was being held aloft by masses and masses of threads that emanated from her body and ran to every corner of the room, attached to the walls and ceiling. Many of them ran out through the windows and off into the village. The Cat had been right – all the threads Binding the villagers were coming directly from her.

Then Arthur caught a glimpse of the tapestry's reflection in the mirror too and he saw something he literally couldn't believe.

The tapestry wasn't a tapestry.

It was a doorway.

Suddenly, there was a deafening scuffle as the four Yarnbulls reached the entrance to the drawing room. Lady Eris looked toward them for just a second. And, in that second, Arthur ran towards the tapestry, knowing instinctively that this is what the Cat had wanted them to do.

"Not so fast, Arthur Ness."

Something whipped its way toward Arthur and wrapped itself around his wrist. A black thread held him tight.

A cruel grin wrapped itself around Lady Eris' face and the sheer evil in that smile sent waves of terror crashing through Arthur's body. She started reeling him in, hand over hand, like a terrified fish. The Yarnbulls, mean-faced, waited at the door and silently watched their mistress as she prepared to put an end to this troublesome situation.

Arthur could hear the voice in his head getting ready to tell him what a failure he was…

All of a sudden, a black shape flew out of nowhere and landed on the black thread connecting Arthur to the witch.

The Cat was back.

"*You!*" Lady Eris stopped still in shock. And now, for the first time, Arthur saw something on her face he never thought he would ever see. *Fear.* He couldn't quite believe it.

Lady Eris was *terrified* of the Cat.

"What are *you* doing here?!" she screeched. "You were dead!"

"I was." The Cat agreed. "But I got better. Here, Arthur, let me give you a hand. Sorry, a paw."

And with that, the Cat swiped a single claw at the thread and snapped it cleanly in two – Arthur was free!

Seeing the boy get free, the Yarnbulls suddenly sprang to life again and squeezed through the doorway, one after the other. Once again, Arthur ran towards the tapestry.

"Wait, the mirror!" Arthur saw it resting against some spare sweeping brushes. He reached a hand towards it but then pulled back at the last second as a huge Yarnbull hoof slammed down onto the floor and smashed the intricate glass and ivory to pieces.

"It's okay, leave it!" the Cat yelled.

Arthur had no choice but to do what the Cat said and he put his head down and ran towards the tapestry as fast as he could. All he had time to think was – *if this isn't really a doorway, this is really going to hurt…*

Arthur opened his eyes.

He was in a castle.

A *castle*.

"I really hope this is the last surprise of the day," Arthur said breathlessly, "because I honestly don't think I can take any more…"

His gaze ran over the many tapestries hanging on the stone walls, the suits of armour dotted about, the great, long banqueting table in the middle of the room… And on the wall he had just emerged from, another huge tapestry, identical to the one they'd just run through.

"Where…where are we?" Arthur asked.

"Escape first, questions later!" the Cat shouted as he darted past.

"Arthur Ness!" came Lady Eris' scream as she emerged from the gate-tapestry. Once again, Arthur felt that hot-cold feeling come over him as his knees began to turn to rubber.

"Come along, Artie!" the Cat yelled as it disappeared off towards an exit doorway. "Less gawping, more running!"

And so, witch and terror-creatures at his heel, Arthur Ness ran. And ran. And ran…

And very soon, he found himself standing at the edge of a cliff – black space at his back, the Cat at his side, a mysterious cable attached to the ground by his feet, Lady Eris and her creatures in front of him… and nowhere to run.

And that's just when the cable attached to the ground began to shake and shake and shake.

A loud **whoosh**ing noise blasted down from above them and Arthur looked up. With wide eyes, he immediately realised that running through a tapestry and finding himself in a castle was *not* going to be the last big surprise of the day.

A galleon – an actual, actual pirate ship – came hurtling down out of the black sky. It's black and red sails billowed, full of air and aggression. An anchor chain trailed from the underside of the ship and attached it to the cable with a huge, metal ring. As the vessel flew down toward the ground, the anchor-ring ran along the cable, making it shake, violently and filling the air with a loud, continuous **thrumm**.

"I know you wanted us to stop for a bit of a gossip, Eris," the Cat said, jumping up onto Arthur's shoulder, "but my taxi has arrived and I really can't keep it waiting. You wouldn't believe how much extra they charge for daring rescues. Seriously, it's just ridiculous."

The end of a rope came tumbling over the side of the ship and Arthur instinctively grabbed hold of it with both hands.

"But don't you worry, Eris…" the Cat's voice was suddenly firm, serious and scary, "…we'll be back."

And the ship swung round in a great spiral and shot back up the cable, pulling the rope tight and then up into the air. Arthur cried out as the ground suddenly disappeared from beneath his feet. They were pulled along at breakneck speed and as they flew up and away from the castle, Arthur could finally see the whole island.

It looked just like the islands on the tapestry back in the house. Floating in the black nothingness. And, just like the pictures on the tapestry, there were more cables coming from the island and going off in other directions.

But, as fast as they were going, the island was soon gone. Swallowed by the darkness.

That was it. They'd escaped!

"Come on!" the Cat called into Arthur's ear over the deafening howl of rushing wind and the thrumming of the anchor-ring. "Best get ourselves aboard. You don't want to fall into the NothingSpace. Trust me, that's a fate infinitely worse than death."

Without even stopping to ask just what kind of fate could be infinitely worse than death, Arthur started to pull himself hand over hand towards the ship.

As soon as they got within an arm's length of the side, the Cat jumped off Arthur's shoulder and landed lightly on the side-rails. And within moments, Arthur had hauled himself aboard and tumbled down onto the wooden deck.

"Permission to come aboard, Captain," he heard the Cat say, the familiar grin in his voice. Arthur looked up. He'd expected to see loads of sailors or pirates or soldiers all over the deck. But all there was to greet them was a single person.

A girl, about his own age.

"Wow, Cat, that were close!" she said. "I were beginning to think you weren't goin' to turn up!"

"Well, Arthur and I had a little bit of trouble with almost being chopped to pieces," said the Cat. "I do apologise."

The girl smiled at Arthur and held out a hand. She looked familiar, but Arthur couldn't quite place it...

"Nice to meet you, Arthur Ness. Welcome to Arilon," she grinned. "Welcome aboard the *Gallopin' Snake*."

And with that smile, Arthur *did* recognise her. It was the same smile that Sam had when he'd first met him.

"Teresa!" Arthur babbled. "You're Teresa Smith!"

Teresa's eyebrows raised a little in surprise.

"That's me. And let me tell you," she smiled a dark, daring smile. "If you thought this were all about a few Yarnbulls in Waterwhistle, you haven't seen *nothin'* yet..."

THREAD TWO

ARILON

THE QUEEN

There's a ship called the *Twilight Palace* and it sails through the black NothingSpace, moving along the Travel Lines between islands. And it never stops. Never once pausing for supplies or food or rest or repair. Sleeplessly, it prowls the empty space between the islands.

People everywhere – sailors and landfolk alike – sit around campfires or at tables in taverns or in the safety of their homes at night and they whisper in hushed tones about the Nightmare Ship. What kind of vessel never needs to stop for repairs? What kind of crew never needs to sleep?

Few people have been aboard the *Twilight Palace* and come back to tell the tale. So, people know very little about the vessel at all.

The only thing they really know is that the *Twilight Palace* – the Nightmare Ship – is the home of the monarch of Arilon. The terrible and frightening ruler of the islands and the sun and the NothingSpace between them.

The *Twilight Palace* is the home of the Queen.

And it's aboard this ship that Lady Eris now finds herself.

Captain Isaac knocks on the door of the Royal Chamber.

"Yes?" comes a voice from within.

"Lady Eris has arrived, your Grace."

"Send her in, Captain."

The Captain, firm and tall (though not as tall as Lady Eris) opens the door and stands to one side. The Noir Lady steps inside and the door is closed softly behind her.

As usual, the Queen's chamber is in near-darkness. This is something Lady Eris is always grateful for. It means she can't see the eyes that stare at her from the walls.

The throne, a golden chair covered in fine, woven silk, sits empty and alone at the far end of the room. The Queen very rarely uses it. Instead, Lady Eris finds her in her favoured position; sitting cross-legged on the floor in the centre of the chambers, her robes splayed out on the floor around her.

In her hands is a small, cloth doll, finely embroidered, onto which the Queen is sewing a leg. Around her, as usual, spread out all over the throne room floor are more silk dolls. Hundreds of them. They are of all sizes and all types. Dolls of men and women, children and the elderly. Dolls of soldiers, dolls of beggars, dolls of kings and queens and dolls of pirates.

Lady Eris knows better than to interrupt the Queen when she is sewing. She waits. All the while, unblinking eyes in the wall continue to stare at her.

Eventually, her gaze still fixed on the doll in her hands, the Queen speaks in a low, rich voice.

"We have a problem, Lady Eris."

"Yes, your Grace."

"The Cat has returned," the Queen says, sewing on. "The Cat whom we had thought finally destroyed."

"Yes, your Grace," Lady Eris says again.

"The human boy is with him."

Lady Eris shakes her head. "Arthur Ness is of no consequence, your Grace. He is weak. Fearful. He is no longer under my roof but he is, as ever, under my control."

"You are so confident, Lady Eris?" the Queen sounds strangely amused. "You do not think the boy will feel braver now he has escaped your clutches?"

"I am sure he *will* feel braver," Lady Eris says. "Still, he will be of no consequence."

"Let us hope you are right, Lady Eris."

Lady Eris doesn't reply and the pair remain in silence for a few moments more. The Queen continues to sew her doll with long, smooth strokes of fine, silver thread.

"How much does he know about us?" she asks eventually. "The boy?"

"I am sure the Cat will inform him of all he needs to know," says Lady Eris.

Then a horrid sound erupts from the Queen – the dark sound of her laughter.

"He will fill the child's head with lies. That has always been the Cat's way." The Queen speaks while her gaze remains fixed on her doll. "The only truths the child will get are the ones the Cat wishes him to have."

Lady Eris takes a deep breath. "In any event, your Grace, Arthur Ness is aware of what I am doing to the inhabitants of Waterwhistle."

"But he does not know why?"

"He does not." Lady Eris reassures her Queen. "And I am confident that the Cat also remains unaware of our true goal."

Silence again. The Queen continues to sew.

Lady Eris glances at one of the walls for a moment and glimpses the eyes. And the faces. And the long, thin bodies. The eyes continue to stare at her with envy and hatred. She looks quickly away.

The Queen draws the thread through the doll one final time. Then she raises it to her mouth and bites the thread, snapping it. (For a second, Lady Eris glimpses the jewels in the Queen's teeth).

The monarch gracefully slides the needle - elaborate gold and emerald - into her robes. Then she places the doll delicately on the edge of a nearby table.

Lady Eris contains her surprise as she realises that she recognises the doll's face.

"You will return to Waterwhistle," the Queen says, looking only at her newest doll. "The human village is key to our plans. The machine grows more complete every day. It is of utmost importance that you attain full and complete control over Waterwhistle and its inhabitants as soon as possible. If even one of them is capable of a single act of bravery, if even one of them can see the Threads or the Yarnbulls..." Her eyes rest on the doll of a little girl and her voice grows quiet, as if talking to herself. "...all could be lost..."

Lady Eris nods, slowly. "And what of Arthur Ness? And the Cat?"

"You will send agents to locate them," the Queen replies, still not looking at Lady Eris. Instead, her gaze floats over her dolls, landing on one after another after another. "When they have been found, you shall return to Arilon and deal with matters personally."

"Yes, your Grace...but..."

"What is it, Lady Eris?"

"I dare not rely on Yarnbulls alone for this. They are nothing but mindless brutes. I need something more... subtle."

The Queen is looking, now, at a doll by her feet. It's a doll of an old woman with bound hands and feet. A dark smile flits across the Queen's mouth.

"I thought Arthur Ness was to be of no consequence..?" Her voice is ever-so-slightly mocking.

"Yes, your Grace," replies Lady Eris. "But it is better to be prudent. To be prepared. We must give them no chance to ruin our plans."

Finally and for the first time, the Queen raises her eyes towards Lady Eris. The Noir Lady is momentarily taken aback, as she always is. The Queen's dark red eyes bore into Lady Eris in a manner not unlike the way Lady Eris' eyes would bore into Arthur Ness. It sends chills through the Noir Lady's body and she wishes silently that the Queen would look elsewhere. But she keeps her tongue silent and forces herself to return the gaze.

"You wish to awaken the Needlemen?" the Queen asks, slowly, deliberately.

Lady Eris nods. "Yes. If it pleases your Grace."

The Queen continues to stare at Lady Eris. Between her eyes and the eyes in the wall, Lady Eris can barely stand it. But it will be worth it…as long as she says-

"Very well. The Needlemen are yours to command."

Lady Eris almost allows herself a sigh of relief. The Needlemen! Hers to command! Let the Cat and Arthur Ness run where they may for now. The Queen's own hunters are about to be set loose. And from them, there is no escape.

"Your Grace is too kind," says Lady Eris. "I will not fail you."

"See that you do not," the Queen replies, her gaze boring deeper than ever into the place where Lady Eris' soul would be if she had one. "I am sure you are well aware of the dim view I take of failure."

Lady Eris' eyes glance again at the eyes and faces in the walls. The previous Noir Ladies. Lady Aerie, Lady Kray, Lady Taranteen and a dozen others. All defeated by the Cat. All of them now stitched by the Queen into the walls of her chambers. Unmoving, unblinking, yet still alive. Forever staring at the Queen they failed.

Lady Eris bows, low.

"My Queen – the Cat and Arthur Ness shall be yours in mere days. And our work in Waterwhistle shall be completed and you will have the final victory."

The Queen says nothing else. She simply produces another set of materials, silks, buttons, threads and sets to work on another doll to sit beside the one she has just finished. The doll of Arthur Ness.

Lady Eris leaves.

THE FIRST JOURNEY

Arthur stood on the deck of the *Galloping Snake* and stared, open mouthed at the black skies above him. The endless darkness enveloped them and crashed against the vast sphere of powerful, white fire that was the Arilon sun. The severe light sitting against the pure darkness had played havoc with Arthur's eyes at first but as they continued their journey away from Lady Eris' castle, his vision had eventually settled down. And soon, he had started to see the true beauty of the Arilon skies.

The overriding feature of their surroundings was, of course, the neverending dark. The purest, deepest black that Arthur had ever seen. This was surely what space looked like, he thought. It was exhilarating (even though the idea of being in space had always terrified him).

Dotted throughout the curtain of dark, though, were the stars - or what looked like stars. They were sprinkled across the skyscape like ever-so-sparse handfuls of fairy dust. Here and there, the stars were bunched together in odd little clusters.

The most visually striking thing though, hands-down, were the cables.

"What are they called again?" asked Arthur. "Travelling Lines?"

"Travel Lines," the Cat corrected. "They connect all the islands of Arilon together. Some islands have more, some have less. Ships are attached to them with an anchor chain that has a ring on the end and they just travel back and forth along the lines, through the NothingSpace."

Arthur marvelled at the sight of the Travel Lines in the darkness. Actually, it was more like he was marvelling at the *lack* of sight of them. The Lines themselves were all but invisible against the black of the sky. Only when you looked towards the sun could you see reflections of them as the sunlight lit them up. It was a bit like shining a torch in the darkness; you could see the floating dust particles but only the ones that passed near the light. You knew the rest of the air was just as full of dusty bits, you just couldn't see them.

Judging from the sheer amount of reflections that were illuminated near the sun, Arthur could tell the rest of the black space must be *filled* with Travel Lines. Clearly, the NothingSpace around them wasn't as empty as it seemed.

"Those points of light you can see," the Cat said, "aren't stars. They're intersections. Whenever the Travel Lines cross over or branch."

Arthur nodded. "Ah, I see, that's why they gather in bunches every so often – those are where the Travel Lines converge around the islands, aren't they?"

The Cat winked, impressed. "You're getting it, Arthur Arthur Ness."

"But, wait a minute…" Arthur was struck by a sudden thought. "There must be loads of ships out there right now, travelling along those lines. Maybe even the line we're on, coming towards us right now. What happens when two ships want to get past each other on the same Travel Line?"

"Simple. They crash into each other, explode and everyone dies."

Arthur stared at the Cat, agape. The Cat shrugged.

"Okay, note to self; don't joke about getting blown up. No, they simply rotate so one's above the Line and the other's below it. Then the anchor rings just pass through each other."

"Pass through...?"

"Well, not through like ghosts. I just mean they open and close in just the right way to let each other past while always keeping the ships connected to the Travel Line."

"That sounds complicated..." Arthur said, clearly unconvinced of the reliability of this arrangement. "And only very slightly more reassuring than the crashing, exploding thing."

The Cat smiled. "Don't worry, Arthur. The anchor rings are very advanced devices and crafted with the utmost care. After all, they're the most important thing in Arilon. Without them, ships wouldn't be able to hold onto the Travel Lines and nobody would be able to go anywhere."

"So... the ships don't actually fly, then?" Arthur asked.

The Cat laughed. "Now you're just being silly! Ships aren't the least bit aerodynamic, Arthur, I don't know if you never noticed. Making them fly unaided is kind of impossible."

Arthur looked up at the ship's sails. They were deep scarlet and black and full of wind, propelling the vessel along through the darkness. The strange thing was, though, that although the sails were clearly catching a gust, Arthur couldn't feel a thing. It was as though there was an impossible wind that only the sails could feel.

It was all so alien and crazy and exactly the kind of thing that should have sent him out of his mind with terror. Instead, Arthur was shocked to find himself suddenly laughing.

"This is all just *amazing!*" he shouted.

"Not too bad, is it? Bit different to Wotsitwhistle."

At the mention of the village, Arthur glanced around back up the deck to where Teresa stood at the ship's wheel, steering the ship to wherever it was they were going. He blushed a little as he remembered what a fool he'd made of himself when he'd come aboard. Stuttering and stammering like he'd met some famous movie star.

He'd tried to speak to her but he'd been so nervous, it had just come out as "heyoblahgle".

She'd laughed at his bumbling attempt at conversation, but not in an unkind way. Not like the bullies at school so often did. There was something about Teresa, Arthur felt. An easy friendliness as strange as it was comfortable. It felt to Arthur as though they'd been friends forever.

The Cat stood up and strode along the side-rails of the ship. He turned to Teresa and shouted out (much louder than a cat that small should have been able to, even a talking one), "Next left, I believe, Smithy!"

"Aye, aye, Cat!" she replied with a mock salute.

The Cat turned back to Arthur. "Best hold on for this bit."

Bemused, Arthur looked ahead. With no moving scenery, it was impossible to judge how fast they were going. But that suddenly changed when a Travel Line at right angles to the *Snake* suddenly appeared out of the darkness ahead and whipped toward them at breakneck speed. The cable lay right across their path, forming a junction. Where the two lines met, there was a tiny pinprick of light. The ship's anchor ring passed over the crossing of Travel Lines and a clacking noise rang out as it did its clever, superfast unclasping. The vessel swung round to the left almost like a toy being thrown around by a giant, playful hand. At the same time, there was a mighty **BUMP** which sent Arthur – who had forgotten to take the Cat's advice – sprawling to the floor.

The Cat laughed, long and loud. Arthur rubbed the back of his head but as he looked up, he saw a hand waiting to help him. He reached up and Teresa pulled him to his feet.

"Sorry about that." She grinned. "We just switched from one line to another. It's the only way you can change direction between islands. I'm gettin' the hang of it but I bet I'm not as good as the *Snake's* actual owner."

"So... the ship isn't yours?" asked Arthur.

"Ha! I wish!" Teresa straightened the black hair-band that kept her slightly chaotic, blonde mop out of her face. She turned to the Cat. "Is that the only Line Switch we have to make?"

The feline nodded. "Yep – we should arrive at Graft in about thirty minutes." He yawned. "Just enough time for me to catch a quick nap, I think."

And with that, the dropped down onto the deck and padded away. "Don't anybody go falling off the ship while I'm gone. See you in a bit, non-cats."

"Graft?" Arthur repeated to Teresa once the Cat had disappeared below decks.

"It's an island. You'll like it," she said. "The islands are *amazing*."

"Have you been to many?"

"One or two," Teresa said. "The Cat's told me about loads of 'em, though. I can't wait to see some more."

"You sound like you love it here."

Teresa grinned so wide, Arthur thought her face might split in two. "I've only been here a short while but... yeah, I really do! I've always wanted to travel," she said. "Get out, get on a boat, see the world. Didn't quite have *this* in mind, of course... Y'know, me dad always said..."

Immediately, upon mentioning her father, Teresa's smile faltered. Arthur realised that behind her fun and bravado, she'd been trying hard not to think of home.

"How... how is everyone?" she asked, eventually

"They're all okay... sort of..." Arthur tried to think of the least upsetting way of putting it. "I mean, they're not hurt or anything. They're under Lady Eris' control but they don't know anything's wrong. They're..."

"They've forgotten me, haven't they?" Teresa walked over to the side of the ship and gazed out into the nothingness.

"Everyone but Sam." Arthur came up behind her. "He's the one who told me about you."

"Sam's still okay?" Teresa jerked her gaze up to Arthur, hopefully. "And...what about me dad?"

Arthur was about to ask who her dad was until it suddenly came to him in a flash of realisation.

"Mr Smith! At the farm shop!" he exclaimed to himself as much as Teresa. "I went there every day for compost!"

Then he remembered what he had been buying the compost for and his smile faded.

"He's... he's the same as everyone else, I'm afraid," Arthur said, eventually.

Teresa nodded and her gaze went back out to the NothingSpace. Arthur knew what she was thinking. Her home, her friends, her family... everything she'd ever known was under the control of Lady Eris.

"The last time I saw everyone," she said, "I was standin' on a bench in the middle of the square. Tellin' everyone to throw Lady Eris out of town. I could see it in their eyes – I were reachin' 'em. But then the Yarnbulls grabbed me and everyone went back to bein' quiet. They stopped seein' me. Didn't even notice as I got dragged up the street, kickin' and screamin'."

"Where did the Yarnbulls take you?"

"To *her*," Teresa almost spat the word. "Lady Eris. She said I were causin' too much trouble and she were goin' to dispose of me. The Yarnbulls took me into the tapestry, into that castle and threw me in the dungeons."

"You were in actual dungeons?" Arthur was aghast. "All this time? On your own?"

"Oh, no," Teresa smiled a little, now. "Not on me own. There were some other Arilon folk in there. Told me where I was, what were goin' on. There were this one fella, Captain Thrace. Told me he'd figured out a way to escape and get to his ship, the *Gallopin' Snake*. Only problem was that you had to squeeze through a hole that were too small for everyone."

"Everyone except you," Arthur grinned. Teresa nodded. Her old energy and enthusiasm was back in her voice now as she recounted her thrilling tale.

"I got out, sneaked past the Yarnbulls and followed the Captain's instructions to where the *Snake* had been impounded by Lady Eris. He told me how to fly her so I sneaked on board and…" She laughed now as Arthur stared on, wide-eyed. "Don't ask me how, but I managed to fly her out of there. Right off the island before anyone could stop me!"

Arthur couldn't believe it. He tried to imagine how scared he would have been trying to sneak past Yarnbulls and steal an entire ship from under their noses. Safe to say, he wouldn't have even attempted it.

"Where did you go?" he asked.

"Well, Captain Thrace made me promise to find a way back in to get him and the others out," Teresa said. "So I flew the *Snake* around a bit – y'know, to get the hang of handling her – then I sneaked back down to the island. I tried to see if there were any way I could get into the dungeons. That's when I bumped into the Cat."

Arthur nodded. He knew what the Cat had been doing there. Spying on Lady Eris. And him.

"The Cat helped me out. Y'know, looked after me." Teresa continued. "We stayed on the *Snake,* just far enough away from the island to avoid bein' seen. And we popped down to the surface every so often to figure out how to rescue the Captain as well as for the Cat to keep visitin' you. He kept tellin' me about you, y'know. About how Lady Eris had you runnin' around in that house for her."

Arthur flushed with embarrassment. Why did Teresa have to know all about that? It wasn't his proudest moment or -

"I thought you must have been really brave," Teresa said, suddenly.

Arthur couldn't believe his ears. "Excuse me?"

Teresa nodded, unmistakable admiration on her face. "I couldn't have spent all that time with her in that spooky old house! But I thought, if you could stand to be around Lady Eris all the time, scary as she is, then I could find a way into those dungeons."

That's when Arthur realised what an odd situation they'd been in. They'd never met and yet not only had they heard of each other, they'd been each others' inspiration!

"So… did you find a way in?" he asked.

Teresa nodded. "I think so. But I didn't get a chance to try it out. I saw you and the Cat running out of the castle and I had to come and get you."

"Oh, yeah," Arthur said. "Sorry about that."

Teresa shrugged, a small grin on her face. "Not a problem. I'm sure the Cat will figure out a way for us to get back there and help Captain Thrace and the others."

The grin faltered for a second and Arthur knew why. They'd help the people in Lady Eris' dungeon but who was going to help the people back in Waterwhistle? Who was going to help her brother and her dad?

In that moment, Arthur realised what it was about Teresa that he liked. She was brave and brash and always full of grins. She could face down Yarnbulls and steal pirate ships all day long. And yet there was one thing she was afraid of – anything happening to her family or the people she cared about.

And Arthur suddenly felt that someone as brave and strong as Teresa deserved to have someone help her out when she needed it.

"We'll stop her," he said, suddenly, surprising himself with the strength in his voice. The tone wasn't lost on Teresa. Her eyes instantly jumped up to his. "I don't know how," Arthur went on, "but… we'll stop whatever it is Lady Eris is doing to Waterwhistle and we'll get everyone back to normal. I promise."

The words seemed to pick Teresa up straight away.

"You know what?" she said. "You're right. Who does she think she is, comin' into our village, spinnin' her spells. Doesn't she know we've got bigger things to worry about? There's a blummin' war on!"

They both laughed and Teresa was suddenly standing up straighter, back to her previous, worry-proof self.

"Hey, an' I'll tell you what else," she smirked, nudging Arthur on the shoulder. "I bet Lady Eris is right scared now that Arthur Ness is on the case!"

And even though she was joking, the way she said his name made Arthur feel ten feet tall.

THE BROKEN CROWN

Before Arthur actually saw the island of Graft, he saw its Travel Lines.

A cable became visible above them, parallel to the one they were on. Then another slightly further away. And then one below them and another to the left. The lines were all beginning to converge on the island, Arthur knew, even though the island itself was still hidden by the darkness. Already, Arthur could see it was going to be much, much bigger than the one they'd escaped from.

The Travel Lines began to appear in ever greater numbers. Arthur marvelled at how they popped into view and filled in the gaps between the already-visible points of light that joined them together. Like some cosmic dot to dot, Arthur thought with a grin.

Just a minute later, he saw his first ship. Some kind of passenger vessel, slightly smaller than the *Snake*. He could just about make out people on board getting their luggage together and preparing themselves for their imminent arrival on Graft. Then another cruiser, even smaller and rounder than the first came into view away to the left. Just as Arthur was beginning to think the *Galloping Snake* was the biggest ship around, though, he looked up and drew in a sharp breath of awe at the sight above him. The massive, hulking underside of another ship passing overhead. He didn't know if it was another cruiser or a merchant trader or something else… but whatever it was, it dwarfed the *Snake*.

There were scores, of ships now, Arthur saw. All looming out of the darkness one by one. Craft of all shapes and sizes moved up and down the lines, switching from one to another via the junction points, illuminated by a hundred tiny points of light.

At first, the lines had all been pointing towards the presence of something unseen, hovering in the Black just beyond the grasp of eager eyes. But soon, an unbelievably huge shape lumbered out of the darkness.

Arthur held his breath in sheer wonder at the sight before him. It was basically a floating horizon, cut away from its surrounding world and placed, hanging, in space. The bottom half was completely flat while the top face was covered in buildings and people, hills and valleys, fields and forests. It was like an infeasibly huge plate crammed with life and shapes and movement ontop and nothing underneath.

Lady Eris' island had been absolutely *tiny* in comparison to this.

"Welcome to Graft," said the Cat, wandering up behind Arthur. "It's a cosy little place, nice and out of the way."

"Little?" Arthur scoffed. "It's massive!"

"There are lots of bigger islands in Arilon," said the Cat. "You'll be seeing them soon, no doubt. But this one's a good place to start."

Even from as far out as they were, it took another half hour or more to finally reach the surface. By the time they got close, darkness was falling over the island and Arthur noticed the sun was in a different relative position than it had been earlier. He stifled a laugh of wonder as he realised the island was actually *rotating*.

Teresa guided the *Galloping Snake* towards what looked to Arthur like the island's main ship port. There were dozens of wooden platforms sticking out from the main dock. Most of them had vessels of various sizes docked there. Teresa picked an empty bay and followed the Travel Line down to it.

Slowly and smoothly, Teresa eased the galleon towards the wooden gantry that waited for them. They finally came to a stop between two huge cargo boats. They were bigger than the *Snake*, Arthur saw. (Though, to him, nowhere near as cool).

As the trio walked down the ship's gangplank and onto the quayside, the hustle and bustle of Graft was beginning to fill Arthur's senses. This was more like London, he thought. Lots of people, lots of noise, lots of smells. Yes, he thought, a great smile on his face, he could definitely get used to this place.

The place looked old-fashioned to Arthur. Almost medieval or something like that. Horse and cart seemed to be the main method of transport. People dressed in simple, roughspun clothes and a few had swords (actual swords!) hanging from their belts. The crowds clamoured on all sides and voices shouted a thousand thousand things. There were smells of food being cooked and sold at the roadside and above them, the streetlights were blinking on one at a time as the nighttime darkness descended. Considering the places didn't appear to have electricity, Arthur wondered just what was powering the lamps.

As alien as it all seemed, it also seemed completely normal. There were farmers, miners, labourers... they could have been taken straight from the towns and cities back home, Arthur thought. The buildings that surrounded them were factories, warehouses and all kinds of places of work. People were streaming out of them with expressions of weariness and happiness – the satisfaction of hard work well done.

"Here on Graft," said Teresa as they pushed through the crowded street, "everyone works hard. The adults work hard at various jobs and the kids work hard at school.When they finish school, they do their homework then they go out to their night-time jobs and they work hard at those, too."

"Sounds like a tough life," said Arthur.

"Indeed it is," the Cat said, leaping up onto Arthur's shoulders. "Oh, you don't mind do you? Lots of feet down there. Anyway, yes, the people of Graft *do* have a bit of a tough life. Which is why, when they've finished their night-jobs, many kids head to places like the one we're going to now."

"Which is where, exactly?" Arthur asked.

Teresa smiled. "The pub."

Arthur waggled a finger in his ear, pretending to clean it out. "I'm sorry, I don't think I heard you properly. It sounded like you said we were going to a pub."

"It's called the Broken Crown," said the Cat.

Arthur's mouth dropped open. "You... you're serious, we're going to a pub?"

"Oh, don't worry," laughed the Cat. "They don't serve alcohol at kids' pubs. But they do have over fifty kinds of pop and more types of juice than you can shake a Yarnbull horn at."

Arthur shook his head. A pub for kids..! He seriously didn't think there was anything else that could surprise him, now.

"Hey, where's my bone?" came a deep voice from behind Arthur. "Where's my bone? Anyone seen my bone?"

He turned round just in time to see a big, hulking dog trotting up the road, nose to the ground. "Where's that blummin' bone got to?" the dog muttered to himself.

A horse, tied up outside a shop, shook its long head as it watched the frantic hound scuttle past and huffed, "Stupid dog."

The Cat roared with laughter when he saw Arthur's face.

"What," he laughed, "you thought I was the only talking animal? We're not all as stupid as the creatures in your world, you know!"

Before long, the trio arrived at a ramshackle building in the centre of town. A wooden sign hung high over the door, swinging softly in the gentle night breeze. And on the sign, the name 'The Broken Crown' with the picture of a crown in two pieces, the gems and jewels, scattered over a rough, wooden tabletop.

The building didn't seem to be in much better state than the crown, Arthur thought. Some of the paint was peeling and one of the window shutters was hanging off. And yet, despite all that, the place seemed to give off an odd sense of comfort and friendliness – probably down to the windows that glowed a warm orange from all the activity inside.

As they headed through the door, Arthur was glad to see his instincts had been correct. The place was absolutely crammed wall-to-wall with kids of all ages. But rather than the rowdy noise he'd heard when going past pubs in London, this place felt like a collection of friends relaxing and swapping stories about a long day.

The Cat directed them towards the bar and they pushed through the throng of people. Standing behind the counter, serving a neverending sea of customers was a big, round man with a bushy moustache and a very grumpy-looking face. He was dishing out drinks while a skinny, young fellow wandered around with a tray, collecting empty cups and glasses.

"Frogham!" the Cat shouted and the big barman looked up at them. Straight away, the sour expression melted away and the big man was suddenly all smiles.

"Cat!" Frogham called back. "You're alive! I'd heard the Queen had stuffed you and mounted you on her mantelpiece!"

"Well, it wasn't a mantelpiece," said the Cat, "more like a trinket shelf. Ah, but wait 'til you hear how I escaped…"

"A-HEM!" Teresa cleared her throat very loudly and both old friends stopped in mid-sentence, staring at her.

"Oh, I'm sorry," she said, sarcastically. "Did me dyin' of thirst interrupt your conversation?"

Frogham laughed a laugh so loud and deep, Arthur could feel it in his shoes.

"Hey, Cat, I like this one!" the barman nodded at Teresa. "Where'd you find 'er?"

"Well, we have a lot of catching up to do so why don't you set us up with something to eat and drink and a nice, private table at the back…" said the Cat, "…and I'll tell you all about it."

BLASTBERRIES
AND CATCHING UP

It wasn't until Arthur started his meal that he realised how ravenously hungry he was. It turned out daring escapes made for hungry work. But as tasty as the meat and potato stew had been, the highlight of the meal was definitely his drink. A tall, cold glass of something called blastberry juice.

"This is delicious!" he said for the sixth time, wiping the sweet, sticky stuff from round his mouth with the back of his hand. He set the glass of juice down and stared again at the swirling orange and crimson lights dancing about inside. "I've never heard of a blastberry before."

"They only grow in Arilon," the Cat said, lapping up his fizzy milk. "You have to pick them wearing metal gloves. In case they explode."

"Ex...explode..?" Arthur looked up.

"Oh, yes," the Cat went on. "Squeeze a ripe blastberry too hard, it could take your whole hand off." He looked up from his milk and smiled at Arthur. "But they're scrummy, yes?"

"Don't worry," Teresa smirked at Arthur's worried face. "Once they've been picked, they're safe. No more boom boom."

"Unless you shake it really hard," said the Cat. "Fizz it right up. People dancing with unopened tins of blastberry juice in their pockets tend to get very nasty surprises. Puts a severe crimp in your foxtrot."

Somewhat nervously, Arthur took another sip of the juice. He fancied he could almost feel tiny explosions as it slid down his throat and into his stomach. But, he thought with a grin, it was that slightly dangerous stinging that just made it all the tastier.

"But…" the Cat said as he finally finished the last of his drink, "…we didn't escape from crazed cow monsters just to talk about blastberries, did we?"

Arthur suddenly realised this was the part he'd been dreading. Flying around on borrowed pirate ships was fun. Lady Eris and Yarnbulls and whatever was happening to Waterwhistle was *not* fun. Arthur had a horrible feeling that the next few minutes were going to make him aware of just how much danger he was really in.

And then they'll know what kind of a scaredy-cat you really are, won't they?

Frogham came bustling over, another tray of drinks in his meaty hands.

"These ones are on the house as well," said the barman, "on account a'your miraculous return from the dead, me feline friend!"

His face was so jolly now, it was hard for Arthur to imagine the grumpy-looking man they'd seen before.

"Right, let's get down to it, then," the barman said as he took a seat at the table. "Young Stick'll keep the punters 'appy for a spell but e' ain't too bright, bless 'im. 'Fore long, he'll ferget to ask the customers for any money, like as not."

Arthur peeked up from his stew and looked Frogham up and down, as much as he dared. He was friendly enough but this was a new person into the small circle. The Cat seemed to notice Arthur's apprehension.

"What we're about to discuss, Arthur," the Cat said, "you'll see there's a conflict going on. And there are sides. And Frogham here, he's on ours."

"Good blummin' thing, too," the barman said, "takin' wanted fugitives under me roof."

Arthur gulped. He knew it. Wanted fugitives.

"Okay, are you sitting comfortably?" the Cat asked, pulling his second bowl of fizzy milk toward him. Arthur nodded, gingerly. He could see Teresa glancing around the pub rather than preparing to listen to the Cat – clearly, she'd already had this talk.

"Right then," the Cat said to Arthur. "Let's start with the islands…"

- THE IDEA ISLANDS -

"You see," he started, "everyone on Arilon lives on the islands. But they're not just pieces of land like in your world. Each island is an Idea. Let's take where we are now. Graft. You see, Graft's Idea is 'hard work'. The people here know the value of putting in a solid day's work and getting the satisfaction of a job well done in return.

"You saw when we arrived that this island has lots of Travel Lines. Well, it's not just the ships that use them. Ideas travel along them, too. Those Lines out there transmit Graft's Idea out to the rest of Arilon. Through them, people all over Arilon feel the Idea of hard work.

"Popular Ideas come from islands with lots of Lines. Hard work. Fun. Greed. And then, there are those Ideas that only a few people feel strongly. Charity. Murder. Bravery…"

"Okay..." said Arthur, "...so some islands have more control over people's thoughts than others, I get it. But... what does all that have to do with the Queen?"

"Well..." said the Cat, looking down into his milk, "...that's where it starts to get rather unfortunate..."

- THE QUEEN -

"The Queen ain't actually a Queen," said Frogham, taking over. "She just showed up, one day and *declared* 'erself Queen."

"Didn't you fight her?" Arthur asked.

"With what?" the barman shrugged. "Arilon ain't got no army. Jus' peacekeepers – and they ain't really set up to deal with that kind a' conflict. See, what you got to understand, Arthur, is that, naturally, Arilon's in a state a' *balance*."

Arthur was confused, "Balance...?"

The Cat moved the salt and pepper shakers so they stood a few inches apart. Then, he pressed a paw down on the curved end of a fork so the handle rose up. Arthur picked up the fork and, seeing what the Cat wanted him to do, rested it carefully across the top of the two shakers, forming a bridge.

The Cat went on. "It's all in the way the islands are connected. There are bad Ideas – like greed or jealousy. But good Ideas, too. Kindness, helpfulness and so on. We feel them all but there are more connections to the good Ideas than the bad ones.

"Yes, some people are more naturally bad than others so they feel the nasty Ideas more strongly, even though there are less connections to them. Those people sometimes do nasty things, so we have the peacekeepers to keep them in check. But, generally, most people are good most of the time."

Arthur nodded in understanding, looking down at the fork bridge. "I see. Balance."

"The Queen changed all that, though," said Frogham, shaking his head. "See, Arthur, she decided that she wanted to control everyone in Arilon. That meant controlling what they think an' feel. So…"

Arthur suddenly saw where this was going. "She started cutting the Travel Lines, didn't she?"

The Cat smiled, impressed.

"That, she did, boy, that she did," Frogham looked sad, all of a sudden. Sad and tired. "She travels around Arilon with 'er fleet of warships, trimmin' and prunin' the Travel Lines. Like she's growin' a plant that she wants to shape just so.

"One a' the first islands she went to was Duseeya. Their Idea is Self-Reliance. They know – so we all know – that if you rely on yerself rather than waitin' for everyone else to do everythin' for yer, then you're in more control of yer life.

"The Queen cut hundreds a' cables from that island. There's only a few left, now. The Idea of Self-Reliance suddenly got a lot weaker right across Arilon."

Arthur nodded. "Well, that must help the Queen," he said. "Nobody thinks its their responsibility to fight her. Everyone waits for someone else to do it. That means *nobody* does it."

"She's messin' with the way people feel," said Frogham, "which messes with the way they *think*. Which messes with the way they *act*."

The Cat knocked the salt shaker over and the fork clattered to the table. Arthur nodded.

No more balance.

"But… but what about you lot?" Arthur asked. "You're still fighting her."

"People are still individuals," said the Cat. "They're still clever or selfish or kind or greedy. Depending on how much of those you naturally feel, you'll feel certain Ideas more or less."

"So, if you're a naturally brave person," asked Arthur, "and the Queen cuts Travel Lines to the Bravery island, then you'll be less brave, but still more brave than others..?"

The Cat grinned. "Precisely. Naturally brave, that's us."

"Yeah…" Frogham took a drink. "Or naturally stupid."

"So…" Arthur mulled the information over in his mind, "…the Queen wants to control all of Arilon. But why? If she already owns an armada and stuff, she must already be rich."

"It's not money that drives the Queen," said the Cat, "It's power. She wants to control everyone just to control them. She has no other purpose, no other desire. She just wants to hold everyone in her hands as if we were nothing but dolls…"

The Cat was staring into the half-distance now, recalling something in his mind as he talked about the Queen. Some memory or knowledge, Arthur thought, that he wasn't sharing with the rest of them.

Another question popped into Arthur's head.

"What about us?" Arthur said. "Me and Teresa? Does it work on humans, too, this cable-cutting thing?"

"Not really," said the Cat, his attention coming back to his surroundings. "Human minds are very similar to ours but you're not plugged into our islands. You seem quite resistant to the Ideas – more likely to stick to your own."

"Do you get many humans in Arilon?" Arthur asked.

"Not many," Frogham said. "But every so often, some humans do fall through to this world, one way or another."

Arthur definitely wanted to hear more about that but thought perhaps now wasn't the time to ask.

"Judging from the activity in Waterwhistle," the Cat went on, "it looks like those travellers have given old Queenie the idea of going on some trips of her own. Looks like she wants to head out into the Human World. And once she gets there, I think it's safe to say she'll set about doing the same thing there as she's doing here."

"But, how..?" Arthur asked. "Our ideas aren't connected together by cables."

The Cat looked as though he was about to say something – but, in the end, whatever it was, he decided to leave for another time.

"The only thing we know," he shrugged, eventually, "is that Lady Eris is Binding the inhabitants of Waterwhistle so she can take their thoughts into her direct control."

"But, why?" asked Arthur.

"I don't know," admitted the Cat as he lapped up the last of his fizzy milk. "That's why we're going to ask Bamboo."

Frogham raised his bushy eyebrows in surprise. "You're goin' ter see Bamboo? You think you'll be able ter find 'im? You know how hard 'e is ter track down!"

"Plus, you told me he were crazier than a sack of cuckoo birds," said Teresa.

"Okay, okay," said the Cat. "Yes, he can be hard to find. And yes, he is a little on the eccentric side. But he's pretty much the best Weaver in the whole of Arilon. Probably even better than the Queen. He should be able to give us some insight into what's going on in Waterwhistle."

Frogham nodded in approval. "Well, speakin' of which, could you ask 'im a couple of questions about me pub? Me packet snacks aren't sellin', see, and I wondered if…" and with that Frogham and the Cat wandered off into the crowded tavern, chatting away, leaving Arthur and Teresa behind like an afterthought.

"Bye, then!" Teresa waved to them, sarcastically. She turned to Arthur and rolled her eyes, smiling. "Sometimes it's better to just leave him to it, I reckon. The Cat knows what he's doin'."

Arthur nodded. Weavers? Bamboo? Islands? Ideas? The confusion on Arthur's face didn't go unnoticed by Teresa.

"Lot to get your head around, isn't there?" she said.

"It all makes sense," Arthur said, "it's just a bit… new."

"I felt exactly the same way when the Cat told me." Teresa nudged Arthur's shoulder and grinned. "Don't worry. I'll look after you. You'll be alright."

Arthur smiled. Teresa did have a knack of making him feel better but it didn't hide the fact that, bit by bit, he was beginning to feel way out of his depth.

Arthur liked the Cat but he did seem a little too reckless and carefree. As though this was all just a game to him. He'd seen Arthur being bossed about by Lady Eris and decided to recruit him into this little war – but what if Arthur hadn't wanted to join? Lady Eris had tried to control Arthur. If the Cat was trying to make Arthur do things he didn't want to do, then how was that any different?

- 102 -

All kinds of confusing thoughts bumped and bashed around inside Arthur's head. Rather than saying anything, though, and making himself look stupid, he kept quiet and finished his blastberry juice.

There was a jingling and clattering of glasses, suddenly, and Stick – Frogham's barboy – came stumbling up to the table.

"Um… any a' yoo seen Mr. Frogham? I thinks we done run out of Stink Juice. Ain't no more comin' out the taps."

Teresa pointed into the crowd. "He went that way, somewhere, with the Cat."

Stick fumbled with the tray of glasses, nearly dropping it. "Oh gosh, okay. Cuz the Stink Juice… it's so popular… people's gettin' all uppity about it…" but by now, he was wandering off, talking to himself, the two children completely forgotten.

Teresa and Arthur looked at each other – and burst out laughing.

"Come on," Teresa wiped the tears of laughter from her eyes, "don't tell me you don't love this place!"

"Well," admitted Arthur, "it's certainly growing on me."

The Cat suddenly popped up onto the table from nowhere.

"Honestly, leave you two alone for five seconds and you start giggling. It's like you're children or something," he said. "Now buckle down. We've got work to do."

"Before you start going on about this Bamboo fella again," Teresa said, "can I remind you I've got a promise to keep?"

The Cat nodded. "Don't worry, I hadn't forgotten. I'm already planning how to rescue Captain Thrace from Eris' dungeons. We owe him. Without him getting you out of there, Teresa, we wouldn't be sat here now." Then the Cat smirked, "Besides, breaking people out of Lady Eris' personal dungeons will annoy her no end. And annoying Lady Eris is like the dot on my 'i'. The shine on my shoes. The cherry on my cream cake…"

Again, Arthur noted how much fun the Cat was having in the face of serious danger.

"Okay," said the Cat. "Let's eat some Orange Rocket Cake, warm up our best action music and figure out how to break *into* a prison!"

SHUTTING UP SHOP
(from the initially happy thoughts of Karl Frogham)

It was good ter see the Cat again. So glad he ain't dead. It'd make fighting the Queen kinda difficult if he was. He's the only thing she's scared of. Heavens, if I knows why.

"You need anything else before I go, Mr. Frogham?" asks Stick.

"I just need yer to go and fetch them barrels of Mudwater in from the back," I say. "Then you can get off 'ome."

"Right you are, Mr. Frogham," says Stick and he disappears out the back door.

I like Stick - hard worker, very polite. Thicker than a plank a' wood, mind, but I s'pose you can't have everythin'.

The front door creaks open and three men walk in. Tall, thin. Look like undertakers. They're wearin' identical black suits which is immediately suspicious since there ain't many folk on Graft that wear suits, not ones this expensive lookin'. They got pristine, white shirts and perfectly straight black ties. And then they got wide-brimmed hats what cover most of their faces. All's I can see are their noses and thin, cruel-lookin' mouths. Their hands are all in their pockets except the one at the front who's carryin' a small, black, leather valise. His bony, white fingers are clutchin' the bag handle like 'is life depends on it. The weirdest thing is they all look exactly the same. Like triplets or somethin'.

"Take us to the cat," the middle one says.

I shrug me shoulders and keep wipin' the bar top down. "What cat?"

"The talking cat," says the one on the left.

"The one with no name," says the one on the right.

"There's lots a' talking cats frequents this establishment," I say, tryin' to hide how nervous I am. "Talkin' dogs, too. Whether or not they 'ave names ain't no business a' mine."

"So you will not tell us where the cat and the human boy are?" the one on the left asks again.

I go cold. They know about Arthur. But I keep on wipin' the bar top and shrug.

"Very well," says the middle stranger.

He puts the black bag down on my countertop and I can finally see his hands properly. Me grip tightens on the cloth in shock when I see his fingers. 'Cause they ain't really fingers at all. They're long, thin, sharp, shiny lengths of metal. Straight away, I know what these strangers are.

Needlemen.

People talk about 'em in hushed, scared voices. They're the stuff of late-night stories and myths. Sometimes, children are told that if they're naughty, the Needlemen will come and get 'em. But no-one believes they're actually real 'cause no-one's ever seen one.

Well... no-one that's lived to tell the tale.

The Needleman clicks open the valise and reaches inside. He takes out a small, rolled up piece a' cloth which he then lays on the bar top I just finished wipin'.

"If you will not co-operate..." says the one on the left.

"...you will be replaced," says the one on the right.

The middle one unrolls the cloth. It looks like a small table mat except it's got all these tiny pictures of faces on it. But the faces are all blank. No eyes, no mouths or noses.

Except one. One of the faces is filled in. And I recognise it. Blessed islands, I recognise it!

But it's too late for me to warn anyone what I've discovered - the Needleman's fingers 'ave started moving. He waves 'em over the mat, super-speed, like he's typin' some infernal words onto an invisible typewriter. The needle-fingers are glistenin' in the dim light of the wall-torches as they burn low. They're shinin' as they start to move so fast, they all just become one big, shimmerin' blur.

I look into the mat again and I can feel it tuggin' me. I feel terrified of something, but I don't know what. Suddenly, threads shoot out of the mat, wrappin' around me. As they wrap around me, I can see them wrappin' around the stranger, too. But as they cover me up, they change him. Change him to look like *me!*

He smiles at me with my face.

Then I fall towards the mat, towards one of the blank faces and everythin' goes bl-

BARRELS DONE
(from the simple thoughts of Mikkal 'Stick' Stikkelson)

I pokes me head into the pub. I thoughts I heard some commotion. Shouting or somesuch. But Mr. Frogham's standing behind the bar, wiping the top down and whistling. Hmph. Must've 'magined it. Always 'maginin' things, me. Mr. Frogham says I should do less 'maginin' and more workin'.

"I'm all done, Mr. Frogham," I say.

He waves to me. "Okay, I'll see yer tomorrow. Tell yer old mother I said 'ello."

I nod. "Yessir, I will."

"Oh, and tell 'er not to worry about 'er back. I'm sure it'll get better with rest."

I frown. "How did you knows about that? I didn't think I'd mentioned it..."

Mr. Frogham looks at me and smiles. It's a strange smile. Kind of looks like he's using his face for the first time, getting' used to how it works.

"Didn't you know, Stick?" he says. "I'm very good at findin' things out. Give me enough time... I'll know *everythin'.*"

CREEPING FEAR

Arthur stood alone on the deck of the *Galloping Snake* and stared at the Travel Line as it stretched away into the darkness. Although he couldn't see it, he knew exactly what waited on the other end of that Line. He knew exactly what it looked like and he knew just how terrified he was of seeing it again.

But, for their plan to work, he was going to have to go to Lady Eris' castle once again.

The burst of bravery he'd felt that led him to steal the mirror from Lady Eris' safe felt like a million years ago, now. And it had largely evaporated by the time he'd jumped through the tapestry with the Cat. By then, he was just running for his life.

The wonder of experiencing Arilon had been so awe-inspiring, he'd forgotten to be scared for a while. But now they were back in the thick of things. Going toe-to-toe with Lady Eris.

Welcome back, fear.

Welcome back? I never left.

Arthur put his hand into his shorts pocket and felt the tin of blastberry juice. He'd put it there for safekeeping, but it was making him nervous, sitting there. He took it out and placed it carefully on the siderails on the edge of the ship (the gunwhales, Teresa had told him they were called – he was going to have to remember the proper names for the parts of the ship).

Leaving the bright green tin standing there against the blackness of the NothingSpace, Arthur reached over to the telescope. Time to check again.

The shiny, brass scope was fixed to the gunwhale and Arthur swivelled it so it was pointing along the Travel Line and he put his eye to the end.

Although Lady Eris' castle was still too far away for the naked eye to see, the telescope somehow punched through the darkness with ease. Just as it had done the first six times he'd looked, Arthur's stomach lurched a little as the dark grey castle came into view. Touching the cold metal, Arthur inched the telescope down a bit, past the castle ramparts and main gate. Then along a bit, off to the side, beyond the courtyard.

No-one was there. Yet.

He moved away from the telescope and took a deep breath. On the one hand, he was glad. He didn't have to make his move yet. On the other hand, it just meant that the moment was still to come. Waiting for something scary to happen was even worse than the scary thing itself, Arthur thought.

The slight swaying motion of the *Galloping Snake* reminded Arthur of the only time, before coming to Arilon, that he'd ever been on a boat.

"Dad! Look!" Arthur pointed into the sky as he held tight to the edge of the small rowboat.

Arthur's father looked up in time to see a formation of four spitfires go speeding by overhead. Arthur grinned from ear to ear. The droning hum was deafening but extremely thrilling. The planes held a tight diamond shape as they passed.

"What formation is that, dad?" Arthur asked.

Arthur's father smiled. "We call that the 'show off to the people on the ground' formation."

As the planes disappeared into the distance – large, black shapes slowly turning into tiny, black dots – the hum softened to a distant buzz and the tranquil silence of the lake returned.

The fishing trip went back to being just Arthur and his dad. He knew why they'd come. His dad was going back to the base tomorrow. He was flying off to fight Hitler. This was going to be their last time alone together.

"When you're up there," Arthur asked, "being shot at... isn't it frightening?"

"Well, you're not up there alone," his father said. "You're in a squadron. Your mates are up there with you. And when the enemy are shooting and your mates need your help... well, there's no *time* to get scared."

Arthur checked the telescope. Again, nothing.

But wait-

Specks, at first. Then, very quickly, the specks became figures. Teresa. The Cat. Some other people.

And Yarnbulls.

Arthur grabbed the tin of blastberry juice and stuffed it back into his short pockets. He ran over to the ship's wheel and span it round. At the same time, he threw the large, wooden lever forward just as Teresa showed him. Instantly, suddenly, the sails filled with the mysterious, unfelt wind and the *Galloping Snake* lurched off towards Lady Eris' castle.

No time to be scared?

Arthur hoped his father was right.

RETURN TO CASTLE ERIS

Almost immediately, the island and the castle emerged out of the darkness. The fear flooded through Arthur's veins with full force as he saw with his own eyes the turrets, the walls, the gates of Castle Eris.

And yet, his grip tightened even more onto the ship's wheel and through gritted teeth, Arthur whispered;

"*Faster… faster…*"

The *Snake* picked up more and more speed as it arrowed down towards the island. The ship's anchor ring whipped along the Travel Line, making a strong, droning **thrummmm** that got louder as the ship picked up more speed.

Arthur could see the others with his naked eyes now. Teresa and the Cat were hurtling as fast as they could towards the island edge, followed by a straggley bunch of strangers (no doubt, the prisoners) and chased by a horde of enraged Yarnbulls.

The strange menagerie of characters was getting nearer and nearer to the island's edge. Any moment now, the Yarnbulls would have them trapped.

Suddenly, the moment was right and Arthur yelled to himself;

"*Now!*"

He pulled the motion lever all the way back and the huge sails fell away to nothing, the mysterious wind, dismissed. But the ship still had loads of momentum – it was slowing down a little but it was still hurtling toward the ground.

And that was where the next stage of the plan came in.

Arthur grabbed the wheel and spun it to the right as hard and fast as he could. Hand over hand, faster, faster. And slowly, the big ship started to turn. Still following the Travel Line, the *Snake* was turning slowly to the right, coming down sideways – almost *skidding* like Arthur used to do on his bike down the Commons road.

For just a second, Arthur imagined what he must look like. A young boy, just ten years old, steering a pirate ship all alone. Speeding into danger. Moments away from being smashed to pieces on the shore of an island. And for just a second, just the slightest moment, did he feel just the slightest touch of...

...excitement?

But then the moment was over as he saw the ground coming up towards him way too fast.

"Come on, come *on!*" Arthur span the wheel until it couldn't move anymore and then he held it in place, the ship fully turned to its side, now, skidding, sliding towards the island's surface and Arthur willed it and willed it and willed it to slow down but the ground was coming too, too fast and Arthur was going to crash and destroy the ship and kill himself and his friends and the prisoners.

"*Stop*, you stupid ship! *STOP!*"

And the *Galloping Snake* bumped gently onto the ground.

Arthur blinked.

A perfect landing!

"Arthur!" came the Cat's voice from somewhere down below. "The ladder!"

Oh. Yes. Right. Rescue in progress.

He ran back over to the side of the ship and unhooked the three rope ladders that were attached to the side. He threw the ends down and they unrolled open, one after the other. The Cat, Teresa and the prisoners all immediately began to scramble up them.

Arthur looked up into the courtyard. The familiar howl of enraged Yarnbulls reminded him that danger was still hot on the Cat's heels.

Time for his next task.

He took the blastberry juice out of his pocket and shook it. Really, really hard.

Arthur could feel the tin begin to vibrate, as though it were filled with rocks, all bashing against each other, fighting to get out. The tin started to jump in his hand. It took all Arthur's strength to keep it from dropping out onto the deck. Arthur grabbed the struggling tin with both hands and held it over the flaming torch next to the telescope.

Very suddenly, the tin got hot. Very hot. And even more jumpy. With a final effort, Arthur threw the blastberry juice as far and hard as he could in the direction of the Yarnbulls.

The creatures had almost reached the *Snake's* hull – just moments away from grabbing the final prisoners as they leapt onto the hanging ladders. Arthur knew his throw would be rubbish. At school, the PE teachers had virtually banned him from cricket. Even before the tin of juice had gone far, Arthur knew his failure was imminent.

"You need to make sure you get a direct hit on the Yarnbulls," the Cat said. In the background, Teresa prepared to leave the ship and head down to the Castle to free the prisoners.

Arthur looked at the juice tin in his hands. "This little tin's going to make the Yarnbulls retreat?" he asked.

"The Yarnbulls are made of yarn..." the Cat began.

Arthur's eyes widened. "Really?"

"You really are a dimwit, aren't you, Arthur Arthur Ness?" the Cat rolled his eyes. "Yes, they're made of actual yarn. And yarn is extremely flammable. One little spark and it all goes up in flames. The Yarnbulls aren't afraid of much... but they're *very* scared of fire."

"And... what if I miss?"

The Cat cocked an eyebrow. "Then you get this ship all to yourself."

BOOM!

The tin exploded directly over the Yarnbulls – exactly where Arthur had been told to put it. He punched the air in celebration as flaming blobs of molten blastberry juice cascaded down over the creatures in streaks of crimson and orange. And just as the Cat predicted, the Yarnbulls shrieked in terror and ran away as fast as they could. Tiny globules of molten berry had fallen on one or two of the beasts and sprouted into licks of flame.

"Wake up, Arthur!" the Cat cried, suddenly up on the gunwhale at Arthur's elbow. Behind him, Teresa and the prisoners were scrambling over the side and dropping onto the deck.

"I mean, we can hang around if you like," said the Cat. "Maybe Lady Eris will hear about us being here and come through from Waterwhistle with tea and chocolates."

At the mention of Lady Eris' name, Arthur jolted his eyes away from the Yarnbulls.

"Right," Arthur said to himself, under his breath. He sprinted up to the bridge and threw the motion lever forward once more. Instantly the sails billowed up again and the ship lurched forward. Arthur span the wheel hard to the right and the *Galloping Snake* lifted up, swinging, turning away from the island. Pointing back towards the welcoming black of the NothingSpace, Arthur pushed the lever full forward and the ship sped up, up and away at full tilt.

Within moments – and for the second time in two days – Lady Eris' island disappeared into the Black behind them and was gone.

"Well done, Arthur," the Cat said, unmistakable pride in his voice. "You did it!"

Arthur held onto the ship's wheel, out of breath, scared and jelly-kneed and he realised the Cat was right.

He blumming-well *had*.

CAPTAIN CHADWELL THRACE

If Arthur had to be honest, the old man in front of him didn't look much like a pirate captain.

He was unshaven, his scraggly white hair was unkempt and wild. He wore a long, dirty overcoat, draped limply over an old tunic and britches And to top it all off, he had two good eyes – not an eyepatch in sight.

Okay, Arthur had to admit, he *had* been locked up in Lady Eris' dungeons for months. But still… he was more Scruff-beard than Blackbeard. Disappointing.

Arthur was shaken from his thoughts by the last of the prisoners as they left the ship.

"Bye, Arthur," the round, middle-aged man (who smelt more than a little of rat droppings) shook Arthur's hand vigourously as he left the ship. "Fantastic flying! Just jiggetty!"

"Jiggetty?" the Cat cocked an eyebrow. "What the heck does *that* mean?"

Teresa shrugged, "It means 'brilliant', I suppose…"

The Cat shook his head, "You non-cats and your nonsense words…"

And with a final wave to Teresa and the Cat, the last ex-prisoner hobbled down the gangplank, onto the bustling docks of the island called Exeo and vanished into the crowd. Arthur looked out over the place, trying to figure out what it was about this place that had been bugging him since they'd arrived. Then he suddenly realised what it was – none of the buildings had any windows. Not a single one.

"Well, then…" came a voice, suddenly in Arthur's ear.

Arthur jumped as a hand landed on his shoulder and he turned to see the tall figure of Captain Thrace standing over him. Arthur gulped. The old man seemed a lot more fearsome close up.

"I have to thank ye, Arthur Ness. That were some mighty fine flyin', 'tis true. Mighty fine."

Arthur nodded, words stuck in his throat. Thrace turned to the Cat.

"And to you, creature, for mastermindin' the operation."

"It's not 'creature', it's 'Cat'," said the small feline. "With a capital 'C'."

Thrace nodded and touched his cap in apology. Then he turned to Teresa and smiled for the first time.

"And to you, girlie, for comin' back for me just like ye promised, I owe a special treasure-chest-full a' gratitude." And he bowed, making Teresa blush a little.

Then he stood up, "Okay. Now all a' yer, get the hell off me ship."

The Cat blinked, puzzled. "I'm sorry – is that some kind of pirate joke? Because if it is, I don't get it."

The old captain kicked open a wooden panel by his feet, pulled something out of it and spun round – and all of a sudden, he was pointing a very dangerous-looking pistol at the Cat and his companions.

"Well, if ye didn't get the last joke," said the Captain, "then ye certainly won't be laughin' at *this* one. Off. Now."

And just five minutes later, the Cat, Teresa and Arthur all stood on the docks of Exeo watching the *Galloping Snake* disappear along a Travel Line and get swallowed up into the black.

"Well…" said the Cat, "…isn't that just jiggetty."

CAPTAIN CHADWELL THRACE ...AGAIN

The cat and the two human children stood on the docks, amid tugboats and liners and transport boats and they looked up into the black sky, utterly dumbfounded.

"He... he left us!" Arthur finally found his voice.

"It's fine," said the Cat.

And Teresa said, "That low down, dirty, double-crossin', backstabbin', stinky-faced, lice-ridden, scruffy-lookin' *nerf herder!*"

"It's fine," said the Cat.

"What's a nerf?" Arthur asked. Teresa spat on the ground.

"I don't know, but whatever it is, it's as low down, stinky-faced and lice ridden as *him!*" She shouted the last word up into the black Exeo sky.

"It's fine," said the Cat.

"Why do you keep sayin' it's fine?" Teresa shouted at the Cat. But the Cat, his eyes never leaving the sky, just smiled. The two children looked where he was looking.

And as they watched, the *Galloping Snake* suddenly emerged from the darkness and came sliding down towards them.

"Because..." said the Cat, "...it's fine."

The galleon descended gracefully, its anchor ring holding tight to the Travel Line and it eventually touched down softly in front of them. The gangplank slid down and Captain Thrace was standing at the top of it. He wasn't looking down at them, though – he was gazing into the distance, like he was trying to work out a particularly difficult piece of mathematics.

"Lady Eris is goin' to be lookin' fer me, ain't she?" he said into the crisp night air.

"Yup," the Cat answered, making himself comfortable ontop of a nearby wooden crate.

"The *Snake's* been used in two rescues off her island," Thrace said, "and she ain't likely to be too happy 'bout that, is she?"

The Cat shook his head as he lazily eyed a mouse scurrying past. "Not at all."

"Prob'ly got every Yarnbull, Sharp-Eye an' Needleman from Aquila to Zeon lookin' fer me."

"Well, let's put it this way…" the Cat looked at Captain Thrace at last. "There's a large target in the shape of Lady Eris' boot pasted right to your backside, Captain."

Thrace went quite pale.

"And how long do you think it'll take Lady Eris' people to find you?" asked the Cat, moving towards the *Snake*, now. "Well, I don't have to ask, do I? The fact that you came back here tells me you already came up with the answer."

Thrace nodded, his voice a little hoarse. "Not very long."

"And that's an optimistic estimate," said the Cat. He was now halfway up the gangplank. Teresa and Arthur, hadn't moved. The Cat continued. "Those other fellow prisoners of yours, they just did little things, didn't they? Said something bad about the Queen, maybe, or were at the wrong place at the wrong time. But you actually defied her, didn't you? Stole money from a ship owned by Lady Eris, I believe?"

"I didn't know it were hers…"

"Makes no difference. Lady Eris doesn't like to be defied. I know. I've been defying her for a long time. Of course, you *could* take your chances. Go on the run on your own."

"I've been on the run by meself fer me entire career!" the Captain tried to jut his chin out, defiantly.

"Ah, yes," said the Cat, almost at the top of the gangplank, "but you've never been on the run from Lady Eris. Trust me… that's a whole different game. Now, you can try and play that game by yourself…"

The Cat locked eyes with Thrace.

"…or you can stick with someone who knows how to win it."

Arthur could literally see the Captain's brain working it all out at super-speed. Trying to determine every possible way forward without the Cat. Arthur knew he'd soon work out that every single one of those ways forward had the same ending – him locked up in Eris' dungeons. If he was lucky.

But would that be enough, Arthur wondered? Captain Chadwell Thrace clearly liked being the master of his own destiny. He might still take the risk of going it alone. Unless…

"They're rich," Arthur suddenly said.

Thrace's gaze suddenly fixed on the young boy.

"Sorry?"

"The Queen, I mean. And Lady Eris," Arthur fumbled his way through, his nerve getting stronger as he went. "They're really, really rich. I mean, you already know that, don't you? Teresa tells me you tried to steal a few jewels. But imagine getting your hands on loads of it. Enough to fill the hold of the *Snake* fifty times over. You wouldn't have to be a pirate anymore. You could buy your own island."

The idea seemed to light something behind the Captain's eyes. Arthur allowed himself a small smile as he dropped his final line on the old man.

"How do you fancy being called *Governor* Thrace?"

That sealed it. Arthur could tell by the look of yearning on the old man's face. Self-preservation was one thing.

Being ridiculously, filthy, stinking rich was quite another.

His eyes flicked between the Cat and Arthur.

Suddenly a great, warm smile erupted across the old man's face and he stood there, beaming at them, arms wide.

"Welcome aboard the *Gallopin' Snake*, me hearties! Congratulations – you're now a part o' me crew!"

The Cat grinned and strolled aboard. "Cheers."

Arthur and Teresa followed the Cat up. Teresa glared at Thrace as she went past, but said nothing. She still wasn't impressed that he'd tried to leave them behind, Arthur saw. He liked that she let him know it. Captain Thrace actually looked a little bit uncomfortable as he caught Teresa's gaze.

"Oh, one thing, Master Ness," Thrace suddenly took hold of Arthur's shoulder as he went by. "I'm not a pirate. I'm a businessman."

"Oh?" said the Cat. "And what's your business?"

"Piracy."

The Cat looked puzzled, "So... doesn't that make you a pirate, then?"

"Oh, no!" Thrace said, eyebrows raised. "That'd be where you're mistaken. See, a pirate sails around, stealin' things off of ships he comes across."

"And what do you do?"

"Me an' me crew ask all nice like if the folk on the other ship mind terribly if we relieve 'em of all their valuables."

"And if they say no?"

Thrace shrugged/ "Then we shoot 'em dead and take the valuables." He held up a finger, "But we *did* ask nice."

"Well," said the Cat, "far be it for the lowly crew to tell the Captain his business, but there won't be any of *that* going on anymore." The Cat fixed Thrace with a hard, threatening glare. "Am I making myself fabulously clear?"

Thrace made a slight bow. "I suppose so. There ain't nothin' wrong with a temporary change of approach…"

"Right then." The Cat sprang off down the deck, all sweetness and light again. "Get the gangplank up, you kids. The Captain is about to give us his first order."

"…I am?"

"Yes. You're about to order us to set sail for Bamboo's island."

"What..?" Thrace's eyes widened in surprise. "An' how are we goin' to find an island what can't be found on account it keeps *movin*?"

Arthur and Teresa looked on in shock. A moving island?

"Fortunately," said the Cat, "I've got directions."

Thrace looked about, clearly wondering just what he'd gotten himself into.

"Your orders, Captain?" asked the Cat. "Not that I'm trying to tell you what orders to give, of course, totally up to you. Your ship and all that."

Thrace paused for a moment. Arthur recognised the look on his face, because it was the same one he'd worn when he first met the Cat. The old man was trying to decide if he should follow the Cat out the window. Quickly, though, he made his decision.

"Teresa, Arthur, get that gangplank up, yer filthy gully-rats. Then Arthur, get yerself up that mast an' check the riggin'. Teresa, I need them rudder-wheels scrubbed an' locked then you're on the helm and waitin' for my instructions. Come on, get to it, yer bilge-eatin' maggots, we ain't got all day!"

He stalked off after the Cat. "Right, then, Cat, let's be havin' them directions. Bamboo's island awaits, so let's get goin'. The Queen's treasure ain't goin' ter steal itself."

A VISIT FROM A FRIEND
(from the busy thoughts of Montgomery Avis)

I have had the most exceedingly productive morning, here in the shop. Yes - *exceedingly* productive. Surely more productive than anyone else here on Graft. I make maps, you see. Absolute top quality, best of the best. And I've been working for weeks to try and manufacture a stronger type of map paper. This morning, I finally cracked it! The strongest, thinnest map paper in all Arilon!

The Queen may be flying around causing trouble, getting everyone hot under the collar and so on. But, at the end of the day, as my grandfather used to say, the more lost the world becomes, the more it will need maps to show it the way.

Ding-a-ling!

The shop door opens and in walks a fellow I haven't seen in ages.

"Mr Frogham!" I grin. "Why, my friend, it's been too long!"

"Yer right," says Frogham. "It has. I need to ask you something."

"Oh, straight down to business, as usual," I grin. "Not even going to ask me how come I'm never in the Broken Crown? Well, I shall tell you - it's the children, you see. Too noisy. They make my ears ache and-"

"Avis," Frogham interrupts, rudely. "I need one a' yer special maps. I need ter know how ter find Bamboo's Island."

Ah. Now, *this* could be awkward.

"Erm...well, the Cat told me never to tell anyone how to get there..." I stammer.

"Come on, Avis," Frogham smiles. "You can tell me. I'm one of the Cat's closest friends."

"Yes, I know," I say. "And as *you* well know, it's for that very reason, the Cat says you must never know. If the Queen ever wants information about the Cat, she'll try to capture his known friends and allies for interrogation. That means people like you, Andreyev Romanov, Big Sally and Little Sally... none of you can know. Me, on the other hand, well... nobody knows I'm the Cat's friend. So they won't come looking for me. It's quite safe for me to have that knowledge."

"These are dangerous times, Avis," says Frogham, darkly. "*No-one's* safe."

Ding-a-ling

The door opens again and in walk two men in dark suits, one carrying a small, black valise. I know straight away who they are. *What* they are. I turn and try to run out to the back of the shop - but a third man, identical to the other two, is already emerging from the back, blocking my way.

I turn back to Frogham. Except it isn't Frogam, is it? Frogham is gone. Gone somewhere no-one will ever be able to get him back from.

The Needleman with the valise takes a cotton mat out of it and lays it on the counter top. It has many blank faces - but two faces are filled in. Frogham's and someone else I don't recognise.

"I'll never talk!" I cry.

"You won't have ter," says the fake Frogham.

And the Needleman's fingers begin to move.

MAP GAZING

Arthur walked slowly and gingerly into the *Galloping Snake's* navigation room, the heavy mug of mudwater held carefully in both hands. The Cat and the Captain were studying a dizzying collection of maps and charts spread out over the large table.

At the sound of Arthur's entrance, Captain Thrace looked up.

"Ah, there ye are, lad!" the Captain bellowed. "I was beginnin' ter think ye'd gone all the way ter the Bog Islands to ferment the mudwater with yer own two hands!"

The Captain looked a lot different now, Arthur realised with a start. Dark britches, a crisp white shirt and all covered over by a long, black overcoat with gold trimmings. Still no eyepatch but at least there was a tri-corner hat. Now, he really *did* look like a pirate.

"Well, come on, lad! Before I die a' thirst!"

Arthur hurried over and Thrace took the tankard of brown, steaming liquid eagerly. Arthur, for his part, tried not to be sick as Thrace gulped down the horrid-looking stuff.

"Is it really from mud water? From a bog?" he asked, trying not to breathe in the smell.

"Don't judge, lad," said the Captain. "Properly filtered, mud water is a right tasty drink for real men of enterprise. Want to try some?"

"Not in a million years," Arthur said quickly. Captain Thrace and the Cat roared with laughter.

The Captain turned back to the table of charts. The Cat was reciting, from memory, a long, complicated string of coordinates that would help them find Bamboo's moving island. Arthur (not at all eager to get back to scrubbing the masthead) turned and looked around the rest of the room.

All over the walls, there were maps and charts and large sheets of paper with rows and rows of numbers on them. And dozens of shelves with rolled up tubes stacked higher than Arthur could reach. Arthur's eye soon landed on the biggest, oldest map of them all.

A map of Arilon.

Arthur moved slowly toward it, entranced by its size and detail. The paper was older and browner than anything else in the room and there were burn marks all around the edge. As Arthur got closer, he could see it wasn't printed but hand-drawn right onto the actual paper. It wasn't a mass-produced map, it was one of a kind. Some of the ink was old and nearly faded out. Other parts of it were darker, having been added more recently.

There were hundreds and hundreds of islands all connected by a countless mass of long, straight lines going in all directions. Each island's name was written beneath it and Arthur's eyes flitted from one to another, reading the strange names and trying to figure out what each island's Idea was.

Duseeya. Votum. Bonitas. But Arthur's eye was suddenly drawn to two islands that were sitting very close together, like twins.

"Phobos and Valia." The rough-as-sandpaper voice of the ship's captain came from just behind Arthur. Captain Thrace (thankfully minus the mudwater) pointed at the two islands on the map. "Phobos, the isle of Fear. And Valia. Isle of -"

"Bravery," Arthur whispered.

Arthur couldn't take his eyes off them. Either of them. After a moment, he turned to Captain Thrace, a little embarrassed.

"Sorry," he said. "It's just… it's an amazing map."

Beyond the Captain, Arthur saw there was no Cat. He must have ducked out for something. They were alone.

"Me father drew most of it," said the Captain, proudly. "I've added the odd bit here an' there. He travelled from one end of Arilon to the other, chartin' everything as he went. Used to tell me stories of all the things he'd seen. I swore I'd see 'em all meself one day. And most of 'em I have. Shardtree storms, Yarnbull fields, waterfalls tippin' off the edge of islands and fallin' away into the Black…"

He moved his head slightly toward Arthur and lowered his voice. "One time, I even saw the Rainhand."

"Rainhand?"

Thrace nodded and shivered at the same time. "Terrible, terrible creature. That's one experience I don't care to be repeatin'…"

"Is it still up to date? The map?" Arthur said, shaking the old man from his dark thoughts. "I mean, with the way the Queen gets rid of Travel Lines…"

Captain Thrace shrugged. "I s'pose I should get rid of it. Get meself one a' them fancy modern maps from Montgomery Avis or someone like that. Don't suppose me father would complain…"

Arthur looked up. "Oh… is he…?"

Thrace cut Arthur off. "Oh, no, he ain't dead. Well, not yet."

"So…why would he not mind if you threw out his map?"

Thrace was silent for a long time and Arthur began to wonder if he'd asked one question too far. Eventually, the old Captain spoke.

"He set sail from 'ome at sixteen. Before long, he got 'is own ship, the *Unicorn*. Went explorin' and adventurin' and everywhere he went, it were on that ship.

"While I were growin' up, each time the *Unicorn* came into port, I'd know I were goin' to get a present – some souvenir he'd brought back from some far-flung corner of Arilon. And I'd get stories of all the places he'd been and all the places he were goin' next. He must'a taken the *Unicorn* further away from the sun than anyone else ever.

"Then one day, the Queen cut a load a' Lines from Cassinus, the isle of adventure. Guess she didn't want people roamin' around, explorin'… just wanted 'em to have simple, borin' lives. Go to work. Go home. Nothin' else.

"Me father came back that very night. Set fire to the *Unicorn*. Made me burn every gift he'd ever bought me. Told me never to set foot on a ship. Then 'e went to bed. This map were the only thing what survived the *Unicorn* goin' up. I found it an' kept it hidden. Soon as I were old enough, I left home, took the map an' never looked back."

Captain Thrace turned to Arthur now, and whispered low and threatening into his ear. "Listen to me, lad, and listen good. There's lots a' things you can't control in this life. Why, the Queen could cut an island off tomorrow that'd make yer own mother stop lovin' you. So you make sure you look after yerself. Ferget ev'ryone else. If there's anythin' worth takin', then take it first, before anyone else. Whatever the cost."

And with that, he turned back to the chart table. The silence was heavy in the room and Arthur didn't know what to say. So he turned and left the old pirate on his own.

ARRIVAL AT BAMBOO'S ISLAND

Arthur stood at the front of the ship and watched Bamboo's Island slowly emerge from the darkness.

It was much smaller than Graft but bigger than Lady Eris' place. Whereas Graft looked like a town, this was more like a village. Instead of large spreads of buildings, it seemed Bamboo's Island had little clusters of huts dotted about here and there. Like they'd been sprinkled by some giant farmer's hand scattering corn on his fields.

As Arthur looked back and forth across the slowly enlargening island, his gaze caught the shiny, metal shape of the snake that formed the masthead at the very front of the ship. The figure that gave the *Galloping Snake* its name was stretched out in front of the vessel, its body, twirling and twisting around a long pole. The creature reached out ahead of the ship, hissing angrily at the skies. It looked to Arthur like something once alive, some kind of airborne serpent, frozen in mid-flight and placed on the front of this ship. It looked pretty angry, to be honest. He didn't fancy being around if it ever woke up.

"Prepare the gangplank, young Master Ness! This ain't a time fer lollygaggin'!" Captain Thrace's gravelly voice boomed out from the upper deck. Shaken from his thoughts, Arthur turned and jogged over to the starboard side of the ship.

"Aye, Captain!" he called back as he started to unlock the wooden walkway that they'd use to get on and off the ship once it landed.

"Keep us steady as she goes, Miss Smith!" he called to Teresa as she stood at the ship's wheel, guiding them down to the surface. Arthur noticed that she didn't reply with an 'Aye Captain'. Just a glare. To Arthur's surprise, Thrace didn't say anthing about it – he just gave a quick, uncomfortable cough and went off to talk to the Cat.

Arthur joined Teresa at the wheel.

"Still mad at the Captain, then?" he whispered to her.

She huffed as she glanced at him. "Stupid old man. Leavin' us behind like that."

"At least he came back."

"Only because he had to," Teresa said. "Only because he were scared of Lady Eris."

Why don't you tell her how scared _you_ are, eh, Arthur?
How much _you_ want to run away?

Filling the silence, Teresa said quietly. "Me mum died when I were really young. Not long after Sam were born. And me older brother, Albert, he's gone off to fight in the war." She kept her eyes firmly ahead, on the Travel Line before them. "I suppose I'm just not that good with people leaving me, that's all."

Tentatively, Arthur found himself putting a hand on Teresa's shoulder. She turned and looked at him. Arthur didn't say anything out loud, but from the touch on her shoulder and the look on his face, Teresa knew what he meant. He was promising to stick by her side. Whatever happened.

She smiled.

"Land, ho!" Captain Thrace called out from the main deck. Keeping the ship steady and slowly reducing the speed,

Teresa brought them safely into the docks. They were a much smaller version of the ones on Graft. Only a couple of Travel Lines came to the island and there was just one other ship moored there. Finally, the *Galloping Snake* came to a stop with a small bump.

"Getting' better, eh?" Teresa said to Arthur with a wink. "Not dumpin' you on your backside anymore!"

Arthur laughed and ran down to the gangplank. Grabbing hold of the winch, he wound the handle round and round, the wooden walkway lowering itself with every turn. Soon, it had connected itself to the quayside.

"Right, everybody off!" called the Cat, striding down the gangplank. "Somebody remember where we parked."

The four members of the motley crew strode down to the quayside and there waiting for them was an old man standing next to a horse and trap cart. Arthur looked to the man as he expected some kind of greeting. A greeting did come, but not from the man.

"Hello, dearies!" said the horse. "My name's Mary! Welcome to Bamboo's Island! Hop onto my cart and we'll get going."

Arthur and Teresa exchanged surprised glances. Although they knew many animals in Arilon talked, it was the first time they'd actually been addressed by one other than the Cat.

In contrast, Captain Thrace and the Cat both jumped up onto the cart without a second glance. Teresa followed them. Arthur got on last, nodding to the old man who returned the nod with a heavy, weary one of his own.

The old cart creaked and bounced along, following a busy road out of the docks and into the evening countryside as they headed toward their destination village.

Arthur looked around him as nighttime began to creep, slowy across the landscape. The countryside was so like Waterwhistle with tall hills sloping down into large, expansive fields that ran for miles in all directions.

"I still can't imagine that all this is sitting ontop of a floating disc in space," he said to Teresa.

"I know what you mean," she replied. "But then, I suppose it's no different to everything on our planet being sat ontop of a ball floating in space."

"So, my dearies," the horse said, "let me welcome you again to Bamboo's Island. My name's Mary and this grumpy old man sat atop my cart is Elian. So, you're here to see Bamboo, are you? Well, that's just grand. Oh, yes, Bamboo can help you. I don't know what it is you're here to see him about, of course, none of my business, I'm just a lowly horse. But whatever it is, I'm sure you've come to the right place. Why, just last week Elian stubbed his toe on the kitchen table leg – oh, he was in a foul mood that day, let me tell you! And the *language--*"

"Horse, will you please just shut *up*?!" said the man, Elian, at last. "Crikey, it's a wonder you've any breath left in you after all your gossiping! And anyway, since when was this *your* cart?"

"Don't you 'shut up horse' *me*, you silly man," Mary whinnied back. "And of course it's my cart. I'm the one pulling it, aren't I? You just sit on it with your big, fat, backside. Sorry about that, people. My person's a bit grouchy."

"For the illionth time, I'm not your person, you're *my* horse!"

And so it carried on all the way through the countryside. Eventually, the Cat took mercy on everyone's ears and interrupted the squabbling couple, regaling them all instead with tales of his adventures and daring escapes from Lady Eris.

Before long, the cart trundled into a tiny village at the foot of a picturesque range of hills. The man and his horse (or the horse and her man) wound their way between the little bungalows and eventually dropped the group off outside a small, round hut in the centre of the village.

Outside, stood a young, dark-skinned boy in loose-fitting white and grey shirt and trousers. He looked a little bit like the Berber or Tuareg desert nomads Arthur had read about in the library.

"Welcome, my friends," said the boy, grinning as they pulled up. "Bamboo is waiting inside for you. Please, come with me."

Arthur followed the others clambering down off the cart.

"Bye, my dearies!" Mary called. "Hope you have a good visit!"

As they trotted away, Elian said something that sounded to Arthur like 'mind your own business, horse'. Mary argued something back but by now, the pair were disappearing into the rapidly descending darkness.

Arthur looked up into the sky and saw the island had rotated fully away from the sun now. As there was no moon, the only light came from the gas lamps that had somehow popped themselves on as the sunlight disappeared. Although he had already seen this on Graft, it seemed somehow more magical here since there were so few people and the whole village was just so peaceful and quiet.

A familiar nudge on his shoulder woke Arthur up.

"Hey, Captain Daydream," Teresa nodded to the door. "You comin'?"

Arthur took a deep breath. Okay. Time to go on the next stage of this wild ride.

"Time to see Bamboo," the Cat said as they entered the little hut. "Only thing I'll say... try not to stare."

"Stare?" Arthur asked. "At what?"

But the Cat just smiled.

BAMBOO

Arthur tried not to stare. He really did. He tried really very hard indeed. But he couldn't help it.

He was looking at a stick doll on a chair.

Teresa, not taking her eyes off the doll, leaned in close and whispered in Arthur's ear.

"So... Bamboo likes dolls? And this is...what? His favourite one?"

Behind the pair, Captain Thrace was slightly less subtle.

"You said, Cat, that Bamboo was crazy," he said in a gruff voice. "You never said he's a doll collector."

The Cat ignored Captain Thrace and stepped forward to the unmoving stick doll.

"Bamboo, my old friend," he said, "it's good to see you again."

Arthur looked about, puzzled. Why was the Cat addressing the doll? Some kind of strange Arilon custom?

The boy who had met them outside went over to the chair and bent his head down towards the doll's face. Arthur realised with some surprise that he appeared to be *listening* to the stick figure.

Presently, the boy stood up, smiled and spoke.

"Bamboo says he is so glad to see you alive, Cat," he said. "He had heard that the Queen had skinned you, turned you into a flag and flew you from the main mast of the *Twilight Palace*."

"Well, it wasn't quite the *main* mast," said the Cat, "just one of the smaller ones. Oh, but wait till you hear how I escaped..."

For the second time since landing on this island, Arthur and Teresa exchanged shocked glances – and this time, Captain Thrace joined them.

The *doll* was Bamboo?

The boy cocked his head again, listening to the tiny figure, even though it wasn't moving or speaking at all.

"Bamboo is very much looking forward to hearing about it," said the boy, "but time is very short and so will have to wait until another day. Before we begin, may I ask if anyone would like a glass of ice juice?"

"Tell the pile o' sticks over there that I'll have a tot o' rum," Captain Thrace was leaning on the back wall, arms crossed, an amused grin on his face.

The boy looked at the Captain. "Bamboo says you should not be so rude."

The Captain grinned wider. "Tell the pile o' sticks over there that I'm sorry."

The Cat interrupted with a warning glare at the Captain. "I think the drinks can wait, Bamboo. You're right – we're short on time. Please tell us the information you have on the Queen."

The boy nodded his head. "Of course. But first, Bamboo would like to speak to *him*."

The Cat was puzzled. "Who?"

Arthur's heart skipped a beat as the boy turned to look straight at him and pointed.

"Him. Bamboo would like a word with Arthur Ness."

THE CENTRE OF ALL THINGS

"I don't understand," said the Cat. "You know about Arthur?"

"Bamboo saw him in the Threads," said the boy. "He knew he was coming."

Arthur felt hot as everyone in the room turned to stare at him. Even the stick doll seemed to be looking right at him, knowingly.

The boy removed two pieces of paper from his shirt pocket.

"Have you explained to the human children what Bamboo is?" he asked the Cat.

Captain Thrace snorted, "You mean he *ain't* a pile of sticks on a chair?"

The Cat ignored the Captain and turned to Arthur and Teresa. "Bamboo is like the Queen and Lady Eris. He's a Weaver."

Arthur remembered hearing the Cat use that word when they were at the Broken Crown.

"What's a Weaver?" he asked.

"I suppose you'd say it's the same thing as being a wizard or a witch. Basically, its someone who has special abilities to manipulate the Threads. You've seen the huge Travel Lines that connect the islands? Well, just like them, all things, all people, all places are connected by invisible threads. Not just here, but in the Human World too. They connect you to your parents, your friends, your toys, places you like going..."

Arthur and Teresa exchanged sceptical glances.

"…invisible threads?" Teresa said in a voice that showed that Teresa and Arthur had switched the 'crazy' label from the stick doll to the talking cat.

The Cat simply smiled and went on. "Arthur, who's your best friend back home in London?"

Arthur thought – most of his friends back in London weren't very good friends. But there was one…

"Mickey."

"Well," the Cat explained, "when you and Mickey were born, a very thin, faint thread would have connected the two of you together. You see, even back then, there was a slim chance that you would grow up and meet each other. The older you got, the more events started to bring you together. Your parents moved to the same town, they sent you to the same school – each event made the thread that little bit thicker. Until eventually, you met one day - I'm guessing your first day of school?"

Arthur nodded.

"Well, when you met, the thread would have become very thick. And the closer friends you became, the thicker the thread grew. Until now you're best friends and it's as thick as your arm. It's the thing that makes you choose each other when it's playtime. It's the thing that will keep you writing to each other when you grow up and move apart."

Arthur nodded – he could see what the Cat was saying. Some things in life, you felt more strongly about than others. Choosing one toy over another, one sweet over another, one person over another…

"And Bamboo can see these threads?" Arthur asked.

"Yes," the Cat nodded. "And through them, he can see how everything connects to everything else. From there, he can figure out certain things that might happen in the future."

"And so can the Queen?" Teresa asked, warily.

"Yes," said the Cat. "Very few people have that gift. They're all a little bit mad because of it." He turned to the doll and smiled, apologetically. "I hope you don't mind me saying..?"

The boy listened, grinned and said, "Bamboo says, no, not at all."

"Anyway," the Cat finished, "we're here because Bamboo has been reading the Threads and discovered important information about the Queen that he felt I needed to know."

The boy was silent for a long time as he listened to the unmoving doll. Eventually, he spoke.

"The Queen has been trying to gain control over everyone's thoughts for a long time now. A few people such as myself and the Cat have been able to fight against her. Fight... but not defeat. She has severed so many Travel Lines, most people are incapable of strong feelings of self-reliance, resistance or injustice. All feelings they would need to fight her. They are too scared. They are *letting* her win.

"But then, Bamboo noticed the threads were beginning to gather together. A new focal point was beginning to emerge from the chaos. The threads were showing him a person who would become extremely important in the fight against the Queen's tyranny."

Arthur felt a flush of anxiety as the boy returned his gaze to him.

"*You*, Arthur Ness," said the boy. "You are the key to defeating the Queen."

"Me..?" Arthur felt numb. "I'm going to defeat her?"

The boy shook his head. "Bamboo did not say you would defeat her – only that you are the key to doing so. If you turn one way, she is defeated. If you turn another, she will defeat *us*…"

"But…" Arthur's mouth was dry with shock, "…but I would never do that..! I'd never help her!"

But, even as he said the words, Arthur remembered how Lady Eris had tricked him into helping to grow the Yarnbulls in Waterwhistle. And he remembered how he suspected something was wrong – but he was so scared, he pretended everything was fine and went on helping her.

"Please remember, Arthur Ness," the boy said, his voice calm and serene, "nothing is for certain. The threads simply show what *might* happen. What is *likely* to happen. But the only ones who can control what *will* happen is *us*. We have to make our own choices and do what we feel we must."

Arthur suddenly felt like he was under some unbelievable, massive weight.

"Why me?" he asked, his voice a little hoarse. "I'm not special."

"You may not have been born special," said the boy, "but circumstances *made* you special. You're just the right person in the right place at the right time."

Yes, Arthur thought, or the wrong person at the wrong place at the wrong time…

Arthur's head was spinning. He looked at the Cat for some help but the Cat simply stared back at him, completely without expression.

"What is it you want most, Arthur Ness?" the boy asked, softly.

"To not be scared all the time," Arthur said immediately, "…and to go home."

"If you wish to go home, simply ask," said the boy. "There are many tapestries and woven rugs in the Human

World and in Arilon that serve as gateways to one another. All you need is to possess the power to step through them, as the Cat does. The nearest such portal is back on the island of Graft."

The boy handed Arthur one of the pieces of paper he was holding. "This is a spell-map that will open that portal and take you to the rug in the hallway of your home in London."

Arthur almost fell over in shock. This crazy stick doll (or crazy boy – he wasn't sure anymore who it was that was crazy) had just handed him a way home! Not to Waterwhistle, but to his actual, actual home in London – to his mother!

"You may leave whenever you wish," said the boy. "The Cat will help you."

Arthur looked back at the Cat who simply nodded, silently. His face was still expressionless. Arthur felt the weight of all the eyes in the room on him. They were waiting for his decision.

Do it! Do it now!
You know you want to run far away from here!
They're giving you the chance! Take it!

Arthur wanted to listen to his fear. He really did. He could almost see the black and white tiles on the hallway floor back home. And smell the varnish on the coat rack that his father had built just before going away. And see his mother, coming to greet him, smiling, arms open wide…

Then Arthur glanced across at Teresa. For the first time since he met her, she actually looked scared. And he remembered his unspoken promise to her.

"I… er…" Arthur mumbled at first, but then cleared his throat and spoke up louder, "I want to stay and help you fight against Lady Eris and the Queen."

Arthur folded up the spellmap and put it into his pocket.

You're going to regret that…

He'd said the right thing, hadn't he? It felt good to say it, didn't it? Teresa and the Cat were smiling at him now. Yes, he decided. It was the right thing to say.

We'll see, scaredy-cat…

"Very well," said the boy, "and so, onto the Queen. As we know, the Queen has been trying to control everyone's thoughts and feelings by cutting the Travel Lines. But, slowly, the Queen has realised the truth – cutting the Lines greatly influences what people feel but it cannot control their thoughts completely. And so she has begun a new plan.

"The Queen is building a machine."

THE AGENCY ENGINE

"A...machine?" the Cat repeated, wide-eyed. Arthur could tell from the Cat's tone that this was an unexpected move for the Queen. Something the Cat hadn't seen from her before.

From the rear of the room, Captain Thrace snorted, "A machine? Is that what you folk are all worryin' about? Just take a hammer to it and smash it to pieces. Job done, let's go for a beer."

"And how do you smash a machine as big as Arilon?" the boy said to the old Captain. "How do you smash a machine that stretches from one side of the NothingSpace to the other? How do you destroy a machine that has a piece, a pipe, a cable in every island, in every building, in every room, in every man, woman and child in all of Arilon?"

Silence. Everyone was stunned.

"That's a big machine," the Captain admitted.

"Such a huge thing in the hands of the Queen..." the Cat whispered in awe. "What is it for, exactly?"

"Usually, when Bamboo reads the Threads," the boy said, "they point towards some idea or purpose. But around this machine, the threads simply...stop. Nothing can penetrate. Its very existence blocks any potential reading of the future. The only thing that has emerged is the machine's name," the boy paused. "The Queen calls it the Agency Engine."

The instant the boy said the name, the mood in the room changed. The words hung in the air like a guillotine blade waiting to drop. Nobody knew what the name meant –

but it was as if upon hearing it, everyone instinctively knew it meant their doom.

Eventually, the boy spoke again.

"The Threads did not show Bamboo how the machine will work exactly. But knowing the Queen, he feels it must be for one end and one end alone," the boy fixed his gaze on the Cat. "Control. The Queen will use it to do the only thing she has ever wanted to do. Take control of everyone, everywhere. Forever."

Everyone sat still for a moment more. And Arthur was already beginning to regret his decision not to leave when he'd had the chance.

"You said it stretches right across Arilon," said the Cat, "but the good Captain is right... It must have a physical location. A place we can actually go to somehow destroy it."

"Bamboo believes that it does," said the boy, "but where that is, he cannot yet tell. However, although the main machine itself is still some distance from full completion, there is one, small part of it that is almost done.

"This part of the machine alone will have the ability to grant power to the Queen such as we have never seen before. If it is activated, no-one will be able to stand against her and prevent her from completing the rest of the Agency Engine. And so, it is this small part which you must put all your energies into stopping for now."

"So tell us, lad..." Captain Thrace leaned forward, taking everything more seriously now, "...where might this part be found?"

The boy cocked his head, listening to the doll and then spoke again.

"Bamboo cannot be sure. It is very difficult to read anything in the Threads directly about the machine. However, they have shown him the location of someone who does possess the knowledge we seek. The machine's creator."

The boy finally presented the second piece of paper he'd been holding. He unfolded it and showed a grainy-looking photo to his audience.

"His name is Zane Rackham," the boy said. "He is a genius. For years, he worked at the University on Doctreena. He was one of its top professors – and its youngest ever. But one day, a couple of years ago, he disappeared."

The Cat nodded. "I remember. We thought the Queen had taken him but we didn't know what for."

"But now we do," said the boy. Captain Thrace took the photo from the boy and looked at it, closely. Turning it over, he read the information about Zane Rackham on the back.

"Says here, he's been arrested by peace keepers," said the Captain with raised eyebrows. "For bein' drunk an' disorderly in the streets. I like 'im already."

"Okay…" the Cat took a guess, "…so he got abducted, the Queen forced him to design this terrible machine and then he escaped."

"And then got drunk?" Teresa asked, suspiciously.

"Maybe it was because it was his first night off in years," the Captain sneered.

"Or maybe," said the Cat, "he was feeling guilty about what he'd done."

"Regardless, he is now being held by peacekeepers on the isle of Labyrinth," said the boy. "But Bamboo has seen in the Threads that even as we speak, the Queen's agents are on their way to recapture him. If you are to learn anything about the Agency Engine, you must get to him before they do."

"Labyrinth?" the Captain snorted. "That's over a hundred leagues from here!"

The boy smiled. "Then it is fortunate that Bamboo also saw Threads connecting the Cat to an old, selfish pirate who was Captain of the fastest ship in the Black."

Captain Thrace clearly didn't know whether to be offended at being called selfish or complimented on the *Snake* being the fastest vessel in Arilon. In the end, he just shifted uncomfortably and said;

"I ain't a pirate. I'm a businessman."

"Yes…" the boy smiled, "…who specialises in piracy."

ARTHUR THE COWARD
(from the secretive thoughts of the Cat)

Well. *That* was interesting.

The Agency Engine.

Well, Queenie, this is a new type of move for you. Bold. It feels like a winner-takes-all kind of play. I don't like it – mainly because it looks like you're already several moves ahead of me. And that just won't do.

"Did you know, I've been everywhere on this island?" chats Mary as our strange, little group trundles back towards the docks. It's the middle of the night, now. Fully dark. Only the comforting glow of gas lamps to light our way.

"Excuse me!" says poor Elian. "I've *driven* you everywhere on this island!"

"And I've carried you everywhere on this island," Mary huffs. "Which means I've done twice the distance."

"You've certainly done twice the talking."

"Yes..." says the horse, "...and twice the thinking. And judging by how heavy this carriage is getting to pull, you've definitely been doing twice the eating."

"And judging by how much my ears ache, you've been doing twice the moaning."

I never get tired of hearing these two bicker. I've met them several times but they never remember me. They're too wrapped up in their own world to take much notice of all the big, strange, dangerous things going on around them. They pretend to get on each others' nerves but truth be told, neither of them would have it any other way.

In a funny kind of way, I think they're probably the happiest beings I've ever met.

Unlike Arthur.

He's barely said a word since we left Bamboo's place.

I lean close. "I'll bet when you followed me out of that window, you never thought you'd end up talking to a stick doll in a chair."

Arthur looks at me with some surprise. "So, he really is just a stick doll, then?"

"Of course he is."

Arthur sits back. "I knew he wasn't alive."

"Arthur, Arthur, Arthur – just because he's a stick doll," I smirk, "doesn't mean he isn't alive."

Teresa gazes up into the starless sky, shaking her head, slowly. "I just can't believe it."

"I know…" I say, "…once you've spoken to a talking doll, a talking cat is just old news. I feel so out of date."

"No, I mean all this trouble, everything what Lady Eris and the Queen are doin' to Arilon. And now they want to come over and do it to me and Arthur's world, too."

"We *will* stop her," I say, trying to sound as reassuring as I can. "I'm rather good at stopping her, you know. I've done it loads of times before."

"She didn't have the Agency Engine before," Arthur says.

I can't argue with him on that.

"But, you're right, Cat," says Teresa. "We're still in the game. As long as we keep fightin', there's always a chance. Right, Arthur?"

Arthur looks at her and a kind of confidence seems to fill him. He smiles a determined smile.

"Right," he says.

I nod and smile at the pair of them. But I'm worried. Yes, it's a kind of confidence Arthur seems to be showing. But it's the wrong kind. The kind you put on because you think you should. The kind you try to feel for the benefit of someone else. Instead of the real kind – the kind you feel from deep inside.

Now, sure, pretend confidence is better than no confidence at all… but…

Well, it's like wearing someone else's coat. Fine, it'll keep you dry in the rain for a little while. But pretty soon, you'll realise it's just not your size. Too big or too small. Too long in the arms. Too tight round the shoulders. And it won't protect you from the rain as well as you thought it would. You'll realise that coming out in the rain with someone else's coat was a big mistake. Without your own coat, one that fits you just right, you'll just get yourself into all kinds of bother and…well…

You find that it's just better for all concerned if you'd just stayed at home.

"Thank you for staying behind, Cat," the boy – Bamboo's Voice – says after Thrace, Teresa and Arthur head outside to wait for our ride back to the docks. "Bamboo would like a word with you before you leave."

"I know," I say, glancing over to the motionless doll. "You want to talk about Arthur, don't you?"

The boy listens for a moment and then says, "Arthur Ness… he is full of fear."

"Yes," I say. "He's been like that since I met him. He thinks of himself as a coward."

"He does not know the truth about bravery?"

I shake my head and sigh. "Nope. And I can't tell him. He has to figure it out for himself. He'll never believe it if it comes from someone else."

The boy pauses and then says, very slowly, very deliberately, "Bamboo was not entirely truthful before. The threads around Arthur Ness are somewhat clearer than he wanted to say in front of everyone."

I don't think I'm going to like the sound of this.

"There will be several times when Arthur must make the right choices and face his fears. One of them will happen very soon. If Arthur's courage fails him and he makes the wrong choice…"

He pauses. I say nothing and force him to spell it out.

"Lady Eris will capture you all," he says, eventually. "And the Queen will win."

I was right. I don't like the sound of that at all.

THE CORNER OF YOUR EYE
(from the defiant but scared thoughts of Sam Smith)

Sam kicked his legs and swung back and forth on the playground swing. He did it just like the other children did. Slowly. Evenly. Without smiling. He did everything to make sure he looked just like every other child in Waterwhistle.

And yet, the five Yarnbulls at the gates of the park were not staring at any other children. They were only staring at him.

The girl on the swing next to Sam was beginning to slow down so Sam stopped kicking too, allowing his swing to do the same. Gradually, and at the same rate as May Nicholls, Sam's swing came to a stop. He glanced across at her, briefly.

May was staring straight ahead, as usual. She could see what was there, in front of her but, somehow, she also couldn't. There was a look in her eyes. Not exactly lifeless, there was definitely something there. It was just that she'd been kind of... paused.

She used to be the loudest person in Sam's class. Girl or boy, it didn't matter, May Nicholls outdid them all for noise. She was always at the centre of everything, the life of the classroom. The other kids called her May-May because it seemed like there was always two of her, so involved she was in everything going on.

There wasn't two of her anymore. There was barely even one of her.

She stepped off her swing and Sam did the same. He followed her to the gates of the park, doing his best to copy the way she walked. No enthusiastic bounce, no skipping, no running. Just a simple, languid movement. Like a puppet being moved by a puppeteer who was himself lifeless.

May passed through the gates and between the Yarnbulls. None of them even glanced in her direction.

They were all watching Sam.

As he walked between them, Sam couldn't stop his heart thumping faster and faster. He'd become well practiced at pretending not to see the Yarnbulls. He kept his eyes fixed on something in the distance – like a window or a wall – and he simply used his peripheral vision to avoid bumping into things. As best as he could figure, that was how everyone else in the village was, anyway. Some outside part of their vision could see the Yarnbulls, that's why they never bumped into them. It was the central part of their vision – and their minds – that ignored them.

So, yes, Sam could move in just the right way, look just the right way and sound just the right way…

But he was still terrified.

The tall, dark creatures stared down at the child as he walked between them. Their massive, horned heads turned to follow him as he passed. Apart from that, they were completely still, like statues. Their huge hands held their weapons motionless at their sides.

And soon, Sam had passed through the group and was heading down the lane. He didn't dare turn back to look at them. If he did such a foolish thing, they'd be upon him in an instant. So he kept his eyes fixed on his father's shop, right at the end of the road, and walked slowly towards it.

He didn't even turn his head when not-quite-whole May turned up Lamb Lane and wandered off towards her house.

Before long, though, Sam was back home, preparing the evening meal for when his father got in. Even at home, Sam didn't dare let his guard down. More than once, he'd looked up only to find a Yarnbull staring silently in from the other side of a closed window. In those situations, he had to work very hard to hide his shock. Failure to do so would have resulted in the Yarnbull smashing through the glass and reaching in for him right then and there.

No sooner had Sam taken the potatoes off the boil than the front door scraped open. Father was home.

As Sam placed the food on the table, he could hear a coat being removed and hung on the peg out in the hallway. Then boots being taken off and left by the door and slippers being shuffled on.

And then, silently as always, Mr Smith entered the room, sat at the table and began to eat.

"Get some salt, Sam," he said, finally, between mouthfuls. Sam did as he was asked and left the salt just in front of his father. Mr. Smith looked up for the first time since entering the room in order to pick up the salt shaker. That's when he noticed it.

"What's that?" he said.

Sam, who had returned to his seat and continued eating, didn't look up. He simply said;

"What?"

"That," said his father. "You've set an extra place."

Sam looked up. Yes he had. On purpose. He looked up at his father. He stared into his eyes. He searched for the slightest glimpse, the merest spark that something was wrong. That he could remember that, yes, there should indeed be three of them.

"Put it away," Mr Smith said. And went back to eating.

"But…"

"Put. It. Away." His tone warned that this conversation was over.

Defeated, Sam moved slowly towards the plate and cutlery. Wordlessly, he picked them up. He watched his father continue to eat and suddenly noticed something that took him by surprise. A small tear in the corner of his father's eye.

He knows, Sam thought. Surely, surely, he knows. Out of his peripheral vision. Out of the corner of his eye. He knows something's wrong. He knows his daughter's missing.

And in that moment, Sam felt joy for the first time in ages. Yes, when he'd spoken to Arthur, he'd felt hope. But now, he felt actual joy. Because he knew something of his father was still there.

And that's when, with a mighty **BOOM**, the front door flew into the room, right off its hinges. Sam did his best not to look up but that didn't stop a procession of Yarnbulls streaming into the house, reaching towards him with their huge, monstrous hands.

THE CORNER OF YOUR EYE
(from the befuddled thoughts of Mr. Smith)

Mr Smith munched on a bit of carrot and gravy and looked up. Strange. Why was there a smashed plate on the floor beside him? And the door was off its hinges. Maybe he'd left it open when he'd come in and the wind had blown it right off. Yes, that must have been it. And it had made him jump, which is why he'd knocked that plate on the floor. Yes, that made sense.

And then he'd started eating his dinner. Of course. He must have decided to fix it all after he'd finished eating. No sense letting his food get cold. He was about to go back to his potatoes when he noticed something that made his brow furrow in bemusement.

There was a half-eaten plate of food at the other side of the table. Why was that there?

But of course, the answer came to him, he must have left it there from last night. Too exhausted after a day's hard work to finish his own dinner.

Yes, there was an answer to everything. Contented, he went back to his food.

As he ate, he felt something trickle out of his eye and down his cheek. A tear? Why was there a tear coming out of the corner of his eye? It wasn't as though he felt sad in any way. No aching sense of loss, no despair. He felt fine.

He wiped the tear away and forgot about it.

LABYRINTH

Arthur, Teresa and the Cat stared in open-mouthed disbelief.

"Arthur?"

"Yes, Cat?"

"You know that map I just had you draw?"

"Yes, Cat?"

"Tear it up and throw it away, there's a good lad."

"Yes, Cat."

As the Cat and Captain Thrace had explained to the two human children, the island of Labyrinth was basically a huge maze. The streets and lanes twisted unnecessarily in hundreds of different directions and crossed each other thousands of times over. To get from one end of a street to the other was never a straight line. In fact just walking down the road was a good way to get very, very lost.

Ontop of that, every single street, path, road and avenue was lined down each side with wide, open gaps. The fissures went all the way to the underside of the island and the NothingSpace was clearly visible through them. In short, if you tried to cheat and cut across paths, you fell straight into the Black.

Regular people lived and worked on Labyrinth and they all embodied the island's Idea – dealing with complex paths. They knew that life could sometimes look very complicated and tricky and if you panicked and ran about, you'd make yourself lost and confused. However, if you kept calm and evaluated your surroundings, you would always, eventually find your way out of trouble.

Because of the nature of the place, it was the perfect spot to build a prison and so the peace keepers had done just that. Labyrinth Prison was a huge facility and sat right in the centre of the island. It was filled with criminals from all over Arilon. It didn't matter if people escaped the building – they would never be able to escape the island. Not before the peace keepers caught up with them.

All this was already known to the trio when they had left the *Galloping Snake* moored up at the docks under the guard of her Captain. And the Cat had been here enough times in the past that he had memorised the path to the prison. One hastily drawn map later and the three would-be jailbreakers had been confident of an easy stroll to the jailhouse to find Zane Rackham.

Unfortunately, very few things in life end up being as easy as they seem at the start.

"I take it those things weren't here the last time you came, then, Cat?" asked Teresa.

"You take it right, Smithy. And you know what? It's just not fair. Not fair at all."

Arthur walked up close to the thing they were staring at. The thing that had thrown such an early spanner into the works.

It was a tall, wooden archway that spanned the entire width of the road they stood on. To go any further along the street, you had to pass under it. However, the street they could see on the other side of the archway was not the street they were standing on.

What they could see was a road in another part of the island entirely. There was a tall, crimson tower right next to them with a banner advertising labouring work at the docks.

Impossibly, as they looked through the archway, they could see that very same tower far off in the distance.

In other words, if you walked through the archway, you would instantly be transported to a road on the other side of the island. What was worse, Arthur could see even more archways dotted along the street, all no doubt leading to various random streets all over Labyrinth. They were everywhere.

And that wasn't all.

Every few seconds, the destination on the other side of the archway changed, like a radio channel being constantly flicked over. One moment, you could see a long, main road. Then the picture suddenly changed to a small side-alley. A few moments later, it was a row of houses. Seconds later again, it was the driveway of a busy office block.

"How are we supposed to find our way through all that…?" Teresa did not sound impressed one bit. "It's bad enough the island's roads are more twisted than a plate of drunken worms and there are gaps of NothingSpace everywhere… now we have to figure out magical, changing doorways too?"

"It's like playing snakes and ladders," said Arthur. "But with no ladders. And snakes that eat you and steal your money."

"This is a big delay we don't have time for," said the Cat. "The Queen's soldiers will be on their way right now. We need to get to Rackham before they do."

Arthur tried to clear his mind and figure this problem out, just like the people of Labyrinth would do. He took a deep breath and squinted against the bright Arilon morning. He didn't think he'd ever get used to the bizarre nature of daytime in Arilon. The top of the island was currently rotated towards the sun so a harsh, white light filled the island – and yet the sky was still black.

Arthur brought his gaze back down again to the streets around him. He watched as an older man in an expensive-looking outfit and carrying a large pile of papers strolled through the archway before them. He left the busy docks behind him and headed into a long street filled with houses. No sooner had he done that than the view of the houses disappeared. The archway now showed a high street, thick with horse-drawn carts going to market. One of the carts rolled out of the archway and trundled past the trio.

"The locals!" Arthur exclaimed all of a sudden. The other two looked at him, surprised at his sudden animation. Arthur carried on. "Look at them..! They know just when the doorways will change and what they'll change to."

"Hey, you're right..." Teresa looked about and saw people standing patiently in front of an archway as it flicked from street to path to lane before they eventually stepped through as it cycled round to their desired location.

"So...we'll just get one of them to help us." Teresa smiled. "I'm sure it shouldn't be too hard."

"Good luck with that," the Cat said, shaking his head. "The Queen has cut so many Travel Lines from Savis, the kindness island, most people just don't help strangers anymore. They'll probably just walk right past. You'd need to find someone extraordinarily naturally kind and the chances of that are roughly zer-"

"Excuse me, are you three lost?" an old lady's voice suddenly came from behind them. The three visitors turned to see an elderly woman holding an umbrella in one arm and a tiny dog in the other. "Oh, dear," she smiled a kindly smile.

"You look even more lost from the front! Why don't you tell me where you're headed, dearies. Perhaps I can help."

Teresa spared a gloating glance for the Cat before replying to the old lady. "Oh, thanks, ma'am. We're... erm... looking for the prison."

"Right you are," the lady said. "None of my business what you need the prison for. Just be careful, that's all I'll say. Some very unsavoury characters in there, you know. You're in luck, though. I live on the other side of the prison and I'm going home right now. Come on. Follow me."

A KIND OF KINDNESS

The old lady's name was Mila Evansworth. Her tiny dog was of the non-talking variety. It was named Trevor. She lived on Astrid Street in District Seventy-Two in a lovely little bungalow. Her mother and father had moved here from Graft and Elysium respectively when they were newlweds because her father had managed to get a job at a bank on Labyrinth. Her favourite colour was Sunset Red.

This and a hundred other things Arthur, Teresa and the Cat learned about the old lady as she led them through archway after archway and street after street. She didn't stop nattering the entire time.

"...and of course my parents had already said I wasn't allowed to go but all my friends were going, you see. And the High-Tones weren't going to tour again so this would be my last chance. I'd heard so much about them but I'd never actually heard any of their music. You see, I'd been ill when-"

"I'm sorry, are you sure this is the quickest way to the prison?" The Cat politely interrupted Mila's story. "Only, we're in a bit of a rush."

"Oh, yes, dear." Mila nodded. "I've walked up and down these streets more times than you've had hot dinners. This is definitely the most direct path. This route used to be a regular one of mine. I used to date a guard from the prison, you see. And we'd both love to go to the docks and watch the ships come and go. Of course, that was before the archways were put in. But once they'd been here a while, you soon got used to them as long as you were patient. Ooh, not like young Franklin Winterbottom. Now there was an impatient so-and-so. And ever so *tall!* You know, once, about fifteen years ago, he…"

Teresa leaned close to Arthur and whispered, "Crikey, there ain't no stoppin' her, is there? She's like a chatterbox tank!"

Arthur grinned. "Remind you of a certain talking horse?"

"I wonder if Trevor really is a non-talkin' animal?" Teresa whispered. "Or if he just can't get a word in and has given up tryin'."

The pair stifled a laugh as they passed under another archway that took them from a tree-lined park into a grey, dingy part of town. Trees, bushes and grassy spaces gave way to ugly, depressing-looking, concrete buildings with tiny windows. The buildings encircled one structure that was more ugly and more depressing-looking than the rest of them put together.

"And here we are," came Mila's cheery voice. "The centre of the island. Labyrinth Prison!"

Arthur had expected some kind of super-tall tower block stretching up into the sky. He was half right. It was very, very tall, but instead of going up, it went down. It had been lowered into a huge, circular gap in the island's floor and was suspended over the NothingSpace. A series of bridges and struts fanned out from the building like hands of a clock and it was by these that the building clung to the island.

It was abundantly clear there was no way in or out of that place except along one of those bridges because with nothing but a long drop into the Black beneath them, prisoners were certainly *not* going to be climbing out of any windows.

"Now, listen, dears." Mila turned to them. "Do you want me to wait for you? I don't mind!"

The Cat stepped up to the old lady. "Mila Evansworth, you've done more than enough for us already. We can't ask you to-"

"Oh, don't be silly!" Mila gave a dismissive wave of her hand. "Without learning the sequences of the archways, you could be wandering these streets for months, if not years! And people round here aren't as friendly as they used to be thanks to... you know... *her*."

Arthur knew just which 'her' Mila meant. Just as he knew that they were lucky to have bumped into this lady. There can't have been many people who would have been as willing to help strangers the way she had. Arthur glanced at Teresa and could tell she was thinking the same thing. They were both feeling a little guilty at making fun of her earlier. With all the Queen's pruning of Travel Lines, people as kind as Mila Evansworth were in danger of becoming extinct.

"Madam," said the Cat, bowing low, "you are one in a million. We'll be two shakes of a lamb's tale, I promise."

"Oh, don't worry about me." Mila settled herself down onto a nearby bench. "I've got Trevor to keep me company until you get back. Did you know that he-"

Ami Stark craned her eyes skyward as all around her, people began to cry out in fear and panic. Some pointed up, some ran about, some gathered up their little ones and whisked them away inside the nearest building. But Ami didn't move. She just watched the *Twilight Palace* emerge out of the Black and sail down towards her home.

Everyone on Savis knew what it meant. The Queen's flagship had been to the island twice before. Her most recent visit just eight months ago. Each time, the Nightmare Ship and its fleet of fighter craft had cut hundreds of Travel Lines. With less than two hundred Lines left, many of the island's inhabitants had packed up their valuables and fled, fearing the Queen's inevitable return.

Ami had berated them and called them cowards. Now, as she stood and watched the Queen's flagship descend towards her home once more, she had to suspect those others had had the right idea after all.

The panicked, fearful cries of the people around her rose to a new crescendo as everyone watched the massive cutting blades slowly unfold from the underside of the *Twilight Palace*, their pristine sheen glinting in the bright midday sun.

Ami Stark grew fearful. Not for herself. Not for the other inhabitants of her island. But for the people out there on Arilon's other islands. Because right now, the Queen's selfishness was again changing minds.

All of a sudden, the old lady stopped talking. Arthur and Teresa watched in bewilderment as both Mila and the Cat staggered a little. It was as if they'd briefly been about to faint. The moment passed swiftly but something was undeniably different, now. When Mila spoke again, she wasn't the Mila Evansworth they had met. That Mila was gone and a new version of her stood in her place.

"Why am I helping you?" she said, her voice suddenly cold and hostile. "You're nothing to do with me! Helping you doesn't get me anything."

She suddenly stood up, the human children's shocked gaze following her.

"I'm off home," she said, gruffly, turning to go, not even looking at Arthur or the others. "You're on your own."

And with that, Mila Evansworth shuffled off down the road. She passed through an archway and the very next second, it changed to another location. She was gone.

Teresa crossed her arms. "Well, that were just *rude!*"

"Are you okay?" Arthur asked the Cat. "What happened?"

The Cat took a moment to compose himself. When he eventually looked up at Arthur, there was something different in his eyes. Just for a second.

"The Queen," he said. "She's at Savis. Kindness just became even harder to come by in Arilon."

"We're never going to find anyone to help us get back, then, are we?" Teresa said. "It's almost like the Queen knew we were goin' to be here."

The Cat glanced at her for a moment. "Wouldn't surprise me. Don't forget, she's a Weaver, too, just like Bamboo. Come on, we'd better get a move on. We don't have much time."

ZANE RACKHAM

The trio walked along one of the massive bridges holding the prison onto the island. As they approached the large, imposing main entrance, they passed a sign noting that the Guards' Stables were located a short distance down a side-path.

"See that sign?" the Cat said.

Teresa nodded. "Stables? So?"

"First rule of an amazing escape," the Cat smiled. "Never enter a place you can't leave *really* fast."

Arthur understood – the Cat paid attention to *everything*.

The three would-be prison visitors finally entered the low-ceilinged reception area. They found themselves in a circular room with a desk in the middle at which sat an officious-looking young man in a dark blue uniform. Behind him was a row of doors labelled 'Gate 1' all the way up to 'Gate 7'.

"Yes, can I help you?" the man said in a nasally-voice as the Cat approached the desk. He sounded very much like he didn't want to help them at all.

"I'm here to see Zane Rackham," said the Cat.

"You have an authorisation code, I assume?"

"Gamma Eight Seven," replied the Cat.

The man ran his finger down one of his sheets of paper, looking for the code. After a few seconds, he raised an eyebrow.

"Ah, here it is," he said, "Gamma Eight Sev-" He suddenly stopped, mid-sentence. His eyes widened in surprise and he went a worrying shade of white. "G-Gamma Eight

Seven..?" he repeated. And then he did something that Arthur and Teresa were definitely not expecting. He stood up and saluted.

"My apologies, your Highness," he stammered, "...of course, sir, you may see who you like, sir. Would you like an escort, sir?"

"Oh, don't bother with any of that stuff," the Cat said with a dismissive wave of his paw. "Just tell me where Prisoner Rackham's holed up and we'll be on our way."

"Of course, sir," the man bumbled and flicked through several sheets of paper before finding what he was after. "Level 18, Sector 5, Cell 22. Use Gate 3. It's a low security cell, sir. Says here he was picked up for being drunk and disorderly but he's a bit... well, not quite right, sir. If you know what I mean."

Arthur did not know what he meant and judging from her expression, neither did Teresa. The Cat, however, simply nodded.

"Thank you, young man. And may I say, you have excellent manners. Come along, non-cats."

And off he headed towards the far wall where the door to Gate 3 was automatically opening for them. The three of them stepped through the door and Arthur realised they were actually in an elevator. Next to the open door, a large, brass dial sat surrounded by a ring of numbers. In the centre of the dial was a green, metal button marked with an arrow.

"Level 18 please, Smithy," said the Cat. Teresa twisted the dial to point at 18 and pushed the arrow button and the lift lurched into motion. As the carriage jarred and bumped slowly downwards, all three stood without talking. Only the winding and occasional creak of the carriage broke the silence. Eventually, Arthur spoke.

"Okay, shall I go first?" he said.

The Cat blinked up at him. "Hm, I'm sorry?"

"Your highness…?" Arthur was flabberghasted. "Your *highness*?"

"Oh, that." The Cat sniffed and turned back toward the elevator door. "I used to be a King. Sorry, didn't I mention it?"

"Let me think…" Teresa said, sarcastically, "…flyin' ships…Travel Lines…evil Queens…no, no I don't think it came up."

"Well, it's not something I like to boast about. As you know, I'm a very modest fellow, I don't really like to brag," the Cat said, casually. "I'm sure I'd have worked my way round to it eventually. Ah, here we are."

The lift bell chimed and the elevator doors opened. The Cat slipped out, leaving Arthur and Teresa still staring after him, dazed.

"Impossible, impossible creature." Teresa shook her head.

"Do you ever get the feeling…" Arthur started. His tone was suddenly quiet and secretive which instantly intrigued Teresa and she turned to him. "…I don't know…" Arthur went on, "…do you ever get the feeling that he isn't completely honest with us about things..?"

"I suppose…" Teresa shrugged. "But I still trust him."

So do I, Arthur thought, *that's the problem.*

"Keep up, non-cats!" the voice called to them from down the corridor and the pair quickly caught up with the apparently royal feline, leaving the elevator door closing slowly behind.

"Second rule of an amazing escape," the Cat said. "Anyone want to take a guess what it is?"

Teresa and Arthur looked at each other and shrugged. The speed that the feline could change topic of conversation baffled them.

Seeing their empty stares, the Cat sighed and pointed with his nose toward a ventilation shaft high up on the wall. "Check to see if you can fit into places you're not meant to go," he grinned.

The children both stared at the shaft entrance. It was big enough for the Cat but way too small for them.

"Ah, here we are," said the Cat from a short way down the hall. "Enter Gamma Eight Seven into that dial will you, Arthur, there's a good lad."

The pair caught up with the Cat and Arthur saw the number 33 on the cell door in front of them. Under the number was fastened a piece of paper upon which was scribbled, 'Zane Rackham'. Next to it was another dial with numbers and letters in concentric circles running around it. Arthur turned the dial slowly and carefully so that it pointed to each part of the Cat's code, pressing the central button each time. Upon confirming the 'Seven', the door suddenly **clanked** open.

"Right," said the Cat. "Leave the talking to me."

The cell was small and dimly lit with just a small, metal bed on one side. On the bed sat a young man, perhaps in his twenties or thirties, Arthur guessed. His eyes and face, though, looked much older. Working for the Queen had not been good for him.

"Zane Rackham?" said the Cat.

"Zane Rackham…?" the man repeated in a strange, slightly wavery voice," …yes, he's here. What do you want with him?"

"I want you to tell me about the machine, Rackham," the Cat's voice was low and steady. "I want to know what it's for, where it is and how I can destroy it."

"…the…machine…?" the prisoner looked from the floor to the Cat and back to the floor, "…to control…"

"I think he's still drunk," whispered Teresa.

"Yes, I know the machine is to give the Queen control," the Cat went on. "I want to know about the small part that's about to be completed. Tell me about the small part, Rackham."

"…the names…" the man said again in his strange, unsteady voice, "…give…her…"

Arthur's eyes widened in realisation at what he was seeing. "He isn't drunk," he said. "I think he's gone mad."

The three of them looked and saw it instantly. Zane Rackham had the look of someone who was there and not there all at once. His terrified mind had retreated somewhere far away, hiding itself from… something. Only the bare minimum of Rackham's self was left to control his body.

"Being forced to work for the Queen," the Cat whispered, "to build that terrible machine… he must have seen something that drove him insane."

"Poor man," said Teresa. "I can only imagine what they did to him."

"I don't have to imagine," the Cat said, darkly. "It will have been terrible, I know that. But, unfortunately, we don't have time to play it nice. Let's see if we can shock it out of him."

And with that, the creature suddenly whipped round and leapt right at Rackham, pinning him to the wall with surprising strength and baring teeth which strangely looked ten times larger than they actually were.

"Rackham!" the Cat suddenly shouted at the young man. "I don't have time for this! Tell me about the machine part!"

"…the names… give… her…"

"Tell me!" the Cat shouted again.

"Wait! Listen!" Arthur said, all of a sudden. "He *is* telling you!"

The Cat looked at Arthur, puzzled, then back at the babbling prisoner.

"…the names…give… her… the names… give her… the names…give her… the names…"

"Give her the names…" Arthur said. "Who's 'her'?"

"The Queen, of course," said Teresa before turning to the Cat. "Right?"

But the Cat wasn't speaking right now. He was staring at Zane Rackham.

"It will give her the names?" he said quietly, eventually. "Which names?"

Zane looked deep into the Cat's eyes. "…all of them…"

The Cat looked stunned. The children had no idea why, but it spooked them. Arthur stepped forward.

"Where's the machine part?" he asked.

Zane's manic gaze turned to Arthur, now, and he whispered, "…Waterwhistle."

Now it was Arthur and Teresa's turn to be shocked. Yet it did make such perfect sense, Arthur thought, he wondered why they hadn't guessed it already. It explained why Lady Eris was so busy in the village. Too busy to even chase Arthur in person.

"Where in Waterwhistle is the machine part being built?" Arthur asked. Rackham's gaze became more wild, more disturbed. The man's eyes literally pinned Arthur to the spot.

"Not in a place… no, not in a place," he grabbed Arthur's arm in a vice-like grip. "In the people. It's being built in the *people…*"

Teresa suddenly burst forward, her voice an urgent cocktail of desperation and anger. "How do we destroy it? *Tell me!*"

The prisoner saw Teresa properly for the first time, now. As soon as his eyes locked on her, his eyes and mouth contorted in pure terror.

"No!" he suddenly shouted, scrambling backwards away from Teresa. "Keep away from me! Keep away! Don't let it touch me! *Keep it away from me!!*"

Arthur and the Cat stared at the scene in shock. Zane Rackham, a grown man, was scared to death of Teresa. Not just scared. *Terrified.*

They didn't have any time to figure it out, though. Because that's when the deafening wail of a prison siren blared out from somewhere up the corridor.

"What just happened?" Arthur asked, fearfully.

"We just ran out of time," said the Cat. He turned back to Rackham. The prisoner was cowering away in the corner of the bed, his arms over his eyes.

"Why don't you step away from him, Smithy, my girl?" the Cat said, warily. "Before he has a complete breakdown?"

Teresa nodded in numb confusion and came back to the doorway beside Arthur. The Cat turned back to Rackham.

"I'd bring you with us, Zane," he sounded almost kind, "but you're clearly too unstable. And… I'm really sorry, but they're coming for you. They're going to take you back to the Queen. But somewhere in your head is the key to destroying this monstrous machine you've created. I know you want it destroyed – you wish you'd never been forced to build it. We'll meet again, Zane. And we'll destroy the Agency Engine together. We will. For now, just... just try and stay strong."

Outside, the ominous sound of boots was beginning to echo through the corridors.

"Come on, non-cats."

The Cat led the pair out of the cell. Teresa was the last one out and she turned and looked back at Zane. The dishevelled young man looked back at her. The fear was still there. But something else, too. Something like... pity?

"...in prison too..." was all he said.

"Come on, Smithy!" the Cat shouted and Teresa ran out behind them. The sound of the soldiers was getting closer.

"How are we going to get out?" Arthur said, beginning to fret.

"We could really use one of them famous escapes of yours right now!" Teresa said to the Cat as the sound of tromping boots pounded ever louder.

"Ah, yes, of course," said the Cat. "The third rule of an amazing escape!"

"And what's that..?" Arthur pressed his back against the wall. He noticed the Cat looking above his head and he followed the gaze... straight to a ventilation shaft. A large one.

"Third rule of an amazing escape?" the Cat grinned at Arthur. "Before you do anything, always crank your action music up to full volume!"

THE CHASE

Arthur hung onto the horse's reigns for dear life while the animal galloped as fast as it could go. Teresa, behind, hung onto his waist and the Cat was just behind her, digging his claws into the saddle to keep from tumbling off.

Hot on their heels, seventeen mounted soldiers of the Queen's Guard chased them. Their crimson and black armour shone brightly in the harsh sunlight but the featureless helmets that covered their entire faces dispelled any ideas of dashing knights. They were fearsome, unyielding wraiths and you did *not* want to look behind and see them hot on your tail.

Their swords remained in their scabbards for the time being. However, this was no cause for celebration. The only reason they were not using their swords was because a couple of them were currently bringing long-barrelled rifles to bear.

"I don't want to ever see the inside of a ventilation shaft again!" Teresa shouted over the thundering din of the galloping horses.

"What are you complaining about, Smithy?" the Cat cried back. "We stayed ahead of the guards all the way to the stables, didn't we?"

"We didn't need the stables – we could have used that rat we bumped into in the shaft," Teresa said. "It was big enough to carry the lot of us!"

A gunshot blasted from behind them and shattered a shop window as they flew past.

"We haven't escaped yet!" Arthur yelled, ducking his head.

"Right you are, my lad!" the Cat shouted. "Down there, Arthur! To the left!"

Arthur had no idea what he was doing. He had never ridden a horse before. He'd never run from soldiers trying to kill him before. And he'd never, ever been this terrified before

But he managed to tug hard on the horse's reigns and the animal turned sharply to the left, sprinting down a side road.

"Smithy!" the Cat shouted over the noise of the horse's hooves on the cobbles. "Grab that rifle! The one in the horse's pack near your leg. Give those soldiers something to think about! I'd do it myself but, y'know... paws."

Teresa pulled the long rifle from its holder but then hesitated.

"I... I don't want to shoot anyone..!"

"You're riding on the back of a speeding horse, bobbing all over the place, holding a rifle almost as big as you are, aiming at well trained soldiers on horseback. And you're ten." The Cat grinned at her. "Don't you worry – you're not going to hit *anything*! But it'll make them duck a bit more and shoot at us a bit less. Go on!"

So Teresa hefted the weapon up, rested the butt against her shoulder, aimed it in the general direction of the soldiers.

"Go on!" urged the Cat. "Just pull the tri-"

POW!

"Woah!" Teresa cried. The rifle had kicked backwards in her hands as the bullet blasted out, almost knocking her off the horse. Black smoke from the firearm filled the air for an instant before whipping away as they continued flying forward atop the captured horse.

"Heck of a kick, eh?!" the Cat shouted. It seemed to do

the trick, though. The gang of soldiers spread out a little to avoid the incoming shot which meant they were too busy concentrating on not running into each other to bother shooting back.

For the moment, at least.

"Now, this is what I call escaping!" the Cat shouted as the horse took them through another archway and into a rainy part of town.

Far from the excitement in the Cat's voice, Arthur was doing his utmost to control himself. He was so unbelievably terrified, his hands were locked tight around the horse's reigns. He couldn't let go even if he wanted to.

The Cat, on the other hand, sounded like he was playing a game in his back garden. Didn't he realise the seriousness of the situation? Couldn't he tell they were potentially just moments away from death? If he wasn't giving the situation his full attention, then surely Arthur and Teresa were in even *more* danger?

And if all that wasn't enough, they also had absolutely no idea where they were going.

"We're lost!" cried Arthur as they galloped through a green, grassy park. "In case you'd forgotten!"

"Of course we're lost! We're riding around inside a giant, floating maze!" the Cat called. "Don't worry, I have a clever plan!"

"Is your plan to just ride around and hope one of these arches opens up to the docks?" Teresa asked. "Because that's not a plan, that's just laziness."

"Teresa, my dear, you wound me with your lack of faith. Don't you-"

"'Scuse me a sec," Teresa interrupted.

POW!

The soldiers scattered again as Teresa brought the rifle back down.

"Sorry," she said. "You were saying?"

Arthur hung on as the stolen horse took them towards a big archway. They dived through it just before it changed. They were now in a rainy part of the city and the archway behind them switched to show a bustling marketplace.

"We've lost them!" the Cat called out. "They could be anywhere on the island by now."

"So could we," Teresa reminded him, shielding her eyes from the rain. "Wow, you really need to bring an umbrella when you go for a walk in this place – never know *what* kind of weather you'll wander into!"

As they approached the next archway down the road, Arthur was beginning to think about slowing their horse down now they weren't being chased anymore. Problem was, he didn't have the first clue how to do it.

Through the archway ahead of them was a row of houses and what looked like a school. As they approached, the scenery flickered and changed.

And, impossibly, there sat the docks. And the *Galloping Snake*.

"And you thought my laziness wouldn't work!" the Cat grinned at Teresa.

Arthur could have sung with joy! He put his head down and the horse raced towards the arch. They were going to make it! Obviously, Arthur had been worrying about nothi-

The archway changed.

No! Arthur couldn't believe it! Not already!

The docks were gone and they were replaced by...

"Watch out!" shouted the Cat.

The arch had switched to show the road they had just

left – the road that still held the Queen's guardsmen. Arthur gaped in shock as he found himself now galloping *towards* the soldiers!

Fortunately, the sudden change had taken the soldiers by surprise too. Before anyone could do anything, both parties found themselves running past each other as they went under the arch. By the time the soldiers were able to react and bring their horses to a halt, they'd run straight past Arthur, Teresa and the Cat – who themselves were now emerging onto the non-rainy side of the archway.

The soldiers, regaining their wits, raised their weapons at their quarry. Unfortunately for them, Teresa's wits were quicker. She was already aiming her rifle at the archway's left supporting strut.

POW!

The wooden column exploded as she hit it dead on. She swiftly aimed at the other strut, on the right.

POW!

Now, both struts were just shreds and the wooden archway creaked and groaned. The soldiers looked up at it, warily, as it swayed to and fro… then with a final sigh, the entire construct crashed to the ground. The rainy street disappeared and the soldiers were gone.

"Nice shootin', Tex!" the Cat bellowed, laughing.

Arthur turned round to see what had happened. That was when everything went very bad.

The horse whinnied in terror as they ran too close to the edge of the road – and the huge openings to the NothingSpace that stretched along there.

The animal reared up in terror as it did its best to avoid falling in. Teresa tumbled off first. Followed by the Cat. And lastly, Arthur. Teresa landed on the ground. The Cat landed on the ground.

Arthur did not.

"Arthur!" Teresa screamed.

"Hang on, Arthur!" shouted the Cat. "Don't let go!"

Arthur's fingers gripped onto the edge of the ground for all they were worth – and the great, gaping NothingSpace yawned out below him.

"Help me!"

"It's okay, Arthur," called the Cat. "Teresa's going to pull you up!"

Even before those words had been spoken, though, Teresa was already on her knees, holding her hand down towards her friend.

"Grab hold!"

Arthur started to reach a hand back up to her -

BANG!

The ground near Arthur's hands exploded in a small puff of smoke and dirt. Teresa fell backwards.

"It's the soldiers!" shouted the Cat. Sure enough, up at the far end of the road, the Queen's men had managed to find their way through another archway and were emerging from it with extreme urgency. Although still some distance away, they were racing up the street toward them, shooting all the time.

Arthur yelled in fear as bullets flew all around him. Little explosions of dirt blew into his face and the **whip** of the bullets whizzing past him seemed to come from all directions at once.

At any moment, he knew he'd be hit. The only way to escape was to let go and fall away into the NothingSpace. But he couldn't do that either. No-one would ever be able to leave the Travel Lines and come looking for him. He'd be alone forever. Alive, and yet, nothing. And at last, he knew why it was a fate worse than death to fall into the NothingSpace.

But it was that or get shot.

Another bit of the ground shattered into a dust cloud right near one of his hands.

"Help me! I'm slipping!" Arthur yelled again. Teresa tried to get to him but loud, cracking gunshots kept forcing her back.

"*NO!*" shouted a deep, powerful, angry voice that Arthur realised with some alarm was coming from the Cat. "Not again!"

And he ran towards the oncoming soldiers. Arthur had no idea what such a tiny cat was going to do to all those massive men in armour but Arthur wasn't really in a position to worry about it.

"Teresa!" he shouted. But there was no answer. Somewhere in the distance, in the direction of the soldiers, Arthur heard an almighty boom, like a crack of thunder. However, he was currently in no frame of mind to wonder what was going on.

Then, all of a sudden, a soldier stepped up to the edge and looked down at Arthur.

This one was dressed differently. Rather than crimson, his armour was a shiny, sky blue. His helmet was different too. Instead of the full-face covering of the Queen's Guard, this one had a 'T' shape opening through which his eyes, nose and mouth were visible.

It must have been some kind of special soldier, Arthur thought. Sneaked up on them from a different direction while they were busy with the regular ones.

It reached down to him. This was it, Arthur thought,

closing his eyes tight. The end. An enormous hand closed around his wrist. What would happen? Would the soldier toss him out into the Black? Or maybe he'd shoot Arthur up close where he couldn't miss.

Arthur felt himself being hoisted into the air with unearthly strength…. and suddenly, the ground was beneath his feet. He opened his eyes.

Teresa was standing next to a second soldier. His armour, helmet and even his face looked identical to the first. But he wasn't holding her and she didn't look captured. The soldier that had lifted Arthur to safety let go of him, gently. Arthur stared numbly from one soldier to the other and over at Teresa. What was going on?

Then Arthur suddenly remembered – the Cat!

He span round to the oncoming Royal Guard… except they were no longer oncoming. They were all lying on the ground. Sprawled and scattered all over the road, their armour ripped open and bits of scarlet metal littered all around. The horses wandered aimlessly around the scene of total devastation. And staggering slowly towards them…

…was the Cat.

"Well, that was quite some exercise…" he panted, "…think I need a lie down now…" and he collapsed.

"Cat!" Teresa ran forward and caught him. Arthur was by her side in an instant.

"Did he really just…" Arthur started, glancing from the small, furry animal to the bunch of ravaged guardsmen, "…I mean…*all* those soldiers..?"

"I don't know," Teresa said. "I wasn't watching, I was trying to get to you. Then these two other soldiers turned up…"

A distant rattling noise interrupted Teresa. The group

looked up to see another mounted squad of Guardsmen coming charging out of the archway at the end of the road. Swords were drawn and rifles were ready as they powered towards the unconscious Cat and his allies.

"Bamboo sent us," one of the blue soldiers suddenly said in a deep voice which Arthur thought sounded vaguely Russian. "He is thinking you might be needing our help. Looks like he is thinking right."

The soldier who had rescued Arthur held out a piece of paper to the young boy.

"Is map. Follow it back to ship," he said.

Arthur took it, warily.

"And we are not soldiers," he said as they both turned to the oncoming attackers and drew their swords. "We are knights."

And they ran into the oncoming soldiers.

Arthur and Teresa watched, mouths open in awe as the two blue knights ploughed into the Queen's guard. They swung their huge swords left and right and scarlet-clad soldiers went flying in all directions, screaming. It was like watching a monstrous ocean wave crashing down onto the shore, blasting away everything before it.

"Come on!" Teresa called to Arthur while cradling the Cat's unmoving body as carefully as possible. "We need to get going!"

Tearing his gaze away from the destruction unfolding before him, Arthur scrambled to his feet and, following the knights' map, led Teresa through the streets.

The paper gave Arthur all the instructions he needed. They ran up and down various roads and waited at the archways for the right amount of time in order for them to switch to the correct destination. And all the while, the only thing going through Arthur's mind was the blackness below his feet as he dangled from the edge of the world...

"Here we are!" Teresa shouted. And sure enough, Arthur had led them right back to the docks. And there *finally* was the *Galloping Snake* waiting for them.

"Wondered where you lot had gotten yerselves to," Captain Thrace leaned casually on the railings. "Stopped for a spot o' lunch with the Governor, did ye?"

That's when he saw the Cat's unconscious body and stood up straight, suddenly aware of the seriousness of the situation.

BOOM!

An explosion rocked the docks and the trio looked up to see the two blue knights came running round the corner at full speed. Even clad in full body, metal armour, they moved extremely fast. Thrace immediately drew his weapon and took aim at them.

"Damn kids, ye've got 'em right on yer tail!"

"No!" Teresa shouted.

Arthur pulled the gun down before Thrace could take a shot. "They're with us!"

Thrace eyed the pair of knights suspiciously as they ran up the gangplank and joined them.

"My name is Iakob," said one knight before pointing to the other. "And this is my brother Iosef."

"Yakob and Yosef, eh?" Thrace tried his best to pronounce the unusual names. "So... ye *haven't* got 'em right on yer tail...?"

That's when fifty horse-mounted soldiers came charging round the corner.

"No, you were right first time," said Iakob. "They are definitely on tail!"

- 186 -

The Captain wasted no more time and raced over to the ship's wheel.

"Pull up the gangplank! Release the clamps!" he shouted. "An' raise the sails!"

Arthur didn't move – he couldn't take his eyes off the advancing soldiers. Every muscle in his body had frozen stiff with fear. Teresa handed him the Cat and ran to help the Captain get the ship in flight.

Arthur watched as Iakob and Iosef ran back down the gangplank and started fighting off the soldiers to slow them down and buy the *Snake* enough time to get going. He watched as the ship finally began to move off, up away from the quayside. And he watched as the knights both launched into unbelievably massive leaps and landed on the deck just as Captain Thrace threw the lever all the way forward, filling the sails with the impossible wind.

And soon, Arthur was watching Labyrinth as it floated away into the dark and was gone. He heard Teresa and Thrace whooping with joy and Iakob and Iosef clasp each other's hands. But he looked down and saw the unconscious body of the Cat in his arms.

Didn't anyone else get it? Didn't they understand?

The Cat was always in control. He always knew what to do and he always found it exciting. But this time, the Cat was lying in Arthur's arms, out cold. He wasn't in control anymore.

And Arthur finally realised the answer he should have given when Bamboo had asked if he wanted to leave.

I told you that you'd regret it, didn't I?

THE HORSE AND HER MAN
(from the somewhat self-absorbed thoughts of Mary the Horse)

It's getting late into the evening as I trot through the centre of the village. We've had a busy couple of days ferrying things to and fro. Fruit. Veg. People to see Bamboo. And do I get a word of thanks from that annoying man sitting back there atop my cart?

"Well?" I ask him. "Do I?"

Elian sighs. "How many times do I have to tell you, horse, there's no point in having most of the conversation in your head and only bringing me in right at the end. I have no idea what you're going on about! Do you *what?*"

"Get any thanks? From you!"

"Thanks for what? For walking?"

"Takes more effort than sitting. Just saying."

"Who do you think lines up all our work?" he asks me. "People don't just come along and drop it in our lap, you know. I have to go out and bring the jobs in. You're lucky to have someone as experienced as me running things."

"By 'experienced', do you mean 'old'?" I snigger. "And by 'running things', do you mean 'sitting on your backside while your poor horse does all the *real* work'?"

"If I'm old, it's because you make me old with your constant nagging."

"I don't nag – I just tell you when you go wrong. Is it my fault you go wrong a lot?"

"Do you know what Bamboo told me once? That in the human world, an old horse is sometimes called a Nag." Elian laughed long and loud. "Now if that's not the most appropriate name I ever heard…!"

"Oh, buzz off!" I neigh.

"Buzz *this*," and I hear and feel the sharp **crack** of Elian's riding whip on my rump.

"Ouch!" I can't believe it! "Right, that's it!"

I stop walking – right there in the middle of the road. Some of the other carts and pedestrians shout at me as they go past. I don't care.

"I'm not going anywhere until I get an apology from you, Elian Mahaan. We've had this conversation before! No whips!"

Hah! See how he likes it now! I'll show him who's in charge. I'll show him what-

Eh?

I can feel the cart shake in that telltale way that lets me know that Elian's jumped off. He walks in front of me, stretching his arms out in front of him.

"Right you are, then, Mary," he says, putting his hands to the small of his back and stretching that too. "You stand there for as long as you like. I'm going to get a beer."

That's when I realise I stopped in front of a pub.

Drat. I could have planned *that* better.

I turn to see Elian strolling towards the tavern, no doubt already tasting that foul ale that those odd, two-leggers like so much.

But then, all of a sudden, three men in black suits appear out of nowhere and approach him. One of them is carrying a little black, bag. They're all a little too far away for me to hear what they're saying over the din of the street.

Then – oh, my stars! – the men are bundling Elian away from the tavern door and down the alley by the side of the building.

Frantically, I look around for help but no-one else seems to have noticed anything. I turn back and am about to call out his name…

…when, all of a sudden, he comes strolling back out of the alleyway all by himself. As if nothing ever happened. Instead of going into the tavern, he comes back over to me.

"Are… are you okay?" I ask. "What was that all about?"

"Oh, just a couple of robbers, wanting my money," Elian says. "I soon saw them off. School boxing champion, eight years in a row at school, didn't I ever tell you?"

I roll my eyes. "You might have mentioned it once or twice…"

Then, I look down the now empty alleyway.

"They were dressed awfully nicely for robbers," I say, doubtfully.

"Yes, Mary, that's because they'd already stolen those clothes from someone else," Elian laughs. "It's what robbers do, you silly horse. I'm… very sorry about using my whip before, by the way. I know you don't like it. I promise not to do it again." He flicks my reigns, lightly. "Come on, then, let's get on."

"I thought you were going for a beer," I say to him, suspicious of his sudden change in mood. "I thought you needed a break from my constant nagging."

"Oh, no," he grins (a strange, new grin, I think). "I like to hear you talk. Why else would I sit here day after day all these years? Come on, tell me everything. I'm a good listener. For instance, I never asked you if you overheard any gossip when the Cat and his friends were here before."

"Ah, well," I whinnie as we start to trot along again. "I think my old ears did pick up a little slice or two…"

And we wander along. It's nice for Elian to finally be listening to me for a change.

THE NAME GAME

The Captain's cabin was awash with noise.

Sitting around the large, square, wooden table was Teresa, the Cat, Iakob, Iosef and Captain Thrace himself. Every single one of them was talking at the same time. The only person at the table not saying a word was Arthur.

When the Cat had regained consciousness, everyone had wanted to know how he'd defeated that entire squad of soldiers all by himself. He'd made some kind of joke and deftly avoided talking about it. But it was clear to Arthur the Cat was hiding something. Some important, serious piece of information that he was covering up with a joke. But, then, Arthur thought, wasn't that just like the Cat? Just like the whole 'used to be a King' thing. The Cat only said what he wanted people to know and he hid the rest.

Arthur's eyes were fixed firmly on the rough, pockmarked wooden table-top in front of him. Somewhere around the edge of his hearing was the nonsensical babbling on about names and machines – but all he could really hear were the non-stop cracks of the peacekeeper weapons. All he could really see was the endless Black reaching up for him...

"Okay, will anyone who is not a Cat please, *SHUT UP!*" the Cat's voice suddenly cut though the pea-soup fog around Arthur's brain as well as the babble of noise in the room. Everyone instantly fell silent and stared at the small, black feline.

"*Thank* you..." he sighed. "Gosh, it's like school on the last day of term! Now, Smithy..." he turned to Teresa.

"…since you asked about the significance of the Queen stealing names, I'll explain."

Arthur's mind was back in the present for the moment so he tried to focus his attention on the meeting. He wondered if all this talk of names had anything to do with what the Cat told him on the night they met – about the way Lady Eris made Arthur feel weak and scared every time she said his name.

"Your name," began the Cat, "is the most important thing about you. It makes you who you are. It carries your core energy. And if someone knows your name, they can control that core energy. They can control *you*."

Teresa wrinkled her nose in disbelief. "Really…?"

"Oh, it's not just an Arilon thing," the Cat went on. "Many cultures in the Human World know this, too. Your all-powerful, scientific, modern-minded people might think this is nonsense but even they know how to manipulate people by the use of their names. They do it all the time.

"Think about it. When you're a bit bored at school and you can't be bothered to listen to the teacher…"

"I'm sure I don't know what you mean!" Teresa winked at Arthur. "I *always* pay attention in school!"

Arthur felt himself smile back at her a little, despite his mood.

"*Teresa Frances Smith!*" the Cat shouted.

Immediately, Teresa stopped smiling, sat up straight and gave the Cat her full attention.

"Sorry," she said.

The Cat smiled. "You see? That worked a lot better than me simply saying 'stop messing about'. Because I used your name. I said it in a certain way. You didn't realise it, but

- 193 -

I manipulated your core energy. I controlled you. Just a little. I made you do what I wanted, which was to stop talking."

Teresa was awestruck. "Wow... you're right! My father's always doing that! Bet he didn't realise he was being a sorcerer..!"

"Now imagine such power in hands of Queen," said Iakob in that strong, Russian-sounding accent. "Imagine Queen with names of all Arilon people in palm of her hand."

"She'd be able to control everyone," Arthur said, nodding. "Completely. No more cutting Travel Lines. No more messing about."

"But..." Teresa said, suddenly, "couldn't people hide their names? Like you, Cat, and the Queen."

"It's not so easy to do," said the Cat. "To a Weaver, your name is kind of like those shops with the huge, signs on the front made out of light-bulbs. It's very, very visible. It takes great skill and cunning to hide it. Being totally brilliant, I – of course – have such skill and cunning. Unfortunately, so does the Queen. Very few other people do."

"So, that is it..." said Iosef. "When Queen completes part of machine in Waterwhistle, she wins. She has control over everyone in Arilon."

The Cat nodded. "Nobody will be able to stop her from completing the rest of the Agency Engine."

"But..." Teresa said, a dark realisation heavy in her voice, "...having control over everyone in Arilon... that's already a huge thing, isn't it? I mean... if just this little part of the Agency Engine allows her to do *that*... what would the *full* power of the machine do..?"

The room was silent, now, as the full force of that question hit home with everyone around the table.

"That…" said the Cat, finally, "…is a question we don't want answered the hard way."

Teresa gulped.

"Still…" the Cat shrugged. "It's better to know what you're dealing with rather than sticking your head in the -"

"I want to go home."

Those five words, so softly spoken, stopped everyone in their tracks. They turned to the person that had said them.

They turned to Arthur.

"…what…?" the disbelief in Teresa's voice cut into Arthur's chest as surely as a knife. But it didn't deter him.

"I want to home," he said again. "I thought I'd be able to help you all. But, after Labyrinth… and now this… I'd just get in the way. I'll end up getting one of you hurt or killed if I stay. It's best if I just…"

That's right, scaredy-cat.
Tell them it's because you're worried about them.
Don't tell them the truth. Don't tell them you're just so scared,
you want to run home and bury your head
in your pillow and hope it all goes away…

Iakob and Iosef watched Arthur, their faces, undersanding. They didn't know the boy well but they could see he was not cut out for this kind of adventure. It was best for him that he go home and leave this to the others.

Captain Thrace's mouth was cocked ever-so-slightly up at one end and it reminded Arthur of one thing. Lady Eris' smile when she saw how right she'd been that Arthur was a coward.

The Cat watched Arthur with a completely unreadable expression. Arthur couldn't decide if it was understanding or disappointment. Acceptance or disgust.

The worst face, though, the one that pained him the most to see... was Teresa's. She was angry and aghast, yes. But under it all, she was hurt.

"I'm sorry..." Arthur said to everyone (but he was looking at Teresa when he said it), "...I'm just... I'm sorry..."

Teresa's chair scraped heavily backwards, cutting through the silence as sure as a bell and she ran quickly from the room, slamming the door behind her.

The Cat finally spoke.

"Captain Thrace," he said quietly. "Please set course for Graft."

HOMEWARD

It had seemed to Arthur that they'd reached Graft in no time at all.

He'd spent the entire jouney sitting below in Captain Thrace's cabin while everyone else went about their business elsewhere on the ship.

Finally, they'd arrived and the Cat brought Arthur up on deck. Iakob, Iosef and Captain Thrace all shook Arthur's hand and wished him luck. (There was a strange look on the old Captain's face, Arthur thought – as though he couldn't quite decide if he was glad Arthur was getting off his ship or not).

Teresa, unfortunately, didn't shake Arthur's hand. And she didn't wish him good luck. In fact, she didn't even make an appearance.

"She's upset..." Captain Thrace said, uncertainly, clearly unpracticed in the matters of crew emotional problems, "...but I'm sure she'll miss ye, just the same..."

Arthur had just nodded and the Cat had led him down the gangplank and into the silent docks. It was the middle of the night on Graft and there was absolutely no-one around. It was very odd to see the place so quiet considering how busy it had been before. He supposed, though, that if people on the island worked so hard all the time, sleep was something they took very seriously indeed.

Thinking about this, he realised he was going to miss Arilon very much. But his decision was the right one. He absolutely had to-

Run away.

The Cat led Arthur in a new direction, away from the Broken Crown. They headed out of the main part of the town and into an area that Arthur quickly realised was full of vegetable allotments. The small plots of green and brown, splashed with the muted night-time colour of the gas lamps all reminded Arthur of his uncle's little vegetable patch. It was strange how even though they were in another world, some things were exactly the same as back home.

Arthur forced himself to push such thoughts from his mind. At first, Arilon had been a totally alien place but more and more, it was feeling familiar and normal. As though it wasn't really another world, just an extension of the one he knew. Like another country or something.

And he didn't like to think of the Queen destroying it.

Before long, they had arrived at a small shed with a wooden rack outside it upon which hung a range of rusty, worn out tools.

In front of the ramshackle, old building, at the foot of the doorway, was a small mat. It was worn and brown, clearly having had the owner's muddy boots scraped across its surface for years. And yet, the picture of a row of carrots that was woven into it was still just about visible – as though the mat simply refused to let it go.

The Cat moved his paw over the mat, copying the symbols on the paper Bamboo had given him.

Then he turned to Arthur.

"That's it," he said, finally. "Step on. It'll take you home."

Arthur stared at the mat. "That's it? No sparkles, no… flashing lights?"

"Portal magic is difficult but pretty unspectacular," said the Cat. "The mat is now a gateway. Once you're through, I'll turn it back into a mat."

"And this will take me back to London?"

The Cat nodded.

Arthur took a deep breath and looked at it. "Okay…"

"Flying the *Galloping Snake*, single-handedly," the Cat said, suddenly. Arthur looked up.

"Excuse me?"

"Your favourite bit. Am I right?"

A small smile crept onto Arthur's face. "It was pretty amazing…" But then the smile faded as his mind turned back to Labyrinth.

"You did very well, Arthur Arthur Ness," said the Cat.

Arthur looked into the Cat's eyes. Once, at school, Arthur had run the hundred yards dash in P.E. He'd come last by such a large margin that the other children were already back sitting down when he'd crossed the finish line. The teacher had told him he'd 'done very well'. But the look in the teacher's eyes told Arthur that the teacher didn't mean it.

It was the same look Arthur saw in the Cat's eyes now.

All of a sudden, an anger rose in Arthur's chest. He'd had enough of Arilon. Enough of the Cat. Enough of the Queen, of Lady Eris. Enough of everything.

He stepped forward onto the mat.

And he was home.

In London.

In the hallway of his own house.

BLITZED

"Mum?"

Arthur shouted at the top of his voice. He was back in his hallway, standing on the old, raggedy mat his dad had brought back from Burma. Arthur had never really liked it but right now it was the best raggedy old mat in the world.

"Mum?!" Arthur shouted again.

That's when he noticed the place was an absolute wreck.

Dark, violent, cracks jagged their way up the walls, furniture was smashed and scattered all over the floor, windows were broken. What was going on?

"Mum, where are you?"

Still, no answer. Through the front door's glass panelling, Arthur could see it was night. But a much darker night than you could ever normally expect in the city. It was the Blackout.

An air raid was in progress.

To make it harder for the enemy bombers to find their targets, all houses had to turn their lights off and put thick curtains on the windows to hide the candle-light. Arthur had even helped his mum put black tape on the windows to keep them from shattering too badly if they got smashed by a nearby explosion.

In Arilon, Arthur thought, the Black was to be avoided at all costs. Here, in London, it kept you safe.

Everything was as he expected it to be during a Blackout with only his mother in the house.

Everything except... no mother.

Arthur went from room to room in the dark. Living room. Front room. Kitchen. All just a crumbling half-wrecked mess. Surely she wouldn't have stayed here alone, Arthur thought? Maybe she was at Mrs. Patterson's down the road? Unless Mrs. Patterson's wasn't there any more. This kind of damage to the house… surely that meant somewhere nearby had been totally flattened.

Arthur went slowly upstairs. The creaking of the steps was the only sound in the cold, dark, silent house. His parents' room was as much of a mess as everywhere else. He went to his own bedroom.

To Arthur's astonishment, it was in perfect condition! Not so much as a book out of place.

Not knowing what else to do, Arthur sat on the end of his bed and looked up at the ceiling – at the mobile he and his father had made. Two spitfires circling round each other, keeping Arthur safe as he slept. He remembered sitting right on that spot, looking up at those planes on the morning he left, just as his mother had come into the room.

"You have to be brave," she said, sitting down next to Arthur. His suitcase was sitting patiently by the side of the bed. His coat-label with the Waterwhistle address rested ontop of it. Waiting for him.

"Brave like dad?" Arthur asked.

"Brave like *all* those pilots."

"But… aren't they scared?"

And Arthur's mother had smiled. "Of course they are."

Arthur was puzzled and was about to ask her how they could be brave and scared at the same time – when

> an insistent **honk honk** intruded from the street below.
>
> "Come on," said his mother, picking up the suitcase and that horrid, hated label. "The bus is here. We need to get to the station, or we're going to miss your train."

Arthur couldn't take his eyes off the paper fighter planes now, as they hung motionless above him. He knew his dad was flying one of them right now, somewhere many miles away. He could almost hear the humming of their engines.

Wait... he *could* hear plane engines. And they were getting louder. But how could-

BOOM!

The entire world shook and the light of a thousand suns came pouring in through the bedroom window. Time suddenly seemed to slow down, come almost to a complete halt... Arthur could almost see the individual cracks moving slowly along the glass, spidering outwards, joining up with each other... time crawled almost to a halt, until time became *now* and all of a sudden everything's happening *right this moment* with powerful clarity and terror.

And time cranks back up to full speed – and the window explodes, sending glass flying everywhere. Arthur lies on the floor, surrounded by bits of razor-sharp window... the tape not having done such a great job on this occasion. But Arthur knows that means the explosion had been very close.

The bright light has faded back to night-time again but with a faint, orange after-glow. Arthur looks out of the window. Fire. Several streets away. The high street. Maybe closer.

In bomb terms, a very near miss.

But then, more humming. More planes. Arthur runs. He gets as far as the stairs.

BOOM!

This one – even closer – and the whole house seems to jump clear off the ground with the shock of the nearby impact as Arthur is thrown down the stairs, head over heels. Huge chunks of ceiling and wall and floor are leaping and falling in every direction.

Arthur knows he's completely unprotected. He has to get out. He runs to the front door and turns the latch, pulling it.

It won't open! Stupid, stupid – this time of night, surely it's been locked. Plus, the shaking of the house has probably shifted it in its frame so it's totally jammed in place. What to do now?

In a flash, it comes to Arthur. Back door!

He turns, runs down the hallway towards the kitchen and the back door but-

CRASH

The entire ceiling suddenly drops down in front of him – Arthur glimpses bits of his parents' bedroom furniture – their bed, their wardrobes – falling into the kitchen before the entire doorway is filled with rubble.

Arthur's mind goes numb and his heart starts to beat even faster. He's trapped! Can't go forward, can't go back. He runs back to the middle of the hallway. No idea what to do, where to go. He looks up. The front door has indeed shifted in its frame – it's dropped down several inches and there's a gap between the top of the door and the doorframe. And through it, Arthur can see the night sky. He can see the glow of fire and draping of thick smoke.

And he can see a plane. An enemy bomber.

Flying straight towards him.

And a dot…

…coming out of the bottom of the plane.

Oh, no.

A bomb.

Coming straight towards his house. Straight towards *him*.

Nowhere he can go. Nothing he can do.

It gets closer. Arthur can almost see the design, the writing on the side of the bomb.

It'll hit in just a second.

Wait, what's that? Something tugging..? Arthur looks down.

He's standing on the raggedy, old rug.

There's something poking out of the rug, grabbing Arthur's shoelace.

A cat's paw.

It pulls hard.

Arthur falls into the rug.

NEEDLED

And Arthur was back. Back in Arilon. Back in the nighttime garden in front of the ramshackle shed, standing on the threadbare, muddy mat that-

"*RUN!*" the Cat shouted with such volume and urgency, Arthur almost fell over.

"But...what..." Arthur stammered. The Cat grabbed his shoelaces and tugged with an amazing, paranormal strength.

"Arthur, run *now!*" the Cat shouted again. "It's the *Needlemen!*"

Arthur's mind was a whirl of questions – Needlemen? What are Needlemen? Why are they here? Why is the Cat *afraid...*

All of which were immediately cut off as Arthur staggered backwards and tripped over the body of Frogham, lying on the ground.

The whirl in Arthur's mind only got faster and more confusing. Nothing was making any sense. So he did the only thing he could think to do when nothing made any sense.

He trusted the Cat.

He got up and his ran for his life.

The pair of them sprinted through the allotments, through cabbages and potatoes and carrots, running from what, Arthur didn't know. All he knew was that he was terrified.

"You took me by surprise, Cat!" Frogham's voice rang out from behind them. "You knocked me down before I could grab yer! You won't get another chance!"

"You shan't escape, feline! Not this time!" Another voice, well-spoken, one that Arthur didn't recognise. But that voice wasn't behind them. It was off to their left.

Arthur looked round as he ran, trying to spot the owner of the new voice. All he could see were sheds and greenhouses and bushes and spades and vegetables all appearing out of the dark ahead of them and disappearing into the dark behind them. The dark that hid their pursuers.

Suddenly-

Thwip!

– a shiny, gossamer-thin wire shot out of the darkness from one side, right across the front of the escaping pair and stuck into a shed on the other side. The Cat narrowly darted out of the way and Arthur barely managed to skid to a halt before he hit it. He could see, even in the dark, as light from the nighttime sun glinted off the wire that it was razor-sharp. If he'd run into it, it might have cut him in half!

Another voice, this time from the other side.

"You're ours now, Cat, you and the boy!"

That one, Arthur *did* recognise – the old man with the talking horse from Bamboo's island. What was *he* doing here on Graft? What were all these people doing, chasing them?!

"Come on!" the Cat shouted and he started to shoot off in another direction – but another glistening wire whipped out of the darkness and embedded itself into a tree right next to Arthur.

The pair turned around to yet another direction but another wire *thwipped* by, cutting them off once again. Then another. And another. And another. From all directions. Hemming them in, closing them off. And before long, there was a massive web of wires stretching off in all directions, glistening, deadly-sharp, in the pale lamplight.

Arthur knew the Cat could still have escaped – he was small, fast and agile – but he went nowhere.

He stayed by Arthur's side.

As they both stood there, trapped, figures began to emerge from the misty darkness. Frogham. An old man in a neat suit that Arthur didn't recognise. And finally, Elian from Bamboo's island, just as Arthur had guessed.

But that wasn't all.

Appearing out of the night were another three or four men in dark suits and wide-brimmed hats. Long shadows were cast down their faces and only their mouths could be seen protruding from the darkness beneath the hat-brims. But even seeing only the mouths was enough because the thin lips on each and every mouth was twisted up in a horrible, horrible smile. The same smiles that Frogham and the other two were wearing.

And so, at last, Arthur's unasked questions were answered.

These were Needlemen.

They were here to capture them.

And the Cat was afraid of them because they could become and replace anyone. Including his closest friends.

"Told yer it was pointless to run," said the fake Frogham. "Time ter come with us."

Raising a massive, meaty hand, fake Frogham pulled delicately on one of the wires and they all immediately flew towards Arthur and the Cat in a storm of lethal, flashing light until Arthur's arms and hands were fastened tight to his body and his feet were bound together with just enough slack to allow him to walk. Looking back at the Cat, Arthur could see a wire had wrapped itself around the Cat's neck and connected him to Arthur, forcing the feline to walk slowly behind.

Panic began to lick at the edges of Arthur's mind and he started to pull and thrash at his bonds.

"Arthur, no!" the Cat cried. "The wires will just tighten the more you struggle! You'll end up cutting your arms off!"

Arthur cried out as the wires began to dig into his wrists, drawing a thin, sharp line of blood. He decided to take the Cat's advice and forced himself to calm down.

Quickly, the Needlemen marched Arthur and the Cat away from the allotments, through the town and back to the docks. As they were about to turn the last corner before the part of the docks where the *Galloping Snake* was moored, the Cat spoke.

"Arthur, I'm very sorry, but you're going to have to be very brave at what comes next. It won't be easy. In fact, it'll be very, very hard. The hardest thing that you've ever had to do. Please just remember who you really are. And remember what you really want."

Arthur wanted to turn his head and look at the Cat. What did he mean? What was he talking about? Remember who he was, what he wanted? But he never got the chance because they turned a corner and entered the docks. And Arthur's body flooded with terror at what he saw.

A ship – collosal in size – was moored next to the *Snake*. It dwarfed Captain Thrace's ship by at least three times and was built entirely of a deep, black wood. Several ropes and cables snaked from the looming, malevolent ship and were hooked into the hull of the *Snake*, holding it firmly in place and keeping it from escaping.

The huge letters on the other ship's nameplate confirmed for Arthur just what he'd expected.

The ship was called *The Noir*.

The Needlemen marched the pair up the gangplank of the massive, imperious-looking galleon and onto her deck. As expected, Iakob, Iosef and Teresa were tied up and held captive by Yarnbulls. As expected, Lady Eris was standing there, staring at Arthur and the Cat, triumph gleaming in her eyes.

What was *not* expected was that Captain Thrace was standing by her side.

"Traitor!" the Cat hissed at the old pirate.

"Oh, don't be like that," Lady Eris said, smoothly. "Captain Thrace might have betrayed your location to me but my Needlemen were on your trail anyway. They had almost caught up with you. Captain Thrace simply made the inevitable happen today instead of tomorrow."

"It's nothin' personal, Cat," said the Captain. "I could see you lot weren't no match for Lady Eris, here. I just didn't want to be on the losin' side. But you *were* right, about one thing," the Captain held up a handful of gold coins. "She *is* rich!"

Arthur glanced around the deck. It was like a bigger, darker, more dangerous version of the *Galloping Snake*. And where Arthur was used to seeing Captain Thrace's ship all but deserted, this one was filled with crew, soldiers and a smattering of Yarnbulls.

"Like it, Arthur?" grinned the Cat as though he was having a conversation over a bowl of fizzy milk at the Broken Crown. "Big ship, isn't it? It's called the *Noir*. Used to be called the *Aerie*. Then they had to change it to the *Kray*. After that, the *Taranteen*. Every time I defeated one of the Noir Ladies, they had to change its name for its new owner. In the end, I got rid of so many of them, they just gave up, didn't they, Eris? Re-named it the *Noir* and had done with it."

The Cat turned his attention fully to Lady Eris now, his voice not as light. Not as friendly. "The Queen's got her head screwed on straight, hasn't she, Eris? She knows how many of her Noir Ladies I've done away with. Just like I'm going to do away with you. Because no matter how many of you creatures she throws at me, I just keep coming. And before you know it, you'll be stitched into the walls of your mistress's chamber along with your predecessors."

The triumphant grin faded from Lady Eris' face and was replaced with something that Arthur had seen back when the Cat had revealed himself to her, right before they'd escaped through the tapestry. She was afraid of him.

The Cat smiled at Lady Eris now, but it had no humour or warmth or friendliness in it at all. It had teeth and terror and it made Arthur feel as though he didn't really know the Cat at all. And that somehow, the way he looked – small and black and slim – was not at all the whole story.

"You know you can't win, Eris. You're evil, your mistress is evil and ontop of that… you've hurt my friends," he growled. "All of which means I will defeat you. You know it's coming. And then it's only a matter of time before the Queen finds herself under my claws once again. And this time, I won't hesitate to finish the job."

Emboldened by her position, Lady Eris r fear away and her mocking sneer returned.

"No more escaping, Cat. No more running. And no more Noir Ladies falling before you. Not ever again. The story ends here." Lady Eris smiled and turned to Arthur. "Is that not right, Arthur Ness?"

She pointed at Arthur and black threads flooded out of the end of her finger and shot straight toward Arthur's head and face and eyes… and the last thing he heard before darkness claimed him was Teresa screaming his name.

THE END OF THE NIGHTMARE
(from the no-longer-scared thoughts of Arthur Ness)

My eyes snap open.

I take a deep breath. And another. Slowly, calm comes over me and I realise where I am.

My bedroom!

Perfectly tidy and not blown to bits. And the morning sunshine pouring through the not-smashed window.

"Arthur?" The door opens and in walks... no... it *can't* be...

"I heard a noise, are you okay?"

With a sudden surge of energy, I leap out of bed and give my mother the hugest, tightest hug I've ever given her.

"Wow, what did I do to deserve this?" she laughs, hugging me back. "I haven't had one of these for a long time!"

"I'm just so glad to see you," I mumble into her shoulder. "I've had the most terrible nightmare."

From somewhere deep inside me, there's a voice shouting, telling me that something's wrong. And I think I can hear a woman's evil laugh. But I silence it all and shut it away. There's nothing wrong.

I'm exactly where I wanted to be all along.

"Well, don't worry. It's over," she whispers back to me. "It wasn't real. You're awake now."

TO BE
CONCLUDED

THE ARILON CHRONICLES : BOOK 2

WILF MORGAN

ARTHUR NeSS

AND THE

SECRET OF

WATERWHISTLE

PART 2

88TALES ALPHA

A long time ago, in a galaxy far, far away, a short, green, wise, old alien told his pupil;

'Named must your fear be before banish it you can.'

or to put it another way;

'It's definitely possible to defeat your fears – but you have to identify them first…'

THE STORY SO FAR

The bad guys are winning.

It had all started in the village of Waterwhistle - where Arthur had been sent to escape the Nazi bombs falling over London. In the tiny, Nottinghamshire village, he was meant to be safe. But things got very unsafe, very fast.

Arthur, scared of virtually everything even at the best of times, found Waterwhistle to be a silent and unfriendly place. He soon discovered, though, that there was a reason nobody spoke. A reason everyone ignored each other; Lady Eris, his terrifying host, was a witch. How did Arthur discover this? He was informed by a talking cat.

Arthur was quickly learning that Waterwhistle was not a normal place.

Nevertheless, the Cat (he kept his name a secret) showed Arthur that Lady Eris had the village of Waterwhistle under a very powerful spell. She had made the villagers afraid. And they were *kept* afraid by Lady Eris' minions, the fearsome Yarnbulls - huge, weaponed, two-legged, horned creatures who kept watch over the village night and day. Waterwhistle was under mystical lock and key.

Arthur learned that The Cat had spent a long time battling the evil Lady Eris - and her even more evil mistress, the Queen. Eventually, chased by enraged Yarnbulls, the feline adventurer dragged Arthur through a tapestry-portal and into the strange world where Lady Eris, the Cat and the Yarnbulls had all come from… the world of Arilon.

Never before had Arthur imagined a place so wondrous; an endless array of huge, floating islands connected by Travel Lines along which sailed thousands of ships. There was no time to stop and stare, though - Lady Eris' forces were hot on their heels. Now they were in Arilon, things only got faster and more dangerous.

The pair met up with Teresa, a Waterwhistle resident of Arthur's age who had stood up to Lady Eris and had been imprisoned in Arilon for her trouble. Then there was the grizzled, old pirate Captain, Chadwell Thrace. And finally, the twin Knights, Iakob and Iosef. The group, aboard Thrace's ship, the *Galloping Snake*, kept one step ahead of Lady Eris while trying to discover the secret of what the Queen was doing to the people of Waterwhistle and why.

But, as mentioned before, the bad guys are winning. Captain Thrace, ever the selfish pirate, has betrayed Arthur and his friends. The Cat, Teresa and the twin Knights are all captured and held prisoner aboard Lady Eris' ship, *The Noir*. And Arthur? The last thing he remembers was Lady Eris pointing at him and dark threads shooting out of her finger towards his face and then…

…nothing.

PROLOGUE

As Hector Smith stood behind the counter of his shop in Waterwhistle, he realised with some surprise that, for the first time in years, he was thinking of Needlemen.

As usual, he was working in the village's farm shop that he had run for many years. And, as usual, he was staring blankly into the distance, not saying much of anything. There was a faint, distant wondering why the evacuee lad from London hadn't been in for his compost lately. But otherwise, things were normal.

He was coated in a general feeling of fear and dread, just like everyone in Waterwhistle was these days. You kept the fear at bay somewhat by not speaking. Not looking at your fellow villagers. Not asking questions about why things felt like this.

And then, all of a sudden, the thought of Needlemen had popped into his head. It made him jump a little. Why now? After all this time?

Everyone in Waterwhistle knew the stories about Needlemen. They knew that Needlemen were fictional. Made-up. Used to scare children into behaving themselves or tidying their bedrooms. Everyone in the village knew about them and knew they weren't real. Perhaps at some point in your life, you had believed Needlemen to really exist and to really be out there, watching you. But as you got older, the thought of them faded and became replaced by a general feeling of discomfort and anxiety. That's what had always covered Waterwhistle. For as long as he'd lived here, that unnamed feeling of dread in the background, a fear that was there and not there. Like a lie you never mentioned. A picture you never looked at. A knocking sound you always ignored.

And then recently, it seemed to Hector as though something had come along and amplified it. Turned the dial up. Turned the anxiety into full-blown fear. A fear so all-encompassing that every person in the village had turned inwards, had stopped talking to each other unless they absolutely had to.

And now, after all this time, he was thinking about Needlemen again. Co-incidence?

Hector tried to think – how did the rhyme go again?

Into the world, they come to see.
They come to us in bands of three.
Don't look, don't look, they come for me.

It was something like th-
Tinkle.

The door to the shop gently opened and in walked three men. In black suits. Black hats. The one at the front was carrying a black case.

Hector's mouth ran dry. His whole body stiffened. His eyes were stuck wide open. His insides turned to mush.

They were… here? Now..?!

But then, he noticed… it wasn't just here, in his shop. Through the windows, outside, in the street. From one end of the village to the other as far as he could see. Dozens and dozens of Needlemen. Sprung out of nowhere.

The villagers all stood around, frozen in shock, the dark figures seeming to have suddenly awoken everyone from their trance. The black-suited men, their pasty, white faces covered by wide-brimmed hats, began to walk, unhurried, towards the petrified villagers.

That's when Hector noticed that there was one Needleman for each and every villager. Each man, woman and child with their own individual, personal nightmare. Hector could see terror rising up off the villagers like steam. The people of Waterwhistle all looked how Hector felt; like a story was nearing its completion – and an ending they had secretly known and feared for a long time was finally being told.

"It is time," said one of the Needlemen. His voice was cold and still and drew Hector's attention back to his own nightmare.

"The words of this story are nearly done," said the second.

Hector could barely speak, "…story..?"

"We do more than just replace people," said the Needleman at the front. He opened his bag. Something inside it seemed to be glowing. "Much more."

The fear grasped Hector's heart and squeezed. It squeezed so tight that his very thoughts started disappearing. Soon, he knew, all that would be left would be the fear. He, the person, would no longer exist.

But then, just before the darkness shrouded him completely, a light suddenly blinked on in the black. A voice. Calling to him, desperately, from the dim shroud of his fading memory.

Dad!

"Teresa!" he suddenly shouted.

But then the story ended.

ARTHUR NESS

AND THE

SECRET OF
WATERWHISTLE

PART 2

THREAD THREE

WAKING UP

HAPPY BIRTHDAY, ARTHUR NESS

LONDON. 1970.

Arthur Ness sat in his office and looked at the birthday card in his hands. Inside the card, in the scruffy handwriting of a child, it read;

Happy Birthday Arthur, 40 Today!

And further down, it read;

Have you noticed the men in hats lately?

It didn't say who it was from.

The little speaker-box on his desk buzzed and the tinny sound of his secretary's voice came through.

"Dr. Felix is here to see you, Mr. Ness."

"Thank you, Martha, send him in."

"Yes, Mr. Ness." A pause, then, "Have you had a chance to think about my birthday? I'd really like the day off to see my mother and-"

"I have no interest in your personal nonsense, Martha," Arthur snapped. "Be in work on that day or be in the job centre the next. Now, stop bothering me with your prattle and send the doctor in."

"...yes, Mr. Ness..."

Arthur put the card back in its envelope just as the door opened and a tall, thin man in an ill-fitting brown suit entered.

"Happy Birthday, Mr. Ness," said Dr. Felix. "I trust I find you well today?"

"If I was well," said Arthur, ignoring the doctor's outstretched hand, "then you wouldn't be here. Please, let's begin. I have a meeting in an hour."

The doctor nodded, politely. "Very well. Let's move right along."

Arthur had been seeing the psychiatrist, Dr. Felix, for two months, now. To be honest, he didn't even want to see the doctor. He wasn't crazy. But Eleanor, his wife, had insisted. She'd noticed that he wasn't feeling his usual confident, satisfied self. He'd been prone to fits of what she called 'worried sadness'. Like he was afraid of something – something big – but he didn't know what. These had been quite disorienting for Arthur himself because they went completely against the one thing that Arthur Ness was known for.

Namely, not being scared of anything. At all.

Over the years, Arthur had grown into a very successful businessman; the head of the largest electronics company in Europe. He had no fear of anything or anyone and had pushed, fought, shouted – and yes – bullied his way to the top.

Arthur would be the first to admit he wasn't always the nicest person in the world. But being afraid of nothing meant he could forge ahead into whatever activity he pleased and usually win at it. It had been many years since he'd felt the need to be nice to anyone. There was just no need.

But it wasn't just the feelings of sadness and depression that had prompted the visits to Dr. Felix. There were the dreams, too. Dreams he hadn't had since he was a boy, newly returned from Waterwhistle. Dreams of flying ships, floating islands and talking animals.

Dreams of a world that didn't exist.

"So," said Dr. Felix, sitting on Arthur's office chair, his pad and pen out, "how have you been feeling this week?"

Arthur himself was sat on a brown, two-seater sofa. The doctor had brought his chair up beside his patient and the two men faced each other. Arthur sighed.

"The same," he said. "Depressed. Down. Like I can't be bothered with things. Like things don't... well, like they don't matter. Like they're not real."

"Mm-hmm..." the doctor scribbled in his pad. "And the dreams?"

"Getting more and more vivid," said Arthur. "Last night I dreamt I was talking to a stick doll."

"Interesting..." said the doctor. He scribbled again. It annoyed Arthur when the doctor did that; said 'interesting' then scribbled.

"I haven't had these thoughts since I was a child," Arthur said, more to himself than the doctor. "Since I came back from Waterwhistle."

"Ah, yes," said the doctor, "back at the start of the war. The evacuations. What can you tell me about your time in Waterwhistle?"

Arthur allowed himself a rare smile. "It was brilliant. The people were friendly, I had lots of children to play with... I was actually quite popular, seeing as I was from London. They were fascinated with the way I talked. They said 'bath' and wanted to hear me say 'barth'."

"It sounds like you had a good time there."

"The best. Then, when I was finally allowed to come back home to my parents, things got even better. My father was a war hero. He'd flown in the Battle of Britain and shot down over twenty enemy aircraft. But he was injured and had to leave active service. He came back home and the three of us were happy. Happier than ever, really, despite the war. I became really popular at school. I deposed the school bully…"

"You took his place, didn't you?" said the doctor, checking earlier pages from his notes, "Tommy…erm… ah, yes, Tommy Watkins. The school bully. You knocked him off his perch, so to speak. And then took his place as 'top dog'."

Arthur nodded, no hint of remorse in his voice. "Oh, yes. Before I went to Waterwhistle, I was a frightened little scaredy-cat. After Waterwhistle, I felt no more fear at all. Not a scrap. So, yes, Tommy Watkins had it coming to him. I wasn't in the mood for his nonsense anymore. And, yes, I took his place. In this world, the fearless are in charge. I didn't make the rules, that's just how it is."

"So, what happened in Waterwhistle to affect such a big change in you?"

"I…" Arthur stumbled, "…I can't remember… There was…"

"A girl?"

"Yes…"

"The one you can't remember anything about?"

"…yes. Because she wasn't really real. I made her up for some reason. I don't know why…"

"Have you been thinking about her more, recently?"

Arthur nodded, slowly. "I'd managed to put her out of my mind, many years ago. But with all these thoughts coming back into my head, recently… yes, she's been coming back too."

"But you still can't remember anything about her," said the doctor, "because she isn't real. Just like the stick doll or the talking cat or the floating islands."

Arthur nodded. "I know, I know… and yet…"

"What..?"

Arthur looked at the doctor, now, something new in his eyes. Something the doctor hadn't seen before. Something Arthur hadn't felt since his return from Waterwhistle.

"There are the men," Arthur said. "The men in suits. With hats. And cases."

The doctor furrowed his brow, flicked through his notes, "Which men? You haven't mentioned them to me before."

"I know I haven't. Because I wanted to pretend they aren't there. They make me feel…" Arthur could barely bring himself to even *say* the word, "…*afraid*."

"And… what do these men do?"

"Nothing," said Arthur. "They just watch me."

"Watch you?"

"I've noticed them over the last few months. Every so often, I'll turn my head and one of them will be there. Standing in a crowd of people, maybe. Or on a bus that's driving past. Just standing there, watching me. Then I'll turn away for a moment and turn back…"

"And they're gone," the doctor guessed.

Arthur nodded. "I feel as though they're keeping an eye on me or something. I haven't told anyone. Not a soul. Not until now."

"Perhaps…" Dr. Felix said, slowly, "…perhaps they aren't real, either."

"Oh? Then how do you explain this?" Arthur handed the doctor the envelope. Curious, the doctor opened it and took out the birthday card. He read the handwritten note inside.

"There's no name," he said, eventually.

"I know."

"Who gave it to you?"

"It was on my desk when I got here this morning. Martha's been in since the office opened but she said nobody else has come by."

"I... see..." the doctor said slowly, putting the card down and scribbling in his pad again, quite quickly.

"Wait a minute..." Arthur said, "...you think *I* wrote it, don't you? Wrote it to myself."

Dr. Felix looked at Arthur with that expression where someone tries to think of the best way of saying something you don't want to hear.

"Let me promise you one thing, Doctor," said Arthur, firmly. "*I did not write this card!*"

The doctor smiled. "Listen, Arthur. I just want to tell you something. You are *not* crazy. Okay? You're just overworked. Anxious. Stressed out, as the youngsters say. You have a very successful life. Take some time off with your wife and take things easy for a while."

"My wife?" Arthur said, anger suddenly tumbling into his voice, "You mean the wife whose lawyer sent me a letter this morning saying she was divorcing me? That wife? Or perhaps you mean my first wife? The one who also divorced me? Would it be one of those two wives you're talking about?"

"Ah... I'm... I'm very sorry," said the doctor, embarrassed. "I didn't know..."

Arthur looked over to the dustbin by his desk. Barely visible under piles of screwed up paper was the green and blue plastic of a model Supermarine Spitfire Mk II. His favourite aeroplane. An exact replica of the one his father had flown thirty years ago. It had been a birthday present from Eleanor last year. Upon receiving the divorce papers this morning, Arthur had relegated it from his desk to its current position.

His life was full of relics like that. Ruins of things that used to be good but which he'd turned sour. His fearless approach to everything had brought him money and power. But his life was full of wrecks and skeletons of all the things he'd messed up along the way. His parents. His marriages. His children.

Had he made a mistake? Was his total lack of fear not quite the best way to be, after all? Could it be that he ought to-

"Sleep, Arthur." The doctor interrupted Arthur's thoughts.

"Hm? I'm sorry?"

"Everything's getting to you right now. Don't let stress and tiredness make you doubt yourself. You're the head of this entire company but you need a break. Recharge your batteries. Trust me…" the doctor put his pad and pencil away and got up, "…everything will be okay if you just get some sleep. Sleep will cure all, Arthur!"

Arthur was unsure, but nodded. He stood and walked the doctor to the door. This time, when Dr. Felix extended his hand, Arthur shook it – but he was distracted.

"What is it, Arthur?"

"Hm? Oh, nothing. Well… maybe nothing. It's just… well, don't you think it's strange?"

"What?"

"That the Second World War is still going on today? In 1970? Don't you think it's strange that it didn't end back in the forties?"

The doctor furrowed his brow again. "Strange? I don't know what you mean, Arthur. Everything is just as it should be."

THE ISLAND OF FEAR
(from the terrified thoughts of Teresa Smith)

The huge, wooden doors creak open and I stand up as straight as I can manage. Don't look scared. Don't look frightened. Push back me shoulders and stick out me chin. I may be terrified but I'm not gonna to show *them* that.

CREEEAK

And there it is. The crowd. And out there, beyond the crowd.

The wooden stage.

The place where Lady Eris said me, the Cat, Iakob and Iosef were all gonna be executed.

"I don't suppose you've got a plan or anythin' have you?" I whisper. The small, black cat near me feet just huffs.

"I shouldn't think so," he replies. "Plans are for wimps."

I sigh. "I were afraid you were goin' to say that."

The Knights, the Cat and me are all stood on the back of a horse-drawn cart. The driver's some old fella, stooped and hunched over the reins and dressed in smelly rags. I know I shouldn't be mean – but he *is* driving me to me execution so I think I can be forgiven a little bit of name-calling.

The driver cracks his whip and the two snorting horses break into a slow trot. We all jolt a little as the cart lurches forward.

We emerge out into the harsh, white sunlight and I try to raise me hand to cover me eyes – only, I can't do it properly because of the ropes we're all tied up with. Me and the Knights have got our hands tied together while the Cat's got a rope round his neck attachin' him to the cart itself. Despite everythin', Iakob and Iosef are standin' tall, motionless and defiant in their sky blue armour (though their helmets have been taken away). And even though the Cat's just sittin', starin' out at all the people, he manages to look mean and rebellious. I try me best to do the same.

As we trundle forward, I squint against the cruel sunlight and see how big the crowd really is. Hundreds and hundreds of people – men, women and children – all turned out to watch. Thing is, they don't look excited or happy or angry or expectant or anythin'. They just look... well, I can't think of a better word than *broken*. Like they don't *want* to be here... but they know they *have* to be here. They've been told to turn up and watch us die. And so they have, in droves. They're too scared to do anythin' else.

Phobos certainly lives up to its reputation. Like all the islands, the sky's black even in the middle of the day. But somehow, Phobos' black sky seems even blacker, even more oppressive. Like a blanket dropped over everything, smotherin' the life out of everyone under it. There's that horrible feelin' of rain just about to come. That fear when you know something terrible's just round the corner, gettin' ready to happen.

The buildings add to it, too. They're all huge. Tall and wide. No cute, little houses. No interesting looking chalets. Just gigantic monoliths with tiny windows, all made out of awful, black stone.

There's Yarnbulls everywhere, too. The giant, upright bull creatures walkin' around carrying axes and swords and hammers. They're starin' at the people of Phobos all the time, just like in Waterwhistle. Unlike Waterwhistle, though, the people here can see the Yarnbulls. They don't have to be tricked into bein' afraid. Their fear's right in front of them, in plain sight.

Waterwhistle…

I can't hardly think about the place without me throat tightening up and tears threatenin' to come to me eyes. My home… Me and Arthur were goin' to save it. I know we could have, too. We might only be a pair of silly children next to all these Knights and Weavers and talking cats, but we could have done it. I know we could have. There was nothin' me and Arthur couldn't do as long we stuck together…

That's all over now, though.

Story's done.

The crowd parts and lets us through. For a moment, I lock eyes with this little girl, a touch younger than me. She looks just as scared as the rest but for a second, I think I can see a glimmer of somethin' else in her eyes. But then it's gone and the crowd swallows her up again.

As we roll on through the people, as they stare at us with dull eyes, as we trundle slowly to the wooden stage at the front, I finally clap eyes on the woman that made all this wonderful magic happen. There she is now, standin' up there, waitin' for us with an evil, triumphant grin on her face. Yarnbulls and Royal Guardsmen stand on either side of her but it's her what wields the real power.

Lady Eris.

And finally, we're at the front. The cart stops.

"Out." One of the soldiers grabs me arm and yanks me up onto the stage. They grab the Cat and the Knights, too. I'd like to see them be so brave if the ropes weren't there. Iakob and Iosef would have 'em all eating their own arms and legs, you just see if they wouldn't.

Unfortunately, the ropes *are* there. So we don't have no choice but to do what we're told.

On the stage, there are four wooden posts in a row. They kind of remind me of the maypole that we put up back in Waterwhistle, every year. The girls of the village (not me, I refused) would dance round it to celebrate May Day. It'd be bright and joyful with loads of multi-coloured ribbons windin' round each other in endless combinations.

Funny how these horrid, dull things could remind me of something so bright and happy.

The soldiers take the rope around me wrists and fasten it to one of the posts. They do the same to the other three. The Knights are tied by the wrists, same as me, while the Cat's attached to the bottom of his post by his collar. It's a very short rope, he can't hardly move. But, still, he doesn't seem the least bit worried. He just sits there, starin' out at nothing in particular, like he's tryin' to decide what to have for dinner.

"Aren't you worried?" I ask him.

He shrugged. "Worried? Why, Smithy, I never waste time being worried. Either everything will turn out alright in the end, or it won't."

"Well, everything's gone wrong," I say, more to myself than him. "It's all about to collapse in on us and there's no way out."

"In my experience," the Cat smirks, "that's usually when the best stuff happens."

A shadow falls over the Cat. We both look up. Lady Eris is standin' in front of us, smilin' that horrible smile of hers. The thing that makes it so nasty is that you don't even get the feelin' she's all that pleased. She's just behaving how she thinks she *should* behave. Really, she's just like the people of Phobos. She's doin' what she's told.

Unfortunately, that means she's tyin' us up to wooden poles and shootin' us up into the Black to experience loneliness, starvation and death. So she doesn't really get too much of *my* sympathy.

"So we have finally reached the end of our little tale, feline," she says to the Cat. Then she turns to me. "You see where you end up when you defy me."

"Yep," says the Cat, "hoping someone would hurry up and shoot me into the Black just so I don't have to listen to you yammering on anymore."

"I'm so glad you have lost none of your legendary sense of humour, creature, even now, at the end," she says. "Especially as your little band has been reduced by two. Any words for me to pass onto Captain Thrace, by the way?"

The Cat barely holds back a snarl. "Tell him, I hope he enjoys his blood money."

"Oh, he is enjoying it immensely," Lady Eris smiles. Then she looks at me even though she's still talkin' to the Cat. "And what of Arthur Ness? Oh, but I forget. He is gone from us forever."

Me stomach tightens and me knees go weak. I try and gasp for air. I want Arthur here, with us, so badly. It feels wrong that we're apart. But this witch woman's right. He's not coming back. Ever.

Lady Eris' smile just widens.

BLITZKRIEG

Arthur drove quickly through the traffic.

His car was a brand new Ford Cortina. It had a 2 litre engine, 98 brake-horsepower and full leather-trim interior. It had been his pride and joy just two weeks earlier when he'd driven it off the car dealer's forecourt. Yet, today, his new car couldn't have been further from his mind.

Outside, the majestic stone arches of the Tower Bridge sailed by as he crossed the River Thames. Distractedly, he fiddled with the tuning knob on the radio. Nothing caught his attention (there was something about the Beatles breaking up but music didn't really interest him). Arthur sighed and flipped the radio off altogether.

He didn't know what was happening to him. Ever since he'd come back from Waterwhistle, his life had been brilliant. He'd been totally without fear. Without remorse. That had allowed him to steamroll over everything and everyone to get what he wanted. His life had been one success after another.

Except, he thought now, perhaps it hadn't been so great. Perhaps the failed friendships and relationships were not as unimportant as he'd previously believed. Perhaps they were actually a string of failures which were just as long – if not longer – than his string of successes.

wwwhhhooooooooohhhwwwwwooooooo

What?! Arthur couldn't believe it. The air raid alarm? In the middle of the day? The enemy never engaged in air raids unless it was under cover of total darkness. He could see it in the faces of the other drivers and pedestrians around him; panic, shock, fear. Everybody instantly knew the same thing.

This was going to be a bad one.

BOOM!

Arthur gripped the steering wheel – the explosion had been just a few hundred yards behind. He turned to see cars flying twenty feet into the air as if they were toys. He looked up. Like a conspiracy of angry ravens, dozens of enemy aircraft filled the sky.

Without waiting another second, Arthur turned and rammed his foot on the accelerator pedal. His car screeched off before anyone else had managed to react. He weaved in and out of the traffic at seventy miles an hour. All around him, people screamed and ran and shouted and hid and stumbled and fell but Arthur just kept going.

BOOM!

The car physically lifted off the ground this time, the explosion was so close. Overhead, the Stuka aircraft soared by, their wing-mounted sirens filling the air with an unearthly wail. And falling from them were hundreds and hundreds of tiny, black-

BOOM!

Blackness. Silence. Muffled noises. Funny head. Dizzy. Eyes open… people running… on ceiling..? Noises getting louder… screaming and fire and explosions and…

Arthur awoke with a sudden jolt and realised his car was upside down he was still in it. Alive. How he'd survived, he had no idea.

His body racked with pain, Arthur crawled across the ceiling of his brand new car (which was now the floor of his brand new car). Hand over hand, he eventually made it to the smashed out window and crawled out. Dusting himself off, Arthur stood.

The city was in flames.

It was early evening and still bright but the smoke blocked the sunlight out. The only light now was the dangerous, orange glow of the fires. The streets were still full of people running in all directions but most of the buildings were either aflame or had just collapsed altogether.

Arthur looked up into the sky. Angry, black, billowing smoke covered the entire view but through it could be heard the unmistakable drone of hundreds of bomber engines. Stumbling, Arthur limped slowly into the middle of the road, his gaze fixed firmly to the sky.

Why was the war still going on, he thought? Why wasn't it over? He had never thought it strange before now. But all of a sudden, the idea that the allies were still fighting Nazi Germany in 1970 seemed not at all right.

Suddenly, the clouds of black smoke parted as if some giant hands had drawn them like curtains. A single Stuka JU87 bomber emerged from the gloom like a dark angel. And it was heading straight for Arthur.

Arthur had been used to not feeling fear for his entire adult life. Right now, staring at an enemy bomber flying towards him, he still felt none. He knew he should run – not out of fear but out of common sense. And yet, still, he didn't. He just looked at the plane. The plane that he felt, more certainly with every passing second, *should not be there.*

For no reason he could put into words, Arthur began to walk towards the oncoming aircraft.

And that's when he saw them.

The men in suits. Loads of them. Watching him. They were lining the streets like some kind of silent, dark parade crowd. Where had they come from, all of a sudden? Arthur knew why they were here, though. He didn't know *how* he knew, but he was sure they were here to stop him walking towards the plane. He felt afraid. Very afraid.

But he kept walking.

All as one, the black-suited figures stepped off the pavement and moved in his direction, hands outstretched. It was the most fearsome thing Arthur had ever seen. Twenty, thirty, more, all striding towards him. All intent on stopping him. Stopping him from what, though?

He kept on walking forwards. The plane came in lower and lower as though it had spotted Arthur and was coming in just for him. The suited men increased their pace, hands reaching for Arthur.

The Stuka opened fire. The **CLATTER-CLATTER-CLATTER** of the machine guns rattled their way along the road surface, the mini-explosions of tarmac swiftly moving in Arthur's direction.

Everything was getting closer and closer and closer…

"*Move!*" came the little boy's cry as he flashed across in front of Arthur, grabbed him by the arm and yanked him away.

Arthur didn't even have time to blink. The boy had a firm grip of his hand and was dragging him at top speed off the road and down an alleyway. For some reason, Arthur let himself be dragged and off they went. Down one alleyway. Up another. Out onto a main road. Down another alleyway. Never stopping. Were they still being chased? Arthur didn't dare look behind. Didn't have time to even if he'd wanted. The boy was pulling him faster and faster, going who knew where. It reminded Arthur of another time, years ago, when he'd been no older than this boy, probably. When a talking cat had dragged him into an adventure he didn't understand...

SLAM!

They were inside, Arthur suddenly realised. Inside where? He looked around. A library? It hadn't been hit and looked in good shape. Just dark and empty. There was something eerie about a library at night. But at least the place had walls and a door and a roof and could keep them out of the madness for a while.

"I think they're gone," the boy said, looking out of the window. There was something familiar about him, Arthur realised now. His hair, his old-fashioned sweater and shirt and shorts...

And it hit him.

The boy turned around and smiled a crooked grin that looked completely out of place on that face.

His face. His ten-year old face.

"Happy Birthday, Arthur!" said the young version of himself. "Did you get my card?"

NIGHT IN THE LIBRARY

"*You* sent it?" Arthur wasn't sure which fact he was more surprised at; that he had suddenly found out who had sent the card... or that it had been sent by a version of him that had not existed for thirty years.

"Of course I sent it," the boy said but he was already looking around them, only glancing back at Arthur every so often. "Who else was going to send you a birthday card? You're a right grumpy so-and-so. And by grumpy, I mean rude, nasty and self-centered. But it's okay." He faced him and grinned that lop-sided grin again. "I'm here now."

"But..."

"No time for buts, Arthur Ness," said the boy, "We're on a really tight timescale. It won't take long for the Needlemen to figure out where we are so we have to move quickly. Time moves differently here, see? We might still have a chance to save them."

"Save who?"

"The others! Keep up, gosh you're thick."

The boy disappeared off into the darkness of the library.

Arthur was bewildered. "I think I understood about three words of what you just said. Needlemen? Rescue who..? What are... hey, come back!"

Arthur looked behind a shelf. The boy was gone.

"Wow, you might be tall but you're slow, Arthur Ness," the voice came from behind him. He jumped and span round. The boy looked at him, curiously.

"Wow, age doesn't suit me at all, does it? I'm all... round and hairy."

Arthur stared at the boy – at the skinny legs and messy hair.

"Are you really... are you really me?"

"I really am," said the boy. "Got to say I'm a little disappointed though."

"Disappointed?"

"That I grew up to be so grumpy. And by grumpy, I mean rude, nasty and self-cen-"

"Yes, you mentioned that already," Arthur snapped. "But... how can you *be*?"

Young Arthur's face grew serious. He spoke firmly and clearly but also rather quickly. "Arthur, listen to me. Those men in the suits. They're called Needlemen. They're very dangerous. Very, very dangerous. Which, of course, means it's very good news they're here."

"Good news? Why?"

"Because dangerous people are only sent to places where there's a threat to the dangerous peoples' boss. That's you, Arthur. You're the threat. Understand?"

"Not in the slightest."

"Good. Understanding just slows you down. Come on," and he grabbed Arthur's hand and led him into the darkness.

"What are we doing here? We need to get somewhere safe."

"Oh, you're way past safe now, Arthur," said the boy. "This place, this world, this entire existence of yours is turning against you. Forget safe. You need a way out."

"So, what are we-?"

"We need a story. That's why I brought us to the library. Surely *that* makes sense."

"A story?!" Arthur all but cried. "You're crazy!"

"*I'm* crazy?" said the boy. "*You're* the one talking to yourself."

Arthur looked about them at the rows and rows of books. In the dark, they were completely indistinguishable from each other. This was the last place he'd expected to find himself in the middle of an air raid. But, then, life as he'd expected it had sort of stopped recently.

He sighed. "Okay, well as long as I'm going utterly insane, let's look for this blumming story. Which one do we need?"

"Well, there's the catch, you see," said the boy, "I can't tell you."

"You mean, you *know*?"

"Of course I know. I'm your subconscious. I know lots of stuff. I know all the things you know but are too afraid to admit to yourself."

Arthur bristled. "I'm not afraid of anything!"

The young boy nodded. "Yes, I know. That's the problem. But listen, we need a story or it's all over. The Needlemen will catch you and that's it. Now, I know what story we need – which means *you* know which story we need. But I can't tell you... you have to figure it out for yourself."

"Why?"

"There's a certain power that comes from the knowledge you figure out for yourself. When someone tells you something, you know it *here*..." he placed a finger on the side of Arthur's head. "But when you work it out for yourself, then you know it *here*." He touched Arthur's chest, right above his heart. "You understand?"

Arthur looked down at the boy's finger then back at his face. And he nodded.

"Right," said the boy, urgency back in his voice. "Find us that story, Arthur. Where are we looking? Oh, and I don't want to put any pressure on you, but I think the Needlemen just entered the building so it'd be really good if you could do this next bit really *fast*."

Arthur's eyes darted back and forth, trying as best he could to read the shelf header signs. Children's, dramas, romances, biographies, histories…

"That way!" Arthur whispered, pointing toward the historical section. He didn't know why… it just felt right.

"Wait…" the young boy only touched Arthur's arm but the tone of his voice made him stop dead still. There was a broom leaning against the wall next to them. The boy silently reached over and picked it up. He then took a small piece of glass out of his shorts pocket. It was a shard of a mirror. There was something familiar about it, Arthur thought. Something about the way different colours danced across its surface when it moved…

Young Arthur tied it with a piece of twine – also from his apparently bottomless pockets – to the end of the broom handle. Motioning for the adult to stay still, the boy held the broom outstretched so the mirror peeked around the corner of the nearest bookshelf.

Arthur felt his heart skip a beat as he saw the reflection of a man in a dark suit and hat. He was silhouetted against the window and the orange and yellow devastation outside.

The boy pulled the makeshift periscope back.

"Not that way," he whispered.

The pair crept in another direction, taking the long way round to the Historical Books section. Twice more, the boy stopped them and stuck the mirror round the corner of a shelf. And twice more, they saw the reflection of a Needleman standing there, searching the library with slow, deliberate movements.

Arthur didn't like feeling afraid. He was sure he'd done with all that nonsense thirty years ago. These Needlemen were the first thing in all that time to make him feel any kind of fear. But as much as he hated it... it also felt... good? No, good wasn't the right word. What was it, then... proper? Normal?

Necessary?

"This way," the boy whispered, touching Arthur's arm. Two steps and they finally reached the Historical shelf.

"Right, find us a book then, Arthur Ness," whispered the boy. "Quick as you can. No time for leisurely browsing."

Arthur scanned the book spines quickly, running his finger over the books on the top row. Nothing. Then the next row. Nothing. The third row. Nothing.

This was stupid. He didn't even know what he was looking for! Why was he listening to this child (who was obviously a hallucination)..? He should be outside, finding a way home.

"Arthur, hurry..!" the boy said, quite loud. Why wasn't he whispering, Arthur thought? The Needlemen would find them! But then his stomach clenched with fear as he realised the reason the boy was no longer whispering.

The Needlemen had already found them.

"Don't turn around, Arthur," the boy said, nervousness creeping into his voice for the first time. "There's no point in turning around. Turning around right now would be bad. So, so bad. Just find the book we need. Find it now!"

Arthur wanted to do nothing more than turn around and look. But the boy was right – what would it achieve? He'd see Needlemen. Two? Three? Five? Ten? (The fear assured him it was *at least* ten). But then what? They'd get him.

He needed to find the story. Now!

He ran his finger along the books. More books. More books.

Nothing.

"Arthur…!" he could feel the boy backing into him, now. That meant the Needlemen had surrounded them. Were almost upon them. He could just see them in his mind's eye… reaching out with their long, skinny arms and their needle-sharp, metal fingers, only their mouths visible under the shadow of their wide-brimmed hats. The one at the front, carrying a bag. Opening the bag…

The Remembered Life of Hector Smith.

"Found it!" Arthur grabbed the book and span round, holding the dog-eared paperback up in front of him. It was worse than he'd imagined.

The library was *filled* with Needlemen.

He held the book higher, pointing it at them.

"What are you *doing?*" the boy shouted, "They're not vampires and that isn't a blummin' crucifix! Just *run*, you great turnip!"

And run, they did.

THE BROKEN BROKEN CROWN

The pub was a broken down mess.

The air raid finally seemed to be over now, but it had taken its toll on the old place. It hadn't suffered a direct hit, but nearby explosions had shaken the watering hole to pieces. Chairs and tables were scattered around, the bar was in two great pieces and broken pipes leaked beer all over the rubble-covered floor.

Arthur had never been in here before but he'd passed it many times and noticed its unusual name.

The Broken Crown.

He didn't know why, but it always made him think of Waterwhistle. This evening, as their flight from the library led them here, it occurred to Arthur that the Waterwhistle connection was no co-incidence.

"Drink?" the boy asked. He was holding a glass under a pipe that was shooting tap water up like a fountain. Arthur nodded and the boy filled two glasses.

"Right," said the boy, handing one of the drinks to Arthur before taking a seat at one half of the bar, "so, I know what you're thinking."

"Sure about that are you?"

"Yes," the boy took a sip of water, "you're thinking that you'd forgotten how handsome you were when you were ten."

Arthur felt a laugh escape his lips before he even had time to stop it.

"I know what you're thinking too," he said to the boy.

"What's that, then?"

"That you're excited to know that you're going to grow up to be such a good looking man."

"Um…not really…" said the boy, "…but it's nice that you think so highly of yourself."

Arthur looked out of the window. "Do you think they'll find us in here?"

"Eventually," said the boy. "But we aren't going to stay here long."

"So…Needlemen." Arthur took a gulp of water. His hands had finally stopped shaking. "Any chance of telling me what the heck they are?"

"Well, as I said," the boy began, "they're here to make sure you stay asleep. The fact they're making such a nuisance of themselves means you're waking up. That's a good thing. That's a very good thing."

Arthur nodded. "It's like the Yarnbulls back in Waterwhistle." As soon as he said it, he looked up to the boy in shock. "Why did I just say that? What does that mean? What's a Yarnbull?"

The boy grinned. "You see? It's starting to come back to you. You're waking up!"

"Waking up from what?" Arthur said, agitated. "I'm not asleep!"

"Yes you are, Arthur," said the boy, "you've been asleep for a while now. The good news is you haven't been asleep for as long as you might think. Like I said before, time moves differently inside the Binding than outside it…"

"Binding?"

"Stop interrupting. Yes, the Binding. You're Bound."

"As in 'tied up'?"

"I said stop interrupting. Yes, as in tied up. By a nasty piece of work with some serious meanness issues."

- 253 -

"But, I'm not tied up..! Look!" Arthur waved his arms about like a demented ape. "I can move!"

The boy rolled his eyes to the heavens. "Clearly, I'm talking to myself… Okay, fine, interrupt away! See how far we get when the Needlemen catch up with you and you start crying 'oh, I wish I hadn't kept on interrupting that devastatingly handsome boy'!"

"Okay, okay… I'm sorry." Arthur mimed zipping his mouth shut. "No more interrupting."

"Thank you," the boy sighed and carried on. "You're Bound, but it isn't your body that's been tied up. It's your mind."

Arthur opened his mouth to say something but a warning glare from the boy stopped him.

"Your mind has been tied up by giving it a world that stops it from thinking. For some, that might be a world that terrifies them so much, they just spend the whole time trapped in a nightmare, unable to string two thoughts together. For others – like you – it's achieved by giving you the world you always thought you wanted. It makes you so happy, you never want to admit it isn't real. You never want to wake up."

"Does everybody get the same dream?" Arthur asked.

"Oh, no," said the boy. "There are as many different dreams as there are people to have them. For some people, it's fame. Others, it'd be riches. I'll bet there are those for whom it would be a place where they're fed endless amounts of chocolate ice cream."

"And for me?" Arthur asked.

"I think, somewhere deep down inside, you've already have figured it out."

"Can't you just tell me?"

"No! It's like I said before – sometimes, for you to really believe something, you need to figure it out for yourself. You've started waking up because you've begun to see the lie of the world around you. That's why you've been feeling weird and started seeing the delightful Dr. Felix. But because of that, the dream is sending the Needlemen to scare you back on track. Your only hope now is to see the whole lie. To uncover the full extent of it. Then you'll wake up completely and the Needlemen won't be able to touch you. Well... not *these* Needlemen, anyway."

"But how do I do that?"

"Remember," the boy stared into his face. Arthur looked deep into his own young eyes. "You have to remember Arilon, Arthur. Remember *all* of it."

"Like...the Broken Crown pub? The one on Graft...?"

"Yes!" the boy started to get excited. "Anything else?"

"Like... like... sailing some sort of ship...the... damn... oh, the *Galloping Snake!*"

"Yes! Keep going!"

"Bamboo, the Weaver..! And Captain Thrace! And Iakob and Iosef. And the Cat!"

"Yes..! And who else?"

"And... and..."

"Yes..?"

"I can't... I can't remember her name..." Arthur looked at the dirty floor, "...I can never remember her name..."

The boy's shoulders slumped. "No... I know you can't. It's because she's the most important part. You have to remember her, Arthur. Or those Needlemen out there will get you and you'll never wake up."

Arthur looked down at the book.

"And this is the key?"

"Yep," said the boy. "It's *your* key. Your key out of this world. And maybe more."

Arthur ran a finger over the cover, wiping off dirt and dust.

The Remembered Life of Hector Smith.

Who on earth was Hector Smith, Arthur thought. Why was he important? Well, time to find out. He opened the book. He flicked through page after page. Then some more pages. A few more. They were all the same.

"Blank," said Arthur. He looked up to the boy. "They're all bla-"

But the boy was gone.

Arthur looked left and right. No sign of him. Dr. Felix was right. He was stressed. He needed to go to sleep. Sleep would fix everything, the doctor had said.

Of course he wants me to sleep! This whole world is designed to keep me asleep! Arthur was well aware the thoughts he was having now made it sound like he was finally going crazy. He looked down at the book cover. It was a picture of the village square in Waterwhistle. Right at the centre was the memorial from World War One.

Well, if he was going to go crazy, he might as well do it properly. He snapped the book shut.

He needed to get to the train station.

WATERWHISTLE

Waterwhistle, it had to be said, was a complete mess.

Arthur stood on the main street and looked up and down the village. Nobody was about. According to the taxi driver who'd brought him over from Nottingham train station, the village was totally abandoned. Years ago, something had happened. Nobody knew what exactly. Some kind of disaster. All the people had disappeared. Not a soul was left.

The police had eventually given up and assumed everyone had left in some kind of mass hysteria. Cars and trucks sat rusted and dead on metal wheel hubs, the rubber tyres long since disintegrated. There was no graffiti, no rubbish – not even vandals went there. Just the buildings, the houses, the shops. All run down. There was even glass in all the windows. Just nobody living behind the glass.

It was, basically, a ghost town.

This wasn't right, Arthur thought. What had happened? It had been such a happy place. He remembered clearly, as if it were yesterday. He used to play with the children right over there, in the park. On his very first day, Lord and Lady Roberts had brought him down into the village to meet the children and they'd all made him feel so welcome.

What could possibly have happened to everyone? And why couldn't he remember it coming on the TV or radio? An entire village disappears after some kind of 'incident' and it doesn't even make national news?

Just the latest in an ever-increasing list of things that had ceased to make sense over the last twenty-four hours, Arthur thought.

He pulled the book out from the carrier bag he'd got on the train. The picture on the cover showed Waterwhistle in happier times. The village square – where he was standing right now – was neat and tidy. Rows of immaculately kept flowers framed the grassy area. Friendly looking people walked around, going about their daily business.

It was a photo from the forties so it was sepia rather than colour. But, curiously, even though it was all browns and oranges, you could still somehow feel how green and bright and colourful the place was.

Arthur looked up from the picture to the reality. No people. No life. No immaculate flower beds. Unlike the picture, it *was* in colour but the colours seemed tired and half-dead. Everything somehow seemed even more still than the cover photograph.

Stuffing the book back in the bag, Arthur turned and headed up the main street towards the hill overlooking the village. Up towards the big house.

It didn't take him long to get there. It had seemed a much longer walk when he was ten. His legs were longer now, though, and he made it up very quickly.

As he approached through the garden, there was a sudden feeling of dread as he looked at the soil all around him. It was covered and overgrown with weeds and wild grass but, just for a second, he had a feeling that bulls were going to come up from the ground. But then the feeling passed and Arthur laughed to himself.

Bulls out of the ground, indeed!

Looking up at the house, Arthur was filled with a sense of happiness. He'd spent many happy days and nights here. Lord and Lady Roberts had been like a substitute father and mother at a time when he'd been missing his real parents like crazy. In fact, Arthur recalled with a small smile, there was the time that Lord Roberts had tried to teach him cricket. Arthur had missed every single ball except the last one. He'd made proper contact with it and it went flying... right through the kitchen window. At first, Arthur had been terrified he'd get shouted at but instead, Lord Roberts had just laughed and laughed and-

No, wait a minute. That wasn't right.

He couldn't remember Lord Roberts laughing. In fact, he couldn't remember Lord Roberts at all. Because...

Because...

...because he had never met him.

He took the book out again and looked at the cover. The village square. Something had happened there, he suddenly thought. Something to do with... something to do with the girl. He still couldn't picture her in his mind but he suddenly had a strong feeling that he needed to get back to the square. If he got there, it would all make sense, somehow. He would see her.

He would remember her.

Clink

Arthur turned his head at the soft noise. He was suddenly aware of how silent the place was. The only sound had come from his own feet as he walked.

But he wasn't walking now.

Clink

Again. Arthur looked for the source of the sound. A bird? A badger, coming out early into the dusky sunset?

Something moved in the window of the house, barely visible behind dirty glass.

Not a badger.

A person. Wearing a hat.

Arthur backed away.

The back door opened. The man stepped out. And another behind him. And still another behind that one.

Arthur turned and ran from the Needlemen as fast as he could. He ran back out through the garden gate (another Needleman! Right at the gate!) and headed back into the village.

He sprinted down the lane, a narrow corridor of bushes – black-sleeved arms reached out from the leaves as he ran past. Sharp, spindly fingers scratched against his jacket but he evaded them and ran down the main street.

As he ran through the village, finally the doors of the houses began to open. But it wasn't Mrs McGugan or Mrs Shepard or Mr Babbage. It was Needlemen. Lots and lots of Needlemen.

The houses were suddenly full of them – they spewed from the doors, running out into the street. They came from round every corner. They came from the park. They streamed out of the garage. They flowed over the little bridge that spanned the brook. They came from every house, every nook, every cranny. Without end, they came.

Arthur ran and ran and didn't stop to look back. He kept heading for the square. When he got there, he'd see her. He'd remember her. She'd help him.

The Needlemen swarmed in from every direction, arms reaching, fingers outstretched, looking to grab him, but Arthur didn't stop – even though his chest was aching and his legs were screaming. He kept going, kept running until, finally, he reached the square. Except…

…the girl was not there.

Arthur felt all the hope drain from him and he came to a stop, staring at the empty space in the middle of the square. Nothing was there except the War Memorial.

Thwip

"Ow!" Arthur shouted as a thin, metal wire flew from nowhere and wrapped itself around him. Before he even had a chance to see where it had attached itself, another one **thwipped** in from a different direction. Then another. And another.

Trapped! No way out. It was over.

"Teresa! Help me!" cried Arthur at the top of his voice, "*Teresa!*"

A hand suddenly dropped on his shoulder.

"I was wondering when you were going to ask for my help!" Teresa said, standing next to Arthur as if she'd been there all along.

With a deft and impossible movement of hands, Teresa pulled off all the Needle Wires and they fell away, harmlessly, to the ground.

"Wh…?" Arthur couldn't stop looking at Teresa. How could he have ever forgotten her?

"Gawping later," grinned Teresa. "Fighting now!"

She tossed him a short, broken broom handle with a shard of mirror tied to the end. She had the same thing but longer – a full broom handle. Just like the one from before, in the library.

A cold hand grabbed Arthur's leg. He swung the weapon downwards and slashed across the Needleman's arm. To Arthur's surprise, billows of black thread came spilling out of the black-suited figure as it fell away and dissolved into nothing in the blink of an eye.

But even as he disappeared, more came through the fading thread to take his place. So Arthur and Teresa swiped and lunged and slashed, knocking the Needlemen back.

The two of them were surrounded by a sea of black suits and dark hats and empty eyes and the sea was neverending. They fought against impossible odds. But they fought.

And fought.

And fought.

Until finally, inevitably, they were overwhelmed.

THE ISLAND OF FEAR
(from the terrified thoughts of Teresa Smith)

"I'm so glad you have lost none of your legendary sense of humour, creature, even now, at the end," Lady Eris says. "Especially as your little band has been reduced by two. Any words for me to pass onto Captain Thrace, by the way?"

The Cat barely holds back a snarl, "Tell him, I hope he enjoys his blood money."

"Oh, he is enjoying it immensely," Lady Eris smiles. Then she looks at me – even though she's still talking to the Cat. "And what of Arthur Ness? Oh, but I forget. He is gone from us forever."

Me stomach tightens and me knees go weak. I try and gasp for air. I want Arthur here, with us, so badly. It's not right that we're apart. But this witch woman's right. He's not coming back. Ever.

Lady Eris' smile just widens.

Before the Cat can say anything, she turns away from us and faces the crowd. At the same time, a Yarnbull at the other end of the platform is pulling on some kind of crank wheel. Its muscles are strainin', the burlap sack material that those things are made of looks like it's going to rip at the seams through the sheer force it's exerting in turning the handle. As the handle goes round, it's turning a massive, ratcheted wheel. And as the wheel goes round, the noise of the ratchet itself rings out over the entire grisly scene.

"People of Phobos!" Lady Eris addresses the crowd. Somehow, her voice is amplified and super-loud, like it's coming out of a huge speaker.

"You know what it is to be afraid. The Queen *wants*
clack clack clack clack
you to be afraid. Your Island has many Travel Lines still
attached because the Queen wants everyone all across
clack clack clack clack
Arilon to feel that fear as well. But it isn't because she is cruel.
It is because she cares about you. If you are afraid,
clack clack clack clack
then you will not do anything stupid. You will not do
anything that will get you hurt."
clack clack clack clack
"The Queen only wants her people to be safe. And that
is why these troublemakers have been brought here.
clack clack clack clack
We are going to make you watch as they are cast up
into the Black, never to return. You will be scared at what
you see –
clack clack clack clack
and that fear will be transmitted right across Arilon. And then
you – and all the people of Arilon – will
clack clack clack clack
remember that to defy the Queen means a terrible fate. And
this thought will keep you safe from harm."

She spreads her arms wide to the crowd with a smile
that could melt the Devil's own heart.

"Because your Queen loves you."
clack clack clack clack CHINK
She turns to the Yarnbull at the crank wheel. Her smile
is gone.

"The girl first."

I look down at the trapdoor I'm standing on. I brace meself, ready for it to shoot upward, to blast me up, right up into the NothingSpace far above where I'll just-

"*YOU!*" screams Lady Eris.

Okay, I weren't expectin' *that*.

I look up.

The Cat's free. Iakob and Iosef have their swords in hand and stand ready for battle. And standing right in front of me, a stupid grin on his face and a sharp knife in his hand, ready to cut me ropes like he'd just done for the others...

It's Arthur!

"I hope you've got your action music ready," he grins, "because this is probably the best rescue you're ever going to see."

I'm not sure, but I think me mouth's hangin' open.

What -

- just -

- *happened?*

WHAT JUST HAPPENED

The back of Arthur's head was hurting. And cold. His back was cold, too. And his bottom. And behind his legs. Cold and aching. And a bit damp. Fighting the aches and pains, he opened his eyes. What was that? A ceiling? A stone ceiling?

Ah. He was lying down.

Arthur sat up, his muscles complaining all the way. He realised he hadn't been moving for a long time. But... how come? He'd been home! Back home and living there for years! Grown up, married, rich...

But... even now, it was beginning to fade, like a dream. What had happened? He could remember Doctor Felix, the air raid, the library, the trip to Waterwhistle, the Needlemen, Teresa... but it was like trying to see through a frosted glass window. It was just a dull blur.

Everything had been so clear a moment ago. He'd figured out what it was that had been keeping him asleep. He'd figured out how to wake himself up. But now, it was all slipping away again back into the depths of his spinning brain. He was beginning to turn back into his old self again.

And yet. And *yet...*

Something *did* feel different.

Arthur got slowly to his feet, testing his legs and then his arms. He was a little wobbly at first but sensation soon returned to his limbs. He looked around for the first time.

He was in a stone cell. Small. Bare. Cold. Damp. No windows. One door.

Slightly open.

Open?

The memory of recent events flashed back to him. Being back on Graft, getting dragged aboard Lady Eris' ship. Teresa, screaming his name. Then the blackness.

Lady Eris had Bound him, he remembered. Well, that would explain the door. If he was out for the count, never to return, why lock it? He wasn't exactly going to wander off.

Except, now he *was* wandering off. Arthur was shocked to find he was actually *smiling* at the thought. Yes, something in his mind definitely felt different.

He stepped through the door. A corridor. Long. Dark. Cobbled floor, stone walls. More doors. Silence.

Arthur closed his eyes for a moment and concentrated on the floor, how it felt beneath his feet. His weight wasn't swaying from side to side. Not on a ship, then. On an island. They must have been offloaded from Lady Eris' ship onto wherever it was she'd been taking them. Which meant only one place, surely. Not Castle Eris. That was just where she lived. She must have taken them to where she *worked*.

He was on Phobos.

Arthur was amazed at how quickly his brain seemed to be working. If he'd ever found himself in a situation like this before, he would have simply curled up in the corner, paralysed with fear. But now…yes, he was scared, but…

He remembered learning to ride his bike. At first, he'd been terrified – what if he fell off? What would that be like? How would he survive it? Well, before long he *had* fallen off. Hard. It had hurt and he'd cried a lot. Every time he got on his bike after that, he wasn't as scared of falling off. He'd done it and knew what it felt like. It wasn't an unknown anymore.

It was okay being afraid of something for what it was. But being afraid of something that hadn't happened yet… that was somehow much worse.

Now, standing in the doorway of his cell, Arthur realised that he was no longer so scared of what might happen if he got caught because he'd already *been* caught. He knew what it was like and he'd survived it. No point in worrying about it anymore.

He stepped out into the corridor. Taking hold of his courage, he began to walk.

Following the corridor for several metres brought Arthur to a corner. He turned and kept going. Another corner and another and another. As he went, he wondered where the others were. He didn't wonder for long.

"Who are you?" the soldier stood, suddenly. Arthur looked around the room he'd suddenly stumbled upon. It was small and had various weapons and pieces of armour stored on wooden shelves. Some kind of store room?

But wait. Those two helmets. Sky blue, shiny metal. And the swords next to them. Long, wide, double-handed. Arthur recognised them instantly; Iakob and Iosef's things. So, not a store room. Confiscated items from prisoners.

"Well?" the soldier took a step towards Arthur.

Arthur's brain worked fast, taking everything in and figuring out what to do next. Then his brain kind of went *ping* like an oven telling him his plan had finished baking and was ready to use. Arthur bobbed his head, putting on a look of fearful obedience.

"Lady Eris sent me, sir."

"For what?"

Arthur pointed at the twins' helmets and swords, "Those."

"Why?"

"I'm to take them to where the prisoners are being held, sir."

"But they're about to be taken out to the execution stage in the square."

Arthur gulped. Execution stage? That didn't sound good.

"In fact," the guard went on, "one of the Yarnbulls is setting up the popper as we speak."

"Yes, sir, that's what I meant. I have to take the weapons out to the execution stage. I expect Lady Eris probably wants to destroy the weapons at the same time as the prisoners, sir."

The guard snorted. "Suppose that makes sense. Nothing keeps the local populace scared like getting rid of troublemakers that look big and powerful. Hammers home to the little people just how powerless they are, doesn't it?"

"Yes, sir," said Arthur.

The soldier motioned, gruffly. "Go on, then. Best not keep her Ladyship waiting. Not unless you want to get Bound."

"Yes, sir, quick as I can, sir," said Arthur. And in his mind… he was smiling.

Just a few minutes later, Arthur was stumbling down the corridor, dragging a large sack containing the twin Knights' helmets and long-swords.

All in all, Arthur couldn't believe how much nerve he was showing. By merely suggesting he knew what was going on, people assumed he knew everything and just blabbed away, giving him exactly the information he needed.

Time to give it another go.

"Excuse me?" he stopped a guard walking along with some official-looking woman, both of whom were in a heated discussion. "I'm looking for where the Yarnbull is preparing the popper..?"

Arthur's gamble worked. The pair were so busy in their important-sounding conversation, the guard pointed impatiently down the relevant corridor ("last door on the right"), not bothering to ask Arthur any uncomfortable questions about what was in the sack.

Still, he had no idea what the execution stage entailed or what the 'popper' was. But he prepared his nerve now because as he reached the last door on the right, he knew he'd reached his destination. And he knew he was about to face his biggest challenge yet.

The Yarnbull was big, scary, mean-looking... all the things that Arthur knew Yarnbulls were good at. At first, the beast didn't even notice Arthur enter. Its back was turned to him as it busily worked away on some kind of heavy machinery on the far side of the room.

All along one side of the long room, there were five huge springs, each one so wide, it would have taken four Yarnbulls in a circle to reach all the way around. The top of each spring was attached to what looked like the underside of some kind of trap door in the ceiling.

The Yarnbull was working on a huge winding wheel. Thick, powerful-looking chains were wrapped around the wheel and went off in two directions. One way, they were attached to each of the giant springs. The other way, the chains went up through a gap in the ceiling and connected to something else. Arthur could glimpse another winding wheel through the hole, one with a ratchet handle.

The wheel with the handle was outside, Arthur could tell. He could glimpse the black sky and hear the murmuring of a gathering crowd.

All of a sudden, it was clear to Arthur how this thing worked. They were directly under the execution stage right now. The Yarnbull would go up to the stage and wind the ratchet wheel and in doing so, this huge wheel down here would turn and cause these massive, powerful springs to coil up. Then with a push of a lever – BANG – all four springs would hit the trapdoors and his friends would be catapulted up into the NothingSpace and left there to die.

Arthur noticed a fifth, unused spring. And he noticed a long, sharp dagger hanging from the Yarnbull's belt. Again, his brain took in all the details and tried to come up with a plan.

This time, Arthur noticed what his brain was actually doing. He was gathering all the information he had and finding out where the gaps were, what details he didn't yet know.

Then he was somehow figuring out what was meant to go into those gaps by seeing how everything connected together. It was kind of like seeing the truth behind things, he thought.

It was a very strange feeling.

Ping.

He was ready. With a gulp, he stepped forward, hoping against hope that he'd figured everything out correctly. If not, this was going to be a very short and painful conversation.

"Yarnbull!" he called.

The creature froze. Then slowly, it turned its huge, angry-looking face towards Arthur. The small, dark eyes, the massive, furrowed brow, the sharp teeth and angry grimace all made the fear scream in Arthur's stomach, begging him to run away.

Instead, he took another step forward.

"I have new orders for you. You will not question them. You will follow them to the letter. Do you understand me?"

The Yarnbull stared at Arthur, long and hard.

Arthur hoped against hope that he'd figured this out correctly. He knew there must be some kind of hierarchy. Just like his dad had told him about the army. It was like a ladder. Someone at the top, then someone the next step down, and someone else a step lower down again and so on. All the way to the people at the bottom.

Since this was Phobos, Arthur had figured that it must be very simple – the more scared you were, the lower down the ladder you came. At the bottom were the people of Phobos, the most fearful. Above them were the Yarnbulls who kept them fearful. And above the Yarnbulls were those without fear. And the ones without fear gave the orders.

All Arthur had to do was convince this Yarnbull that he was not afraid of it. He stood still, his shoulders back, his back straight, his chin up and stared the Yarnbull right in the eye. And…

The Yarnbull slowly nodded.

Arthur couldn't believe it! It had worked! He had to literally stop himself from jumping up and punching the air with glee! (Especially as that might break the spell, somewhat…)

Arthur had scrunched his fear up into a tiny ball and pushed it way down into the pit of his stomach. But fear is a powerful, springy thing and he couldn't hold it down for much longer.

He kept his eyes locked onto the Yarnbull's and took another step forward.

"I have some instructions for you and you must listen carefully and follow them *to the letter*. But first of all…" Arthur pointed at the Yarnbull's long, sharp dagger, "…you're going to give me that."

ENIKA
(from the downtrodden thoughts of Enika Ardenne)

I hate coming here.

But Lady Eris says come. So me and momma and a thousand other people, we all come. Come to watch some people who was stupid enough to fight against the Queen. Come and watch them get tied to posts and chucked out into the Black.

Serves them rightly, so it does.

Our life here on Phobos, it's not too great. We don't sing happy songs all the time like they do up on Gravisus. Or dance around, having parties like on Laytans. We live an' work in fear.

And that's just how it should be. Fear keeps you safe. Someone who's scared, well, they ain't out puttin' themselves in harm's way, are they? They're at home or at work. Keepin' their heads down. Stayin' out of trouble.

It's what we get taught every day. They tell us at school. They tell us at work. They tell us at home. I've been told every single day since I was born.

So, why is it, then, that I don't believe a word of it?

I don't say nothin', of course. That'd be suicide. Every so often, someone just ain't as afraid as they're supposed to be. The Yarnbulls come for 'em and they ain't never seen again.

Well, that ain't fully true. Sometimes you do see 'em again – when they get brought out, put up on that stage and then blasted up into the Black to die alone.

Yep, that's a lesson that the rest of us don't forget.

So I keeps my thoughts to myself. I know bein' afraid all the time ain't right. But I also know that to do anything about it is stupid. You'll get caught. People always get caught.

So, I do what I'm told to do. When I'm told to come to watch some silly folk get catapulted into the Black, I come and watch. Even though I don't want to.

There's somethin' about these folk, though, that strikes me as bein' a bit different from the normal breed of troublemaker we seen in the past.

The cart trundles past me and I step aside to let it through. I look up at the people on there – two Valian Knights… (well, those Valians are *always* out lookin' for trouble). But then there's a cat just sittin' there, all calm and dignified. Like a king or somethin'.

And then I lock eyes with the girl. Just for a second, we're staring right at each other. She just looks like a normal girl but I get the feelin' she ain't like any normal girl I ever met. There's somethin' about her that's big and strong and…

And then the moment passes and the cart rolls away. And before long, all four of 'em are up on the stage, tied to the shootin' posts.

Lady Eris talks that same talk she always does. The Queen wants us to be safe. The Queen's lookin' after us. I know it's all nonsense – I know the Queen just wants to control us. But, for the first time, I don't feel like I should be keepin' it to myself. I should be-

Woah.

What in the Blessed Islands is happening?!

One of the kid helpers has just sliced the ropes off the cat and the Knights. The Yarnbull has pulled the lever but instead of the troublemakers flyin' off into space, the fifth post's trapdoor sprung up and popped the Knights' helmets and swords up onto the stage!

And now… the kid's thrown off his hood an' cloak. It's some boy. And he's cuttin' the girl free!

And Lady Eris… she looks so mad, she's fit to bust a blood vessel!

Everyone around me's just starin' in shock. Not movin'. Somethin' comes over me and I pull my hand out of my momma's and force myself right down to the front.

Lady Eris is facin' 'em. She's really angry. I can just about hear the girl sayin' somethin' while the boy's cutting her free.

"But... how come you're here?" she's sayin'. "You were Bound!"

He was *Bound*? And he's *free*?

He grabs her and they both duck as a crimson-armoured Royal soldier goes flyin' past their heads - thrown by one a' them Knights.

"Gawping later," the boy's grinnin'. "Fighting now!"

All five of 'em – the Knights, the cat, the boy and the girl – they all form themselves into a circle, back to back. I swear, I ain't never seen nothin' like it. They're a team, those folks. Ready to fight together an' die for each other if need be. And more'n anything in the world, I finds myself wishin' beyond wish for just one thing.

I want to be in that team.

Unfortunately, as the soldiers all start to move towards 'em, their swords pointed out like a hundred shiny ways to die, I don't think I'll ever get the chance. Because that team ain't gonna be around for much longer.

Lady Eris, her eyes literally sparkin' thunderous rage, she's comin' toward 'em and I've seen her wieldin' that magic of hers before. Between her an' those soldiers, this rebellion's gonna be pretty short-lived.

I mean there's the soldiers on the stage. And Lady Eris. Then beyond them, there's loads more soldiers in the huge, dark towers of Phobos stretchin' for hundreds of miles in every direction. An' above us, there's a big chunk of the Queen's fleet floatin' around.

There's no way out of this.

And I find that I'm disappointed. Turns out I was right all along. Fightin' against the fear, it don't get you nowhere but caught.

Right...?

"Coming back from beyond," says the boy, "getting Iakob and Iosef's weapons back, freeing you lot... that was easy."

The soldiers advance, weapons raised. Me an' the rest of Phobos watch with bated breath.

"Getting us off this island..." he gulps, "that's going to be the hard part."

THE HARD PART
(from the excited but scared thoughts of Teresa Smith)

"So, Arthur Ness…" Lady Eris is standing right in front of us. The royal guards are surrounding us, a hundred swords pointed right at us. But it's only Lady Eris we really see. "You're back. I'm impressed."

Arthur's not replying. He's looking around. Up. Seems a bit distracted. A bit frantic. What's he-

"I expect this is all very new for you, Arthur Ness," Lady Eris keeps on talkin'. If she's annoyed by the lack of attention Arthur seems to be payin' her, it don't show. "All this daring bravery business. Seemed like a good idea to begin with, I suppose?" With one hand, she motions to her armed men. "How about now? Are we still feeling just as brave? Palms getting sweaty? Legs feeling weak? Fear not. In a moment, I shall order my men to strike and all your troubles will be over."

"When are you going to learn, Eris?" the Cat says, "There's no version of this that sees you come out on top. It's not even me outsmarting you this time. It's just a small, human child."

Lady Eris flashes the Cat a hateful glance – that also seems to be hiding something else.

"Who says I've been outsmarted?"

Suddenly, Arthur puts his fingers to his lips and lets out a piercing whistle. Why? What's he-

THUNK!

The Yarnbull pushes the lever in front of him. Me mind reminds me we're all still standin' on one of the trapdoors just as there's a loud **TWANG**.

The ground disappears.

Not just the ground – the stage, Lady Eris, the people, the buildings, all of it whips downwards in an instant, shrinking away to a pinprick.

Me stomach lurches right down to me feet and I suddenly feel twenty times heavier than normal as we shoot up into the air very, very high and very, very fast.

What's Arthur *doin'?* Why did he signal that Yarnbull to flip us up? I know we had to escape from Lady Eris, but… why did the Yarnbull listen to Arthur at all? And… are we slowing down already..? Slowing down and…

…and stopping…

For a sickening second, me stomach lurches again and we all hang high in the air, motionless. Phobos is spread out beneath us like a giant map.

And then, we start to fall.

Right onto the hard, metal deck of a ship.

"Ow!" Me head bangs on the cold, rusty floor. When I look up, though, there's a hand reaching down for me.

"Sorry about that!" Arthur smiled, "Bit bumpy!"

He pulls me up. The Cat and the Knights are getting up too, dazed and confused at what's just happened.

"You timed it…" I mutter, "…so this boat would be going past at just the right moment..! You planned this whole thing…?"

Arthur shrugs. "Most of it was planned. Some bits, I kind of made up as I went along."

"For the sake of my sanity," gasps the Cat, "please never tell me which bits were which."

Iakob and Iosef clap Arthur on his shoulders, congratulating him and the Cat is beaming like a proud parent. But Arthur looks at me and the smile fades from his face. Despite everything that's just happened, he suddenly seems nervous.

"Teresa..." he's stumblin' for the words, "...I'm.... I wish I'd never..."

I grab him by both shoulders. He looks bemused. I turn him round so he's facin' away from me. He seems even more bemused. Then I point at the four Royal Sprint Craft that are racing along the Travel Line right towards us.

Arthur stops being bemused.

"Oh, right," he nods. "Talking later. Escaping now."

He races over to the tugboat's steering wheel on the upper-front deck. Iakob's already there, hands on the controls.

"It's okay, Iakob," he says firmly. "I've got this."

The Knight frowns. "Are you sure you don't want me to-"

"No, no, I know what I'm doing..." Arthur sets his shoulders, nervously, "...kind of."

Holdin' firmly onto the wheel with one hand, he shoves the drive lever forward and the tugboat's sails instantly fill with that strange, impossible wind. They billow and flap and with a bone-thuddin' lurch, we shoot forward.

The boat seems pretty sturdy but it's small. The thing's pokey and round and banged together with rough, rusty metal panels. Every dent and bash the little thing's taken over the years shows up nice and bold and it has to fight for every bit of speed Arthur can coax out of it.

The Royal Sprinters, on the other hand, are sharp and sleek and they scythe through the air like daggers. Their anchor-cables whip along the Travel Line at a blinding speed while our tugboat's anchor-ring thrums along the Line with a hefty **chugchugchug**.

"Arthur Arthur Ness!" the Cat leaps up onto the deck next to Arthur. "Not that I'm not glad to see you, because I am. And not that I mean to sound ungrateful for the rescue, because I'm not. And not that I mean to sound miffed that someone has finally upstaged me in the 'being awesome' stakes – because I don't care about being the best at daring escapes. Not really. Well, okay, a bit. Actually, a lot but let's pretend I stopped at 'a bit'."

"I assume that there's a question on its way soon?" Arthur's hanging grimly onto the wheel. "Like, *very* soon?"

"Yes…" says the Cat, "…where in the Blessed Islands are we *going*?"

"Ah, that's easy," says Arthur, "we're going to-"

"Incoming!" Iosef suddenly shouts. We all turn round in time to see a tiny, black dot coming out of one of the chasing ships. In just a very short second, the tiny, black dot becomes a not-so-tiny and very mean-looking cannonball and it's hurtling right at us.

"Hang on!" Arthur yanks the wheel to the left. The tugboat lurches to the side, hanging desperately onto the Travel Line as the ball of metal races past and off into the gloom.

"Cat…" Arthur murmurs, his face white as a sheet, "…may I please request permission to panic?"

"Absolutely not," the Cat says. "You only have so much panic available to you for each crisis. If you panic too early, you use it all up. Save it for when you really need it."

"What we need is weapons!" I shout over the rush of wind. "We need to shoot back!"

Without waiting for another hint, Iosef rushes over to the aft of the boat. There's a whole load of who-knows-what covered up by sheets of black, dusty tarpaulin. He throws the coverings off, one at a time, to reveal various pieces of junk, machinery, wooden crates, two halves of a cannon-

"Bingo!" I shout. Iakob looks at me, puzzled, as his brother starts to pull the weapon pieces together.

"Bingo?" he says, "What means 'bingo'?"

I shrug. "It means 'just what I wanted'…"

"Ah…" Iakob nods his head, one eyebrow raised. His brother's not quite so pleased at the timing of this little language lesson, though.

"Iakob? Little help?"

The Knight rushes over to his brother and the pair of them lift the heavy cannon barrel into place and fix it on.

"Good news, we have cannon," says Iosef. "Bad news, we have no cannonballs."

Iakob and I glance around. He's right. But then, I spot something. I grab one and hand it to Iakob.

"Will these do?"

"Fireworks?" Iakob takes them with a doubtful look on his face. He turns them over and examines them and all of a sudden, a grin comes over his face. "You know… I think is probably *better* than cannonballs…"

Iosef swivels the cannon round, testing the levers and controls.

"Is seeming to work…"

"I think the most important question, here," I say, "is *will it fire?*"

Iakob grins. "Is time for finding out."

He lights three fireworks and stuffs them into the cannon firing chamber and slams the hatch shut. Iosef aims the ramshackle weapon at one of the chasing ships and pulls the firing lever…

BOOM!

The cannon jolts and the fireworks scream out towards the lead Sprint Craft. The ship swoops to the side and dodges the incomin' missiles. But any satisfied grin the helmsman has don't last for long as the fireworks explode just yards off the ship's starboard bough. A hundred flaming balls of crimson fire rain down on the Royal vessel, scorchin' the hull and settin' parts of the sails aflame.

Iosef turns to me and grins. "Bingo!"

I give the pair the thumbs up and run back over to Arthur and the Cat at the front of the boat.

"Okay, Arthur," I gasp, "the lads have got the means to give those Royal busybodies somethin' else to think about. What now? You got any plan left?"

The Cat looks at Arthur. "Yes, plan, what she said."

"Well," Arthur begins, "I was thinking that we'd-"

"*Arthur!*" I scream, pointin' right ahead of us.

Arthur rolls his eyes, "Always with the interrupting…"

Emergin' out of the increasingly darkening sky is another ship, a frigate, switchin' onto our Line. Passin' over the junction point, the ship swings round and accelerates in our direction. Its forward gun lowers down until it's pointin' right at us.

"Okay, Arthur, you win," the Cat gulps. "*Now* would be an excellent time to use up some of your panic."

IMPOSSIBLE

"Panic?" Arthur said, a crazy idea suddenly springing into his head. He glanced at Teresa. She grinned back. He instantly felt better. He turned back to the frigate bearing down on them. "That sounds like an excellent idea. Let's make them do *that*."

He swung the boat's wheel hard to the right as sharply as he could. The metal slug jerked to the side so hard, and shrieked so loud, Teresa was sure it was about to tear itself apart.

As it jumped to the side, Arthur pulled the anchor lever, disconnecting the anchor ring from the Travel Line – and the ship leaped into the evening air.

"Oh... my.... stars...!" wailed the Cat as the boat sailed through the sky, completely unattached to anything. Everyone's hearts jumped into their mouths. Suddenly, another Travel Line appeared out of the dark just ahead of them. As they sailed over it, their anchor ring snapped onto it and the tugboat swung round onto its new path.

Back on the original Line, the frigate and the Sprinters suddenly found themselves racing toward each other with no tugboat between them. They each pulled up hard to avoid crashing. They were not successful.

"Woo-hooo!" yelled Teresa. "That was *amazing!*"

The Cat was speechless.

Iakob and Iosef were speechless.

Arthur – despite being the one who had pulled off the feat – was speechless.

But he was also grinning.

Teresa turned to the Knights. "Um… boys…"

They both turned to look where the girl was staring. More Royal ships on their new line, coming up fast behind them.

"Ah ha! Is time for more shooting...!" Iakob grabbed two fistfuls of fireworks. Iosef swung the cannon round toward the latest pursuer.

"Am planning," he stared grimly down the gun barrel, "on lots more Bingoes."

"That... was some trick, Arthur," the Cat sounded impressed, his eyes flicking from Arthur to Teresa and back again. But there was something else in his voice now, too. Something Arthur couldn't put his finger on.

"Best put your foot down," Teresa warned, pointing at more incoming ships. So that's what he did. Pushing the speed lever forward even harder, the tugboat put on an extra burst of speed.

As they fled across the evening sky, high above Phobos, more cannonballs rained down from pursuing ships. Travel Lines covered Phobos like strands of spiderwebs and those Lines carried enemy craft scuttling around them like a horde of angry spiders trying to catch a very tricky and annoying little fly.

"There!" Teresa pointed at a Sprinter bearing down on them. "Above, to the left!"

"And two behind!" the Cat yelled. The Knights blasted the ones to the rear and the sky was bathed in explosions of light and colour that set the enemy ships on fire wherever the white-hot metal fragments could catch hold. Arthur span the ship around again, bounding down onto another Line, confounding the chasing ships. None of them dared emulate the stunt; the risk of plummeting to the ground miles below or drifting off into the Black just above was too great.

"Two in front!"

"One above!"

Arthur leaped again, narrowly missing an incoming shot.

"Another one, dead ahead!"

Arthur weaved the ship underneath the Travel Line as the frigate passed over them. At the last moment, his anchor-ring popped off and continued to swing around in a circle until it hit another line and they were whipped away in another direction once again.

"This is amazing beyond words," the Cat breathed. "Not amazing beyond *me*... but, y'know, still pretty good..."

"We might just make it out of this alive!" Teresa laughed.

"No! What are you thinking, Smithy, don't say that!" the Cat was aghast. "You must never say that! That's number three in the top ten things you must never say in a crisis situation! Don't you know that's what someone says right before it all goes horribly wrong?"

"We're out of Line," said Arthur.

The three of them looked ahead and saw their Travel Line stretch out into the sky – and then stop. The severed end swayed back and forth lazily in the darkness.

The Cat looked at Teresa. "I hope you're happy."

Iakob came running over.

"I thought I hear someone saying we are running out of Travel Line."

"You heard right," said the Cat. "One of the Lines the Queen has cut."

"Well..." the Knight looked down the boat at Iosef and then back to the others, "...if is just me and my brother, I say we fly boat off end of Line and fall into NothingSpace.

They never take us alive. But with children on boat... I'm sorry, but I think is time we give up."

"No!" Teresa said, "We're not giving up! Not ever!"

"But... there's nowhere else to go..." Arthur said, the end of the line getting ever closer.

"I've been from one end of Arilon to the other, Arthur," said the Cat, "and you know what I've discovered? There's *always* somewhere else to go."

Teresa touched Arthur's shoulder. "As long as you have the right people to get there with."

She smiled at him and he smiled back. He saw the three remaining Sprint Craft bearing down on them from behind. He turned back to the front and saw the end of the Line approaching.

You tried and failed. That's why you should never try.

Drawing strength from the touch of Teresa's hand still on his shoulder, Arthur batted his scared voice away, grabbed the wheel tight and put his hand on the speed lever.

"Just so you know," he said to everyone, "I have absolutely *no* idea what I'm doing."

He threw the lever as far forward as it would go and the tugboat lurched forward at its top speed. Teresa held on firmly to the railings, the Cat next to her. Despite the buffeting of the boat, the Cat kept perfect balance. He stood perfectly still and never took his eyes off Arthur.

Iakob, now joined by Iosef, held onto the opposite railings, staring straight out to the loose Travel Line end. As they got closer to it, shortening the remaining Line, the end went from waving slowly to whipping frantically like an angry snake, faster and faster, shorter and shorter. Then the Line suddenly disappeared under the front of the boat…

…and the boat…

…just…

…kept…

…going.

"Wh… what..?" Iakob couldn't believe his eyes. "We are still flying…?"

"How you are doing this?" said Iakob, eyes wide in disbelief. "You are making new Travel Line as you go! This is not possible!"

Arthur had no idea how he was doing it. He was just… doing it.

"In all my lives…" the Cat whispered. But for once even he was lost for words.

"So, since you're controlling the Line and not the other way around," said Teresa, "where exactly *are* we heading?"

Arthur nodded. "Well, I thought we'd visit Valia. I've always wanted to go there."

Teresa looked over the edge at the pursuing Royal ships - only to find they weren't pursuing anymore. They were obviously as shocked as everyone else. They'd come to a dead stop where the original Line had ended and were just watching this impossibility unfold before them.

They couldn't do anything as Arthur flew off into the Black – defiantly drawing a line all the way from fear to bravery.

"Enika! Where are you, girl?"

The crowd was dispersing now, at the behest of some very insistent Yarnbulls. Enika's mother wasn't leaving, though. Not without-

"Momma!" the girl suddenly popped into view.

"Come here, young lady!" her mother grabbed her arm, relief and anger washing over her at the same time. "You are in such trouble!"

"No, momma. It's not me who's in trouble."

"What in blazes you talkin' about, child?"

Enika pointed up into the dark sky. A few other inhabitants had noticed and were also looking. The ones who had already started to disperse saw that their fellow islanders were staring at something up in the sky and they too stopped and looked. And so more and more people took pause and cast their gaze upwards.

Finally, Enika's mother followed her daughter's finger. And that's when she saw it. Faint, at first. So faint, if you weren't looking for it, you might not even make it out. But, staring intently, she could definitely see it.

A ship, flying away from Phobos.

Making new Travel Line as it went.

"Impossible…" she whispered, her eyes wide.

A little way off, a group of Royal Soldiers and a Yarnbull were trying to move along a bunch of islanders. But the men and women were so entranced by the spectacle in the sky, they barely even noticed the massive creatures.

"You see?" said Enika. "It's not us who's in trouble." She directed her mother's gaze to the soldiers and Yarnbulls. "It's them."

THE FOREST

Hundreds of thousands of miles away from the scene of the miraculous escape from Phobos, there lies a forest. The forest sits on a ship.

The ship is called *The Twilight Palace*.

The Queen's personal ship and flagship of her Royal Fleet sweeps slowly but purposefully through the NothingSpace. No other vessel is near – sailors right across Arilon know that it is bad fortune to lay eyes upon the Queen's ship. Every sailor knows the fear of flying alone in some remote part of the Black only to see the fearsome visage of the Nightmare Ship emerging from the darkness. Sailors usually avoid any area their telescopes cannot see into. To run into a trap set by pirates or buccaneers is bad.

To run into the Queen is worse.

"Your Grace?" Lady Eris stands a few metres behind her mistress and creator. In the aftermath of Arthur Ness' escape, she had been summoned to report on the event. Her journey had been but a single step through a tapestry. Mere moments after her summons, here she is.

Even though Lady Eris has been standing ready for some minutes, though, the Queen has not acknowledged her presence. She simply stands, gazing into the trees.

These are not normal trees. The trunks and branches, all gnarled and twisted, do not bear any leaves or fruit. Instead, millions of shiny, metal wires hang from them. They stretch from branch to branch and from tree to tree. They look as though they have been spun by a billion tiny spiders. Or by one very big one.

To those few who are aware of its existence, this place is known simply as The Forest. Lady Eris is aware that the Queen knows it by another name. But she never says it aloud. Names are a precious commodity in Arilon and not foolishly squandered.

It is both a beautiful and fearsome place, Eris thinks, and the Queen is often to be found here. Strangely, she seems most at ease with herself when she stands among its deathly, razor-wire branches.

Nevertheless, Eris has work to do and precious little time to do it.

"Your Grace," she says again. "You wished to see me?"

"You are on your way back to Waterwhistle," the Queen says, softly. Her voice is deep and rich and there is a sinister sparkle behind her words. Barely audible, like bells in the distance.

"Yes, your Grace," says Lady Eris. "The boy will be heading back there soon. I must be ready for him."

The Queen reaches up to a low-lying branch and runs her finger softly along one of the many wires that enshrouded it. Lady Eris is sure she will cut herself on the razor wire – yet there is no blood.

Though her face is turned away from Eris, she knows that the Queen's eyes are closed.

"He will be armed," she says at last.

"I expect he will have those fools in tow, yes, but-"

"I do not refer to his pitiful band of followers," the Queen's calm voice interrupts. "He will be armed with a weapon. One which you are not prepared for."

"Weapon?" Lady Eris' face shows her surprise. "Of what kind, Majesty?"

The Queen takes her finger down from the wire and turns to face Lady Eris for the first time. Her eyes drill into whatever passes for a heart in the Noir Lady's chest.

"What will be, will be," the Queen says. "I have faith in you, Eris."

"Your Grace is too kind."

"Do the Needlemen continue to hunt the child?"

"In their hundreds. I plan to keep only a small number back," says Eris. "Just enough to achieve our ends."

The Queen touches another wire, this one hanging down, limp and loose, from an overhanging branch. She closes her eyes while touching it. Eventually, she lets go and returns her gaze to Lady Eris.

"Send them back to Waterwhistle," she says, "Their presence in the human village is of more importance. Acquiring the weapon will be difficult for Arthur Ness. He may yet fail without our interference."

Lady Eris nods. "Very well. If that is what my Queen deems best."

There is an odd tone to Eris' voice. The Queen does not miss it. "You do not agree?"

Lady Eris tries to make herself agree with the Queen. But the words do not come.

"I would hear your thoughts on the matter, Eris. Your Queen demands it."

"Very well," Lady Eris draws a slow, deep breath. "I believe it is a mistake to allow Arthur Ness too much freedom. We should send as many Needlemen as we can spare. I only need a few back in Waterwhistle, now. The village is completely under my spell."

The Queen looks at Lady Eris for a long time. Eventually, she moves. She walks around Lady Eris, slowly. The Noir Lady can feel her eyes looking her up and down as a beast assesses its prey.

"There are many paths to the universe, Eris. Not just one. Each moment brings multiple possible outcomes. And each of those potential outcomes have further multiple outcomes of their own."

As the Queen circles Eris, the Noir Lady keeps her gaze fixed firmly ahead.

"We do not have the luxury of relying on a single plan," the Queen continues. "Should your plan fail, we need another. And should that plan fail, we need another. And another. And another. Each time, we close off one more possible outcome. One more possible future. Until the only future that exists is the one we want. The one *I* want."

She has returned to the front of Lady Eris. Her gaze reaches into Lady Eris' eyes and freezes her solid.

"Recall the Needlemen. And should you ever feel the need to question my authority again, please do so. And then prepare yourself to be emptied and stitched into the walls of my throne room. Are my words understood?"

Lady Eris tries her best to control the terror coursing through her body as she bows to the Queen.

"As my Majesty commands."

With nothing more than a movement of her dark eyes, the Queen dismisses her Noir Lady. Soon, she is alone. She returns to the comfort of the Arthur Ness Forest.

VALIA

The sheer number of cut Lines took Arthur by surprise. Even though Iakob had warned them what it would be like, it was still a shock to see. A massive expanse of waving, disconnected Travel Lines stretched across the horizon as far as the eye could see, like some swaying, underwater forest of seaweed.

From the number of Lines, it was obvious how well connected Valia had been to the rest of Arilon. Now, thanks to the Queen, only two Travel Lines remained. One of them went out into the Black but Iakob had told them it was heavily mined with explosives to prevent anyone using it to leave or approach the island.

The other Line stretched up towards another, nearby island.

"Pavidus," Iakob had said, "The island without fear. Is also called Isle of Dead Monsters. Is connected to Valia by single Line and to Phobos by single Line. That is it. Nobody from either island goes there."

His tone had been dark and almost... fearful.

"But... I thought *Valia* was without fear," Arthur had said. "Isn't that the point of bravery?"

Iakob had been about to say something but the Cat had called him away to check some part of the boat that looked as though it were about to fall off.

Arthur looked up at Pavidus now. Apart from the sun, it was the brightest dot of light in the blackness. A sudden desire swept over Arthur with a surge so swift and powerful that it left him almost shaken – he *had* to go to Pavidus. It was as though someone had shone a torch on him and revealed a gaping hole right in the centre of his being. A hole that had always been there but he'd never noticed. He had no idea why, but he knew that the Isle of Dead Monsters was the only place in the universe that would help him fill it.

"Bring us in nice and easy, Arthur," the Cat was suddenly by his side. "Wouldn't want to come all this way only to crash. Saw that happen once."

"Were you driving?"

"I don't have any fingers, Arthur."

"Oh, so of course you weren't driving."

"No, no, I *was* driving. I don't have any fingers. That's why we crashed."

Arthur concentrated as he drew close to one of the many severed Lines, its frayed end waving back and forth slowly in the dark sky.

"Here goes nothing…" he said under his breath.

"Hang on to something, everyone," the Cat said. "We're about to join two Travel Lines together – something that hasn't happened since the original creation of Arilon. There's no way of knowing how such a cataclysmic event will turn out. It might not work or it might destroy the ship in a cataclysmic ball of fire so cataclysmically hot that-"

"Okay, all done," said Arthur.

"I… what?" the Cat looked round. The tugboat was indeed sliding contentedly down a newly connected Travel Line.

"Ah. Well, yes…" sniffed the Cat, "…good. I knew it would be fine. It was those others who couldn't get enough of the word 'cataclysmic'."

The small tugboat slid down the Line and headed towards the surface of Valia – the first vessel to do so in over a year.

Iakob and Iosef ran towards the bough of the boat and stared out towards the looming island, not quite believing that after all this time, they were finally going home.

While the boat was still halfway up, Arthur could already see visible signs of a crowd gathering on the surface. Several minutes later, as the ground loomed tantalisingly close, the throng had swollen to huge proportions. However, unlike the crowd that had watched them depart from Phobos, this crowd was cheering.

The old, rusty, battered tugboat sailed down past several Lines that were connected to the ground nearby and whose severed ends hung, gently swaying in the evening sky. No sooner had the vessel touched down than Iakob and Iosef leaped out and into the mass of people. They were usually so stoic and solemn, Arthur thought. It was strange to see them so overjoyed.

Arthur and Teresa stood at the edge of the boat, near the gangplank and stared at the mass of celebrations around them. The people themselves were a mix of all kinds – old, young, men, women and children. Smart, official-looking types rubbed shoulders with ruddy, barrel-chested farmers. But they all had a kind of steel to them, Arthur thought. Like any one of them – even the smallest, thinnest 10-stone weakling – wouldn't hesitate to walk into a fire if it needed to be done.

"Cat!" a woman's voice, impossibly loud, boomed its way out of the tumult of the crowd. Arthur and Teresa couldn't tell exactly where it had come from and they scoured the sea of cheering faces, quizzically. The Cat, though, suddenly sprang down from the side of the boat and disappeared into the crowd. The people around the feline immediately moved outwards, opening up a gap (though the Cat would have quite nimbly navigated the sea of dancing feet). Emerging from the crowd came Iakob and Iosef, helmets off and grinning. And between them, the apparent owner of the booming voice.

"Ludmilla!" the Cat greeted the new arrival. "So good to see you again!"

Ludmilla was a short, plump lady with fire-red hair, tied back in two tight buns. Very friendly face, Arthur thought, round and jolly. It seemed baffling that such a small woman could be the mother of two huge monsters like Iakob and Iosef. Nevertheless, Arthur could definitely see their grit and determination in her hard, steel blue eyes. Friendly she might be. But you'd get on her bad side at your peril.

She opened her arms in welcome and greeting as she approached the Cat.

"Am so pleased you looked after my boys! Is long time since I am last seeing them! And since I am last seeing you, also!"

"Let me introduce Arthur Ness and Teresa Smith," said the Cat. "They belong on this island, Ludmilla. They're two of the bravest non-cats I've ever come across."

"Very pleased to be meeting you!" the small woman embraced the children one at a time with a grip that literally took their breath away. "We never give up hope, you see," she addressed all three of them, eventually. "We were being trapped, yes. But we know eventually the Cat would help us. And now we complete unfinished business with Queen. We twist Royal jewels out of her Royal teeth!"

The Cat grinned. "I cannot tell you the joy it would bring me to see someone do that!"

Ludmilla spread her arms wide again. "But plenty of time for this, later! For now, come..! We celebrate! We eat!"

"Well…" said the Cat, already trotting off toward a camp fire where a toothless old lady was roasting fresh fish, "…since you insist."

The next few hours seemed to go in a bit of a blur for Arthur. As tired as he was after his recent escapades, the adrenaline rush from all that had happened was still high. And the constant activity on Valia did nothing to calm him down.

The celebrations had obviously started some time ago, probably as soon as the Valians' long-range telescopes had spotted the tugboat coming towards the island. There were several huge fires dotted around the arid, desert landscape. People danced around them, cooked meat on them or just laughed and chatted by them.

As evening became night, more and more people arrived from all corners of Valia. The ebony-skinned warrior clan from the south had come. The thin, lithe forest dwellers from the western lands had travelled too. The Tinies from the North had made the trip, decked out in gold and steel armour and with permanent grimaces on their small, round faces. All hosted by the Towering Knights of the Eastern Sea. This was Iakob and Iosef's homeland. And with the exception of Ludmilla, Arthur could see how the tall, imposing people round here had come by their name.

Everyone had come together to celebrate the end of their long exile from Arilon… albeit by just a single Travel

Line and visitors no more magnificent than two human children and a talking cat.

Eventually, Arthur was full. He couldn't eat another chicken leg or drink another glass of blastberry juice. He found that, eventually, the exhaustion was beginning to catch up with him and he needed some fresh air and a little bit of peace and quiet for a few minutes. Leaving the Cat chattering away to a group of children about his latest stupendous escape, Arthur sneaked away from proceedings.

There was a nearby clearing with an ancient-looking ruin of a fort wall which he'd spotted earlier – but when he got to it, he realised he wasn't alone.

"Halt, who goes there?" Teresa called down to him. "If you didn't bring chocolate, I'll be forced to chuck stones at you!"

"Sorry, no chocolate," Arthur grinned. Then he remembered something and reached into his pocket. "But I have fruit!"

Teresa mock-scowled. "Is that supposed to be some kind of twisted joke?"

Arthur shrugged. "It kind of tastes like chocolate."

Teresa seemed to think about it. Then, "Okay. You can come up."

A hand came down to help Arthur up and in short order, the pair of them sat atop the ancient, ruined wall. For a while, they just stared at the night sky. In Arilon, although there were no stars, you could often see the small pin-pricks of light of nearby islands or where Travel Lines crossed each other. However, Valia had no working Travel Lines to speak of. And the only nearby island was Pavidus so the sky was almost completely empty.

Again, Arthur felt a longing to go to the fearless island. A longing so strong he couldn't explain it. But he pushed it from his mind. Aside from needing a break from the crowd, there was another reason he'd slipped away. He had to do something that he'd been avoiding since coming back from…well, wherever he'd been.

"Teresa, I-" he tried to think of the words to apologise. "That is, you must… I mean, I can't…"

Teresa rescued him with a gentle hand on his shoulder.

"I would have done the same thing," she said.

Arthur stared at her, incredulous.

"You had the chance to see your family again," she shrugged. "Life-threatenin' danger on the one hand, goin' home on the other. Not exactly the hardest decision in the world, is it?"

Arthur didn't know what to say. Teresa was always so brave and gung-ho that he forgot she was scared, too. Maybe even as scared as him.

"I've been thinkin' about it since we got here," she went on. "Yeah… I think I would have done the same thing. I'd give anythin' to see Sammy and Albert and me dad."

"I'm so sorry I left you," Arthur said.

"I know," she smiled. "But what matters is you came back!"

Arthur nodded, still not entirely sure he could quite believe the journey he'd just been on.

"You were there, you know," Arthur said, almost sheepishly, "in my dream or whatever it was."

"Really?" Teresa seemed amused, "What was I doin'?"

"Being really annoying, mostly," Arthur grinned for a moment. "Actually, you were saving my life. If not for you, I'd have never woken up."

"So I saved you and you saved me. Seems to be the pattern," Teresa said. "Since we met, we've been a team, haven't we? Helpin' each other. It's the strangest thing... like we've known each other all our lives. Am I bein' weird..?" Teresa suddenly felt a little foolish. But Arthur shook his head, straight away.

"No, I know exactly what you mean," he said. "I felt it when we first spoke. Remember, when you said me being in the house with Lady Eris had inspired you... and I told you that it was hearing about you that made me brave enough to see the Yarnbulls..."

Teresa put a hand on Arthur's arm. "We're meant to be a team, Arthur. I believe it. No matter how bad things get. No matter how dark and hopeless. You ain't ever goin' to be alone. Not ever."

Arthur put his hand over Teresa's and stared into her eyes. He'd never felt as close to anyone in his life before. He'd fancied one or two girls at his school but this didn't feel like that. It felt much more... important.

"Well," he said, eventually, "now all we have to do is save Waterwhistle. Should be easy."

"Of course it'll be easy! What chance does that witch Eris have against the dream team, eh?" Teresa laughed. "And besides, no matter how hard the road gets, we're not goin' to give up. While we can still stand, we can still fight. If she wants to win this thing, she's goin' to have to work blummin' hard for it!"

Arthur smiled. Somehow, when Teresa said it, the idea of two children defeating the Queen's assembled hordes of beasts and witches didn't sound entirely ludicrous.

He dropped one of the pieces of fruit into Teresa's hand. "How about a toast?" They bumped the fruit together like champagne glasses. "To the dream team," he said. And they both took a bite.

"You know what," Teresa said, munching away, "you're such a big, fat liar – this tastes nothing like chocolate."

THE SUN AND THE STORIES

By the time Arthur and Teresa got back to the celebrations, the night was even darker (if such a thing were even possible) and yet everything was even louder and busier. At least three more delegations had arrived from other parts of the island, including a tribe of very tall, skinny people, covered in some kind of dried, ivory white paint.

"I don't know about the Bravery island," Teresa nudged Arthur as some olive-skinned, forest-dwelling warrior-woman went whirling, dancing past, "but this certainly looks like the party island."

"Non-cats!" called a familiar voice from the crowd. The pair saw the Cat sitting around a small fire with Ludmilla, Iakob, Iosef and two other people they didn't recognise. Teresa plucked a couple of pieces of barbequed meat from a table as they passed and gave one to Arthur.

"How does it feel to be back from dead?" Ludmilla asked Arthur as he and Teresa sat on the warm, dry earth.

"Well, I wasn't exactly dead..." Arthur began.

"You were Bound," said Ludmilla loudly but not unkindly. "Is same thing!"

"Nobody ever comes back from being Bound," Iosef agreed. "Once Bound, is forever."

"Well, let's not get carried away here," said the Cat, indignant, "I may have known it done once or twice..."

"It was by *you*, by any chance?" Ludmilla laughed.

"I'm sure I wouldn't want to brag about it if it *had* been by me…" the Cat looked away with mock-disinterest. The group laughed.

"But truly, you have done a special thing; this is true," another man that Arthur didn't know said. He was one of the dark-skinned warriors that had arrived earlier. He wore bright, white robes, not unlike the ones that the boy who spoke for Bamboo had worn. A black belt held the robes together as well as having built-in knife sheaths all the way around. Arthur spied long, deadly-looking bone knives tucked away in a couple of them.

"I'm sorry, where are my manners..?" said the Cat, "Arthur, Teresa, this is Yide Kallon, Lord of the Kio people."

The pair nodded hello as Yide bowed to them.

"And this," the Cat motioned to the woman, "is Alenne. She is the High Priestess and leader of the Elm folk from the Western Isolde Forest Expanse."

Her skin was a strange colour that Arthur couldn't even recognise. One moment, she looked like a very light brown but then she would turn slightly and look almost green. She was slim and tall and her clothes were made of some kind of metal, woven so finely it looked like cloth.

"The sun shines on you," she nodded.

"I think that to wake from being Bound, you must be a great seer of truth," said Yide. "Being Bound is being lied to. To break free, one must have the ability to see *past* the lie. To see right through to the true working of things. It is a rare talent; this is true."

A seer of truth, Arthur thought. Him? He tried not to laugh. And yet… he remembered how his thoughts had figured out and deduced all kinds of things during his escape from the dungeons on Phobos. Could he really have these skills they were going on about? But, no, he shook his head. Not him. He wasn't anyone special.

"Thanks," he said eventually. "It's nice of you to say and all, but really I'm just bumbling along. Making it up as I go. Honestly, I have no idea what's going on half the time. I mean, take that place up there."

He pointed to Pavidus.

"I didn't even know it existed. I knew about Phobos and Valia, but nobody mentioned Pavidus to me."

"Is because this place is somewhere we do not go," said Ludmilla. "Is bad place."

"Really?" Arthur was confused. "How can fearlessness be bad?"

"Fearlessness isn't bad," said Alenne, "but it makes bad things happen."

"So… why not just cut it off?" Teresa asked. "It only has one cable and it leads here. Cut it off and set it adrift."

"Because we need Pavidus," Iakob said, "Phobos and Valia and Pavidus, they are like three arguing brothers. They despise each other. And yet, they need each other."

"Why is it called the island of dead monsters?" Arthur asked. "Iosef mentioned that earlier."

"I think it's best, Arthur," said the Cat, "that we don't worry about Pavidus. We have much more pressing concerns elsewhere."

The Cat used a tone that clearly said this conversation was over. Arthur let it be over. For now.

"Cat is right," said Ludmilla. "Is to Castle Eris we must now turn our attention. And to Waterwhistle."

At the mention of the village's name, both Arthur and Teresa felt a chill. Surrounded by the strange beings and environments of Arilon, it was easy to forget the small village back in Nottinghamshire, if only for a moment. The mention of it reminded them of a home they missed. But it also reminded them of the peril that awaited them there.

"Everything points to Waterwhistle," the Cat said. "The machine that Queenie is building-"

"The Agency Engine," said Arthur.

"-the Agency Engine, right… it's almost complete. There are still several pieces to go, but one of the most important remaining bits is in Waterwhistle. Between Bamboo and Zane Rackham, the machine's designer, we know that once the piece in Waterwhistle is finished and activated, the Queen will get the names of everyone right across Arilon."

Ludmilla nodded. "She gets names of everyone in Arilon, her power will grow beyond all imaginings. Arilon will fall. Human World will be next. Once she conquers humans, is game over."

"Should she activate that first part using the human village, nothing will be able stand in her way to stop her completing the rest of the machine," said Yide.

"If gaining control over everyone is Autumn…" Alenne said in her sing-song voice, "…winter will be cold indeed."

Arthur nodded. Though she said it in a strange way, her meaning was clear. What kind of diabolical plan involved getting control of everyone as simply a *first step*?

"So…" Teresa said, "…we head back to Waterwhistle and stop Lady Eris from completing the machine? And save the village while we're at it?"

"Sounds easy when you put it like that, Smithy," the Cat grinned.

"The Queen and Lady Eris will be ready for us," said Yide. "They will surely expect an attack."

"Good," said Ludmilla, beating a tiny fist into a tiny palm. "I look forward to punching her in nose. Hard."

"The battle will be short," said Alenne. "The wind will howl furiously, ravaging the big tree and the little tree. But the big tree has more leaves."

Ludmilla nodded, "Alenne is right – any convoy we can cobble together is being nothing compared to the size of Queen's fleet."

Yide frowned. "We will fight, anyway."

"Of course, of course," said Ludmilla. "But only if is no other way. We do not run headlong into pointless battle where is only certain death waiting. We are not The Fearless."

Arthur's ears perked up. "Who are The Fe-?"

"Yes, her forces are larger," the Cat jumped in, "but we will be able to gather more than just the people from Valia. Word of our escape from Phobos will start to spread right across Arilon. More people will join us, trust me."

"We trust you, Cat," said Yide, "as always. But from one end of Arilon to the other, people are scared; this is true. They will not fight."

Arthur thought of the villagers of Waterwhistle and couldn't help but agree with the warrior-lord.

"They may surprise you," said the Cat. But then he sighed. "Still, you're right. Even then, it may not be enough. We're missing something. I can't put my finger on it..."

"What do you mean?" asked Teresa.

"Lady Eris is not going to be defeated by fighting," the Cat said. "She has too many ships, too many soldiers, too many Yarnbulls, too many of everything. But there's a way past her forces, I can feel it. A chink in her armour. But it's something small. Something she would never suspect. Something… I don't know… non-threatening."

Everyone was still and silent. They knew what the Cat meant but they had no idea what could possibly fit such a description.

Arthur looked down at the book.

"And this is the key?"

"Yep," said the boy, "It's *your* key. Your key out of this world. And maybe more."

Arthur ran a finger over the cover, wiping off dirt and dust.

The Remembered Life of Hector Smith.

"How about a story?" Arthur suddenly said.

Everyone looked up at him with varying degrees of shock on their faces. For a moment, Arthur wondered if he'd said something monumentally stupid.

"A story…?" asked Ludmilla, "We fight Lady Eris with a story?"

"When I was Bound," Arthur began, "there was this book. I was told it was important – the only way I'd be able to get out of there. And it was. The picture on the cover helped me remember Teresa. It's how I woke up…" Even now, Arthur couldn't really remember what it was about Teresa that had opened the door to his escape. At the time, it had seemed so clear. But now…

He shrugged and got back to the present.

"Anyway, I got the impression that it had only served part of its purpose. The cover helped me before but the pages were empty. I think there's more about that book that I still have to discover."

Arthur wasn't really sure of what he was saying. It was like feeling his way through fog. He thought that perhaps there was something there but he couldn't be sure. Maybe he was just talking nonsense. The others were certainly looking at him as though that's exactly what he was doing, he thought.

All except the Cat. He was grinning.

"A story!" he said. "Brilliant! That's it! That's the missing piece of the puzzle!"

A look of realisation slowly came over the faces of the others.

"Yes…" said Alenne, "…potentially the most powerful magic in all Arilon… why did we not think of it…?"

"Truly you are a seer, Arthur Ness," said Yide.

Okay, now they were making Arthur nervous. It had been weird when they didn't seem to agree with him. But now they *were* onside, it somehow just made it twice as weird.

"I know I suggested it," said Arthur, "but I don't really understand. How can a story be of any use…?"

"Don't you know about the Sun and the Stories?" the Cat shook his head, "What do they teach in schools nowadays?"

Teresa rolled her eyes. The Cat cleared his throat.

"It is said by some, that the Arilon sun is the home of the creation force that brought Arilon into being. It lives inside that big, ball of flame and looks out into Arilon. And in there with it are stories. Pictures and words written and drawn on the inside surface of the sun. They tell the entire story of Arilon – from its start to its end. If you could survive inside the sun and look out, you would be able to see the past and read the future. But, of course, surviving inside the sun would be impossible. Mere beings such as us are not meant to know such things."

Teresa raised an eyebrow. "Magic stories?"

The Cat looked at her. "All stories are magic, Smithy, didn't you know? They have a life of their own. Only, sometimes, they don't do as they're told by their creator. Sometimes, they escape."

"From the sun?" Arthur asked.

"Yes, indeed," the Cat went on, "Every so often, one of the stories manages to get free and escape. Stories hate to be cooped up where no-one can get to them, you see. They do their best to spread out as far and wide as they can manage. They do it by jumping into someone's head. If the story is good enough, the person will tell it to other people. And each of those people will tell the story to yet more people. That's how stories spread. And they need to spread to survive."

"If story is never told," said Ludmilla, "it dies. And once story dies, is impossible to bring back."

"Some wise human," said the Cat, "once said that no story lives unless someone wants to listen. And the stories we love best live in us forever."

"So…" Arthur thought aloud, "…this story I saw. The one we need. It escaped from the sun?"

"Yes, almost certainly."

"Please, young Arthur," said Alenne, "do you recall the title of the story?"

Arthur nodded. "The Remembered Life of Hector Smith."

"Hector Smith?" Teresa stared at Arthur, her eyes wide in shock. "That's my father!"

THE ISLAND OF DEAD MONSTERS

Arthur couldn't believe it. He may actually get away with this.

The craft he was in was the smallest one he had yet seen in Arilon. It was literally the size of a rowboat. It reminded him of the little thing he and his dad had sailed out in the day before his father had left to go to war.

The Valians had no way of getting off their island but they still had plenty of boats and ships lying around, waiting to be used. Iosef had shown him one of the docks earlier that night, during the festivities. Unknown to the Knight, the only reason Arthur had been asking was so that he could wait until everyone was asleep and then do what he was doing now.

Stealing a boat and sailing it up to Pavidus.

He hadn't been able to stop thinking about the island even though there was so much important stuff going on elsewhere. They had talked at length about battle plans and how quickly they could cross Arilon and get to Lady Eris' island. And Arthur had listened and nodded and paid close attention. But part of his mind was only thinking of the Isle of Dead Monsters.

Arthur slid the speed lever slowly forward. This boat was so small, he had been able to sneak away pretty quietly. Still, he didn't dare go too fast in case the sound of the boat's anchor ring on the Travel Line woke anyone up. The docks were well away from where the festivities had been so there was nobody very close by. Nevertheless, Arthur didn't want to take any chances. He couldn't afford to have anyone stop him.

He drifted slowly up into the night sky. The Valian docks disappeared below and soon the island was behind him and growing smaller by the moment.

As soon as Arthur felt he was far enough away, he threw the speed lever all the way forward and the boat lurched on, slipping swiftly towards the nearby island.

Arthur couldn't say exactly what was driving him to go there. Thinking about it now, he felt that maybe it had something to do with the world he'd lived in when he was Bound. Being back home. Being old. Well, he smiled to himself, he supposed forty wasn't *so* old. It wasn't like he was a shuffling, white-haired, little old man with a walking cane. Like… fifty.

For Arthur, the memories of that world were like the memories of a dream when you wake in the morning. The more you chase them, try to recall them, the further away they run. But he knew he needed to catch those memories. He had to remember exactly *how* he'd woken up. And somehow, Arthur knew the answers lay on Pavidus.

It didn't take long to get there – the island was already filling his forward view. It was smaller than Valia (which itself was much smaller than Phobos). But even from this distance, the place looked grim.

As far as the eye could see, there was nothing but ruins. Burnt-out, abandoned, neglected husks of buildings scarred the landscape from one horizon to the other.

Arthur shivered. What kind of place *was* this?

The boat floated down to the surface and Arthur brought it to a silent stop just a foot above the ground. All around, the rough terrain was covered by scraps of decayed wood and metal. It took several seconds for Arthur to realise what he was looking at. Pieces of ships and boats. There was not a single sail-worthy vessel. Every single one had been smashed up.

Not derelict, not caught in a fire, not the result of a battle. Smashed. On purpose. And done in such a way that made them impossible to fix or fly.

This made Arthur think two things.

The first thing was – how had he so quickly realised that? Was it this 'truth seer' thing that Yide had mentioned? Did he really have some kind of... ability?

The second thing (and this was the one that really put a chill up his spine) was that the destruction of the ships would surely not have been done by the island's own inhabitants. It must have been someone else, almost certainly the Valians. So, what could possibly be on this island that made the Valians, the bravest people in Arilon, want to make sure nothing got off it?

Nearby, Arthur could see the other Travel Line that was connected to this place. It stretched straight up into the sky and disappeared towards a bright dot in the blackness – Phobos. But around the foot of the Line, where it was attached to the ground, there was a concentrated pile of wood and metal all mixed together. This pile of wreckage seemed somehow different to the rest of the rubble lying around. Arthur shook his head – none of this made any sense.

Arthur didn't like the looks of things but he was certainly not going to go back now. He crept noiselessly out of the boat and, leaving the docks behind, he headed into town.

Things didn't look much better inland. In fact, they looked a whole lot worse. The buildings were truly derelict. Run down. Many of them were missing roofs, walls or windows. It reminded Arthur of the streets back in London – wrecked remains of the nighttime bombings. Was that what had happened here? Some kind of massive attack or catastrophe?

Arthur walked down the main street, past house after house and building after empty, rotted building. It was like a giant graveyard. Soon, he came to a temple of some kind. It was a huge place with large, imposing walls and tall, thin windows. The edifice jutted out of its surroundings like a giant, broken knife. Still not sure where he was going or why, Arthur decided to go inside.

The interior of the place was dark and cavernous. Arthur thought he could probably fit his entire school building in here. Old, withered lamps containing weak, flickering flames were dotted around the walls.

The place was impressive but it was the main centrepiece that really took Arthur's breath away. A massive statue, probably as tall as Arthur's house, sat at the front of the temple, glaring back into the open expanse where hundreds of worshippers once sat. The carved image was of a man sitting on a throne. A *three-headed* man sitting on a throne. One head was a man's head, one was a lion's head and the last was the head of a serpent.

Like everything else, it was decrepit. Crumbling. Bits of it were missing, fallen off, strewn around the floor. What was left was eroded and overgrown with ivy and moss in some places.

"That's Makari."

Arthur span round, his heart in his mouth. The speaker of the words was standing in the doorway to the temple, silhouetted by the streetlights outside.

"He's not a god or anything. People don't worship him. He's just a mythical monster from scary Arilon folk stories."

The man started to walk towards Arthur but he walked very slowly and with a limp. He was hunched over and wheezing just a little. As he periodically passed through the pools of light cast by the flickering lamps, Arthur could see hair as white as the Arilon sun.

"In the stories," the man wheezed as he continued limping toward Arthur, "he used to lead armies of serpents and lions across the Black, looking for unsuspecting islands to attack. They'd come shrieking down from the heavens and render your entire island a desolate mess."

Arthur glanced away from the old man for a moment and up at the statue. He tried to imagine that thing coming down out of the heavens, ready to lay waste to your home. When he turned back, the old man was even closer. He carried on talking.

"Down the road a way, there's another temple with another shrine. It's for a monster called Ch'nay. It looks like a kind of spider but has hands at the end of each leg. It's as run down and derelict as this one."

The closer the man got, the more ancient he looked. It was taking quite some effort for him just to make the walk. Just then, and with a bit of a start, Arthur noticed a second person still by the door. They were staying out of the way but looking on, carefully. They were silhouetted just as the old man had been and Arthur couldn't tell if it was a man or woman. Whoever it was, they stood, motionless, arms folded, staring at Arthur.

"As I mentioned, they didn't build these monuments in order to worship these creatures," the old man went on. "They built them and then allowed them to decay. The people on this island are called The Fearless. They fear nothing and no-one. By having these huge monuments to Arilon's most feared creatures and then just ignoring them, it shows that they are not frightened of them. That was a long time ago, when things actually got built on this island. Nowadays, the Fearless are… different."

The old man was right in front of Arthur, now. There was something familiar about him. His eyes. The way his mouth moved when he talked…

The old man smiled, a kind smile.

"I expect you're wondering who I am."

Arthur nodded. "I am, a bit."

The man didn't say anything. He just kept looking at Arthur as though he were looking at something he found amazing and yet sad at the same time.

Arthur nodded to the statue. "Is that why they call this place the Island of Dead Monsters?"

"One of the reasons," said the old man. "The island has no fear. Monsters, by definition, are things that frighten us. Hence, nothing here is truly a monster. Well…" the man shifted on his walking stick, "…nothing except The Fearless themselves."

Arthur suddenly noticed the words the old man was using. "Wait, you're not from here, are you?"

The man laughed. The laugh made him cough. He coughed and laughed until his eyes watered.

"Oh, no…" he said eventually, "…no, I'm a long way from home." He looked at Arthur, now. "Like you."

That's when it hit Arthur like a thunderbolt – how could he have not seen it before?

"You're... you're *me!*"

The old man nodded. "Yep, 'fraid so."

"But... but how? Why? ... I... I..."

The man laughed again but this time managed to avoid a coughing fit.

"The Travel Lines running through Arilon," he said, "they don't just travel through space. Some of them – a very few, and you really have to know where to look – but, some of them travel through *time.*"

Arthur was still too dumbstruck to speak properly but, somehow, what the old man said made sense. Arilon was all about the linking of things that were related. Most things were related across space. But surely, some things were also related across time.

"There's a Time Line not too far from here. It's what brought me here and it's what will take me home again as soon as we're done talking."

"But... why have you come?" asked Arthur. He glanced up at the unmoving figure by the door. "And who's that?"

"I'm afraid I can't answer the second question," said the old man, "but as to the first, I'm here to give you some advice. Some very important advice."

"You know," said Arthur, "when I was a grown up, I got visited by a young version of myself. Young like I am now. And now, I'm getting visited by an even older version of myself. I'll tell you what, there'll soon be enough of me to field an entire football team."

The old man nodded. "Yes, of course...! It was our birthday. I remember like it was yesterday..."

"It *was* yesterday."

"Yes. So it was. You know… you're going to have some *amazing* adventures. See things that will make everything so far seem like a sideshow. You'll endure dangers. Make rescues. *Get* rescued more than a couple of times. You and the Cat and Teresa…"

The old man's words seemed to catch in his throat. He stopped for a moment, as though he was having trouble composing himself. Eventually, he carried on.

"But there's going to come a time, Arthur, when it will all come crashing down. Things will be at their bleakest, their most dark. You'll be overcome by despair and hopelessness. It's at this time you will turn to the Cat. You'll need him like you've never needed him before."

The man stepped forward and put an ancient, wrinkled hand on Arthur's arm. He looked Arthur straight in the eye. When he spoke, he spoke with the tone of someone who had practiced what he was going to say for a long, long time.

"Remember these words, Arthur. When you find yourself at the edge of the world, when the RainHand is upon you in all its terrible glory, when the Queen is offering to save your life, you will be forced into a terrible decision. A horrible one. One that you alone can make. But it's at this moment you will have to do something else, just as hard." He took a deep breath, "You must kill the Cat."

All feeling drained out from Arthur's body.

"*What..?!*" He stepped back from the man, wrenching his arm from the old man's grip. "I can't do that! I'd *never* do that!"

"Please, Arthur, listen to me – the Cat is not to be trusted at the best of times. But on that day, at that moment, you must listen to *nothing* he says. And you *must* kill him."

Arthur looked at the old man again, his face contorted with distrust. But this old figure was definitely him. It wasn't a trick. He could just... feel it.

"Did you do it?" Arthur asked, eventually.

The old man looked at the ground, sadly.

"I did not."

"And..?" said Arthur, "What happened? How did it all end?"

The old man said nothing. He looked back up at Arthur.

"You need to go back to Valia now."

"Why?"

"Because the Fearless are coming."

Arthur felt his blood run cold. The Fearless. The people that Valia's bravest Knights wanted to keep away from.

"But... I must escape, mustn't I?" he said, "I mean, I'm talking to myself as an old man. That means I must escape the Fearless and everything else. I must win."

"Two things, Arthur. First of all, you must always remember that all things are likely but nothing is certain. Just because Bamboo or the Queen can see something, it doesn't mean that thing will definitely come to pass. We still have to make it happen by our actions or inactions. In the same way, just because I survived my adventure doesn't mean you'll survive yours. You have to manage that yourself. Everything that happened to me was because of choices I made. The same will be true for you."

"And the second thing?"

"Just because I'm still alive doesn't mean I won."

Arthur looked at him. Then at the figure by the door. The old man coughed and Arthur's gaze darted back to him.

"Look after Teresa," said the old man. "She's more important to you than you know."

The old man patted Arthur's hair and then his shoulder with great affection and he smiled a sad, wistful smile. Finally, eventually, he nodded his head.

"You'd better run now. They're coming."

THE FEARLESS

Arthur could hear shouting coming from far away. It wasn't normal shouting. It wasn't words. It was just noises. Angry, angry noises.

"I think you're right," Arthur said to the old man. "We need to leave. Come on."

"I'm sorry," said the man. "We're from different threads that briefly touched. This is where we part ways again."

Arthur suddenly noticed the figure by the door move their arm, throwing something impossibly fast. There was a **thwip** noise and a sudden pinching sensation in his neck.

"Wh…?" was all he managed before he fell backwards, a stinging pain running right through his body. He crashed into a pew and then to the floor. He opened his mouth to cry out in pain. And then…

…the pain was gone. Fled from his body as if it had never been. Gasping deeply, Arthur sat up.

The old man and the mysterious figure were gone.

But the shouting was getting louder.

Struggling to his feet, Arthur staggered back along the aisle towards the doorway and peeked out. Running towards the temple was a crowd of men and women. They were wearing rags, their skin was dirty and their hair was wild. They were carrying sticks, broken-off bits of chairs, rocks… anything they had been able to lay their hands on. And they were running towards Arthur.

Fear and urgency suddenly filled Arthur's body and he pulled the heavy, wooden door shut as fast as he could.

Heaving with all his might, he managed to scrape it closed at the exact moment the Fearless reached the temple. **THUDS** and **BANGS** sounded from the other side of the door as they collided with it, hurling themselves against it, using their own bodies to try and smash their way inside the temple. Frantically, Arthur dragged the huge metal bolt across and locked himself in.

Slowly, he backed away from the door, staring at it fearfully as yells and shouts and whoops and snarls emanated from the other side.

Surely they couldn't get in. *Surely...*

Arthur stood alone in the crumbling temple with the huge, derelict statue of the three-headed monster behind him. The Fearless banged and bashed. They tried to get in through the windows that were on either side of the great door – but Arthur breathed a sigh of relief as he saw they were too thick. They smashed against them with their sticks and rocks, not caring how futile their actions were. Even with no apparent way in, the Fearless continued to fling themselves at the temple, undaunted by anything so troublesome as several feet of stone, wood and glass.

Arthur could see them pulling each other out of the way in their attempts to get to the windows. That's when he realised that they weren't a team, all trying to work together to get at him. They were just a pack of individuals, all out for themselves.

And, suddenly, finally, it hit him.

Over the years, Arthur had grown into a very successful businessman; the head of the largest electronics company in Europe. He had no fear of anything or anyone and had pushed, fought, shouted bullied his way to the top.

Arthur looked over to the dustbin by his desk. Barely visible under piles of screwed up paper was the green and blue of a model Supermarine Spitfire Mk II. His favourite aeroplane. An exact replica of the one his father had flown thirty years ago. It had been a birthday present from Eleanor last year.

His life was full of relics like that. Ruins of things that used to be good but which he'd turned sour. His fearless approach to everything had brought him money and power. But his life was full of wrecks and skeletons of all the things he'd messed up along the way.

"Teresa! Help me!" cried Arthur at the top of his voice, "*Teresa!*"

A hand suddenly dropped on his shoulder.

"I was wondering when you were going to ask for my help!" Teresa said, standing next to Arthur as if she'd been there all along.

So Arthur and Teresa swiped and lunged and slashed, knocking the Needlemen back.

The two of them were surrounded by a sea of black suits and dark hats and empty eyes and the sea was neverending. They fought against impossible odds. But they fought.

And fought.

And fought.

Those people out there had no fear. No fear of anything at all. No fear meant you were happy to do everything on your own and there was no need to band together with other people. No need to band together meant no need to seek or give help. Everyone just out for themselves. Everyone just fighting each other all the time.

No wonder the place was so derelict – the Fearless had done it themselves through endless fighting. Ruined everything they had originally held dear.

So, Arthur thought, if complete lack of fear was bad, and having total fear was bad, perhaps the answer was somewhere in between; you needed to have *some* fear but not let it overrun you.

Fear made sure you got help from others if you needed it. And other peoples' fear meant they would come to *you* for help. Fear made people come together to help rather than to fight.

Fear also tried to keep you safe by stopping you running headlong into danger. But if you had to do that anyway – say, if someone needed help – then you could ignore fear's warning and force yourself to run in. And *that*, Arthur finally realised, was bravery.

Being brave – like the Valians – didn't mean having zero fear. It meant being scared of something but *doing it anyway*.

Teresa embodied these things better than anyone. She had come to Arthur in his Binding dream because he'd realised that being Fearless had just ended up ruining his life. He'd finally accepted that he *was* afraid and needed help.

Even when the pair were fighting off the swarming tide of Needlemen, Arthur saw that Teresa was scared. She was always scared, just like him. But she forced herself to do what had to be done and that's what made her brave. Now that Arthur understood Teresa, he was no longer pretending to be brave – he knew how to be brave for *real*.

And that's why he'd woken up.

Feeling scared? Well, you should be.
You need to get out of here, Arthur. You need to run!

For the first time, his scared voice wasn't trying to bully or tease or intimidate. It was just trying to give advice. It was trying to help.

Fear wasn't a monster anymore. That monster was dead. Now, it was an ally.

Now, it was going to help him be brave.

CRACK!

Unbelievably, the massive door began to buckle under the weight of the Fearless piling themselves up against it. Despite looking impenetrable, the Fearless' sheer inability to give up meant they were managing to break the giant door down.

Quickly, Arthur looked around. There had to be another way out. A place this big had to have a rear entrance.

CRUNCH!

The door was beginning to splinter and come away from the hinges. Arthur was horrified to see arms begin to reach round the edge of the door.

Don't just stand there, you great lollipop!
You waiting for Christmas or something? Run!

Arthur thought it was ironic that his first action upon learning how to be brave was to run... but sometimes, running was just the wisest thing to do.

He turned and sprinted towards the back of the temple and rounded the statue. There was a stone archway through which Arthur could see... absolutely nothing. It was dark as a crypt. It probably *was* a crypt.

Nowhere else to go, though, is there?
Go down there, you may get grabbed by something.
Stay up here and you definitely *will.*

It was a shadowy, murky corridor, but it was also an easy decision. He threw himself into the darkness and ran.

The corridor beyond the doorway was narrow and there was virtually no light at all. Reaching his hands out in front of him, Arthur felt for the wall and any twists or turns of the corridor. Several times, it shunted him left or right and more than once, he ran face-first into a brick wall. Eventually, though, he spied the tell-tale strip of light along the ground that told him he was looking at a door that led outside. He scrambled towards it, trying not to trip over any final obstacles and when he was close enough, he threw himself forward.

Arthur all but tumbled out into the street as he sprang from the doorway. There were no Fearless here – they clearly hadn't thought of coming round the back. Apparently, being fearless didn't stop you from being stupid.

He crept carefully up to the front corner of the building and spied round. The animalistic islanders were pouring into the front of the temple, stampeding over the remains of the door as it now lay, useless, in the dirt. Arthur breathed a sigh of relief. It looked like he'd escaped just in time.

The way back to the docks was along the main street but that would put him in direct sight of those Fearless still waiting for their chance to get into the temple. He kept his nerve and waited. They had to all disappear before he could go.

Suddenly, though, Arthur started to hear echoey shouts and yells emanating from the corridor behind him. Arthur had been afraid of this. They'd found the archway behind the statue and they were coming through the corridor.

There were still a few Fearless clawing their way in through the shattered doorway but the shouts behind him were getting louder all the time. Any second now, they'd come out the rear door and find him hiding there. Arthur couldn't wait any longer. He put his head down and sprinted as hard as he could up the road towards the docks. The three or four Fearless still outside spotted him straight away. They howled like the enraged animals they were and immediately gave chase. At the same time, the first few appeared from the back door and joined in the chase too.

Arthur ran down the long, straight road. The howls from the chasing Fearless trumpeted out behind him.

Those creatures will definitely catch you before you get to the docks. They're faster than you.

Arthur's scared voice was right. He wasn't going to outrun the Fearless on this long, straight road. He needed a new approach.

"We're going to get you, you little weasel!" the bullies shouted. Arthur ran down the Commons Road, bombed out buildings on either side, as Tommy Watkins and his cronies chased him. They were two years older than Arthur at school. And two years bigger and faster.

He ducked down a side alley. And then another. And then another. And soon, he'd lost them entirely.

Yes, he smiled. They were bigger and faster. But he was smarter.

Some strategies worked just as well, Arthur found, against mindless barbarian hordes as they did against school bullies. He ran up and down the narrow alleys, twisting this way and that, confounding and evading his pursuers at every turn. At one point, he burst around a corner and dodged the outstretched arms of a huge, muscly man by mere inches. Ducking under the attacker's grasping reach, Arthur disappeared down another side-street and could hear the enraged howl somewhere behind him as the Pavidan searched fruitlessly for his prey.

Soon, the yells of the Fearless started to fade as they fell farther and farther behind. Arthur stopped to lean against an old shop-front and catch his breath. He never thought he'd be grateful for all those times Tommy Watkins had chased him home from-

Wait.

The screeches and shouts were starting to get louder again. And worse, they were coming from different directions, all around him. They'd split up. That wasn't good. Not one little bit.

The only thing in Arthur's favour was that he knew they weren't working as a team – they hadn't split up as part of a clever plan to trap him. They'd all individually decided that their prey had gone down a different path.

If they *had* been working and hunting together, Arthur thought, they'd have maybe figured out that he was going for the docks and organised themselves to stop him. Arthur wasted no more time. He double-checked his bearings and ran straight for the docks.

As expected, he got there ahead of his pursuers. With a relief he couldn't even begin to describe, he ran towards his boat, still sitting there, patiently waiting for him.

Arthur clambered in and was just about to throw the speed lever forward when he heard a noise. It was coming from above.

Wwwwweeeeeeeooooooooowwwwwww

A wooden cage came shooting down the other Travel Line – the one connected to Phobos.

CRASH!

Arthur ducked down and covered his face as pieces of wood went spinning in all directions. What was happening *now?* What had been sent from Phobos to this forsaken place? Arthur uncovered his face and peeked over the side of his boat.

Oh, crumbs. Just when Arthur didn't think things could get any worse.

It was a Yarnbull.

THE FEARLESS, PART 2

A Yarnbull. Fantastic.

But then, Arthur became even more astounded as he realised it wasn't just any Yarnbull. It was the one he had forced to help him in his escape. The one that had been working the popper. Arthur was surprised to realise that, for the first time, he noticed that Yarnbulls did actually look slightly different from one another. This one had slightly smaller horns and a leaner face than others Arthur had seen. And it had some kind of scar across its face that looked to have been sutured with large, untidy stitches of thick, black thread.

The creature looked somewhat disoriented after its journey and abrupt landing. But, why was it here? As quickly as he'd asked the question, though, Arthur realised the answer. It wouldn't have taken long for Lady Eris' people to figure out the Yarnbull's part in Arthur's escape. The fact that it had been commanded by a child would only have served to prove to them that it was no longer frightening enough to carry out its duties. And so it was sent here. To the island of dead monsters – there to languish with all the other no-longer-frightening creatures.

To be at the mercy of the Fearless.

As if in answer to Arthur's thought, the first few Fearless came running into the docks from the main street. Immediately, they saw the new arrival. There was no stopping, no expression of shock or surprise. To them, one target was as good as another.

As one, the deranged inhabitants of Pavidus ran straight at the creature. None of them came in Arthur's direction and he realised that they hadn't seen him, hiding as he was in the boat.

Immediately, the Fearless fell upon the Yarnbull. Though it was many times bigger than they were, there were at least twenty of them and more arriving all the time. They jumped on him, clambered on him, struck him with their sticks, rocks and bare hands. He staggered as he tried to fling them off. One went flying but was replaced by two more.

Arthur turned to the boat's wheel. This was his chance to escape. Leave them fighting it out while he got away from there. He put his hand on the lever.

"I have no interest in your personal nonsense, Martha," Arthur snapped. "Be in work on that day or be in the job centre the next. Now, stop bothering me with your prattle and send the doctor in."

"...yes, Mr. Ness..."

Arthur took a deep breath. What kind of person was he? A cold, uncaring one like his older, fearless self?

If you help him, he might just turn on you.

He knew that. But he couldn't just leave. Especially when it was his fault the Yarnbull was here in the first place.

That wasn't the kind of person he wanted to be.

"I can't believe I'm doing this..." he muttered to himself. Arthur reached over the edge of the boat and scooped up two metal poles off the ground. Then, forcing his nerve to hold, he stood up and began banging the two pieces of metal together.

CLANG! CLANG!

"Hey come and get me! You

CLANG! CLANG!

stupid dunces! Yes you, ugly! I'm

CLANG! CLANG!

talking to you! Come and

CLANG! CLANG!

get me! I'm right here!"

As one, the Fearless stopped. As one, they fell away from the still body of the Yarnbull. As one, they ran towards Arthur.

This is the part, Arthur thought, *when an actual plan would have come in really useful.*

"Oh, heck…" Arthur took a step backward as the deranged islanders surged towards him, but there was nowhere to go. Their crazed bellowing was all he could hear.

No. Not *all* he could hear…

The heavy **thrummm** of an anchor-ring running along a Travel Line blared down from above and Arthur looked up in time to see a huge Valian boat racing down toward him.

Arthur squinted against the rising sun as the silhouettes of Iakob and Iosef launched themselves from the ship above him. Their battle-cry temporarily drowned out the noise of the onrushing Fearless as they dropped past Arthur and slammed into the ground with an almighty **CRACK!** Their initial impact scattered the Fearless. Their lightning-fast follow-up attack scattered them more.

"*Arthur!*"

Arthur looked up to where the Valian boat had come to rest, just meters above his head. The Cat's small, black face poked over the side, looking down at him. A rope ladder was tossed over and unfurled down toward him.

"Come on!" the Cat yelled.

Arthur reached up and grabbed it before turning to see where the twin Knights were. More Fearless were streaming onto the docks. The noise of the battle had called them as surely as if a flare had been shot into the night sky.

Arthur could tell from the quick glance the twins gave each other that there were too many of them. There was no chance of victory, here. And yet, they gripped their sword handles, raised their shield-arms, crouched into battle-stance and turned towards the oncoming horde.

Arthur let go of the ladder.

"Arthur!" the Cat yelled, "What in the name of the Blessed Islands are you doing?!"

He grabbed one of the metal rods he'd used to distract the Fearless earlier and jumped down to take his place in between Iakob and Iosef.

"What am I doing?" he echoed the Cat's question. "The right thing."

The fearsome tidal wave of Fearless swarmed towards Arthur and the two Knights and it was abundantly clear that they would not survive the impact.

The Cat shouted something else but Arthur never heard it because the feline's words were drowned out by an almighty

BOOM!

as the Yarnbull landed directly in front of the three of them, arms outstretched, and took the full force of the attack.

The huge creature then shifted stance, put his head down and charged headlong into the oncoming storm.

Fearless were flying in all directions as the Yarnbull smashed them this way and that. Mighty arms swept through the sea of islanders and four of them were flung away in one go. Another brutal swipe and yet more Fearless were sent flying. A swoop of the Yarnbull's huge head and the lethal-looking horns laid low another dozen.

Despite such a herculean effort, though, some of the Fearless managed to skirt around the snarling beast. Fighting their shock at the Yarnbull's intervention, the three comrades brought up their weapons once again and met the aggressors with as much force as they could muster.

Arthur immediately started swinging – smashing at the knees of any Fearless that got too close. The fear swept over him but he used its power and fed it into his muscles, his arms, his legs and it powered him on, swipe after swipe. Until, suddenly, inevitably, a fist came through from the chaos and Arthur went flying across the ground.

Head spinning, eyes watering, buzzing noise bouncing around in his skull, Arthur had no idea which way was up. He couldn't defend himself. Surely, finally, this was it.

"Keep away from him!"

Teresa?

Arthur opened his eyes. Teresa had jumped down into the middle of the fray and stood firmly in front of him, facing down the Fearless. And the Fearless...

...stopped.

The hordes of grown men and women stood back, frozen still, looking at the ten year old girl. Their faces were still wild but their eyes betrayed the impossible.

Their fear.

Nobody moved. Not Arthur, not the Knights. Certainly not the Fearless. They just stared at Teresa. She took a step toward them.

The Fearless took a step back.

"Arthur!" the Cat called down. "The ladder! Quickly!"

"Not without Teresa!" he yelled back.

"I'll be right behind you," she said to Arthur, her eyes never leaving the transfixed throng in front of her. She was trying to sound brave but Arthur could hear the tremor in her voice. The fear would overcome her soon. They had to move right away.

"Go up, back to Valia!" Arthur shouted up to the Cat. "We'll follow in this boat. We can't leave it here..!"

The Cat disappeared and Arthur heard muffled voices. Very soon, the Valian boat began to rise back up the Travel Line.

Arthur clambered into his small boat and started the impossible wind blowing. Iakob and Iosef stepped on board, their gaze still fixed on the immobile horde, always afraid – as Arthur was – that the spell would be broken at any moment.

Suddenly, Arthur realised they'd forgotten someone.

"Hey!" he called the Yarnbull. The creature lifted its massive head in Arthur's direction. "Come on! Get in here!"

"Arthur!" Iosef said in alarm. "You cannot! That creature-"

"-just saved all our lives," Arthur said. He turned back to the Yarnbull. "Come on, we have to leave and you're coming with us."

Not wasting another moment, the Yarnbull clambered into the tiny boat, its massive frame and weight causing the vessel to wobble momentarily. But it held itself upright.

"Teresa, come on!" Arthur called, his hands on the boat's wheel and speed lever. As quickly as she could, Teresa jumped into the boat and Arthur threw the speed lever forward. The Fearless surged forward as though some invisible elastic band had been cut. But it was too late.

Their prey was already halfway up to the Black.

ONWARDS

Everywhere was alive with activity. It was like watching bees, Arthur thought. A hundred little figures all moving left and right, up and down, back and forth. Fetching and carrying, loading supplies, checking weapons. And all to one purpose.

Valia was getting ready to set sail.

"So, we are all being clear, yes?" Ludmilla stood at the front of the room, staring out at all the faces looking back at her. Behind her was a large chalk board with so many arrows, circles, plans and writing, it made Arthur's head hurt.

"We are all knowing what is to happen? What is each of our jobs?"

"We set sail," Yide Kallon spoke up, his belt of knives swaying at his hip, "for Lady Eris' island. We try to gather as many ships as we can along the way."

"Our fleet is small," said Filesse, "and yet it will gather others to it. The gentle breeze will become the howling wind."

"And when we reach the island, we will meet the entire Royal Fleet," said the Cat, "assembled for just a single purpose – to completely and utterly destroy us down to the last toenail. How exciting!"

"But even if they destroy our entire fleet, we will still be winning," Ludmilla said, looking right at

Arthur now. "As long as they do not realise you will be bringing the *true* weapon."

Arthur gulped.

"Ready to board?" the Cat dropped down next to Arthur, making the young boy jump.

"Cripes, Cat, I wish you wouldn't do that."

"What's the point of being a little cat if you can't sneak up on people?"

"We are what we are," said Arthur, "you can't choose. You were born a little cat. Live with it."

The Cat looked like he was about to say something serious and Arthur wondered if he'd overstepped the boundary. Where the Cat was concerned, it was difficult to know up from down. But then the familiar grin came over the feline's face.

"So, are you?" he said.

"Am I what?"

"Oh, please at least *try* to keep up. Human brains are so big and clunky. Are you ready to board?"

Arthur looked over to the small, metal, rusty tugboat. It swayed gently in the air. It was a stumpy, fat, shapeless thing. And yet, given all they'd been through on it during their escape from Phobos, Arthur almost felt like it was home.

"We going, then?" Teresa popped up out of nowhere. Arthur jumped again.

"Seriously, are you lot trying to give me a heart attack?"

Teresa was confused. "...what?"

"Our boy Arthur here has a nervous disposition," the Cat explained. "Right now, it appears to be very easy to make him jump. It's actually quite fun. Shall we do it again?"

"Is it any wonder I'm nervous?" Arthur said, irritation in his voice. "This whole island is setting sail to fight Lady Eris' forces entirely on the basis that I thought we could make a weapon out of a blumming bedtime story!"

"A story," Teresa reminded Arthur, "that you saw while you were Bound. That has something to do with my father. It can't be co-incidence!"

"Of course it could!" Arthur snapped, "My sleeping brain might have just remembered Mr Smith from when I was in Waterwhistle and inserted him into the dream for some reason…"

"And I suppose you already knew Mr Smith's first name was Hector?" said the Cat. "Tell you over a cup of tea, did he?"

Arthur had to admit that had *not* happened.

"Don't forget, Arthur," said the Cat, his voice quite serious for a change, "there's something going on with you that we can't ignore. As Yide said-"

"I'm not a seer of truth!" Arthur argued. "I mean, really? Me? Next, you'll be telling me I'm from the planet Krypton!"

"After all the things you've done," the Cat said, "you still doubt yourself? The way you figured out how to make that Yarnbull follow your commands back on Phobos?"

Ah, the Yarnbull, thought Arthur. Another thing that had jangled his nerves.

The Yarnbull was lying down, covered in bandages. It was so long, the doctors had had to push two beds together. The medic's hut was small, dim and quiet – all combining to make the creature seem even bigger. Like one of the huge statues in Trafalgar Square, Arthur thought.

"Even lying down, injured, he looks fearsome, doesn't he?" Teresa whispered. For some reason, Arthur had never thought of referring to the creature as a 'he'. He supposed it was because Yarnbulls had always come across as mindless robots, following the bidding of Lady Eris or whoever. Not creatures with their own minds. And yet, here was one that had, for some reason, decided to help Arthur. Even though it was Arthur's fault that it had been exiled to Pavidus in the first place.

Upon their return to Valia, the Yarnbull had collapsed. Apparently, it had been more seriously injured during the battle than anyone had realised.

"Not surprising he's so badly wounded, I suppose," said Teresa, quietly. "He did take a hundred Fearless right to the face..!"

Arthur smiled. "Actually, that *was* pretty awesome."

"Well, I hope it was worth it," the Cat, suddenly next to the pair, said in a quiet yet unmistakably angry voice. "You run off to the Isle of Dead Monsters on your own, almost get yourself pulverised by a thousand crazy people with bad breath problems…"

"It was," Arthur said, suddenly.

"Sorry?"

"Worth it," he said. "It was totally worth it."

"Because…?" Curiously, the Cat no longer seemed angry. Now he seemed curious, like he was hoping for a specific answer from the young boy.

"I finally learned how to be brave. I learned that being afraid is a good tool, when you don't let it rule you completely."

"Well, well, Arthur Arthur Ness," the Cat was suddenly smiling, relieved and proud. "I was beginning to wonder if you'd *ever* figure it out!"

Arthur blinked, "You mean…"

"I've been waiting for you to learn what bravery is all about ever since I met you." The Cat's small, green eyes stared at Arthur. "I have a very nagging feeling that all our lives will one day depend on it."

"So… why didn't you just tell me?" Arthur asked – but immediately the words of his younger self came back to him. Some things you have to figure out for yourself if you're going to really believe them.

"I was *hoping* you'd take yourself to Pavidus. It's probably the only place in Arilon that could have taught you what you needed to know," said the Cat. "It's a very dangerous place but, let's be honest, compared to what's to come, Pavidus is a trip to the beach. With ice creams."

"The ships are all being in position to connect to Arthur's new Travel Line," Ludmilla strolled toward the trio. Her two sons were in tow as were Yide and Arlenne.

"You are all being ready too, yes?"

"I don't know…" the Cat turned to Arthur, "…are we?"

Arthur took a deep breath. "Well, I'll never be more ready than I am right now," he held his hands up, "so we might as well get on with it."

Ludmilla let out a blast of a laugh, "Ha! That is great wisdom, Arthur Ness. I am glad to have been meeting you." And she gave the boy another bear hug, followed by one for Teresa.

Yide touched his forehead towards Arthur and Teresa and Arlenne gave them a small, delicate nod.

"It has been a great honour to meet you, citizens of the Human World," said Yide, "and I suspect there will be many more surprises in the battle to come."

"If we don't get killed inside the first five seconds, *that'll* be a surprise," Teresa muttered, half-smiling, to Arthur.

"Destiny shall be on our side," said Alenne, the breeze catching her auburn hair. "What will be… will be."

Ludmilla huffed. "If by this, you mean we will twist Lady Eris' head off and use for basketball… then yes. I am agreeing."

Arthur stood and listened as final plans and arrangements were made and confirmed. All around them, the Valians worked to move their ships from their old, mined Travel Line across to the new one Arthur had re-connected. As soon as Arthur and his crew began their ascent, the Valian ships would start to attach themselves and follow them up and out. Arthur was then to make a new branch of Line that would connect them to the rest of the network and the Valian fleet would head towards Castle Eris while Arthur's crew would set off on a different course and go looking for the story.

Standing aboard the tugboat now, Arthur made sure everything was secured ready for the trip.

"You okay?" Teresa touched Arthur's shoulder.

Arthur looked around. Teresa. The Cat. Iakob. Iosef. They were a crew. A team. He'd let them down once before. He didn't want to do that again.

Don't be afraid, he thought to himself. Then he looked up to Pavidus, a bright spot in the sky. He corrected himself – okay, be a *little* bit afraid.

"Let's do this," he said.

"Great," the Cat said, striding past. "Well, then…" he nodded toward the wheel as Arthur took hold of it.

"…Onward!"

Arthur threw the speed lever forward.

THREAD FOUR

RETURN TO WATERWHISTLE

THE BIG HOUSE

Sam woke up.

Where was he? The ceiling was high and ornate. The walls were large and various portraits of stern, well-dressed men and women looked down on him. On one wall, there was a huge tapestry. A patchwork of pictures. They looked like a thousand different islands, connected by lines. Some with lots, some with a few. Looking back at the portraits, Sam realised he recognised one of the stern-looking faces – it was Lord Roberts.

Sam went cold. He realised where he was. He was in the big house.

Lady Eris' house.

He sat up and tried to clear his head. How did he get here? The last thing he remembered was serving dinner to his father. He had put three plates on the table.

Three?

Of course! He'd set a place for Teresa. He'd been trying to jog his dad's memory. Trying to make him remember he had a daughter. Ever since she'd been taken by the Yarnbulls, everyone had forgotten Teresa ever existed. Now, he was the only one who remembered her.

But it hadn't worked. The Yarnbulls had been watching him. Somehow, they had suspected that Sam wasn't under the spell like everyone else.

So they took him.

Came right into the house and grabbed him as he was serving dinner. For a moment, his father had seen the Yarnbulls. His eyes had gone wide in shock and fear and anger. He had lurched forwards to grab his son back from them. But the Yarnbulls were big and strong and they were not letting Sam go. They didn't even have to hit his father, they simply walked out with Sam. And the moment they were gone, the fight was over. Sam could see through the window as he was carried away, huge hands over his mouth to stop him from crying out. He could see his father simply sit back at the table and eat his dinner. He'd glanced at the plate of food Sam had dropped and was probably confused as to why it was there.

Yet, he simply shrugged and went back to eating.

And so the power of the Yarnbulls worked. They scared you so much, you forced yourself to ignore things.

And now Sam had been brought here, to the same place as his sister before she had disappeared. The big house.

Suddenly, the door began to slowly **creeeak** open. Sam gulped hard and braced himself. This was it. He was about to come face to face with Lady Eris. The woman who had stolen his sister. The woman who held the entire village in the palm of her-

Wait.

"Who… who are you?" Sam muttered. But even as he asked the question, he realised that he knew the answer. His father had described them a thousand times. Black suits. Black hats. Pasty white faces. One of them carrying a black, shiny case.

"You know who we are, Samuel Smith," said the Needleman in front. The two behind him stood still and said nothing.

"You know why we are here," the front one spoke again.

"You…" Sam had to fight to breathe, had to fight to speak, "…you've come to kill us."

"Kill? No. Not to kill," said the Needleman. "We have simply come to ensure that which *must* happen… *does* happen."

Sam forced his eyes away from the three horrible apparitions. He glanced back at the still open door. The third Needleman closed it.

"You are wondering where are the Yarnbulls?" said the first Needleman again. "They go where they are needed. Now, that is no longer Waterwhistle. Now, that is somewhere else."

Sam looked back at the creature before him.

"The situation is all about Fear. Fear is like a crop. Lady Eris sowed it. The Yarnbulls guarded it. Lady Eris grew it. And now the crop is ready." He fingered his dark bag. "We are here to harvest it."

"Your village is under our control," the second Needleman spoke for the first time.

"Everyone here is no more," said the third.

Sam's eyes widened in horror.

"Oh, no, we don't mean dead," the first Needleman said, reading Sam's expression. "We simply mean that their minds are no longer their own. They have been completely given over to fear. Given over to *us*. They now have no power to do anything for themselves. Observe."

The Needleman's bag opened and he produced a sheet of white material with a flourish. He held it out and Sam could see an image projected on to it – just like at the movie theatres. The picture was of the village square. It was night and everyone was standing around. Not walking. Not talking. Just standing. With their hands over their faces. A flock of birds flew across the moon on the picture. Sam looked out of the window and saw the moon high in the sky – and the same flock of birds were flying across it.

"Wait a minute… that's what's happening in the village? Right *now*?"

"Yes," said the Needleman, simply. He rolled the sheet up and placed it silently back into his case. "However, as I am sure you will have already noticed, you are not with them."

"And she needs to know why," said the second Needleman.

She? Sam's heart began to thud. He knew who they meant.

Suddenly, Sam's attention was drawn to the tapestry. His eyes widened in shock as a hand came out of it, then an arm. Then a leg. A body. A face. The figure emerged from the tapestry and stepped into the room as though it were an open doorway. The person looked down at the boy and smiled a dark and ominous smile.

Lady Eris had arrived.

"Samuel Smith," she said with a voice so icy, so sharp, it clawed down his chest and grabbed at his very soul. "Your sister was not held by my spell. She saw the Yarnbulls. She was brave. The spell does not work so well against those who are truly brave. So she was removed."

Sam gulped as Lady Eris' dark eyes passed over his face and bore into his mind.

"You were not held by my spell. You saw the Yarnbulls. However, you are *not* so brave. So why, Samuel Smith, does the spell not work so well against *you*?"

Sam couldn't bring himself to speak. He tried not to look into Lady Eris' soulless eyes.

"There is something very wrong about your family, Samuel Smith," she said. "Very wrong indeed. And I intend to find out what it is."

Sam shrank back in the chair as the four dark figures stood over him.

Lady Eris reached toward his face.

QUESTS AND REGRETS

Captain Chadwell Thrace stood on the foredeck of the *Galloping Snake*, the skull and crossbones fluttering high atop his ship, his cutlass drawn and pointed at the small, trading ship trying its best to flee.

And he cried one word.

"Fire!"

A deafening **BOOM** blasted towards the trading vessel and the cannonball flew right past its port bough, as planned. A warning shot. Thrace grinned. Their first and last.

"They're still running, sir!" cried the helmsman, up on the steering deck, his expert hands on the wheel. All around him, Thrace's crew ran about, tending to their shipboard duties. The sails. The rigging. The cannons.

"Still running?" he cried. "Good! Always makes things more fun when you've got to spill a drop of blood or two."

"Aye, sir!" agreed Mister Quinn, the first mate. "The men are ready and waiting for any drops a' blood what need the spillin'!"

Thrace turned to face his second-in-command and the men standing behind him. Ten or twelve of the most bloodthirsty brigands money could buy were standing, swords in hand, ready to board the unfortunate trader and relieve him of his goods.

Not that he needed the goods, Thrace reminded himself. The money he'd gotten from Lady Eris for… well, the money he'd gotten had been considerable. He could have retired to his own island if he'd wanted.

But he was a pirate. His father had been an explorer and where had that gotten him? The Queen had cut and tweaked enough cables and his father's passion had evaporated into the Black, literally overnight. He'd torched his ship and settled into the life of a dull landlubber with nothing to show for it.

No, he wasn't going to go the same way. Thrace knew what life was all about. Get what you can, when you can. Nobody else is important, nobody else should stand in your way.

He didn't have to answer to anybody.

"Target their sails!" cried the Captain. "Prepare to fire…!"

"Gunner!" cried the First Mate into a metal mouthpiece lodged in the side of the ship. His voice ran into the mouthpiece, through the pipes and right through the ship to below decks where the gunners sweated and worked, heaving cannonballs into place and pointing the huge weapon at their target. "Prepare to fire!"

"Preparing to fire, aye!" came back the tinny voice.

Captain Thrace held his cutlass aloft, "Fi-"

"Cap'n! Cap'n Thrace!" the squeaky voice of Ensign Beeker pierced the moment. Thrace turned to see the young crewman come running forward, a scrap of paper in his hand.

"It's a message, sir! From Lady Eris!" the crewman huffed and puffed after running all the way up from the communications room. "She says we 'ave to stop wha'ever we're doin' immediately! We 'ave to make fer her island right now to join her fleet for a battle or somethin'!"

Thrace turned back to the fleeing trader.

Nobody told him what to do. He controlled his own destiny.

I don't answer to nobody.

He sighed, wishing that were true.

"Make fer Castle Eris," he said, trying not to let his disappointment show to his men. "Best speed."

He sheathed his sword with a dull **clank**.

Meanwhile, many thousands of miles away, a woman held a piece of paper in her slender hands. There was a story written on it.

It told of a quest. A small, rusty boat set sail from an island, far, far away. It had an unlikely crew. Knights and children and a cat. A rag-tag bunch who would ordinarily not have much to do with each other. Fate had thrown them together and they now fought for a common cause.

They were looking for something. For some*one*.

They travelled in great haste, for their time was short. They sailed to the island of Exeo. There, they spoke with a drunken sailor who had travelled far and seen much. Unfortunately, thanks to the rum he now drank, he could remember little.

From the scraps of information they gleaned from him, they went then to Quiess, the isle of silence. The people there do not talk or make any sounds at all. To communicate with the islanders, the strange crew from the rusty boat had to learn to use the Quiess Talking Paint – it turned their thoughts into words that were silent, yet that all could hear. The silent islanders told the crew to travel to the isle of Brica and look for a shipbuilder named Zachary.

When the crew arrived there, Zachary was not to be found. They were led on a wild hunt looking for the man. They travelled across the island of Raptor, the land of thieves and Tego, the hidden isle. It is so called because of its cave network where mile after mile of underground caverns hide any people who do not wish to be found. But the kidnappers could not hide there long – not with such determined hunters on their trail. And so, eventually, the boat's crew tracked the bandits to their hideout on the southern peninsula and rescued Zachary from their greedy clutches.

In boundless gratitude, the master ship builder informed them that the person they were after was the Blind Dressmaker. Fortunately, he knew exactly where she was to be found. And so the band were guided toward their ultimate destination. Ora. The Frontier island.

Here, people lived on the edge of discovery. They were the ones who stared out towards the unknown and made it known. They were the explorers, the adventurers, the ones with all civilisation at their backs and nothing but darkness before them. And that was just how they liked it.

Upon arrival at Ora, the misfit crew were taken to a village and a cowboy named Joshua led them, finally, to the house of the person they had travelled so far to find.

The End.

KNOCK KNOCK

The woman with the story in her hand had visitors at her door. And so as one story ended, another began. The woman smiled; such was the way of all things.

She put away the paper and opened the front door.

"Well, hello," said the Cat. "You would *not* believe what we've had to go through to find you."

The Blind Dressmaker could not see them but she knew who they were.

"I'm sure I wouldn't," she smiled. "Please come in."

THE BLIND DRESSMAKER

Arthur and Teresa couldn't take their eyes off the woman who greeted them. She was tall, with golden hair and a slender, kind face. She wore plain, practical clothes like most of the people on this island – and yet, she had a real aura about her; warm and welcoming.

The shop was small and the crew were forced to stand close together, somehow emphasising their mismatched nature. Arthur stared at the woman as she cast her eyes over the group, taking their measure. She seemed to be taking in every detail of their appearance so intently that Arthur forgot for a moment that she couldn't see. He realised that although she was moving her eyes around, it was her ears that were doing all the work – scanning the room and its new inhabitants. Painting a picture.

For a moment, her eyes seemed to land squarely on himself and Teresa and it felt for all the world as though she could see the pair, clear as day.

"That is one beautiful dress," the Cat said, looking at a long, flowing, ivory gown that was hanging on a dressmakers' mannequin in the centre of the shop. It was clearly their host's current project. "Bit big for me, of course but beautiful nevertheless..."

The lady turned her gaze towards the Cat's voice.

"It's for a wedding on Graft," she said. "The bride is very excited. She works in the coal mines and this may be the only dress she wears in her entire life. I want it to be extra special."

"I thought you looked after stories," Teresa said. The woman looked in her direction and smiled.

"I'm afraid I've been telling them a little about you, Dressmaker," said the Cat.

Her smile did not fade. She walked slowly towards Teresa and held out a hand to the girl's face.

"May I?" she said.

Teresa nodded, unable to speak.

The Dressmaker ran her fingers softly over Teresa's eyes, nose, cheeks, chin. Arthur couldn't decide what kind of smile the woman had on her face – it looked happy and sad all at once.

"I do look after stories," she said eventually, removing her hand from Teresa's cheek. "But I am a dressmaker by trade. I've been doing it all my life."

Teresa looked about the shop. There were dresses of all kinds hanging on racks and hangers. Long, short, plain, colourful. One dress was made of a shiny material – but as Teresa looked closer, she could see that it was actually thousands upon thousands of tiny, sparkling stones sewed together. It made her head spin.

"They're so beautiful," she whispered, almost to herself.

"Would you like to have a go?" the Dressmaker smiled at Teresa.

"Me? No, I-"

"Nonsense. I won't take no for an answer," she insisted, gently. "Come. Try this one."

The Dressmaker led Teresa by the hand to a small, wooden machine. Arthur had never seen anything like it. It was a sort of loom but it held threads of different colours out in six directions, like a star. The Dressmaker showed Teresa how to use it – how to feed the threads in from any of the six arms and bring it into the middle where a multi-coloured pattern was being formed. But rather than a flat piece of material with the pattern on it, it was a three-dimensional piece with finely woven, brightly-coloured branches reaching out in different directions. It was the most complex and stunning thing Arthur had ever seen.

"Like this?" Teresa started moving the loom's levers. The colours started to snake in from the outside to the middle. The strands of colour moved at different speeds and settled on the emerging pattern at different points. A glittering array of colour began to form in the centre of the loom. It was like watching the creation of Arilon itself.

"Wow, Smithy!" said the Cat. "You're a natural!"

And so she was, Arthur saw. Teresa was picking up the workings of the machine as though she'd been doing it every day for her whole life.

"Very good," the Dressmaker nodded.

"But… I don't know what colours to do."

"Whichever ones you feel," said the lady, her eyes looking at the emerging star but also not looking at it at all.

Teresa let go of the loom handles and slumped back in her seat. "But… how do I know what to feel…?" She was beginning to look increasingly lost and frustrated. Arthur stepped up and put his hand on her shoulder.

"Just relax into it," he said. "Think of home."

Teresa took a deep breath and closed her eyes. Slowly, she took hold of the machine's levers. She waited a second… and then she moved.

The colours had been creeping in before but now they were flying in. They whipped in from one arm and then another and then another. Reds and blues and greens and yellows, all winding together with an easy, relaxed speed. Relaxed... but unstoppable and strong. In hypnotic waves, the pattern began to grow and stretch its arms as though coming to life, reaching out to the watching eyes, wide open with wonder.

"Amazing..." Iakob said, "...I know little of such things but..."

"...is beautiful!" finished Iosef.

The Cat nodded, as amazed as everyone else. "Not bad, Smithy! Not bad at all..."

The Dressmaker just smiled, her eyes closed. She looked as though she were listening to the most serene orchestral music. It was like she could *hear* the pattern coming to life.

Arthur's attention suddenly fell to a small tapestry on the other side of the shop and quietly moved over to it. It was a picture that seemed familiar to him; a countryside landscape with a church and a horse and cart. It took Arthur several seconds to realise why it felt so strange... it was precisely because it *wasn't* strange. It wasn't a picture of anywhere in Arilon. It was a countryside scene from the Human World.

"Oh!"

Arthur span round at the alarmed noise the Dressmaker had made. He saw that everyone was still looking at the pattern Teresa was weaving. But it wasn't beautiful anymore. What had been a smooth, colourful spiralling star was now a crooked, jagged, dark scratch. What had been warm, outstretched arms were now snaking, evil-looking tendrils. It almost looked like a spider, reaching out to grab the face of anyone who got too close.

"How did that happen?" Teresa instantly let go of the machine and put one hand over her mouth. "It's horrible!"

Her voice was trembling and Arthur was shocked to see she was actually holding back tears. She looked up at him. "It was when you moved away. I didn't feel the same."

"Sorry," Arthur stuttered, "...I saw a... never mind... I'm sorry..."

"Never mind," said the Dressmaker, guiding Teresa away from the loom, a reassuring hand on her shoulder. "It was your very first go. I think you did splendidly."

Teresa managed a small smile. Arthur looked at the Dressmaker and – he wasn't sure as it happened so fast – but he thought the tall woman and the Cat exchanged a brief glance. However, considering one of the people was blind and the other was a cat, Arthur found it impossible to decipher just what that glance meant.

"Well, I'm all for arts and crafts and finding new skills," said the Cat, suddenly, "but we are on a bit of a tight schedule. Got a bit of a battle to go to. Don't want to be late, not when we're bringing the cheese and cocktail sticks."

"You came for a story," said the Dressmaker. "I know. You're right. We had better get started."

A door behind the shop counter opened. Arthur supposed the Dressmaker must have pressed something or moved some lever, though he hadn't noticed her do it.

"We will wait out here," said Iosef. "Keep eye out for undesirables."

"If any of those undesirables happens to be a mouse, try not to smash the shop up trying to get it," grinned the Cat.

Iosef sighed and rolled his eyes, "Was just *one time*..."

The Dressmaker led the Cat and the two children into a back room. Immediately, Arthur could see what he had expected to see in the first place.

Lots and lots of books.

Books of all shapes and sizes lined the walls. There were big, leather bound tomes but also pamphlets so thin, you could barely tell they were there. Arthur gaped as he saw a set of books that were all covered in fur. And there was one very thick book that had several smaller books slotted into it. Floor to ceiling and trailing off into the dark, there were books everywhere.

It was a small space, smaller than the shop. Yet somehow, it was so full, it seemed bigger than the biggest library. Arthur felt that he could keep walking along the shelves and never get to the end.

"We're looking for a particular story," said the Cat. "It has Needlemen in it."

"This story," said the Dressmaker, looking into the darkness, "is it an escaped one?"

The Cat looked at Arthur – who jumped as he realised the conversation had just been handed over to him.

"Escaped…? From the sun, you mean?" Arthur stammered. "I don't know. It's to do with a village. In the human world. A village called-"

"Waterwhistle."

The way the Dressmaker spoke the village's name filled Arthur and Teresa with longing. They so wanted to get back there.

"It's called The Remembered Life of Hec-"

"Hector Smith," the Dressmaker said the words at the same time as Arthur.

"Yes…" he said, "…how… how did you know?"

"It's… a very special story," she said. She turned to them and held out a book. Arthur hadn't seen her pick it up – she must have done it at–

Arthur's heart stopped.

It was the book from his Bound dream. The very same book. With the very same picture on the front - the village square and the World War One monument.

"This is a very special story. It is indeed one that escaped from the Sun," said the Dressmaker. "It is one of the billions that depicts some small part of the fate of Arilon."

Gingerly, Arthur took the dusty, hardback book from the Dressmaker and opened it. Unlike his dream, these pages were not blank. It was a fully written book, cover to cover. Arthur's heart skipped and his breath caught in his throat. He had dreamed of this book and now it was here in his hands! Maybe there was something to this seer business after all, as crazy as it sounded. More importantly, maybe it meant that, somehow, this book really did hold the key to defeating Lady Eris and saving Waterwhistle.

As Arthur scanned the pages, though, his excitement very quickly turned to confusion.

"I... I can't read it!"

"What do you mean?" Teresa craned her neck round to glance at the pages. "The words are in English, I can see that from here."

"Yes, I know," said Arthur, "...but I can't read them! It's like my brain is just... blocking them out."

"It's not your brain," said the Dressmaker, "it's the story. This is a good thing."

"A good thing?" Arthur said. "How?"

"If you gave that book to any random person in the street, they would be able to read it. But all they would see is this-"

The Dressmaker took the book from Arthur and read from it;

"Once upon a time, there was a man called Hector Smith. He was born in Macclesfield in the North of England. His best friends at school were Bert, Freddie and Elsie.

Hector's father worked in a silk factory and that was the job that awaited Hector when he left school. But then, in 1914, the Great War broke out and Hector, Bert and Freddie all joined the army and went over to France to fight..."

"Stop!" Arthur said.

"What is it?" the Dressmaker said, though she wasn't annoyed. In fact, she sounded expectant.

"It's...weird."

"Boring's more like it," mumbled the Cat.

"Weird?" said the Dressmaker. "How so?"

"It just seems...wrong."

"It goes on," said the Dressmaker. "For many more pages. It tells a very long and, frankly, boring story about Hector's life in Macclesfield and later on, in Waterwhistle."

"But it's a lie!" said Arthur. He was surprised to see the Dressmaker smile.

"Yes, it is," she said. "As I mentioned, that is the story anyone else would see. Because that is what the story would want them to see. But the fact you can't read those words means the story doesn't want you to read them."

The Dressmaker stepped close to Arthur, now.

"It wants you to read the *truth*."

"The real story?" Arthur said, quietly.

The Dressmaker gestured to some large cushions propped up on the floor.

"Please," she said, "all of you. Make yourselves comfortable."

Bewildered – but a little excited – Arthur, Teresa and the Cat all took a seat on the cushions. They were very, very comfortable, Arthur found. Immediately, he felt like going to sleep. He suddenly jerked up in alarm, though, as the Dressmaker took out a needle and some thread from her pocket.

"You… you're not going to…?"

"Relax, Arthur," she said, "it is a kind of Binding I'm about to do. But very different from the horrible kind you have already suffered. What Lady Eris did was to Bind you into yourself. Instead, I am going to Bind you temporarily into the story."

Arthur looked at her warily.

"How do you know about that?" he said. "We never mentioned it."

"I spend a lot of time reading," the Blind Dressmaker said. "There are lots of things I know."

"But, if you're blind, how can y-"

"It'll be okay, Arthur, don't worry," the Cat interrupted but in a surprisingly comforting voice. Arthur trusted the Cat, as always. But he found that he trusted this woman too, despite her mysteries. Arthur nodded and sat back.

The Dressmaker started moving her hands in a way that reminded Arthur of the time he had spied Lady Eris Weaving in her bedroom back at the big house. The thread flew through the needle and span around in the air. Coloured lines suddenly sparked out of the thread and danced around the four of them in swirls and eddies, running through each other and knitting together into a slowly emerging sea of orange.

"Stories are not just words on a page," the Dressmaker was saying, "the worlds they tell of really exist. A book is like a window into that world. But with the right magic, it's possible to step through the window and actually enter that reality. There, you will not just see the story. You will be *in* the story. You will *breathe* the story. It will surround you."

Arthur was starting to feel very sleepy now and the Dressmaker's voice was beginning to feel very far away, even though he could still hear every word.

"But beware," she said. "It is the job of any powerful story to change you. To alter your mind. And this is a very powerful story indeed..."

And Arthur opened his eyes.

THE REMEMBERED LIFE OF HECTOR SMITH

As Hector Smith stood behind the counter of his shop in Waterwhistle, he realised with some surprise that, for the first time in years, he was thinking of Needlemen.

From as young as he could remember, growing up among the silk mills of Macclesfield, Hector had been afraid of Needlemen. Afraid of their black suits and white faces. Their black hats. And the black bag that one Needleman could always be seen carrying.

"Eat your greens," his Nan would say, "or the Needlemen will come and get you." Or sometimes, his mother; "Tidy your bedroom, Hector, the Needlemen hate messy rooms!"

There was even a rhyme that was sometimes pulled out to aid in the eating of greens or the tidying of bedrooms;

Into the world, they come to see.
They come to us in bands of three.
Don't look, don't look, they come for me.

One time, when he was five or six, Hector had asked what the Needlemen looked like. "Ooh, they're terrible and creepy. They've got black suits," said his Nan. His dad mumbled from behind his newspaper on another occasion. "Um… and black hats, I think." And another time, still, he'd asked his mother; "…and black bags, they've got, too. You never want 'em to open those bags, mark my words."

When Hector asked what happened when a Needleman opened his bag, the answers weren't as cast iron. "No idea," puffed his father through his tobacco pipe. "Haven't a clue, stop bothering me," his mother huffed as she scraped soaking wet bedclothes on her washboard. "Nobody knows," said Nan, mysteriously. "One thing's clear, though… once a Needleman opens his bag, nobody ever sees you again."

As much as his parents and Grandmother mentioned Needlemen from time to time, Hector had assumed they must have heard about them from various different places, the same as it was with all silly stories. Hector remembered now, though, that he was fourteen when it finally occurred to him that no-one he'd ever met had ever actually heard of Needlemen.

On the way home from school, he, Bert, Freddy and the new girl, Elsie, were talking about what they were going to do this Halloween. Bertie and Freddie lived near Hector and the three of them had been friends since infant school. Elsie was new. Her family had moved up to Macclesfield from a small village in Nottinghamshire. She lived not too far from the three boys and had taken to walking home with them. The Terrific Three had become the Fabulous Four.

"Oh, my-" Teresa put both hands over her mouth, "That's my mother!"

Teresa, Arthur, and the Cat were standing across the street from the four young people. The Dressmaker stood with them. She had told them that they could stand and remain unobserved but if they interfered too much, they risked changing the story. And if that happened, they might lose the very information they had come for. She had also warned them that they may see things that would surprise them. This certainly came into that category for Teresa.

"Both me parents… they look so young! Teenagers!" She didn't know whether to laugh or cry. "And me mum… there's only one picture of her in the house, from when she married dad… but I'd know her face anywhere, even that young…!"

"I appreciate this must be somewhat strange for you, Smithy," said the Cat, "but you're making us miss the story."

"Actually," said the Dressmaker, "you're making us *part* of the story. If someone were reading this now, they would be reading everything we're saying. And whatever we have to say is *not* part of this story. Please. Be silent."

Teresa still had her hands over her mouth and was still staring, wide-eyed at the teenagers ambling up the other side of the road.

"Sorry," she said very quietly.

"I'm going to dress up as Frankenstein," said Freddie.

"Again?" Bert and Hector wailed at the same time. "Freddie, every single year, it's the same thing!"

"I like the old fella! He's blummin' brilliant!"

"Actually, it's Frankenstein's monster you'll be dressing up as," Elsie said, "Victor Frankenstein is the man who created him. The monster is never given a name."

"Hark at Jane Austen!" Bertie cooed.

"What?" Elsie smiled, a little sheepishly. "I just like the book, that's all. I think it's sad. The monster gets created and everyone misunderstands it – then, before you know it, the poor thing's public enemy number one and everyone's chasing it down, trying to kill it. And really, it was all Victor Frankenstein's fault. Everyone's always too busy chasing the monster. No-one ever blames the person who *creates* the monster..."

Hector liked to listen to Elsie talk about books. Or plays. Or school. He suspected that even listening to her talk about paint drying would sound like the sweetest music. He sighed, inwardly, and wondered if he'd ever get the nerve to tell her that he was in love with her.

"Alright, so what are you going to dress up as, then?" Freddy challenged Hector.

"Haven't a clue," Hector shrugged and grinned. "Maybe I'll go as a Needleman."

"A what?" Now it was Bert and Freddy's turn to exclaim in unison. "What the devil's a Needleman?"

Hector's eyebrows raised in surprise. "You've never heard of Needlemen?"

"Not unless it's someone who comes to the house to help mother sew her dresses!" Bert guffawed.

"Well, you know…" Hector fumbled, "…they're like… you know… the bogeyman, but… well…"

"Sharper?" Freddy joked.

The conversation went on like this for a few more minutes before eventually turning to other matters such as Christmas and school and the trouble brewing over in Europe. Eventually, Bertie and Freddy waved goodbye as they turned up their street, leaving Hector and Elsie to walk the last bit of the journey alone. As they rounded a corner and left the jolly duo behind, Elsie suddenly said;

"Eyes of dark and three by three – watch out, watch out, they come for me."

Hector jerked his head up in shock as he realised that this was the first time Elsie had actually spoken since he'd mentioned the Needlemen.

"That rhyme!" Hector said. "You know them! You've heard of the Needlemen!"

Elsie nodded. "Yes. My mother and father sometimes used to use them to make me tidy my room and things like that."

"Yes!" Hector said, excitedly. "Yes, exactly the same with me!"

"Only… you're the only other person outside of my village who's ever heard of them," Elsie said, quietly.

"Well, now that I think about it… I think you might be the first person outside my family whose ever heard of them, too!" said Hector. "How strange..!"

Hector was grinning, excitedly. It was like finding a long lost relative or something. He was quickly noticing, though, that Elsie seemed a lot less enthusiastic about the whole thing than he was.

"The stories always terrified me," she said, softly, "I could never sleep after anyone mentioned them. When we moved up here, I noticed that nobody had ever heard of Needlemen and I was overjoyed! It's just some stupid Waterwhistle thing, I thought. But now, you…"

The words stuck in her throat and Hector wished he hadn't been the one to upset her like this. But it felt so important to have found someone else who knew about the Needlemen.

"It's okay, though, isn't it..?" Hector blustered, "…I mean, they're only made up. It's not like they're real."

Elsie fixed Hector with a cold stare that made him shiver. "Does it *feel* as though they're not real?"

Hector was about to laugh it off. But when he thought about it – really thought about it – he had to admit that, yes… they did feel real. Like ghouls or phantoms. All the more frightening for the fact that nobody else knew about them.

"Please let's not talk about them again," she asked, her eyes boring into his. "Ever."

Hector nodded. "Okay. Fine. I promise."

And Hector kept his promise. Over the following years, he never mentioned Needlemen once. Not when he and Elsie finally started courting and going out together. Not when he asked her to marry him and she said yes. And not when they had to postpone their wedding because the trouble in Europe suddenly got very big and messy. Some Duke's plane was shot down and all of a sudden, all of Europe was at war. And very soon, it seemed like the whole world had joined in.

"Wha... what just happened?" Arthur said. "Where are we?"

The four of them were no longer standing in a cosy, urban street in the north of England. Now, they were standing in a field. But not a nice, green bit of countryside. Everything around them was pure desolation. The sky was thick with black smoke that burned the eyes and choked the lungs. The grass had been scorched away, replaced with mud and stone. Giant craters pock-marked the landscape and sprawling lengths of barbed wire wound over the entire scene like some kind of poisonous snake.

"Wait... I know where this is..." said Arthur.

"Yes," said the Dressmaker, "but nothing here can hurt us. Not as long we stay out of the story."

In 1914, Hector was drafted into the army and was sent to fight in France. He spent months in trenches fighting German soldiers who were hiding in other trenches just meters away. The only break came on Christmas day in 1914 when Hector found himself stationed in a trench in Ypres, near Belgium.

Hector's fellow soldiers all wanted a break from the non-stop fighting and killing. And – to everyone's surprise – so did the German soldiers. So, for one day, they all defied their superior officers and put down their weapons. For one day, the war stopped.

Both sides emerged from their trenches and met the enemy face to face. Hector was surprised to find that the supposed inhuman enemy were actually a collection of frightened, young men who longed to go home. Just like Hector and his comrades.

They talked and joked. They exchanged souvenirs and shared drinks. They even had a game of football.

Eventually, though, the end of the day approached and the soldiers knew that reality would soon be forced upon them once again. They said sad farewells and began to return to their trenches, ready to start killing each other again tomorrow.

Hector was one of the last. He had lingered, talking to a German soldier called Bastian. The Englishman and the German shared a passion for growing vegetables and they had been swapping tips and advice for getting the biggest, most orange carrots. They hadn't noticed the sun beginning to dip or the mist starting to roll in.

By the time Hector and Bastian had hurriedly shaken hands and said unhappy goodbyes, the other British soldiers had already disappeared into the gloom. Hector hurried after them and did his best to catch up, but the fog kept rolling across in ever thickening, billowing swathes. Very soon, Hector was hopelessly lost.

Fighting against a slowly approaching panic, Hector swept left and right, willing his gaze to pierce the thick blanket and show him the way back to his trench. And that's when he did finally see someone. A figure, barely visible, facing away from him. Maybe it was Bert or Freddie or one of the others. He rushed toward the dark shape. As he got closer, though, he slowed. This wasn't right. The person was wearing a hat. And a suit. And was carrying a bag.

Teresa gasped and grabbed Arthur's arm. He was glad she'd done it because he'd been about to do the same to her. The memory of being surrounded by hundreds of Needlemen with just Teresa at his side still clung to his mind and refused to let go.

For a moment, Hector froze. Could this be? Could it really be? Surely not! He stood, frozen to the spot, not knowing whether to walk toward the figure or run away from it.

Eventually, he decided to see if it was real.

"Hello?" he called out. The figure didn't move at all.

"Hello?" Hector called out again.

The head tilted. Then turned a little. Hector glimpsed an ear. A jaw. Then the figure turned fully and looked at the young soldier with eyes that somehow had no light of life behind them. And in the dark, behind the figure, another two shapes, identical to the first, began to emerge from the mist. And their dead eyes were all on him.

Eyes of dark and three by three
Watch out, watch out, they come for me

Hector found, suddenly, that he couldn't breathe. Desolation fell on him like a black cloud, thicker and more vile than any poison gas he had yet experienced on the battlefield. Sensation drained from his fingers, his hands, his arms, his entire body. He couldn't move his legs and he fell, hard, into the mud.

Hector tried to yell, to call out. Nothing came. The three figures moved slowly towards him. Slowly but inevitably, like the falling of night. Hector scrabbled backwards, his terrified gaze never leaving them for a moment.

Pain, sharp and sudden, flashed through his arms and back and he realised he'd managed to snare himself on barbed wire. He gasped and struggled like a caught fish but he was going nowhere. And the Needlemen strode nearer, still. Dark suits and pallid, white faces. Not smiling, not sneering. No expressions at all. And now the lead figure's arm was raised, his spidery, long, sharp fingers reaching out. Closer, they came. Closer. Just inches from Hector's face. The fear pressed down on the young man like a giant hand and squashed him to the ground. He squirmed like a stuck insect. The Needleman's cold, metallic fingers brushed against Hector's face.

"Hector!"

A hand fell on his shoulder at the same time as his name was called. Hector yelled and turned his head, his face a picture of fear, his heart, all but stopped. But it wasn't a Needleman. It was Bert.

"Hey, chap! We nearly lost you! Come on, the trench is this way."

Hector turned back to where the black figures had been standing but there was nothing there. Weak with a cocktail of fear and relief, Hector managed to free himself from the barbed wire and stumbled back to the trenches, his childhood friend helping him all the way.

As planned, the fighting resumed the following day and for one thousand, three hundred and eighty-six days after. Miraculously, he, Bert and Freddy all survived the entire war, right up until Armistice day on the eleventh of November, 1918 when the Great War ended. All three boys went back home to Macclesfield. Hector – having had enough of loud noises and bright lights to last a lifetime – agreed to move with Elsie back to her home village.

And so the pair travelled to Nottinghamshire and bought Elsie's parents' old house in Waterwhistle.

They were very happy there. They started a small vegetable shop and Hector, remembering what he'd learned from Bastian, grew the biggest and best carrots anyone had ever seen. Hector set up a shop and, along with lots of other fruit and veg grown in the area, sold enough super carrots to create a comfortable life for himself and Elsie.

In time, they had a son, Albert. He was their pride and joy and they couldn't wait to give him brothers and sisters to play with. But before they could, Elsie had fallen ill. The illness was fast and devastating. And then it was over and Hector was alone.

"But… wait, that's not what happened!" Teresa stared at her mother's grave in disbelief, her father standing silently on the other side. Tears streamed down the girl's face. "She had more children before she died! Two more - me and Sam!"

She turned to the Dressmaker, "This isn't real! It's another lie!"

"Yes," the Dressmaker nodded. "It is a lie. And a painful one for you, I know. But this story is all about that lie. Remember why we're here. This story is trying to tell us something important. Be patient."

Teresa turned back to her father, standing alone, devastated on the other side of the grave. All she wanted to do was rush over and hug him. But, according to this story, he wouldn't even know who she was.

In 1939, when the whole world went to war again, Hector's son, Albert, went off to fight and Hector was alone in Waterwhistle.

As he stood now, in his farm shop, a small smattering of customers wandering silently from shelf to shelf (never speaking, as people in the village seemed to do nowadays), he realised that he'd kept his promise to Elsie. They had never spoken of the Needlemen again. Yet, somehow, they were always there and not there. Like a lie you never mentioned. The picture you never looked at. The knocking sound you always ignored.

Even when you did all you could to forget about them, the Needlemen never truly went away.

But now, for the first time in years, they fought their way from the back of his mind right to the front.

But, why now? After all this time?

Tinkle.

The door to the shop opened and in walked three men. In black suits. Black hats. The one at the front was carrying a black case.

Hector's mouth ran dry. His whole body stiffened. His eyes were stuck wide open. His insides turned to mush. They were... here? Now..?!

But then, he noticed – not just here. Through the shop windows, outside, in the street. From one end of the village to the other as far as he could see. Dozens and dozens of Needlemen. Sprung out of nowhere. One for every man, woman and child of Waterwhistle.

And they all knew that a story was nearing its completion – and an ending they had secretly known and feared for a long time was finally being told.

"It is time," said one of the Needlemen in front of Hector.

"The story is nearly over," said the second.

Hector could barely speak, "...story..?"

"We do more than simply replace people," said the Needleman at the front. He opened his bag. Something inside it seemed to be glowing. "Much more."

The fear grasped Hector's heart and squeezed. It squeezed so tight that his very thoughts started disappearing. Soon, he knew, all that would be left would be the fear – and he, the person, would not exist.

And then it was...

THE END

And, all of a sudden, the four figures were alone in the farm shop. No Hector. No Needlemen. No villagers outside. Everything was empty and silent.

"That's… that's it?" asked Arthur. He was confused, "It's like Teresa said… that wasn't real. That's not what happened."

"Yes, it is…" said the Cat, "Think, Arthur, Smithy… what's this story called?"

Arthur shrugged. "The Remembered Life of Hector Smith."

"That's right," said the Cat. "The *remembered* life. As far as Hector Smith is concerned, this is exactly what happened. He had one child. He had one child because…"

"Because I got taken by the Yarnbulls!" Teresa suddenly saw what the Cat was getting at. "Everyone forgot about me! But… what about Sam? My dad didn't forget about Sam…"

"He must have," said the Cat. "I'm sorry, Teresa. I'm so sorry, but something's happened to Sam while we've been away. Something that's made Hector forget him, too."

"Sam…?" Teresa whispered, her eyes were wide with fear and shock and anger and just for a moment, they were as dark and unfathomable to Arthur as Needlemen's eyes.

Arthur put his hand on her shoulder – but she shrugged it off.

"Get away from me!" she backed away from everyone. "While we've been running around this stupid place with its stupid floating islands, my family have been slowly wiped out. My whole village…" the words stuck in her throat.

"Teresa," the Dressmaker said her name quietly and only once. Arthur had almost forgotten she was there but the first word she said had an extraordinary effect on Teresa – she stopped and looked at the woman.

"Your whole village," said the Dressmaker, "has been covered with Needlemen. The story has told you this. More than this, it shows something else."

"*What?*" Teresa was barely holding her tears and temper in check. "*What* else has it told us?"

"That, from the day they were born, every person in Waterwhistle has been trained to fear the Needlemen," said the Cat. "Can't you remember? Hector's friends had never heard of the Needlemen. Nobody Elsie had ever met outside of Waterwhistle had heard of them, either. It's like everyone who was going to end up living in Waterwhistle by the end of the story was targeted from the moment they were born. The Needlemen integrated themselves into their lives – and *only* them. To make it so that the Needlemen became the very private fear of all the people who live in Waterwhistle today, now, in 1940."

"They went... back in time?" Teresa didn't look like she believed the words even as she said them.

"Of course..." Arthur said in realisation. "Yes, it's possible to travel the threads of Arilon in time as well as space..."

The Cat looked sharply at him. "So it's rumoured."

An unspoken question hung in the air – *where did you hear that?*

"But why?" Teresa said, still edging backwards. "Why do that?"

The Cat tried to cast his mind around for ideas. "I don't know... maybe it's..."

"It's the Agency Engine," said Arthur, suddenly, the idea dropping into his mind like a stone plopped into water. "It runs on fear. I'm sure of it. Powerful fear. The kind of fear that can only come from seeding a village full of people so they spend their whole lives being afraid of a day they know deep down is coming. A very special day. The day the Needlemen come to town."

Arthur looked from Teresa to the Cat to the Dressmaker and back to Teresa.

"To stop the Agency Engine," he said, "we have to stop the Needlemen."

Silence fell over the quartet for a moment as the enormity of the task sank in. Then, suddenly-

"No," Teresa shook with an anger that had gripped her heart and was fighting to explode from her body. "My family is gone. My *whole* family. And I'm going to fix this. I'm going to get them back."

"Yes," said Arthur, "that's what we're going to-"

"No! I'm going to get them back *now!*"

She turned away from the others and closed her eyes, her fists clenched.

"Teresa, no!" the Dressmaker reached out for her. "Don't-"

But it was too late.

Teresa vanished before their eyes.

Arthur and the Cat stared at the space where Teresa had just been standing, their brains not quite believing what their eyes had just seen.

"Where… where did she go?" Arthur was incredulous.

The Dressmaker was the most calm and composed of the three, but even she was clearly shocked at what had just occurred. "She's gone back into the story."

"But…" the Cat shook his head, "how does she even have the power to do that?"

"Right question. Wrong time," the Dressmaker said, stern urgency in her voice. "We have to get her back – now!"

"But… why?" asked Arthur, "It's just a story. She can't really change anything."

"Haven't you been listening?" the Dressmaker turned to Arthur. "This is a special story – one from the Sun. It tells a story about the real world. It's *linked* to the real world. One wrong move in here could be catastrophic out in reality."

The Dressmaker began weaving the bright orange thread around again, enveloping the three of them.

"We have to stop her before she really does knock herself out of existence," she said. "And maybe all of us with her."

REWRITE

At a speed so blindingly fast it made Arthur's head spin, the trio soared backwards through the story.

...grasped Hector's heart and squeezed. It squeezed so tight that...

In an instant, the farm shop had melted away into a whirlpool of images and sounds that scooped Arthur, the Cat and the Dressmaker up and sucked them into it like leaves in a hurricane. The three flailing figures found themselves flying through a huge maelstrom – a massive tunnel that stretched off into infinity. Hazy images were projected onto the walls of the tunnel that showed all the different parts of the story. The scenes blew around like swirling eddies in a river, chopping and changing at lightning speed.

...had a son – Albert. He was their pride and joy and they couldn't wait to...

The noise was deafening. It was the roar of everything that had happened in the story but now happening at once, constantly, never stopping. It threatened to drive Arthur insane.

"Where is she?" cried Arthur over the din.

"I can't see her!" the Cat shouted.

...travelled to Nottinghamshire and bought Elsie's parents' old house in the...

"What I want to know," the Cat shouted, "is how come she even has the power to move around in the story on her own!"

He looked at the Dressmaker but she didn't say anything. Her keen eye was scouring the storyscape for any sign of-

...noticed the sun beginning to dip or the mist starting to roll in.

By the time Hector and Bastian had hurriedly shaken hands and said unhappy goodbyes, the other soldiers were already disappearing into the ...

"There!" the Dressmaker pointed. Arthur looked but couldn't see anything except the thousand tiny, moving pictures that surrounded them in the swirling storm of story events. The Dressmaker motioned with her hands and one of the pictures suddenly grew and filled the space beneath them, pushing the others away to the side.

The fields of France during the Great War sprawled beneath them. Miles of trenches, endless, rolling lengths of barbed wire. Arthur strained to see what the Dressmaker had pointed out – a little dot, running towards one of the sections of metal-teethed wire. Running towards where a soldier lay stricken, his jacket caught in the wire – and where three suited figures were stalking slowly toward him.

The Dressmaker made another motion with her hands and the three were suddenly on the ground.

"Teresa!" Arthur shouted to his friend, but she wasn't listening or else hadn't heard. She just continued to run towards her stricken, immobile father.

"Why did she come here?" Arthur huffed as ran.

"This was the moment in his life when her father was the most afraid of the Needlemen," said the Dressmaker. "She means to help him."

Lightning fast, the Cat whipped round in front of Teresa. She skidded to a halt, sharply, noticing their presence for the first time.

"Smithy, *stop!*" the Cat cried in a voice that brooked no argument. "This is not the way to go about things!"

"Oh no?" Teresa said, her voice sour. "Lost your family have you? Lost everything in the world? Had it all taken away from you?"

"*YES I HAVE!*" the Cat roared. That made Teresa and Arthur both stop in their tracks. Behind the four of them, the young Hector wriggled, unaware of their presence, as he tried to free himself from the barbed wire.

"I have lost my family, my home, my kingdom and a lot more besides!" the Cat snarled. He was as angry as Arthur had ever seen him. "And I know the only way to get any of those things back is to figure out how to beat the Queen! And I know the best way to *lose* all those things forever is to let my anger get the better of me and rush in blindly!"

Teresa looked at the Cat for a moment. Arthur, too, saw something different about him. He had often thought that the Cat wasn't taking things seriously enough. But here he saw a creature that joked and messed around because he had to – if he let his rage and sadness overtake him, he would be no use to Arilon or himself.

"Stop, Smithy, think…" the Cat breathed. "We can do this. Only Hector and the villagers will have forgotten Sam but we can still remember him. If we can stop Eris, he'll come back, we just have to-"

And that's when the Needlemen passed near them. The mist seemed to part as the three dark shapes drifted by in the gloom. They walked straight past the four invisible visitors and on towards Hector. The young man's eyes widened as the three figures got closer to him, images from his childhood nightmares brought to life right here, in the middle of hell on earth.

Teresa was suddenly galvanised into action. She turned to the Cat. "I'm sorry Cat, but I can't take the risk. I have the chance to stop them now. Maybe I can make a difference…"

"You may do, child," the Dressmaker suddenly spoke. "But it may not be the difference you intend. I still don't know how you're managing to do any of this but you must remember one thing - this story escaped from the Sun. It's a special story that charts the events in Arilon. If you alter it, then events in the real world will alter. But this story is not fully the truth. It's based on the memories of your father and those memories have been altered by the fear the Needlemen created. You can't be sure anything you see really happened. And you can't be sure what effect changing it will have on the real world."

Teresa seemed to listen to the Dressmaker more than she had listened to anyone else so far. But then she turned and saw the Needlemen approaching her young father as he writhed in a futile attempt to free himself from the wire and escape the approaching phantasms.

"You're right, I can't be sure," she said. "But I have to try."

"Teresa," Arthur said. She turned to him but then he didn't know what to say next. He knew she wouldn't be turned away from this. But he was scared at what it might mean if she went ahead.

She touched his shoulder. "Hey, don't worry! We're a team, remember?"

She took something out of her pocket and placed it in his hand.

"I found this on the floor when I got here a minute ago. Buried in the mud. Didn't seem right. Don't know why it were here... but I think you need to have it."

Arthur looked down at the object. It was a smeared and dirty piece of shiny, reflective mirror. When he looked up, Teresa was running toward the Needlemen.

"Hey!" she shouted, waving her arms. "Come on! Look at me, you big baboons! Come and frighten me if you can! Give it your best shot!"

Hector scrabbled backwards, cold earth squeezed between his fingers as he tried to force himself away from the three evil shadows.

"Come on!" shouted Teresa, almost caught up with the Needlemen, "Hey!"

Hector put an arm up to cover his face. He could feel total fear swelling up inside him and threatening to take over his entire-

"I'm talking to you!" came a girl's voice. Hector looked up. A young girl of about ten had appeared from nowhere and had thrown herself in front of the Needlemen. From the expressions of the three, they were as surprised as he was by her presence.

Hector looked at the girl – her back was mostly to him but he could glimpse part of her face. He didn't recognise her... yet he felt as though he knew her. He couldn't explain it. One thing he did know... he immediately felt braver.

"I'm not going to lie," she said up at them. "I'm terrified right now. I can feel the fear running through me veins and fixing me to this spot. But let me tell you something in simple words so you don't misunderstand. You – are – not – passing!"

For a moment, the Needlemen stood frozen to the spot, looking down at this girl. Their expressions didn't change. It looked like they'd been turned to stone. The girl began to wonder if she'd managed to somehow stop them.

And then – as one – all of them reached out toward her.

Immediately, the story started to fall apart. Big chunks of the sky crashed to the ground. Arthur yelped as a huge piece of the ground was broken by part of the Waterwhistle farm shop bursting through out of the soil.

"Watch out!" cried the Cat as a huge fissure opened up in the ground – it whipped past the trio as if it were a huge zip being opened. Out of it flew buildings that lined the street

Hector and Elsie had walked down with Bert and Alfie. Story debris flew in all directions.

Arthur couldn't see Teresa, her father or the Needlemen anymore.

"The story is collapsing!" the Dressmaker said. "We have to get out, now, or we'll be wiped from existence!"

She grabbed Arthur and the Cat and the three of them flew into the air, dodging machine guns and cars and huge bits of houses.

Eventually, Hector moved to Waterwhistle with Elsie…

They flew and they dodged.

Many times over the years, he remembered the awful moment on Christmas Day back in France. The three shapes coming toward him…

Upwards, higher and higher.

…and sometimes, he got the feeling that there was someone else there with him. But it was like catching quicksilver. The thought came but went again. There couldn't have been anyone else. Just him. And the Needlemen. And the fear.

"We're almost out! Hang on!"

...standing alone in the shop when the door opened... Needlemen, in his shop! The fear came over him... everyone outside was already still... he was the only one left... the fear overcame him... soon there would be nothing left of him... the darkness shrouded him...

And the three of them landed back on the floor of the Dressmaker's back room with a loud **thud**.

For a moment, all they could do was sit there and catch their breath. The Dressmaker rose first.

"Are you both... okay?"

"Phew," the Cat shook his head. "That was close! I'm fine. You okay, Arthur?"

Arthur nodded. "I didn't think we were all going to get out of that one...! All present and correct, though, I think."

"Leave nobody behind, that's my motto," the Cat joked, "or it would be if I had a motto. Shall I get a motto? Somebody please stop me from saying the word motto, it sounds weird now. Motto."

The door suddenly burst open and Iakob and Iosef burst in.

"Are you alright?" Iakob said. "We hear big bump and think you are being under attacked!"

"No, it's okay," said the Cat. "Put your swords away. There were a couple of mean-looking picture books but I think we handled them."

Iosef straightened and relaxed, his sword going back into its sheath. "Very funny."

"We're fine," the Cat assured him. "Three went in, three came out. Told you there was nothing to worry about, didn't I, Arthur?"

Arthur looked down at his hand. For some reason, he thought he should have been holding something. Something small and cold and … shiny? But the thought soon left him. He hadn't taken anything in so he couldn't have been bringing anything out.

"Well, we really must be on our way," the Cat said to the Dressmaker. "I think that was very useful. We now know that the Needlemen seeded Waterwhistle right from the start so that all the people there today would be susceptible to them. Be so afraid of them that when the time came – as it now has – Lady Eris could take over the village and use their fear to start up the Agency Engine."

Arthur nodded. "Now we know how to stop it. Get rid of the Needlemen from the village."

Iakob raised a sarcastic eyebrow. "Oh, this is all?"

"I'm glad I could help," the Dressmaker said. Her voice sounded strange somehow, Arthur thought. Like she was sad about something but wasn't sure what. "I hope you are able to defeat Lady Eris. And the Queen."

And with that, the two knights, the boy and the talking cat all left the shop and continued with their adventures. Adventures, she knew, that would be told in another story.

She went behind her counter and took out a small, wooden box. Like most small, wooden boxes kept in secret places, it hid a variety of personal treasures. But, in this case, one thing in particular stood out. A photograph.

The Dressmaker didn't know why she suddenly had the urge to take it out, but take it out she did. Of course, she couldn't see it – but she knew what was on it. The image was imprinted in her mind and she saw it now, as clearly as the day it was taken. A long time ago. When she had a different life. A different face.

The picture of her and her husband, Hector. And their son, Albert. And their youngest son, baby Samuel.

Herself. Her husband. And her two children.

RUMOURS

From one end of Arilon to the other, people are talking.

Fess – The island of business and endeavour.
A dinner party

"So, you know what I heard? I heard some people escaped Phobos. Right from under the nose of Lady Eris."

"Now, Governor, with all due respect, that doesn't sound likely, does it?"

"No, I heard the same thing as the Governor! And apparently, the old King of Ends was involved, too!"

"Now, that's just pure nonsense. The King of Ends is a fairy story, he isn't even real."

"Actually, he was real but he was killed when his Kingdom was destroyed."

"No, he wasn't killed. He got turned into a gnat. Or a bat. Something like that."

Graft – The isle of Hard Work
A mining team

"Alright, Puck, if they got away, how did they do it? On the back of a flying horse? Pass the toolbox."

"You won't believe this – but they made new Line."

"You're right, laddie. I don't believe it. Toolbox!"

"Oh, sorry, here. Anyway, it's true! I heard it from a Caturan trader at the docks. He's done business with dozens of ships and islands in the last Halfday and apparently, it's all anyone's talking about!"

"Come on, Puck, you know they're all weird on Phobos. You can't trust a Phoban. They're too scared to tell the truth about anything."

"Well, they're not too scared to leave! Not anymore!"

"Flibbety Gibbets, now I know you're talking fishtails. Leave? Of their own accord?"

"Yes, indeedy, or may the Man in the Sun strike me down on the spot if I'm lying!"

Doctrina – The isle of education and learning
A lecture

"Leaving?!"

"Ssh, keep it down! The teacher'll hear us. You want to get us thrown out?"

"Sorry. See? This is me whispering."

"Doesn't matter, forget it."

"No! Tell me…! This is amazing..!"

"Okay… well, yes. Apparently, some Phobans are getting in boats and trying to get to the new Line and follow it off the island. But the soldiers are fighting them back. It's chaos, apparently. A real uprising."

"But… why don't they just go up on one of the existing Lines? Phobos has got almost more lines than anywhere else."

"Some people *are* doing that but apparently, most people want to go up the New Line because it's the most direct way to get to Valia."

Autela – The Cautious Island

A son helping his father repair the garden wall

"Oh, Valia. I wondered when *they* would come into this. If there's any trouble, you can always guarantee a Valian won't be far away!"

"Dad, that's just nonsense!"

"Valia was cut-off for a reason, you know! They're a dangerous element, best left to their own kind and kept away from the rest of us."

"Well, they're off the island, now. Sailing against Lady Eris. There's going to be the mother of all battles! I know it's best to take a step back and think things through… but you know what? I wish I could be there with them!"

"You're going nowhere, lad, and don't you forget it! Anyway, how can new Line be made in the first place? The Travel Lines were woven at the time of Creation. Once a Line is cut, it's cut. I don't like what the Queen's doing any more than anyone else, but there it is. No-one in Arilon can make new Travel Line."

"Ah, well, that's just it. It wasn't someone from Arilon that did it. It was a Human."

Savis – The Kindness Isle

The Stark Household

"Human? Ami, you know humans don't come to Arilon."

"They do from time to time, Uncle. And this one can create new Travel Line. It's a sign! Things are going to change. The Queen and Lady Eris are no longer going to have things all their own way!"

"You don't know how much I – wait, what's that?"

"My travel bag."

"Why do you need a travel bag?"

"Because I'm going travelling."

"Can I ask where?"

"…"

"Ami Stark, I asked you a question!"

"There's a group gathering to the South of the city. They've chartered a boat. We're going to join the Valian fleet attacking Lady Eris' island."

"*YOU'RE WHAT?!*"

"They have the courage to face the Queen – why should we do any less?"

"I promised your parents I'd look after you, Ami, you can't just-"

"Yes, Uncle, and you know I'm grateful. More than I can ever say. But I cannot just sit by and let others suffer while there's something I can do to help. Now the Valians are attacking Lady Eris, there *is* something I can do. I can join them!"

"You do realise you'll be the only ones joining them? It's not some Arilon-wide revolution, you know. It'll just be a rag-tag bunch of Valian ships and a small boat of idealists from Savis. No-one else will be foolish enough to join in."

"Well… I suppose we'll just have to see about that when we get there."

"But… but you're not thinking straight…! It's just this random flush of courage some people are talking about. They say they feel just a tiny bit braver… it's making people go a bit doo-lally…"

"Where do you think that feeling has come from, Uncle? It came from the new Line that the Human has made into and out of Valia. The bravery island is just that tiny bit more connected to Arilon, now. And people are feeling it. Now's the time to act on it, Uncle! Now's the time to stand up to the Queen. You're the kindest person I know... you know what I'm saying is right."

"...of course it's right... I just don't want to lose you the way I lost your parents..."

"Uncle, you know as well as anyone the devastation the Queen has brought here to our island. I can't promise I'll come home safe. But if I stay here and do nothing... if everyone stays at home and does nothing... then very soon, *none* of us will be safe."

AUDIENCE WITH THE QUEEN

"Everyone is talking, your Grace," says the Needleman. "They are talking about Arthur Ness."

The Queen – who has been walking slowly along the deck of her ship – stops and turns to the three suited men.

"What do they say?" she asks. Her words are clipped. Curt. Irritated.

"They say he brings bravery back to Arilon."

The Queen's eyes stare, unmoving. The black pupils, ringed with an unnerving shimmer, drill into her loyal agent. However, unlike Lady Eris, the Needleman does not feel any discomfort at all.

The Noir Ladies are created by the Queen. Through magic as ancient as it is terrible, she gives them form and breathes life into them. They feel. They have emotions.

The brutish Yarnbulls are also one of the evil monarch's inventions. She conceived and created the grotesque seeds that the horned creatures grow from. Though lacking in intelligence, they also possess a modicum of emotion.

The Needlemen are another matter entirely.

"Bravery," she says eventually, the faintest hint of metallic jingle submerged within that rich, deep voice. "Bravery is the first step toward death." She turns away and looks out towards the Black. "As they will soon learn."

"Lady Eris' forces are massed," says the lead Needleman. "They await the arrival of Arthur Ness."

"Arthur Ness…" the Queen says the name in such a way that makes it impossible to determine her feelings.

"He has set Arilon to talking, this much is true," she says, her gaze still resting on the infinite NothingSpace stretching away into the distance. She reaches into her robes and carefully produces an item from within. She stares down at it.

"There is no part of the great scheme of things that is closed to me. And yet, it is ever the nature of the Threads to change as the will of those that makes them changes. We must be ready for all eventualities."

"Lady Eris is confident everything will progress as it should," says the Needleman.

"I am glad of her confidence," the Queen looks back at the suited figure. "Please return to her and make sure she is fully aware how… eagerly I await her success."

The Needleman nods. "Yes, Your Grace."

The slightest inclination of the Queen's head and the Needlemen know they have been dismissed. And so, the three of them calmly step off the deck of the ship as if they were going out for a morning stroll. They drop down onto the Travel Line below and – upon hitting it – vanish into three dark spots of light, almost invisible, and disappear into the distance, following the Travel Line to their destination.

The Queen looks down at the item in her hand, the one she earlier removed from her robes. It is a doll she previously made. A doll of Arthur Ness.

"Soon, we shall meet, Arthur Ness. And then shall begin your *real* test. Have a care – your end-times approach."

And she drops the doll over the side and watches it disappear silently into the Black, never to be seen again.

ATTACK ON CASTLE ERIS

It was black and it was silent. The calm before the storm. Nothing moved. It was as if Arilon itself was holding in a breath, waiting for the signal to release it and exhale... and for all chaos to break loose.

At least, that's how it felt to Arthur.

He looked to his left and right. Ships from Valia. Loads and loads of them. Maybe two hundred. More than he'd seen in one place at one time so far. They travelled in long, patient rows on several dozen Travel Lines all heading toward Castle Eris.

There were small, fast corvettes and clipper ships, their light weapons ready to annoy, harry and hassle. Then there were the medium-sized frigates who would have the task of backing up the clippers with extra firepower. But they would also assist the final type of vessel – the huge galleons. There were only ten or twelve of these but they were the backbone of the Valian fleet. They would take the bulk of the enemy fire and allow the smaller ships to nip in and do their thing.

And then, Arthur thought with a sigh and a shiver, there was his boat. Tiny, metal, banged up and dented. Rusty, slow, sluggish and noisy. Barely any decent weaponry or ammunition to speak of. It didn't even have a name that he knew of. And yet, Arthur had to remind himself, it was the only vessel in the history of Arilon to have made new Travel Line. And surely, that had to count for something.

"Taking it all in?" the Cat strode silently up behind Arthur and took up residence on the gunwales. Somehow, the feline balanced on the thin railings without any effort. Which was good since losing his balance would have resulted in him dropping off into the NothingSpace.

"It all seems so peaceful," Arthur said, glancing again at the two hundred, silently sailing ships above, below and to both sides of them. "I know that's weird, seeing as we're going into battle."

"And certain death," the Cat added. Arthur turned to him, horrified. The Cat shrugged. "Okay, okay, *almost* certain death."

Arthur turned back to face the Black ahead of them. He could already see in his mind's eye the shape of the building they were heading towards.

"I don't know if I can make it through this battle, Cat," he said. "Not without-"

He paused as the rest of the sentence got stuck in his mind. Whatever he was about to say, he had no idea what it was. "It feels like something's missing," he said, eventually.

The Cat nodded but, unusually, didn't say anything. Every so often, one of them would say something that seemed to suggest that they were expecting someone else to be there. And yet, at the moment of saying it, they would suddenly realise that everyone was already present.

Whatever they thought they were missing, they were clearly imagining it.

"Land, ho!" the cry came from Iakob, up front at the ship's bough. The sky-blue armoured Knight had been staring through the telescope for some time. But now, he had spotted what they were all waiting for.

"Land, ho!" he cried again. "Castle Eris in sight!"

With the naked eye, it was still just blackness before them. But Arthur knew that the telescopes could see deep into the NothingSpace. All around him, Arthur knew the two hundred ships' crews were getting ready – loading their weapons, testing their steering controls, perhaps even drawing their swords in anticipation of being boarded by enemy soldiers. They were preparing themselves.

With a deep breath, Arthur tried to do the same.

"Message from *The Unbending Sword*," Iosef took out a strip of paper from the telecom. "Is from Mother."

Arthur was fascinated with the ship-to-ship communications machines they used in Arilon. Back home, the armies and navies used radio to talk to each other, but Arthur had no idea how these Arilon devices worked. He assumed they probably used the Travel Lines somehow.

He'd seen them put to use – messages were typed onto a keyboard and sent to whichever ships you specified. The closer they were, the quicker the message got there. When it arrived, it printed out on a thin strip of paper. Just like the paper Iosef was bringing over to him and the Cat now. Iakob, fresh from checking the cannon (now complete with actual cannonballs to complement their fireworks) joined them too.

"I hope it's that Salmon Soufflé recipe I've been asking her for," said the Cat.

Iosef read the message, "To all brave Valians, cats and human children. Telescopes is seeing about a thousand Royal Vessels. Is reason to be happy, yes?"

"*Happy?*" Arthur repeated, incredulous. "Being outnumbered five to one is a reason to be *happy?*"

"Yes!" grinned Iosef before Iakob joined in and they both said at once, "*Is making it really easy to find an enemy to hit!*"

Arthur looked at the Cat who was just rolled his eyes. "It's a Valian thing."

Iosef read on. "Attempts to get other Arilon people to join us is failed. Is no matter. Is for them we fight. They who cannot defend themselves, we defend them. We are being their shields. Their swords. Their armour. So, is for them we say *Forward!* Even into battle that will overcome us, so long as we try… we say *Forward!*"

As if on cue, the galleon just above and ahead of them, *The Unbending Sword* – the flagship of their fleet and the ship upon which Ludmilla herself stood – billowed and puffed out its sails. And forward, it sped.

All around them, ship after ship puffed out its sails as the Captains ordered them to go to battle speed. Arthur fancied he could hear them all crying out *Forward! Forward!*

"Ready, Arthur?" the Cat asked him. Arthur looked at his companion and, with a bit of a start, realised that the Cat and the Knights were waiting for him. Waiting for him to give the word. As if he was the captain of this ship.

Arthur took a deep breath and then said, simply;

"Forward."

ARILON STANDS
(from the book 'The Battle of Castle Eris', written 200 years later)

It was a massacre.

As the Valian fleet stormed forward through the NothingSpace, the Royal fleet began to emerge from the darkness. What must have been dark, shimmering, foreboding outlines of nearly eight hundred vessels – galleons, battleships, frigates, sprinters, clippers and more – sprang from the Black. Even the most battle-hardened Valian warrior must have thought twice about continuing forward.

Yet continue forward they did.

The first volley of blasts came from the Royal light vessels. They took the oncoming Valian fleet head on and unloaded an estimated one thousand tonnes of cannon upon them. Many vessels fell in that first advance, ship hulls splintered and smashed and crew members fell and scattered into the NothingSpace.

But even that initial devastating blow was nothing compared to what came next. According to the diary of Eli Kamaron, an officer aboard the Valian ship, *Furious Angel*;

"The first attack from the Royal Ships was just to draw us in; this is true. We returned fire and charged forward with full speed, knocking aside the burning wrecks of our fallen comrades as we went. But then we realised there were more ships coming in from the sides. They had us caught in a trap. We were at their mercy. When they opened fire, we stood no chance."

It was a classic pincer movement. The Valians would have had very little time to properly plan and prepare for the battle. If they had perhaps had some Torians with them, they might have had a better tactical plan. However, records show that no people from the strategy-thinking island were present in the attack, which is a great shame.

As it turned out, many more Valian ships began to take a severe and heavy beating in the minutes that followed. Another diary entry from a survivor – this time, a gunner aboard a small vessel whose name is not known – said the following;

"The evil wind howled all around us – the Royal Fleet poured its full metal down on us. To my left, the 'Sentinel' disappeared beneath a storm of fire and I saw many figures sail away into the Black, like leaves on a river. To my right, the Galleon named 'Here I Stand' was under intense, severe hail. Three Royal frigates pounded it but it took their power and returned it double. Though aflame and battered, it destroyed those three royal ships and scattered their crews to the winds.

But no sooner was this feat accomplished than four more Royal ships took the place of their destroyed comrades. But still, 'Here I Stand' continued to fight, even as it was being chopped at as the lumberjack chops at the oak.

And in between these howling beasts of destruction, I saw with my own eyes the tiny tugboat upon which the human boy and the cat (the rumoured King of Ends) flew. They were but a spec of dust against the thunder and lightning – but they did not falter. They forged on. And from their example, I drew heart and kept my cannon firing."

And so here was the crux of the battle. The tiny, unnamed tugboat upon which stood Arthur Ness. Though various accounts from different sources and crew members of various Valian ships claimed that he waved or saluted them as he flew past, it's unlikely such a thing actually happened. Reliable records – including the Smith documents – indicate that Arthur Ness at this stage was still very scared and full of trepidation (despite his feats at Phobos and Pavidus). More likely, he was keeping his head down as ships exploded all around him. He was probably extremely terrified – after all, this entire battle was being fought with just one aim; to get him back to Waterwhistle so he could face Lady Eris and stop activation of the first part of the Agency Engine.

However, the battle had gotten off to a disastrous start. Arthur Ness had no idea how he was going to stop Lady Eris should he get through to Waterwhistle – and it didn't look likely that he'd even get that far. He would not have felt incredibly optimistic about things.

This, however, was about to change.

It began with a slight glimmer in the Black.

The first people to spot it wouldn't have realised what they were seeing to begin with. They might have thought it was the glare of the battle shining off some distant Travel

Line junction points. They may have turned back to the fight as it continued to rage around them. But those who continued to watch would quickly have realised what was causing the shimmering. As the slight shifting of lights amalgamated together into forms and shapes and very suddenly, the combatants – Royal and Valian – paused their fight to watch hundreds upon hundreds of Arilon ships burst from the Black.

There were ships of all kinds and from all corners of Arilon. Many of them weren't even battle ships and most of the people on board were certainly not trained sailors or soldiers. They were just people.

Ami Stark, Savis (recovered journal)

"We arrived and what we saw was like nothing we could possibly have been prepared for. It was like Arilon had been cut open and fire and pandemonium was pouring out. I'm sure many of us wanted to run away. But we couldn't let the Valians sacrifice themselves for us. We had to stand alongside them. It was our duty to Arilon."

Ennika Ardenne, Phobos (interview)

"My ma and me, we came on board this ship even though they told us not to. I mean, what do we know about battles an' war an' such? But I got a job runnin' and fetchin' ammunition fer the crew an' my ma was loadin' and cleanin' the ship's guns. We don't know much. But we know what it's like to be afraid. An' we don't want that no more."

Mikkel 'Stick' Stikkelson, Graft (interview)
"I ain't never flied on no ship before. Ain't never even left Graft, no sir. Not a day in my entire life. But somethin' done happened to my boss, Mr. Frogham. He maybe never knowed it but he was the bestest friend I ever done had. An' I know that if we don't do nothin'… well, I ain't never been one for words an' such… but, well, it just wouldn't be right. Whatever happened to him, well, it'll prob'ly just go right ahead an' happen to the rest of us eventu'lly. So, even if we can't do much – whatever we can do, then I guess that's what we gots to do."

Jonni Evansworth, Labyrinth (journal)
"My gran told me that she'd met Arthur Ness – not that any of us knew his name then, of course. That was before he'd created new Travel Line at Phobos. But gran told me she'd started to help him before suddenly coming over all queer and faint. Then, just like that, she hadn't wanted to help anymore. Later on, she realised it was because the Queen had cut more Lines from Savis, the kindness island. But by then it was too late to go back and help. The battle, though, was my chance to help. My chance to say to Arthur Ness and everyone that even

though the Queen tries to control our thoughts and feelings, she will never control our hearts."

Arthur was later described as feeling 'moved and humbled' by all the people of Arilon that had shown up that day. They had come to offer much needed ships to the battle against the Queen's forces. But more importantly, they had shown that the people of Arilon cared. That they may have been afraid but they didn't let that stop them from standing up against terrible evil and tyrannical oppression.

The rebel forces were still outnumbered three to one but that was, obviously, better than five to one. Arthur Ness was probably feeling a bit more hopeful about things and possibly even gave orders to the two Valian Knights – Iakob and Iosef – to surge forward. To use the distraction of the suddenly arriving ships to mask their progress. After all, they were too small and insignificant. Nobody would even be looking for such a small craft among all that destruction.

Unfortunately, somebody *was* looking for them. And, unfortunately, that somebody had found them.

The *Galloping Snake*, captained by Chadwell Thrace suddenly swung into view, right in front of Arthur Ness' little fishing boat. Eyewitnesses all tell the same tale of what happened next.

The *Galloping Snake* opened fire once with a deadly volley. The tugboat was instantly reduced to a flaming wreck. Arthur Ness, the Cat, Iakob and Iosef were seen hanging on by their fingertips.

The pirate vessel opened fire for a second and final time. When the smoke cleared, the tiny, metal boat was gone.

And so was its crew.

BATTLE
(From the conflicted thoughts of Capt. Chadwell Thrace)

I don't answer to nobody.

Seems I've been repeatin' that to meself a lot, lately.

"Captain Thrace, how gratifying to see you came so promptly when called upon," says Lady Eris. The great, ugly brute of a Yarnbull behind her grunts, menacingly. Lady Eris smiles. "Truly, you are an individual upon which one can count."

Somethin' in the pit a' me stomach twists but I keep me silence. Me First Mate, Mister Quinn, is standin' just behind me and I'd be shocked if he ain't eyein' that Yarnbull just a bit nervously.

We're standin' in the courtyard of Castle Eris. Tufts of moss and weeds spring up between eroded flagstones. The Castle itself reaches high up above us. And in the black sky above that, clinging to the Travel Lines, are ships. Hundreds upon hundreds of ships.

As to the Castle itself, of course, I'm no stranger to it. Spent near enough a year here, rottin' in one a' the Castle's deepest dungeons. A fact I'm sure ain't lost on Lady Eris. We didn't have to meet here. In fact, we didn't really have to meet at all. She just wants me to stand here. To remember me time in the dungeons. To remember who put me there. And to remember that, despite me apparent freedom, it'd only take a word from her to put me back.

I try not to look at the Travel Line what's anchored to the ground just a few feet away. If I looked at it, I might remember how I'd escaped from the cell in the first place – and who had been responsible fer *that*.

"Quite a fleet yer gatherin', Lady Eris," I say eventually, glancin' up into the sky above us. "Expectin' a bit o' trouble?"

"A bit."

"Ye've got near a thousand ships up there, all told," I say. "Seems to me like yer expectin' more'n a bit."

Lady Eris smiles. It ain't a nice smile.

She walks slowly along the courtyard, forcin' me to fall in beside her. Mister Quinn follows behind me, enjoying the company of the massive Yarnbull.

"I take it you've heard the ridiculous rumours spinning from one end of Arilon to the other?" she says.

"Rumours?"

"About our friend, Arthur Ness."

That twisting feeling in the bottom of me stomach comes back.

"The ones about 'im makin' new Line?" I say, once I can trust meself to speak.

"Indeed. I'll grant you, he escaped from Phobos. And that in itself is a great achievement. We applaud him. But the idea of him making new Travel Line…"

"I've been from one end o' this world to the other. Seen a lot o' strange things on a lot o' strange islands. But nothin' as strange as *that*. Once Line's gone, it don't come back."

"Exactly," says Lady Eris. "I just wish all those imbeciles across Arilon shared your logic. Instead, one or two of them have decided to join this fool's crusade buoyed by

- 413 -

the stories of a human boy who can make new Travel Line. In a lot of ways, this battle is really a fight between common sense and foolishness. And you're no fool, are you Captain Thrace?"

A million words came to me mind, but in the end, I just lower me eyes to the ground as we walk.

"No," I say.

"Of course not," Lady Eris goes on, ever so politely. "And so I need a man of your calibre to stop the barbarian hordes at the gates. To protect reason and logic, the very fabric of Arilon itself. Who else to lead my forces?"

I raise me eyebrows. "Lead..?" I weren't expectin' *that.*

"Oh, I have many Captains and Commanders and they are fine soldiers who have attended many battles. This engagement, though, I expect to be… unique. And it requires a unique man to lead it. A man of the greatest strength and guile. One who can see who his real allies are and who will not hesitate to destroy his enemies. Are you that man?"

She asks it like a question – but I know full well, it's a question with only one acceptable response.

"Aye," I nod, slightly. "I reckon I am."

Lady Eris smiles. "Good, I'm so glad. Return to your ship and make plans for the battle. You will find some of your crew have been replaced by a squadron of my soldiers."

"What? I don't need yer flamin'-"

"But Captain," smiles Lady Eris, as innocently as I'm sure she's able, "however will my people learn from you if they cannot be in your presence during the battle? I hope you didn't think it was because I want to control you! I just want my men to learn from your shining example."

I can hear the words. But I know exactly what she's *really* sayin'. And I know I can't do anything about it.

"Aye," I say, eventually. "Aye, that'd be fine."

Lady Eris smiles.

Less than two hours later and I'm standin' aboard the deck of the *Snake* as we speed into battle, explodin' ships lightin' up the dark skies around me.

"Fire!" I shout.

The *Snake's* guns burst with flame and spit blindin' hot metal at our target.

"You missed!" cried Lieutenant Ekker, one of Eris' Royal scurvies. I've only known him for an hour. I already hate him.

"Missed, did I?" I round on me unwanted second-in-command. "Tell me again our job here, lad."

"To destroy the-"

"Nope. Just two words into the sentence and yer wrong already. Our job is to protect Lady Eris' island. Make sure none a' these lubbers gets past."

"The best way to do that," says Ekker, defiantly, "is to destroy them!"

"The best way ter do that," I roar, "is up to *me*, since *I'm* the Captain. Correct?"

Ekker glares at me but I can see he don't fancy a direct challenge to the Captain's authority. Most likely because he don't fancy bein' thrown overboard as is the right of any Captain faced with a potential mutineer.

"You... are correct," he murmurs.

"I am correct...*what*?"

"You are correct, *sir*."

"Right, then," I turn back to the battle. "Now we got that straightened out..."

Three Valian ships are tearin' down the Line toward us. One of 'em spins off onto an adjoining Line that splits off in another direction.

"Take aim!" Lieutenant Ekker calls into the comm tube, "Prepare to-"

"Belay that order," I shout. "Ahead, full speed!"

"We... we're going to ram them?" the Queen's man gulps.

"Nope," I say as we race towards the oncoming ships. "We ain't..."

I've done this more times than I can count and I ain't come across a pilot or captain yet that can match *my* nerve.

The two rebel ships are racin' towards me and I can just imagine the two Captains. They're waitin' for me to stop. I don't. I can see 'em in me mind's eye – their first officers are shoutin' at em to change course, just as mine's shoutin' at me.

At the very last moment, just before we're all about to smash into each other, the other two ships spin off onto branchin' Lines.

"Gunner!" I shout into the brass tube. "Take 'em out – masts only."

The *Snake's* side facin' guns flash once, twice and all three of the Valian ships rock violently as their masts snap and collapse, their sails flailing uselessly. We leave the ships flounderin'. They're stuck and they ain't goin' anywhere.

I ignore the distrustful looks them Royal dogs are givin' me. We've been in this fight over half an hour and we ain't destroyed so much as a rowboat. Disabled, blocked and damaged. But not destroyed.

I don't care what they think. And, I'm surprised to find, I don't much care what Lady Eris thinks, neither.

I'm the master of me own ship.

"*Fire!*"

That weren't me. It was Ekker.

It was aimed at the small, steel tugboat that's suddenly swung into our path. All of a sudden, everything seems to happen very fast, one thing after another.

First, I notice somethin' that makes me heart stop – the tiny boat (the smallest vessel we've seen so far) has got just a few figures on deck. A couple of tall figures in shiny, sky blue armour. Very familiar armour. They stumble and stagger left an' right as the *Snake's* volley smashes into the side of their boat.

Quickly, I whip out me telescope an' peer through… and see just what I was afraid I'd see. Me heart both leaps and dives at the same time.

"Again!" cries Ekker, "Destroy them!"

"No!" I cry out but me voice is drowned out by the boom of a second blast. The glare of the explosion's blindin'. As the smoke clears, all that can be seen of the tugboat is the tiny pieces of metal flying away into the Black – and the tiny figures of the two knights, a black cat and a young boy.

"You see, Captain?" Ekker turns to me, "That's how you do i-urgh"

The gurgle at the end is on account of me sword pokin' out his back.

The other Royal soldiers freeze in disbelief as their boss' body slumps to the deck – my loyal crew of brigands, on the other hand, do *not*. This is the moment they've hopin' for.

"*Get 'em!*" cries Mister Quinn.

And in just one second, the entire ship is awash with chaos. Pirate against soldier. The clang of swords and the thud of fists rings out. Pandemonium is everywhere.

Everywhere except in my head. *My* mind is very clear and focused. I'm doin' just one thing.

I dive for the wheel – now abandoned amidst the fightin' – and fling the ship in the direction of the rapidly disappearing figures. I pull a wooden plunger and the anchor ring disconnects from the Travel Line.

And the *Gallopin' Snake* dives off into the Black after Arthur Ness.

CATCH

Faster and faster the ship flew through the Black, attached to nothing, clinging only to hope.

As the fighting raged around him, the Captain gritted his teeth and willed the ship to go as fast as it ever had. The tiny figures were almost lost against the massive expanse of Black. If they went much farther, he would never be able to find them. Nobody would.

"Come on!" the Captain urged his ship, "I'll not let that boy be lost a second time..!"

And, suddenly, there they were. Four figures – he could see them clearly. The two Knights, the Cat... and Arthur.

He span the wheel so the ship would swing round and scoop the falling figures up... but nothing happened.

"Wha-?" Thrace span the wheel one way. He span it the other. Then he finally realised. He wasn't flying. He was falling. He was as lost as the people he was trying to save.

Of course. How could ye be so stupid? Why would ye dive off the Line to save 'em? Ye've damned yerself, you old fool!

Thrace tried his best to ignore his scared voice. He'd listened to it more than enough recently. Ever since getting out of Eris' jail, in fact. It was what had made him initially abandon the Cat and the children after his rescue. It had stopped him lending more of a hand on Labyrinth. It had convinced him to betray them all to Lady Eris...

No… now was the time to put that damnable voice out of his mind as much as he could physically manage.

He ran through the soldiers and pirates dotted around the deck – they were no longer fighting on account of plummeting into the NothingSpace – and grabbed a length of thick rope hanging on a hook by the ladder. There were several hoops of rope at various points around the ship that could be used to rescue any unfortunate that fell overboard into the Black. He ignored the fact that the *Galloping Snake* was in just as much need of rescuing as anyone else right now.

He flung the rope out, towards the figures as they floated as close to the ship as they were ever likely to get unaided.

"Grab on!" he shouted. Iosef didn't need telling twice. Or even once. He reached out and grabbed hold of the rope at the first attempt. Quickly, he fed it through his hands and sent it to Iakob, next to him. He was already holding the Cat. He fed it through his arm and sent it backwards to Arthur.

All attached, Thrace began to pull. He had to fight against their momentum, which was now carrying them away from the ship. He placed his feet as firmly as he could on the deck but straight away, he could feel the irresistible force dragging him towards his doom.

Yet, still, he would not let go.

The old Captain strained and pulled and heaved. His feet scraping the deck as they slid closer and closer to the gunwale. Another moment, and he'd be right over the edge. Well, he thought, if that was how it would have to be, that was how it would have to-

"Hold on, sir!" Mister Quinn cried, taking the strain of the rope. "I've got you!"

"We all do!" cried Ensign Beeker who was heaving behind Mister Quinn. And behind him, the free end of the rope was no longer free – several other members of the crew all had hold of it, all pulling behind their Captain with all their might.

Only at that moment did Thrace realise the loyalty of his men – and that this loyalty had led his crew to be damned alongside himself. He'd flung the ship into the Black on a fool's errand to save people the rest of his men had never met and were probably not bothered about in the slightest. They would have been within their right to throw the Captain overboard.

And yet, they were helping him.

"Heave!" cried Mister Quinn. And heave they did. And again. And again. And again. Until, eventually, Iosef set foot on the deck. And Iakob. And the Cat.

And Arthur.

They all stood there, staring at the Captain. The Captain stared back at them.

He tried to think of what to say. Of why he'd been foolish enough to betray them. About why he'd suddenly realised he had to try and save them. But in the end, he didn't need to say anything – because Arthur simply held his hand out and said;

"Thanks."

Dumbstruck, the Captain took Arthur's hand and slowly shook it.

"Yer welcome."

"Well, now that's all sorted," said the Cat as if nothing had happened, "we do appear to have the slight problem of drifting through the Black towards our certain deaths."

"Wait…" Iakob said, "now we have ship! Arthur, you make Line, yes? Like before?"

Arthur shook his head.

"I don't think it won't works that way. When I did it before, I had some Line to start with. Out here… there's nothing to grab onto. I can't do anything."

You're on your own, Arthur.
You can't do anything on your own.

Arthur's could always count on his scared voice to be there when things were going wrong. Strangely, though, it wasn't fear that overcame Arthur right now. It was sadness. Sadness from feeling so alone. But why? Everyone was here with him.

He walked over to the ship's wheel and span it. The ship didn't move to the side, it just kept falling. The battle was now a rapidly shrinking firework in the distance.

"What's the matter?" asked the Cat, popping up next to Arthur. "Apart from all the, you know, certain death and everything?"

"I feel… lost." Arthur sighed. "Like something's missing. Something I really need."

"I…" the Cat's face dropped for a moment, "…I know what you mean. I've felt like that since we left the Dressmaker."

Arthur span the wheel again. Again, nothing happened.

"I can't do anything by myself."

Captain Thrace came and stood with them. One of the shiny, metal buttons on the pirate's jacket glinted and caught Arthur's eye. Arthur turned and looked at it. It was shiny and reflective. Like a…

...like a mirror...

Suddenly, a feeling came over him. Arthur had no idea where the feeling came from or what was causing it. But it was warm and powerful and it promised to never leave him, no matter how bad things got. No matter how dark or how hopeless, Arthur would never be alone. Not ever.

Arthur span the wheel again.

The *Galloping Snake* turned.

WATCHING THE IMPOSSIBLE
(from the spying thoughts of a Sharp Eye)

Hundred of year ago – long before Queen have arrive in Arilon – there was being many thousand of Sharp-Eye.

When Queen come, she hunt and kill Sharp-Eye by the thousand. No matter which secret, hidden part of any island where is Sharp-Eye living and grazing peacefully, she come and destroy all.

She leave just few hundred alive. And every single one of us…

…now is working for her.

Now, in this today and age, very few people ever see us. But just because they no see us… not mean we no see them.

"Sharp-Eye!" I hear Lady Eris say in her cruel voice. "Get closer. Show me the Valian ships approaching in the lower right sector."

I be out in middle of battle. Is nobody seeing me. They too busy and I too small. I being about a foot high. Round, metal body. Thin arms. Is having no legs like other Arilon peoples. Instead, is having a wheel. With wheel, I be balancing upon the Life Lines (that which other Arilon peoples call Travel Lines). And I be rolling along very fast. I be having perfect balance. Is natural for Sharp-Eye to move along Life Line, just like walking along grass for other Arilon peoples.

Very fast, I be arriving at part of battle Lady Eris wants to see. How is she seeing? I is telling you.

Unlike other Arilon peoples, Sharp-Eyes be having just one eye. Also unlike other Arilon peoples, our eye is able to be *lent*. Is able to be removed from my head and placed over another's eye. Then, when I be pointing my eyeless face toward something, is other person who sees.

We is being very sneaky and quiet and fast and small. And is able to be letting others see what we see.

It is being this ability for why Queen slaughter and enslave us. We are making for her the perfect spies.

Lady Eris is right now being on her island. On her left eye is being mine own eye. Is silver and bright and is covering her eye like a shell. Through me, she be looking and seeing battle unfold right in front of her.

When I is being first called to Lady Eris, I is telling her my name. She no caring for that. What use is she having for knowing my name? Is carpenter giving name to hammer?

"Ah, I see. Excellent..." she says. Through our connection, I be feeling her satisfaction. Is feeling like horrible spiders running all over me. "Those Valian vessels are attacking one of my galleons – but they serve only as a distraction from another attack about to be launched from behind it."

I be feeling her no-worrying. She is knowing the Captain of her galleon being very clever and experienced. And, she is being right. I be showing her the big ship's guns firing on vessels in front – but at last moment, a single canon is being poking out of back and shooting small, fast ships about to attack from behind. They are being destroyed, completely.

Lady Eris is being very happy (which I is feeling and is making me itchy). I be showing her entire battle. In the starting, her ships outnumber Valian ships by five times. Is big smiling, I feel from her.

But then is surprise – Arilon peoples from many islands. Ships in every size. All leaping from NothingSpace to assist Valians. But even with more ships, rebels is still being outnumbered by three times.

Is still smiling I was feeling from Lady Eris.

But, suddenly, is no more smiling I feel.

"Sharp-Eye!" she is snapping. "Show me the *Galloping Snake*. What does that ridiculous pirate think he's doing?"

I wheel closer to pirate galleon is being called *Galloping Snake*. There, I see is disabling ships. Is not destroying, like other Queenships. Is a curse I about to feel from Lady Eris when all in a sudden, mine eyeless face is seeing small, metal boat. Slow. Old. Is having many holes and dents. For truth, is being miracle for this boat even to fly at all.

"Show me who is on that boat!" Lady Eris is being hissing. I look close. Even with mine great distance from boat, I is having no problem seeing individual peoples on board. I showing her two armour men. One boy. One cat.

"Arthur Ness…" she is saying.

I am not knowing what is being an Arthur Ness. I is seeing what I is being pointed at. But I is not understanding. And – for truth – I is not really caring.

But what is happening next is being surprise, even to me.

Galloping Snake is destroying small boat. Then *Galloping Snake* is jumping off Travel Line after survivors of small boat. *Galloping Snake* is surely lost forever in NothingSpace. I is feeling Lady Eris being speechless.

"Well…" she is saying when she is finished being speechless, "…I did not see *that* coming."

Several moments later, I am thinking, she was also not seeing next thing coming, either.

From nowhere is a shape emerging from the darkness. The darkness – which once is swallowing something, is *never* giving it back – is spewing out the *Galloping Snake*.

At first, I is feeling Lady Eris wondering how ship is managing to make new Life Line. But then, she is seeing through me, something that is an impossible to accept.

The *Galloping Snake* is not being connected to a Life Line. The *Galloping Snake* is flying.

From Lady Eris, I am being filled with feeling of horror. She is with feeling of horror because is seeing a thing that is not possible. Reality is having rules and in front of us, these rules is being broken.

As pirate ship is being flying through middle of battle, Lady Eris is being not only one who is stopping and staring. All ships – Royal and rebel – is being paused in their fightings. All Arilon peoples on those ships is knowing the same thing – they is watching with open mouths at the end of impossible. From this day on, is being nothing the same ever again.

But, suddenly, movement. Not all of the Arilon peoples are being stopped by sight. A Valian ship – on which is being short, stumpy woman with bright red hair – has regained the wits before everyperson else.

She commands ship and it fires on nearby Royal Frigate. The shot is being devastating. Royal Captain – who is being too distracted by impossible flying ship to be sending defensive commandings – is suddenly finding lower part of hull is gone. Guns, equipment… all inner workings of ship is being floating out into the NothingSpace. Is now tilting to one side as short, Valian woman is doing destroying frigate's sails. Royal Frigate is being stopped dead.

And is now leaving big hole in Lady Eris' defences.

As *Galloping Snake* dives toward Castle, Royal ships finally is waking up from shock. Is trying to turn guns on pirate ship. But hundreds of rebel ships is being abandoning their own battles and swinging in to protect flying ship. Battle is being flipped upside-down. Rebel ships is now being the ones stopping Royal ships getting to island. Is forming shield to protect *Galloping Snake* and focussing fighting on this point instead of all over battlefield.

And now, *Galloping Snake* is being very close to Lady Eris' Castle.

"Sharp-Eye," Lady Eris is saying, "return."

Is doing as I am told, I scooter back to Castle super-fast. I am arriving just before pirate ship.

Lady Eris is being waiting for me on highest castle ramparts and by the time I am arriving with her, the *Galloping Snake* is approaching the courtyard below.

And now, I am being in front of Lady Eris and she is reaching to remove my eye from her eye. In last moments of connection with her, I am being feeling her excitement and anticipation at coming battle – but am realising there is not being any anger and annoying-ness from her. I is thinking this is strange.

Then connection is gone. Am feeling small dizzy as Lady Eris is tossing mine eye toward me and it being spinning through the air, showing me ground and sky and ground and sky and ground and...

I am catching it. Putting it back into mine head. I am looking up.

Lady Eris is already being gone. Is no thank you. Is no 'you may leave'. Is just gone.

Am hearing loud **clunk** noise and am turning to look down into courtyard – *Galloping Snake* has reattached anchor ring to Life Line and is being touching down on island. Gangplanks and ladders is being opening and dropping from side of ship and lots and lots of pirates is being spewed forth, with cutlasses and pistols out, straight into wall of Yarnbulls that is being waiting for them.

Is looking like will be great battle.

But such things is not for me holding any interest. I am simply returning to the cages with other Sharp-Eyes and is being waiting for my next command.

SLAM! *CRASH!*

Thump-Thump-Thump-

THUMP! Nothing at all

SMASH! *Bang!*

had prepared Arthur *ROAR!!*

Bang *Crash!*

Rumble for this. *Thump*

THUD! BANG!

"Keep up, Arthur!" the Cat bellowed, although Arthur couldn't see him. His voice was coming from somewhere in the sea of Yarnbull hooves and pirate boots that covered everything that Arthur could see.

"You don't want to get left behind! Not in this mess!"

The noise was deafening – Arthur had no idea how the Cat's voice was even managing to reach him through the almighty pandemonium. Everywhere Arthur could see, there was either a frightening pirate with teeth bared and cutlass held high or else there was an axe-wielding Yarnbull, roaring and swinging with the destructive power of a hurricane.

Simply put, of all the moments of Arthur's life to that point, he had never been so scared of any of them as he was of each one that came along now. Each moment was even more terrifying than the moment before it.

How was he ever going to handle this? The feeling of everything happening around him was pressing in on him, making it hard to breathe. But then Arthur realised that it wasn't everything around him that was pressing in on him – it was the *fear* of everything that was happening. He was afraid of being hit or being stamped on or being swiped by a pirate cutlass or…

Arthur took a deep breath. These were all things that had not happened yet. Yes, they might happen. There was actually quite a good chance of one of them happening. But they hadn't happened *yet*.

And while there was time, there was hope.

"This way, Arthur! Hurry!"

Arthur caught a glimpse of black shadow darting to the right, down a side-corridor. Arthur ducked a swiping Yarnbull axe and dived down after him.

Things were a little quieter down there. The rocky, cobbled floor gave way to a smooth, shiny marble. There were marks on the wall where it looked like pictures or portraits used to be.

Memories flashed back to Arthur of the last time he was in this castle, running along, following the Cat. Except this time, he was going in the opposite direction.

"How do you know your way around this castle so well?" Arthur panted between breaths as he sprinted to keep up with the lighting-fast feline.

"Been here once or twice," came the curt reply as their route darted to the left. The pair burst out of the corridor into another part of the main hall. Silence gave way to noise, peace gave way to pandemonium and the pair plunged back into the thick of battle.

Ahead of them, Arthur glimpsed Iakob (he could easily tell them apart, now – he was amazed he ever thought they were identical). The Valian Knight was back to back with a hulking, burly pirate (by the name of Kaleb, if Arthur remembered right). The pair of them were smashing Yarnbulls all over the place. A few of the huge creatures managed to get some blows in but the pair shrugged them off and kept going.

Arthur followed the Cat in between two Yarnbulls and a group of pirates. The entire pile came crashing down – Arthur was inches from being crushed but skipped free at the last second.

"Nearly there!" the Cat called. And Arthur could see he was right. He recognised this bit of the hall. Not far from here was the – yes, there it was! The banquet hall with the long table and suits of armour. It had been nearly the first thing Arthur had seen upon entering Arilon. Which meant the tapestry was nearby.

"Arthur, *duck!*"

Arthur didn't even wait to see what was coming towards him. The voice was Iosef's and if Iosef said duck, Arthur was not going to argue. He flung himself to the ground just as a Yarnbull sword whooshed over his head. An almighty **CRACK** rang out and the Yarnbull itself suddenly flew into Arthur's field of vision, its arms and legs flailing everywhere. The Knight vaulted over Arthur's head and gave chase.

The Yarnbull got to its feet and turned to face Iosef. It brought its sword up and **CLANGED** together with the Knight's broadsword. That's when Arthur noticed the statue the pair were fighting next to. Well, what was left of it. There were four legs, each one broken off at the knee. The rest of the creature – whatever it was – had been smashed and taken away. But just by looking at the size of the feet and how far apart they were, it was clear the beast had been something massive.

"Arthur!" called the Cat over the ongoing din, "Do you have a colouring book?"

"A colouring book…?"

"Well, from the way you're standing around taking all the time in the world, I thought you might be on holiday or someth-"

BANG!

Arthur's world turned upside down and inside out. Everything went black and then bright white and eventually faded back to normal and only then did he realise he'd been hit.

"*Arthur!*" the Cat's voice rang out desperately but the small, black creature was hidden from view. The Yarnbull that had hit Arthur was now stood over him, blocking the view of everything else. Arthur wanted to shake his head but it felt like it would drop off if he did. Was he still alive? How could he be? It must have only been a glancing blow from the Yarnbull, he realised. Otherwise he would simply not have a head to shake.

"Arthur! Run!" the Cat shouted. Arthur glimpsed the small shape sprinting towards the Yarnbull. Another four Yarnbulls were running towards Arthur now, joining the first. The pounding of their hooves was getting louder and louder – outdoing even the pounding that was still going through his head.

Somehow, he scrambled to his feet and started to run for the tapestry. All five Yarnbulls were close behind him, though, and gaining. He wasn't going to make it.

He slipped. The Yarnbulls pounded ever closer. He scrambled back to his feet but turned as he did so. The creatures were almost directly on him. The lead Yarnbull roared with jaws so wide and close, all Arthur could see were teeth and death. He had nowhere to go. It was all over.

And then, there was the Cat.

"It's okay, Arthur Arthur Ness. I've got this."

And the Yarnbull's axe came down on the cat in an instant.

"*NO!*" Arthur cried as his friend disappeared beneath the massive weapon.

Rubble and smoke mercifully obscured Arthur's view of the Cat's body but by then, the other Yarnbulls had caught up with them and were crowded around Arthur and the spot where the Cat had been killed.

BOOM

The sudden explosion sent Arthur spinning backwards – but somehow, he was the lucky one. The Yarnbulls were all flung through the air as though they were rag dolls thrown away by an angry child. And, as the smoke cleared, in the centre of all that devastation was the biggest, scariest, meanest-looking creature Arthur had ever seen. It was a cross between a rhinoceros and a jaguar and even on all fours, it was nearly as tall as a Yarnbull. But it was *much* wider and longer. Each leg was like a tree trunk. Its body was like a tornado ready to explode and the teeth and snarl and eyes… Arthur was simply dumbstruck in the face of such anger and power.

Wait, its feet…

They were the same as the statue's feet he'd noticed a few moments ago. It was the same beast! But why would this creature have a statue here? One that had been destroyed…?

And it suddenly came to him at the same time as the creature spoke in a deep, snarling voice that was totally alien and at the same time instantly recognisable.

"You still here Arthur Arthur Ness?"

The huge beast turned to the assembled hordes of Yarnbulls. The creatures took a step back. Then the Cat roared a deafening, ear-splitting battle-cry. The Yarnbulls responded and they all rushed towards each other and the explosion of force that erupted from their collision ripped stones out of the walls.

But by then, Arthur had already leapt into the tapestry.

Arthur stood, legs shaking. All was silent. All was dark. His feet were on carpet instead of stone. The walls were wallpapered. The window showed a starry, moonlit night. He was back in the living room. Back in Waterwhistle. He was back home.

But he wasn't alone.

He looked around to see the room was full of Needlemen. Lady Eris stood at the front of them, smiling a smile that was not nice at all.

"Welcome back, Arthur Ness. We missed you."

THE SECRET OF WATERWHISTLE

It's over. You lost.

Arthur scrunched his scared voice up and stuffed it into a box at the back of his mind. That was best for now. Now wasn't the time to listen to his fear. Not even a little bit.

It was a tall order, though.

After coming to greet Arthur, Lady Eris had turned and swept from the room, leaving behind a simple two-word command; "Bring him."

Two Needlemen had bound Arthur's wrists with their razor-sharp metal wire and a third had taken the wire and led him from the room. The other two walked behind as they passed the many dozens of Needlemen that filled the Big House.

Out through the hallway that Arthur had cleaned and swept a thousand times. Out through the kitchen where he had washed a hundred pots and pans. Out through the garden where dozens of Yarnbulls – all, now gone – had been grown, partly by his own frightened hand. They had passed through the alleyway, flanked by hedgerows. And finally, they had reached the road leading into the centre of the village.

Arthur's blood ran cold. All along the edges of the road like milestones stood the villagers. They stood, frozen still, with their hands over their faces, as though hiding from some unspeakable fear. And it was clear just what that fear was. Behind each villager stood a Needleman, its left hand on their left shoulder and its unmoving eyes locked on the captive human.

Despite their hands covering their faces, Arthur easily recognised the individuals as he marched by. Mrs. Pettifer, Mrs. Shepard, Mr. Babbage, Mr. and Mrs. McGugan. Everyone was there. The entire village, held immobile and captive by fear.

It filled Arthur with such dread and terror that he couldn't stop his fears from tumbling back into his head all at once. All he could do was take deep breaths and keep walking.

On they marched, along the high street, past the Post Office, past the garage – all the while, going past more and more villagers, faces hidden, standing still as if hollowed out and placed there by someone else. Well, Arthur realised, that was exactly what had happened. Whatever Lady Eris was in the process of doing to the villagers when Arthur had arrived, she had obviously now completed. The village of Waterwhistle belonged completely and utterly to her.

Eventually, they turned the final corner and there was the village square. All around stood the remaining dozens and dozens of villagers, each with their own personal Needleman behind them, touching their shoulder, staring at them.

Arthur realised that this was the spot where he had first seen the Yarnbulls. Except, now, the huge beasts were long gone. What was here was much worse.

The way the Needlemen's hands rested so lightly on their captives' shoulders reminded Arthur of something. Of some*one*. Someone who had done that same gesture. A hand on the shoulder to share their strength. This looked like that except the Needlemen were not sharing strength, they were soaking it away.

In the centre of the square, by the First World War memorial stood Lady Eris, staring at Arthur, her face, impassive. Finally, the trio of Needlemen brought Arthur to a stop directly in front of her. The lead one stood to one side while the other two stayed behind, each with a hand on Arthur's shoulders.

Arthur looked up at Lady Eris, but, unlike on Phobos, during the rescue, he now found it very difficult to hold her gaze.

"And so, we return, Arthur Ness. Back to where it all began. With you, small and scared, looking up at me. And with me holding you in the palm of my hand."

"No, Lady Eris, not exactly where we started," Arthur uttered as bravely as he could. "I'm not the same, scared boy anymore."

Eris looked at Arthur intensely. "We shall see." She raised a hand to the silent village around her. "You should count yourself honoured. You are the guest of honour on this, Waterwhistle's final day."

"You think you can control everyone," Arthur said. "You're wrong. I fought against the Yarnbulls. So did Sam."

"The Yarnbulls?" the Noir Lady laughed. "Mere beasts. They fulfilled their purpose."

"What purpose?"

"I know you have spoken to Zane Rackham, so you know of the Agency Engine. You know that the first part of the Engine is located here, in the people of Waterwhistle. You have learned that once this initial piece of the Engine starts, it will give the Queen control over every being in Arilon. And you know that when the entire machine is finally active, her Majesty will be granted a power you cannot even imagine. You will all be nothing more than dolls to her – to be placed wherever and however she pleases.

"Many years ago, The Queen determined that here, today, in this place, the first true step toward turning on the Agency Engine would be taken. So she embedded the Needlemen into the childhood nightmares of every man, woman and child that would today find themselves living in Waterwhistle. The fear was planted.

"Then I came and brought with me the Yarnbulls. I nurtured the fear, cultivated it. They maintained it so that it matured, tall and strong. The fear was grown.

"And now, the day that the Queen long ago prepared for has finally come. The fear will now be harvested. The fear will be cut from the villagers and used for the purpose for which it had been grown all along. Unfortunately for them, the people of Waterwhistle are now so full of fear, that harvesting it from them will leave nothing behind. Nothing but empty husks."

Lady Eris looked at Arthur. "So you see, you creatures – you poor, pathetic human creatures – are nothing more than the soil in which we grew our fear. You are nothing more than… compost."

Arthur's head was spinning. It was all largely information he already knew, of course, but… hearing Lady Eris lay it out like that… all the more cruel for its simplicity. It felt all the more real. And all the more inevitable.

Arthur had no idea what he could possibly do to defeat her now. He was alone. The Cat was gone, Iakob, Iosef, Captain Thrace. None of them were likely to get through all those Yarnbulls at the Castle.

And yet, someone had once said to him, while he could still stand, the fight wasn't over. And so he pushed on his fear as hard as he could. He squashed it down into his stomach, deep into himself, and slammed a trapdoor on it. It fought and screamed and bashed at the door, threatening to make things a thousand times worse. But Arthur did his best to keep it locked away.

He looked up at Lady Eris.

"So... what's next?" he forced the words out. "You have the fear, ready to harvest. How are you going to use it to turn on the machine?"

Lady Eris smiled and pointed towards Mrs. Shepard's garage. Inside, a tractor sat that Mrs. Shepard had obviously been working on; its engine compartment was open and tools lay all around. The engine itself was exposed.

"Are you aware of how your motor vehicle engines work?" she said, like some evil version of Arthur's schoolteacher. "They require petrol to make them run. But they cannot start simply with the petrol. To bring the engine to life, you need a spark of electricity. That will set fire to the first bit of petrol and begin the machine's operations. The machine will then take over – the energy from the exploding petrol runs the machine and allows the burning of yet more petrol which runs the machine and allows the burning of yet more petrol... and so the cycle continues, forever."

She turned back to Arthur.

"The Agency Engine is fuelled by fear. The village of Waterwhistle will provide that initial fuel to be burned. But before that can happen, we need the spark... that intense spark that will set the entire machine in motion." She leaned closer, her eyes boring deeper. "We need *you* Arthur Ness."

Arthur felt the heat drain from his body.

"M-Me..?"

One edge of Lady Eris' lips turned up ever so slightly. "Why do you think the Queen brought you to Waterwhistle in the first place?"

And the trapdoor burst open and Arthur's fears poured out and swamped him.

Despite the miracle of the flying pirate ship and news that Arthur had managed to make it inside the castle, the battle in the NothingSpace above Castle Eris raged on.

"We are being overrun in the Sunward quadrant," Ludmilla shouted to her ship's first officer. "Tell *Furious Angel* to follow us. We go to help."

Alexandr Fipps, the First Officer, put in the message which was relayed to the nearby Valian ship, the *Furious Angel*, one of the largest galleons from the Bravery Isle. Then it and Ludmilla's vessel, *The Unbending Sword* turned and headed along the Travel Line towards the section of the battle where the Royal Galleons were overrunning various rebel vessels. Some were Valian but there were also a few small Graft ships as well as one from Savis which was heavily damaged. It was about to fall off the Line altogether and the crew of young people (who looked as though they'd never been in an argument before, much less a naval battle) were busy being evacuated to a Graft vessel. The Royal Galleons were not willing to allow such a rescue to go ahead and they continued to pound all the ships to ensure that it didn't.

"We shall take those two largest Galleons," Ludmilla called to Mister Fipps. "Tell the *Angel* to get in and help protect the rescue operation. They need the extra firepower."

And the two ships swooped in.

Ludmilla knew they were hopelessly outgunned. They had lost far more vessels than the Royal Fleet and they'd had far less to begin with. But everyone knew that the only reason they were there was to get Arthur Ness back to the human village and stop Lady Eris. Nothing was more important than that. If the Noir Lady succeeded in getting the first part of the machine up and running, all would be lost.

Open-mouthed and in shock like everyone else, Ludmilla had watched the flying pirate ship sail impossibly through the middle of the battle. More proof, if any were needed, of the extraordinary abilities this human boy possessed. If anyone could stand up to the Queen's despicable power, it was certainly him.

Nobody had any idea if Arthur had made it all the way to the Tapestry and back to Waterwhistle. For all they knew, he had been killed – along with her sons – as soon as they had attacked the castle. But, equally, he could have made it all the way through and was moments away from victory and relying on them to keep the Royal forces from getting into Waterwhistle.

Even though the only thing Ludmilla wanted to do was leave the fight and go and find her sons, she knew there was more at stake. So she and the others would keep fighting even to the last ship to give Arthur the chance to save them all.

"We got 'em on the run, Ludmilla!" cried Mister Fipps. Ludmilla smiled – they were indeed prevailing. Everyone had been rescued from the Savisian ship.

"All guns target Royal vessels!" she cried. "Let us be showing these people what is real bravery! We shall-"

"*Ludmilla!*"

The cry of fear that came from Mister Fipps made Ludmilla's blood run cold. She had seen her First Officer and friend face down an entire pack of Bull Wolves with just a broken sword. He didn't frighten easily.

She turned to see what he was looking at.

It was a ship.

Ludmilla certainly didn't scare easily either. But she was scared now.

"…brought… brought me here..?" Arthur couldn't compose his thoughts. "…but I was sent here by the government… it was random…"

"Please, Arthur Ness, have you learned nothing about the threads that connect the universe together?" sneered Lady Eris. "Nothing happens by chance. When the threads are very complicated, it might *seem* random. But every action can be traced along its thread-line to the thing that caused it. And if you are a Weaver, like the Queen, you can affect that delicate tapestry. Cause certain things to occur. And she wanted *you*. Here. Today."

"But why me?"

"Because you were the most scared person she could find!"

I told you, Arthur. You have always been a little scaredy-cat. And the Queen was able to see it, even from a million miles away in another world. And now your fear has doomed everyone!

Arthur held his head, trying to force his scared voice away.

"The Queen knew your fear would be greater than anyone else's. Your fear could provide the spark to ignite the Agency Engine."

"But… I'm not scared!" Arthur shook his head. "I mean, I am… but I learned to be brave! I sneaked into your room! I stole the mirror…"

"Oh, you mean the mirror I left in the safe? The safe which I left open? At the same time as I happened to leave my door open when you were outside scrubbing the floor?"

Arthur felt the ground fall away from his feet.

"You... let me steal it?"

"I *made* you steal it!" Lady Eris revelled in her victory. "I knew that if I insulted you enough, you would feel a brief pang of defiance and want to prove that you weren't as scared as I thought. I showed you the mirror and dared you to steal it. And you didn't disappoint me."

"But... I escaped into Arilon..." Arthur argued, hopefully.

"Because that's exactly where I wanted you to go," Lady Eris dashed his hope away. "It was always the Queen's intention that you would go on your little adventure. That the Cat would fill you with hope, with thoughts of bravery. That you would think yourself the hero. The courageous warrior. That you would return here with hopes of having grown into a bold hero to defeat me."

"But... why...?" Arthur whispered – though deep inside, he already knew the answer.

"When you arrived here that rainy night, Arthur Ness, you were terrified, this is true. You thought that perhaps everything was too big and frightening for you to have any control over. But that was just normal fear.

"Now you have had all those adventures, faced your inner demons and finally, after all these years, emerged from your chrysalis, transformed into a new, courageous butterfly. Except, everything was a lie, caused by me. You faced nothing. You learned nothing. You have been transformed into *nothing*.

"Before you were scared. Now, you are desolate. Beyond all hope. And you finally realise what you really are and will always be. *Useless.*"

Arthur had slumped forward on his knees. The Needlemen's hands were still on his shoulders but he could barely feel them. His own hands trailed uselessly in the dirt. Lady Eris was right. What was he thinking? How could he have believed, even for a second, that he – Arthur Ness – could save the universe? He'd laugh at himself if he didn't already feel so completely defeated.

Though he couldn't see her, Lady Eris' voice sounded as though she had stepped very close to Arthur.

"And so, finally," she hissed, "you are ready. You are the key to starting the machine that will end all things. You always were. *You* are the secret of Waterwhistle."

Arthur looked up at Lady Eris, now. But all hope had gone from him. The villagers had been turned into puppets – but he had always been one, right from the start. *He* felt hollowed out, now. Ready to be used in the purpose for which he had always been intended.

> "*You*, Arthur Ness," said the boy, "You are the key to defeating the Queen."
> "Me..?" Arthur felt numb, "I'm going to defeat her?"
> The boy shook his head. "Bamboo did not say you would defeat her – only that you are the key to doing so. If you turn one way, she is defeated. If you turn another, she will defeat *us*…"

Lady Eris held her hand out towards Arthur's face and splayed her fingers wide. The two Needemen still stood behind him, their hands on his shoulders. Arthur didn't resist. How could he? Everything he thought he'd achieved had been a lie. Escaping to Arilon. Waking up from being Bound. Making ships fly. He hadn't truly achieved any of it.

"It is time, Arthur Ness," said Lady Eris, her use of his full name taking away the last of his will. "It is time for your story to end."

Wait… Arthur thought *…story?*

For a moment, the Needlemen stood frozen to the spot, looking down at this girl. But then they – all of them – reached out toward her.

"You leave her alone!" Hector lunged forwards and knocked the lead Needleman out of the way before his metallic fingers could touch the girl.

All three of them looked up at him in horror and he swiped again and they vanished from sight as if they had never been.

And all of a sudden, Hector was alone. There were no Needlemen. No girl. Had she even been real? She must have been, he thought. Without her, he would never have been able to stand up to the Needlemen.

He still feared the terrible men in dark suits. But as long as he remembered that girl, he knew there would always be a part of him that could fight them.

(from the suddenly alive thoughts of Hector Smith)
Wait a minute! How could I have forgotten that part of the story? There was a girl there with me… of course there

was! And her face... I didn't see it, but I'm sure it was... could it really have been... *her?*

The words of the story came to Arthur in a flash. A part of the story he had forgotten. He looked up and saw Hector in the crowd. His hands were no longer covering his face. And from his expression, Arthur knew he wasn't the only one who had suddenly remembered how the story *really* ended.

"Prepare to mark the end of the universe, Arthur N-"

Lady Eris stiffened, her face a sudden picture of pure shock. Arthur's hand was gripping her wrist.

"Don't keep saying my name," he looked her in the eye. "You'll wear it out."

And from his trouser pocket, as if it had always been there – and perhaps it had – he pulled the piece of broken mirror that the girl in the story had given him. And he swiped it across Eris' wrist, cutting her hand clean off.

The shriek of terror that erupted from the Noir Lady's lips pierced the nighttime sky. She staggered backwards, clutching her wrist with her remaining hand. Yet, there was no blood. Just dark threads spilling from her wrist, reaching out like a million, gossamer-thin tentacles.

Arthur stood, the mirror in his hand, its colours shifting and changing in the moonlight. The two Needlemen behind him shrank away, a sudden fear in their eyes.

"You will pay for this, Arthur Ness!" shrieked the witch. "This entire village will pay!"

"We have already paid," Hector suddenly said. He pulled a mirror shard from his pocket, just like Arthur had. "However, I think we are due a refund."

He held the mirror fragment up and looked at the Needleman behind him. As soon as Hector locked eyes with the suited figure through the glass, the Needleman cried out in silent agony and then exploded in a puff of night-black threads.

"Fear can't stand it when you look it right in the eye," shouted Hector. "Everyone, remember your stories!"

(from the no-longer-sleeping voices of Waterwhistle)
"…that girl… she helped me lock the Needleman in the closet… how could I have forgotten that…?"

"…of *course* I wasn't alone on that boat…!"

"…wait…! There was a girl *with* me at the well… we pushed the Needleman back down it, together…"

"…the Needlemen in the forest… that girl helped me stand up to them… how could that have slipped my mind all these years…?"

The villager next to Hector slowly removed her hands from her face, reached into her skirt pocket and pulled out a mirror fragment. And the one next to her. And the one next to them. All along the rows of villagers, up and down the square, along every street and lane. Each and every villager suddenly found they had a mirror fragment in their pocket. Each and every villager looked at the Needleman behind them and the creature they had feared since childhood exploded into the night.

"How… how is this possible..?" Eris couldn't believe her eyes.

"How is 'this' possible? Which 'this' are you referring to, Lady Eris?" Arthur asked. "By 'this' do you mean Waterwhistle fighting back? Or perhaps you mean 'this'..."

Arthur held out the mirror fragment to the side of him and dropped it.

Right into Teresa's hand.

"You know, Arthur," said Teresa, "I think she might mean this one."

Lady Eris' eyes widened in horror.

"You..! How..?"

"I went into the story, Eris," said Teresa. "And I re-wrote it. I helped me dad. Couldn't totally stop 'im being afraid, but I did help him realise it were possible to stand up to fear with a bit of help. Damn near destroyed the entire story, mind. Almost wrote meself out of existence. But I escaped into Mrs. McGugan's story. And then Mr. Babbage's. And Mrs. Shepard. I helped 'em *all*, Eris. Every single last person in this village."

Lady Eris couldn't believe what she was hearing. This girl..! This one, human girl...!

"Everyone forgot me, Eris," Teresa went on. "The more I re-wrote the stories, the further I got from the real world. But I didn't stop, I kept going. You know why? 'Cause all along, there were this one tiny, tiny thread keeping me connected to reality. And through it, I were gettin' strength from the one person I knew couldn't never, ever *properly* forget me."

Eris' eyes flitted from Teresa to Arthur.

"Come on, Eris," Arthur smiled. "You didn't think I'd permanently forget my own sister, did you?"

"Your... your sister?" Eris couldn't believe her ears.

"I know…" Arthur smiled and nodded, "… I only just figured it out, too. Crazy day."

Teresa locked her gaze on the shrinking Noir Lady, "What can I say, Eris…" she said, "… looks like you just discovered the *real* secret of Waterwhistle."

Eris staggered backwards, cradling her severed wrist to her body, her hair a mess, her face terrified and enraged all at once. Her plans had all failed, had all come apart at the seams. The only thing she could think of to say now was;

"*Kill them!*"

She turned and ran away as the remaining Needlemen charged towards Arthur and Teresa. Arthur dodged an incoming clawed hand, the sharp, metal fingers shining in the moonlight. Teresa swiped at the Needleman's arm with the mirror fragment and cut it clean off. The Needleman disappeared in a puff of threads.

"Here," Teresa tossed the mirror shard to Arthur and pulled out one of her own. "Think you might need this."

Arthur grinned briefly at her, "Thanks, sis."

"Talk later," she said. "Defeat evil now."

The pair turned back to back and faced down the oncoming Needlemen. Just like in his Bound dream, Arthur remembered. The pair of them beating back the attacking hordes – doing together what neither of them could do alone. Together, they were unstoppable. Unlike in his Bound dream, though, this time, they weren't overwhelmed. Because this time, they had help.

"Charge!" yelled Hector and the people of Waterwhistle surged forwards. Their own Needlemen defeated, they rushed towards the village square to help their young saviours. They were scared. They were terrified, in fact. But they knew that the fear you can't bear to face is always stronger than the fear you look in the eye. Especially when you have help. They poured forward into the sea of dark suits and hats, mirror shards swinging, shining in the moonlight.

And very soon, the Needlemen were gone from Waterwhistle.

"*Dad!*" Teresa ran forward and leapt onto her father, flinging her arms around his neck. "*Sammy!*" she cried as her brother joined in. All the villagers crowded round, hugging, laughing and crying.

Arthur was happy for them but he didn't have time to join in the celebrations. He turned and ran as fast as he could up the road and up towards the big house. Because he knew that's where she'd be.

"You're not getting rid of me that easily!" Teresa was suddenly running beside him. "Not again!"

Arthur grinned briefly and together, they ran all the way to the house, through the garden, in the kitchen door, through the hallway... and together, they burst into the drawing room.

And there was the tapestry. And there was Lady Eris.

And there...

...and there...

...was the Queen.

"Greetings," she said, slowly, "Arthur Ness."

AT LAST

The Queen stood motionless and stared at Arthur Ness. It was impossible to tell if her expression was a smile or a scowl of hatred. Somehow, it managed to look like both at the same time.

Arthur couldn't believe he was actually seeing the Queen for the first time – after all the talk about her, she'd almost stopped being real. But here she was. She was incredibly tall, just a touch moreso than Lady Eris. Her face was long and her expression, completely unreadable. Her eyes were a colour Arthur couldn't even describe and the crown on her head was just a simple, jewelled band of silver keeping her long, white hair in place.

Most of her body was hidden from view by a long, white robe, encrusted along the trim with cold-coloured jewels. She stood completely motionless. She didn't even appear to be breathing.

Next to her, Lady Eris stood. Her hair – usually so immaculate – was a matted, dishevelled mess and hung down, covering half of her face. She stood hunched over, cradling her injured arm, out of breath. Utterly defeated.

"And so, Arthur Ness," the Queen said, simply. She turned to Teresa. "Here we are."

Arthur stood motionless. He had the strangest feeling. Lady Eris had emitted pure fear. But the Queen was different. Being near her made you feel... he couldn't even describe it. It was like being hypnotised. You couldn't move, you just wanted to stand and look at her. Listen to her. She was captivating in every way. She reminded Arthur of the Venus flytrap that would entice the insect toward it before slamming its jaws shut and devouring the unfortunate creature.

"It has been some time since last I saw you, Arthur," she spoke in a slow, rich tone that held Arthur as motionless as the sight of her did. He thought he heard the soft tinkling of faraway bells behind her voice. "I tried to start the Agency Engine today. And you defeated me. Such is life. Congratulations. Enjoy your victory. I came not to fight you. Not today. I only came to retrieve my property."

And with that, the Queen touched the ragged shadow of a woman that stood, defeated, by her side. The terrible scream that issued from the Noir Lady's lips sent shivers down the spines of the two children. And in an instant, billions of tiny threads erupted from her body and wrapped themselves around her. It looked for all the world as though she was being scribbled out by the crayon of an angry child. The black threads completely consumed her and with a final shriek of terror, she was gone.

Arthur stared at the empty space. "Is she…?"

"She is not dead," the Queen answered. "She is far worse than dead. She is suffering eternal punishment. You shall not see her again. Eris was the last of the Noir Ladies. The time for such proxies is past. When next we meet in battle, it shall be face to face. And I look forward to it."

The Queen raised a hand and suddenly, the two mirror-shards wrenched themselves from Arthur and Teresa's grip and flew into the monarch's open palm. With a sudden **crash**, the window splintered and dozens of identical mirror-shards – presumably the ones the villagers had been holding – all came bursting through from outside. They all fell into the Queen's unmoving hand and arranged themselves, mixing, matching, re-ordering and finally bonding together. In just a few short moments, the Queen held a fully-formed mirror that glinted ever-changing colours in the moonlight. The mirror – Arthur realised with a shock – that he had stolen from Lady Eris' safe.

"As I said," the Queen spoke, hiding the mirror within the folds of her robes, "I came to retrieve my property."

"The mirror's yours?" Arthur couldn't stop himself blurting out.

"Lent to Lady Eris to entice you into stealing it as part of our plan to manipulate you. It is more than a mere mirror. It is a powerful device." The Queen stared straight at Arthur while she spoke. "It appears your sister was able to activate its power when she was trapped inside the story. She managed to manipulate the device and use it to help you all free yourselves from the Needlemen's grip, despite not really understanding what she was doing. Her power grows strong as does yours, Arthur Ness. You are a formidable team indeed and I admit defeat to you today."

The Queen then glanced for only the second time at Teresa. Her scowl was very much in evidence now.

"But in the end, I always win."

And then she was simply – gone.

Arthur and Teresa stood there for a long, long moment.

Suddenly, the tapestry flashed and a small, dark shape burst out. Arthur and Teresa cried out in shock and scrambled backwards. Then they saw who it was that had joined them in the big house.

"Did I miss all the fish?" said the cat, normal-sized again. "What happened?"

Eventually, Teresa turned to Arthur.

"I'm not sure, but, for now, at least..." she whispered, a smile daring to sneak onto her face, "...I think we won."

THE END FOR NOW

"Mum! Dad!" Arthur ran and ran along the train station platform and didn't stop until he was in his parents' arms.

"Arthur! Oh, Arthur!" his mum grabbed him and kissed him all over his head, face, ears and anywhere else she could reach. His father reached around them both and hugged so tight it felt like he was never going to let go.

This was the best part. Better than beating Lady Eris, better than flying pirate ships through space, better than everything. Being back home, back in London with his mum and dad. Not because he'd run away like the first time. And not a dream like the time after. For real. Back home for real.

"I've been sick with worry..!" his mother said, finally, her voice thick with tears, "...but I've got my boys back now! We're all together again!"

That's when Arthur really realised for the first time that it hadn't just been him who'd been alone and afraid. Each of them had been away from the other two and had no idea if they'd each survived their respective adventures. They'd each had important tasks and they had all forced themselves to go on despite the fear of what may have been happening to the others. Forcing themselves forward through the fear. Arthur smiled – looks like there was some Valia here as well.

"So, little fella," said his father at last, "how was Waterwhistle? Meet anyone interesting?"

Arthur shrugged and grinned up at his parents.

"Yeah," he said, "one or two people."

"*Sister?!*"

"I know," said Arthur, "it's-"

"*Sister?!*"

"Cat, this is kind of a-"

"*Sister?!*"

"Okay, if you say that word one more time, you're banned from my planet."

The Cat took a deep breath. He looked around the modest Smith household. He started to say something. Then stopped. Then his mouth moved and no sound came out. But his lips looked very much as though they'd formed the word '*sister?!*'.

"Okay, Cat, I'll tell you what," said Teresa, "we'll tell you about the whole 'brother and sister' thing if you tell us about that whole 'turning into a great big cat monster' thing."

"Ah, yes," said the Cat, "that."

"Yes," said Arthur. "That."

"I'm sorry…" came the deep voice from the other side of the dining table. Arthur, Teresa and the Cat looked up. Hector had not moved in several minutes. "I'm sorry…" he repeated, slowly, "…I'm sure the story of the talking cat turning into a giant battle beast is an enthralling one… but, personally, I'm a bit more interested in the fact I have an extra child I didn't know anything about."

The room was silent.

"To be honest," Arthur said eventually, "I don't know much, myself. I just kind of… realised. People keep saying I have some kind of 'seeing the truth' power… I suppose it must have come from there. Right at the point where the memory of Teresa popped back into my head. I realised why we'd been so drawn to each other. Why we felt as though we'd always known each other, like long lost friends. I think I knew it all along, really. Like we were…"

"Connected," Teresa finished. "It's like we was connected."

"Well…" said the Cat, "…you're both the same age so that would make you twins. You don't get much more 'connected' than that."

"But, you can't be," Hector said, "Elsie… your mother… she went into the hospital to have you, Teresa. I had to wait outside the delivery room. Then they came to get me, brought me inside. Said I'd had a baby girl and they gave you to me. I were so happy. But there was definitely just one of you!"

"Are you sure?" the Cat asked.

"I think I'd have noticed!" said Hector. "I think Elsie might have mentioned it, too!"

The Cat was silent, thinking, figuring out. Teresa shook her head.

"Lady Eris said there was something strange goin' on with our family," Sam said, eventually. "She said she wanted to figure out how come we kept muckin' things up for her. Arthur and Teresa being twins and no-one knowin' anything about it… maybe that's got somethin' to do with it?"

"But… I just don't know how it could have been possible…" said Hector again, his level of shock not receding at all.

"Well, I don't care what you say, dad. From

the moment Arthur said it, I knew. It's like he'd flicked a switch I didn't even know I had. Turned on something I'd been waiting for all me life without even realisin' it. He's me brother sure as eggs is eggs."

Hector looked at Arthur for a long time, his face stern and perplexed. Then, quite suddenly, a change came over his expression. His face softened and his eyes widened.

"Elsie..!"

Arthur blinked. "I'm sorry?"

Hector's eyes were still fixed on Arthur's face. "I don't know how I didn't see it before... your eyes... your cheeks... your ears... I don't know how it's even possible, but... I'd know her face anywhere..."

And with that, he reached over the table and swept up both children in his arms in a giant bear hug.

"It's a blummin' *miracle!*"

And for the next several seconds, Hector Smith – the man Arthur had known as the grumpy farm shop owner who had sold him bags of compost – let out a long, overjoyed laugh and danced with his three children round and round the room like a man drunk on overwhelming joy. Eventually, exhausted with elation, he collapsed onto an armchair. Breathing heavily, he wiped his brow and stared blissfully at Arthur, Teresa and Sam.

"I started the day thinking I only had one kid and now I've got four! You're mine, I know it. I don't know how it happened and I don't care. All I know is Elsie would be so, so proud of all three of you for what you did today. She'd love you all so much."

Arthur felt his throat tighten. For the first time, it hit him that he would never meet his mother. He suddenly found himself wanting to go back inside the story with the Blind Dressmaker just so he could look at Elsie's face again, knowing now who she was.

Wait - his *mother!*

Teresa seemed to have the same thought at the same time.

"Your parents!" she said. "Your... I suppose they're your adoptive parents... have they ever..."

"Never said a word," said Arthur.

"You can't blame them," said Hector. "It's a difficult thing to deal with. Different people deal with it in different ways, I expect. I'd imagine they'll tell you in their own time. When they think you're ready. Don't think badly of them."

Arthur didn't think badly of them. Quite the opposite. He was dying to see them again. And, no, he decided... he wouldn't mentioned any of this to them. He'd wait until they were ready to tell him themselves.

After everything that had happened – good and bad – all he wanted to do now was go home.

"Well, here we are," Arthur's father said as they rounded the corner where the Commons Road met Victoria Street. Arthur's street. And just a dozen metres up, there was Arthur's house. Well... what was left of it.

"Are you sure this is a good idea, Duncan?" Arthur's mother said. "For Arthur, I mean? It might be too distressing…"

"Abbie, he insisted," Arthur's father tried his best to sound confident.

"I'll be fine," said Arthur, his eyes not moving from his family home. "We convinced the board to let me come back to London for the weekend so we could do this. It's important. We need to do it together." He turned to them. "As a family."

The three of them turned to look at the house together. It was still mostly standing. From the outside, at least. The roof had caved in and all the windows had blown out. The bomb that Arthur had seen coming toward the house – the one that the Cat had saved him from by pulling him back through the mat at the last moment – had landed just behind the house. The back garden was all but gone as was the alleyway that ran between the houses on their street and the houses behind. Arthur remembered riding his bike down there many a time. Now, it was nothing but pebbles and ash.

"I can't believe it…" Duncan's voice was a little hoarse.

"This is the third time I've seen it," said Abbie. "It doesn't get any easier."

Arthur watched as his father took his mother in a hug. "I thank the Lord you were trapped in the Tube Station that night."

"Well, it didn't seem so good at the time, spending the night underground with two hundred strangers," Abbie laughed a little, "but I was certainly thankful for it when I got here in the morning. I can't imagine what it would have been like to be here during the attack."

Arthur supressed a shiver. He didn't *have* to imagine.

- 462 -

"What do you think, laddie?" Arthur's father put a reassuring arm round his shoulders. "It's like a different world, isn't it?"

Arthur nodded. He'd been to a different world. And his father was right. This was every bit as strange as that had been.

"Good evening, Cat!" said Mrs. McGugan as she went by.

"Mrs. McG," the Cat winked at the old lady. "How's Waterwhistle's most beautiful sweet shop proprietor?"

"Oh, stop," Mrs. McGugan giggled. "Arthur, Teresa, Samuel – I hope you're all enjoying the festivities!"

The three children waved at the lady as she disappeared back into the crowd of people eating, drinking, laughing, dancing and generally having a good old knees up.

Waterwhistle was partying.

Arthur still couldn't believe what he was seeing. He'd been so used to seeing the village as a silent, unfriendly, hostile place. To see Mr. Babbage dancing a jig with Mrs. Shepard was more outlandish than anything he'd seen in Arilon.

"This is the Waterwhistle you've always known, isn't it?" he said to Teresa without taking his eyes off the spectacle.

"Nope," she said. "This is *better*. The village was always friendly… but there was… something. A shadow. An unspoken fear…"

Arthur nodded, "The Needlemen."

"But that's gone now," said Sam as he watched three local ladies trying to convince Captain Thrace to dance. "Teresa's right. This is better than ever."

Arthur had to agree. Just twelve hours ago, they had overthrown Lady Eris and the Needlemen. There had been much disbelief. Much crying and laughing. Many deep sighs of relief. And then someone had suggested that any good war needed a proper victory celebration. Or, in this case, a street party.

And so in a mere eight hours, the villagers had pooled every bit of food and drink they could find – despite the rationing making such things in short supply – and stacked it on a hundred different tables borrowed from a hundred different kitchens. The village square was the scene of the celebration to end all celebrations.

The villagers' quick acceptance of the Cat was quickly followed by the arrival through the tapestrry of Captain Thrace, Iakob, Iosef, Ludmilla, Yide Kallon, Alenne and many more. Arthur had worried that they might not face a warm welcome, considering what the previous visitor from Arilon had done. But no sooner had the Cat explained that these people had stood up to great evil and great danger to save Waterwhistle than the villagers drew them in with open arms.

"Now then, Cat," said Teresa, "I believe you owe us an explanation regardin' you turnin' into a giant battle-cat monster thing."

The Cat looked as though he were about to joke

or laugh his way out of it – or perhaps just wander off altogether. But suddenly, his expression grew serious and sad.

"That giant, battle-cat monster thing is me. My real, true form. What I used to look like.

"It all started with a battle. A huge one. The Queen had not long arrived in Arilon from who-knows-where. She was an unknown quantity so she took us by surprise. Her forces attacked my kingdom and the maelstrom of conflict that followed made today's fight look like two babies fighting over a squeaky toy. Trust me. It was horrific.

"Eventually – as any respectable war should – it came down to just two people slugging it out in a battle-scarred field. Me and Queenie. Toe to toe, face to face. My claws against her magic. But in the end… well, her magic won.

"She tried to kill me but for some reason, she couldn't. So she transformed me into the most useless, pathetic, harmless version of myself. What was once grand and mighty and powerful became… a pet. Something that an old lady would stroke on her lap. Something that would not be any threat to her as she continued her domination of Arilon."

"Except, you *have* been a threat," Teresa said. "A constant one."

"Yes, my dear Smithy," the tiniest grin returned to the Cat's face. But it was a grin that promised menace, not mirth. "That's because the Queen failed to realise that it doesn't matter what's on the outside. It's what's on the inside that counts. And inside, I'm still my old self. And always will be."

Arthur nodded. He had finally understood that about himself too. He felt he had finally come to accept that perhaps there was more to his inner self than a scared, little boy.

"But what about back at the castle?" he asked the Cat. "How did you escape being killed by that Yarnbull? And then how did you change back to your old form?"

The Cat looked Arthur dead in the eye. "I changed back to my old form because I *didn't* escape being killed by the Yarnbull."

Arthur and Teresa both gasped in shock.

"You mean…" Teresa's hands covered her mouth, "you were really…?"

"I have nine lives, you see. Like any cat. And every time I die, the curse is temporarily lifted. I change back to my true form for a few minutes. It's a rare opportunity to put my claws to good use – so I do try to pick my times of death as carefully as I can."

Arthur ignored the Cat's attempt to lighten the mood because an image had suddenly popped into his head – the image of crimson-clad royal soldiers lying ravaged and beaten all over the road.

"Back on Labyrinth…" Arthur whispered, "…when I was hanging over the edge of the NothingSpace. Right before Iakob and Iosef showed up. All those soldiers… did you…?"

The Cat gave Arthur and Teresa the warmest smile they had ever seen from him.

"Listen… every so often, not all the time but once in a while, you come across some non-cats that are worth sacrificing a life or two for."

The three friends stared at each other for a long time – and that's what they were, Arthur realised. Friends. After all they'd gone through together and done for each other, what else could they possibly be *but* friends.

"I know you've just told us that deep down, you're really a great and terrible war-king…" Teresa grinned, cheekily, "…but I hope you don't mind if I give you a cuddle right now."

"My dear Smithy, I'd never turn down one of those."

And turn it down, he didn't.

Arthur had a stupid grin on his face as he watched the sister he'd never known hug a magical, multi-lived king from another world. He wondered if any of his classmates had had such an eventful evacuation as him.

"Is private hugging?" cried Ludmilla, bursting forth from nowhere. "Or is possible for anyone to join in?"

"Sorry, Ludmilla," the Cat grinned as Teresa put him down, "I just reached my hug limit for the month. But I will keep you in mind the next time a hugfest window presents itself in my calendar."

Ludmilla let forth another of her laughs that reminded Arthur of a cannon blast. Then she turned to him and Teresa.

"Children, you make impossible happen today. Queen is dumped on royal backside! Is fantastic! For this, and for the lives of my sons, I want to give you my undying thanks and gratitude. Okay, I am believing Queen will not like this and war in Arilon is inevitable, I cannot doubt. But war will kindly wait until after this party is being over, I think!"

Teresa looked fearfully in the direction of the big house. "But... if things are happening in Arilon, shouldn't we-"

"We eat," said Ludmilla. "We drink. We dance. We enjoy hard-fought victory. One thing in war is always certain – more battles await. More danger. More... tragedy. These things are rushing toward us even as I speak. Do not rush toward them. They will be here soon enough." The woman held up a glass of ginger beer for Teresa. "Yes?"

Teresa grinned and nodded. She took the glass. "Yes."

Arthur took another glass offered. "Yes!"

"Fight Queen later," said Arthur. "Enjoy party now."

"Okay, is decided!" smiled Ludmilla, "Is not the end." She clinked all the glasses together. "But is end for now."

Arthur stepped into his bedroom. It was not entirely level. The floor dipped in the middle and not a single thing was the right way up. Somehow, though, the mobile of the spitfires still hung over his bed. Battered, burnt. But still flying.

"Nice bed."

Arthur span round, his heart in his mouth – and there was the Cat, relaxing on his bed, comfy as you like.

"How… how did you get here?" Arthur tried his best to keep his voice down. His parents were still downstairs, picking through what was left of their belongings, looking for anything of sentimental value to take away with them. It really wouldn't do to make them aware of the cat from another world that was visiting their home.

"Oh, I stowed away on the back of a gigantic, musical flea that-"

"Okay, okay, you know what, forget I asked," Arthur grinned.

"Done," the Cat nodded. "I just thought I'd drop by. Make sure you're okay. When you get back to Waterwhistle, I won't be there. I… may not see you for a while."

"What… how come?"

"Ludmilla was right when she said war would come to Arilon. The Queen is really making her presence felt over there. There are sides brewing – those loyal to the Queen versus those who want to fight her."

"Loyal…?" Arthur couldn't believe it. "Who in their right minds would fight *for* her?"

"Nobody in their right minds," said the Cat. "That's the thing when you go about cutting threads and shaping peoples' thoughts. You can get an awful lot of people not in their right minds."

"So… Arilon's heading for a civil war?"

The Cat sighed. "Afraid so. But Arthur, we have a lot to do. As soon as I can get back, you have to come back with me to Arilon."

"Of course," said Arthur. "I can't wait to start giving the Queen what for."

"Well, that will have to wait, I'm afraid. We have something much more important to sort out first."

Arthur creased his brow. "What?"

The Cat spoke in a low, serious voice. "Teresa."

With everything that had happened, Arthur had totally forgotten about it – but it came back to him now

"It's about what happened with Zane Rackham, isn't it? And the Fearless," said Arthur. "The way they were all really terrified of her."

The Cat nodded. "Rackham had so lost his mind, he barely even registered that we were there. Yet as soon as he clapped eyes on Teresa, he all but climbed out of the window to get away from her. And the Fearless, well they're not afraid of anyone or anything… and you saw what happened with them."

Arthur remembered the terror in Zane Rackham's eyes as clearly as if the crazed inventor of the Agency Engine were in front of him right now. When he looked at Teresa, he was definitely seeing something the rest of them weren't. And whatever it was, it was something that had struck fear into the Fearless.

"Whatever it is about our little Smithy that's causing this reaction," the Cat went on, "she appears to be completely oblivious to it. I want to keep this between you and me for now, Arthur, because… well, my instincts tell me Teresa's in real trouble. We need to figure out what's going on and help her before it's too late."

Arthur glanced up to his spitfire mobile and then back to the Cat.

"We *will* help her." Arthur promised. "None of us would be here if not for her escaping from Lady Eris' dungeons. She's saved us… *me*… more times than I can even count. This time, we save *her*."

"That's the spirit, Arthur," the Cat smiled at the young boy with pride. "Lady Eris may have engineered your trip to Arilon but you achieved much more than she could ever have imagined. More than *anyone* could have imagined. I hate to admit it, but you even surprised me!"

"Well," Arthur shrugged, "I suppose Arilon wasn't as dangerous as I first thought."

"Oh, no," the Cat suddenly frowned, "it's *every bit* as dangerous as you first thought. Arthur, you've barely scratched the surface of Arilon – there's a lot more for you to get to grips with. And if we're going to save our Smithy, you're going to have to get to grips with it *fast*. But you'll do it, Arthur. I had faith in you from the first moment I clapped eyes on you, standing there, dripping wet in Lady Eris' hallway. And I always will."

Arthur smiled at the Cat.

"Hey, laddie, what's going on in here?" Duncan Ness' head popped round the cracked, splintered door. "You talking to someone?"

"Oh, er… just this cat," said Arthur, hastily. "Must have snuck in, you know, what with us having great big holes where our walls used to be…"

Arthur's mother came in. "Oh, what a cute, little thing!" Abigail Ness reached forward and tickled the cat under his chin. Arthur had to fight back a grin as the Cat – dethroned King, rebel leader, ten foot long creature of terror and destruction – purred.

"Arthur was talking to the wee fellow," said his dad.

"Talking?" Abbie grinned. "How funny. Imagine if he talked back."

"Come on," said Duncan finally, "I think we've gathered all we can. Let's get back to Mrs. Wilson's before it gets dark. This war's not over yet."

And Arthur Ness followed his parents out of the room. Before leaving, he glanced back around for one last wave goodbye-

-but the Cat was already gone.

THE END

A word from the Author

Hello Reader!

It's me, your humble storyteller here. Many thanks for reading 'Arthur Ness and the Secret of Waterwhistle' and I hope you enjoyed it!

The story started life when I saw a French poster of a black cat (do a web search for 'prochainement le chat noir poster' and you'll see the one I mean). It then started to take form after my kids pestered me to write a story for them (instead of all my usual thriller novels for adults). And so, 'The Cat in the Carpet' was born. It went through several different versions (getting longer all the time!) until it became the story you have just read – so thank you for taking the time to jump in to Arilon with the Cat (sorry... he can be a bit of a big-head at times, it's not my fault).

The current plan is that the Arilon Chronicles will be told over the course of four two-part adventures, 'The Secret of Waterwhistle' being the first. By the end of the fourth adventure, the mystery of the Queen and the fate of Arilon will have been fully revealed... as well as all the consequences that brings for Arthur, Teresa and the Cat...

Arthur, Teresa, the Cat and the rest of the gang will be back soon but in the meantime, if you want to find out a bit more about Arilon and get some hints as to what the Queen has in store for our heroes before the next book comes out, head over to www.arilon-chronicles.com. You can learn about the people and locations of the Arilon Chronicles by reading the ever-expanding Arilon Encyclopedia. Also, you can take the '10 Minute Writing Schools' for young (and not so young!) writers and you'll even have the opportunity to write your own story set in Arilon and see it displayed on the site.

For more great books for younger readers (such as The Cotton Keeper) or for those pesky grown-up types (such as The Assassin's Wedding) please drop by www.88tales.com and take a look around. Look forward to seeing you there!

Again, thanks for reading ARTHUR NESS AND THE SECRET OF WATERWHISTLE!

-Wilf

Comments from some of the children who were kind enough to read 'The Secret of Waterwhistle Part 1' whilst it was still being written…!

I liked how in the first two chapters ('The Big House at the End of the Village' and 'Lady Eris') it was in Arthur's point of view but in the third chapter ('Out of the Tapestry') it was in the cat's point of view. I also enjoyed how you made up the names for the bad creatures. I didn't have anything I didn't like! **– Jocelyne, 9**

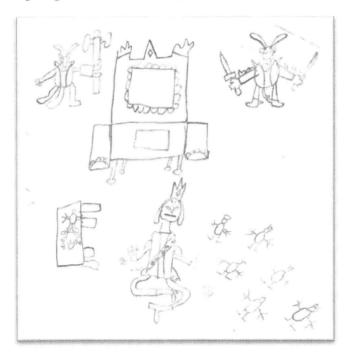

The Queen in her throne room, sewing dolls, flanked by two Yarnbulls –
drawn by Kaleb, 8

I like the story so far, it was full of action and a lot of good ideas and characters. Lady Eris' creatures are good and I like the Cat because he was brave and very cunning, also he could talk. 9/10 good so far – **Joe, 10**

*I thought the story was very exciting and you could follow the plot well. I thought the cat was described well and was quite humourous. Lady Eris and her creatures were described well which made them sound scary. I really want to find out what happens next. 9/10 – **Sam, 11***

Sketch idea for the cover of 'Secret of Waterwhistle Part 2' – **Wilf, 40-and-three-quarters**

The Queen of Arilon stood alone in the darkness.

Her private quarters aboard the *Twilight Palace* were filled with small dolls, stitched in silk. But right now, she ignored them all. Her thoughts were not on anything inside her cabin.

The Queen's dark eyes gazed out of the cabin's porthole, out into the endless night of the black Arilon skies. The Travel Lines, illuminated by the blinding light of the Arilon sun, could be seen criss-crossing away to infinity but even there, the Queen's thoughts couldn't be found.

Behind the Royal flagship, seventy-three vessels, large and small, sailed. On the same Travel Line as the *Palace* but also on other, parallel lines. A fleet of unimagined and terrible power, and still only a fraction of the resources at the Queen's disposal. Many unfortunates – those whose minds were not yet in the Queen's hands – were foolishly inspired by the Valian-led victory at Eris Island. They believed the time to overthrow her supposedly wicked rule was finally at hand.

War was already blossoming all over Arilon in a thousand battles, like flowers blossoming in spring. Soon it would engulf the entire world. And, like everything, it would serve her puposes.

But even that was not what the Queen was thinking about right at this moment.

Instead, she thought about the two children she had encountered this evening. The two children who she had waited for many years to see again. She thought of all the toil and heartache that awaited those two. And she thought of the sweet revenge that was, after all these years, finally within her grasp.

On a wooden table behind her, one doll resided alone. It lay ripped in two, neatly down the middle, each half looking forlornly at the other.

The Arilon Chronicles continue in
TERESA SMITH and the QUEEN'S REVENGE

Made in the USA
Columbia, SC
03 July 2017